Black Mahler
The Samuel Coleridge-Taylor Story

by

Charles Elford

**Grosvenor House
Publishing Limited**

Charles Elford is hereby identified as author of this
work in accordance with Section 77 of the Copyright, Designs
and Patents Act 1988

The book cover picture is copyright to Charles Elford

Yellow Chrysanthemum photograph by Will Gray

This book is published by
Grosvenor House Publishing Ltd
28-30 High Street, Guildford, Surrey, GU1 3HY.
www.grosvenorhousepublishing.co.uk

A CIP record for this book
is available from the British Library

ISBN 978-1-906210-78-6

...a true story.

For John Kriworuchko

CHAPTER 1

Early morning sunshine streamed in through the stained glass above the panelled, front door and dappled the mustard and terracotta patchwork of cool tiles. A large bunch of fresh, yellow chrysanthemums graced a half-moon table under the dark wood mirror and the stairs gently creaked as she hurried down.

Avril stuffed the vocal score into her bag and looked into the mirror. She pulled the wide-brimmed hat over her mane of reddy-brown curls, tucking in her fringe. At least one new freckle had manifested during the night. She gazed into her own eyes. It was rather ridiculous to wear a hat, she thought, when that year's summer was such a scorcher.

It was August 1932 and he would have been approaching his fifty-seventh birthday – instead, it was twenty years since his death. She pulled a large feathery-headed bloom from the vase.

Outside and the chorus of birds were in fine voice. The pavements were unwashed by rain and dusty and that heady, pine scent from sun-baked suburban hedges was beginning to fill the air.

Fifty minutes later and Avril had emerged from South Kensington underground station with the chrysanthemum in her hat. She was briskly walking up Exhibition Road towards the Royal Albert Hall but adopted a slightly more ladylike pace as she grew nearer, and she straightened the creases in her dress.

A small queue had already formed at the box-office window. It was nearly opening time. Rehearsal was about to start. A rush of panic flipped her tummy over. She hadn't wanted to draw attention to herself but she would be rather spectacularly late. She would have to 'excuse me' her way past the seated knees of fellow choristers as they waited, in irritated silence, for her to find her place. Breaking back into a trot and with one hand on her hat, she passed the queue and rounded the building towards the artists' entrance and disappeared from sight.

A poster flanked the box office window – a print, in the Deco style, of a Red Indian standing with his arms outstretched in front of mountains and rivers and forests of pine. 'Samuel Coleridge-Taylor's 'Song of Hiawatha' – Opens Tonight', Dr Collard read as he waited, second in line, behind a rather frail gentleman who straightened when there was a sound behind the glass.

The ticket girl appeared, humming tunelessly. She positioned herself on her swivel stool at the window and unlocked a long, narrow drawer of coins to her right. She had all the time in the world as she popped a large, chewed box of reserved tickets marked 'A to L' on the desk to her left. She reached down for a second box that was equally well stuffed with the other half of the reservations. She looked at her fingernails then insincerely smiled at the elderly gentleman through the glass as she removed the 'Box Office Closed' sign.

"Good morning, Sir."

"Yes, good morning," the old man said. "A ticket has been left for me, I believe. The name is Beckwith – J Beckwith."

"For tonight is it, Sir?"

"Oh yes. Rather. Thank you, dear. Although, now I come to think of it, it may be in the name of Walters. Colonel Herbert Walters?" he twittered.

Her fingers walked casually over the flaky contents of the box. Her other hand mused casually in the air until she decided to rest her chin, too young to be quite so world-weary, on her hand and sighed. At last she found it and read the envelope note.

"Here you are, Mr Beckwith. It's already been paid for by the look of things. Enjoy the performance."

"Thank you, dear. Yes I shall."

Mr Beckwith decided that the delay he had caused, or rather that she had caused, didn't quite warrant a full apology, so he simply smiled to the man behind him as he went on his way.

A minute later and Dr Collard too had his ticket safely stowed in his breast pocket. He drifted towards Kensington Gardens. He had a whole day to kill. The buses and motorcars would be reduced to a more pleasant hum from a sunny bench in the gardens. All the old, horse-drawn trams had long since been replaced by the electric ones, but over the past couple of years these too were being slowly usurped by the trolley buses with their pneumatic tires. Motorbuses were becoming very popular too. All these advances were happening rather too quickly. He couldn't keep up with it all; perhaps a sign of his own encroaching old age – a curse poor Coleridge had been spared.

He found his bench in a sunny spot and sat down. He closed his eyes. He felt the sun on his face – the sweet scent of chopped and drying grass and warmed earth, his toes toasty-warm in their creaky leather, but thought interrupted the careless nothingness once again. Time gathers such a pace as you near the final destination, he concluded – when there was so much more distance behind you than was probably left in front. An aeroplane buzzed overhead. He looked up and watched it for a moment, until it buzzed off. His eyes closed again, he tilted his head to feel the sun full on his face again and silence. Beautiful silence.

It had been silent on Bandon Hill that morning, as he had waited for the sun to rise. It used to be such a beautiful place to walk but they had cleared the woodlands to make way for London's burgeoning dead and the bluebells didn't like to grow there anymore – too muddy for bluebells.

He heard footfalls on the fine, shingle path and opened his eyes as they neared. An old lady, looking rather glad to find a bench, smiled at Dr Collard and made herself comfortable. He smiled back and returned to his dozing. He was quite prepared to share his perfect spot. But then the rummaging started, the hunting for something in her bag, as elderly ladies often do. She was trying to do it quietly but it just seemed to drag out the pain – like someone trying to crunch a boiled sweet behind you at the pictures – crunching slowly; but silence does not automatically come with slowness. He heard her tutting and muttering in mild irritation as she rummaged. She had travelled all the way from Bournemouth the previous day and had stayed over at Claridges. She was determined to be one of the first in line to collect her ticket. He opened his eyes and sighed – slowly, so that she wouldn't hear.

She was proud to have met the composer, Samuel Coleridge-Taylor, on precisely two occasions, she would tell – both occasions, many years before. The first time was at the Royal College of Music on the day of his graduation and the second was some years later, following a concert he had conducted. What a fool she had made of herself over him that day.

"There you are," she said in triumph. Dr Collard couldn't help looking over, cheekily expecting it to be her marbles she had thought lost but it was an old piece of paper, perhaps a letter, folded neatly. "Why is everything always in the last place you look?"

He smiled at her.

"Perhaps," he said, "because once you find what you're looking for, you stop looking."

She looked at him. She chuckled.

Unbeknownst to either of them, they had shared a seat once before. It had been a pew in the back of that ghastly little chapel, all those years ago, in that place – that cemetery that spread over and stole the whole of his Bandon Hill.

"What a simply glorious day," she said with a sigh but her companion was rising. "I haven't driven you away, I hope?"

"Not at all," lied Dr Collard. "Places to be, you know. Good morning."

"Goodbye."

She watched as the man walked away. A whole bench to herself – what a splendid result. She looked down. Her fingers slowly slipped between the folds of the paper, her forearms resting on the sides of the bag on her lap. It was more than twenty-five years old. It had been years since she had held it – that precious treasure. Her hand trembled. She was almost sure that the young woman to whom it rightly belonged would be singing that evening. To hear that music again, she thought, after so many years would be such a wonderful thing, but the real reason for her travelling all that way, and at her age, was to deliver her most precious treasure, and the message it contained to the composer's only daughter.

She didn't know what the girl would look like and didn't know how she would find her. All she did know was that she would. She knew she would recognise her. The young woman was sure to be singing and that was a start; and of course she remembered the name of Coleridge-Taylor's daughter. It was a Welsh name – it was Gwen.

Avril entered the magnificent auditorium of the Royal Albert Hall to join the chorus of more than two thousand strong. Choral societies from all over the country had prepared for months and this was the day that they would come together for the first time to rehearse as one – a single day of rehearsal before the two week run opening that evening. To her relief it looked like they were a long way from starting. She relaxed.

People were strewn all around, wherever there was space, many standing and all still in their hats and coats. They chattered excitedly as they waited for Dr Sargent, the conductor, to arrive.

Avril took off her hat and touched her hair with the heel of her hand. Behind her, she could hear the ladies and gentlemen of the orchestra tuning up, assembling clarinets, polishing flutes, tightening and relaxing strings. Somebody moved and Avril turned to see that separating the chorus from the audience, and by a staged area, was a large, dark lake that reflected the ceiling. Everyone was looking around. Everyone was awestruck. There was a narrow footbridge crossing it to the conductor's stand and in the lake, the moon was reflected.

Avril's eyes drifted up to the gaping, circular Hall's domed ceiling. Vast cloths were hung all around the upper circle reaching up to a centre point; frozen in sail-like billows. It gave the impression of a wigwam's interior but of a cathedral's scale. The bottom edge of the great swathes, were exquisitely painted with wispy, dawn clouds drifting dreamily across a pale, eggshell blue sky. Higher up, the mid-section was streaked all around with purple and blue, turquoise-green, and coral pink of the setting sun. He mouth fell open and her skin chilled cold with goose-bumps. Higher still and the cloth cone bled into inky, blue-black night, with starry constellations and a waxing moon.

Somebody behind jostled her shoulder again. The Hall smelt of paint and somewhere a man was hammering. Many of the others were looking over her shoulder to the chorus seating. Avril turned.

Hiding the great organ pipes from view, at the back of the cavernous Hall, was a backdrop of twelve hundred square foot, slung from one side of the Hall to the other. There was thunder in those painted mountains with their snow-capped peaks and the palisades of vast and ancient pine forests on the slopes that met with the dew and damp of prairie meadows below. It was the majesty of an unspoilt and perfect wilderness, with innumerable echoes and curling, blue smoke of the wigwam village fires.

Avril and the rest of the multitude in the centre of that most ornate cave, watched as dustsheets protecting the chorus area were removed to gasps from the whispering crowd. A hillside of bushes and log chutes were revealed, down which would pour a cascade of water, ending in falls that would splatter on rocks and ripple the lake.

This was the Golden Age made real – the Land of the Dakotahs when the land belonged to itself. This was the wigwam of Hiawatha's father, the Great Spirit – the West Wind, Mudjekeewis.

Mr Beckwith slowly walked towards the Natural History Museum. He patted the breast pocket that held his ticket. How proud he felt to have been the great man's first music teacher. He was meandering in these rambling and absent-minded reminiscences when suddenly he heard the unmistakable sound of a marble being dropped, bouncing once or twice and then rolling – rolling along towards him. He stopped.

Down a cobbled back lane, a scruffy, little lad had stood up with pained expression. The boy knew he couldn't catch the wayward marble before it was lost forever down some drain or other, but it rolled towards Mr Beckwith and the old man just managed to catch it under the creaking rubber of his right shoe.

The boy beamed and trotted over. The old gentleman had saved his favourite marble from almost certain death. The old gentleman lifted his shoe and the urchin retrieved his marble. The boy looked up and in that moment, Mr Beckwith's own skin goose-bumped. It was him. Well of course it wasn't but it really was most disarming never-theless. The boy had exactly Coleridge's smile; a smile of uninterrupted and perfect joy. He was about six; about the same age as little Coleridge would have been when he had first encountered him back in 1881 or so. He was strikingly similar, except of course that this little boy was white and Coleridge was black. At least, he presumed the boy was white – under all that soot and grime.

That day, half a century ago, six-year-old Coleridge had been playing marbles too; playing happily on his own, on the pavement outside Mr Beckwith's Croydon home like some grubby little church-mouse, in grey shorts and with those great, big, beautiful brown eyes. And on the pavement by the brown mouse's kneeling knees was his tiny, tattered, scratchy violin case.

Mr Beckwith had been standing at his front door with his last student of the day when he noticed the little black boy in the street. Mr Beckwith was just twenty-two, but was already well established in the music world of South London's newest suburbs and was regularly engaged to compose incidental music for the local theatres there.

Deirdre, his pupil, had no real talent, just like most of his adult students. She was being made to study music by her family who believed that the ability to play an instrument was fitting for a young lady of her class. Not that Mr Beckwith thought that she would ever really fit into the class that her family clearly aspired to. He hated teaching adults, with their desperately unrealistic expectations and their giving up so soon. He hated Deirdre.

He limply helped her on with her coat, relieved that he no longer had to hear her scrape away at the melody on her defiled violin; each note played to set a new tempo and expose a new nerve end. Deirdre would hit a note one of two ways; either with the pained and ferocious purposefulness or a croquet ball savagely malleted through a hoop, or in such quick succession with some other poorly chosen ones, that it sounded like someone falling downstairs with a tray full of cutlery. Thankfully though, after torturing the poor piece to her satisfaction, she would normally despatch it fairly swiftly with an unclean but sharp ring of the neck.

"Thank you again for the tickets. We thoroughly enjoyed it and all agreed that you're wasted on the Croydon Grand."

"Thank you, dear. Yes," he said, watching the small boy at the end of his path and not really aware of what she was saying, or what he was saying himself.

She talked incessantly and had no awareness of the signals used in polite society, that lead a person to know when to stop talking, when to listen and when to make your excuses and fetch your hat. Mr Beckwith knew that this alone would lead to her inevitable exposure as a fraud. Not that Polite Society would point the finger and shout, 'fraud!' at her for pretending to fit where she patently did not. Instead, Polite Society would merely smile a half-smile and watch over tea-cup brims as the poor wretch clung onto the preferred class by her bleeding fingernails whilst the burden of truth hanging from her rather swollen ankles grew ever more weighty. Would she never shut up?

"So I won't see you next week but the week after next at the same time if that suits? ...Mr Beckwith?"

"Pardon? Oh yes... next week. That's fine."

"You really do belong in Drury Lane you know, but I suppose you wouldn't feel the need to teach so much if that were the case. Drury Lane's loss!"

She laughed. So did he. He didn't know why. Nor did she.

"Yes, goodbye, er... Drear.... Deirdre."

She started down the path and managed to sidestep the small boy in her path without a glance.

"Goodbye," she said, cheerily waving the back of her hand at him without turning as she clacked her way down the pavement.

The little boy was deeply engrossed in his game as Mr Beckwith approached him with a friendly smile. The child looked up for a moment and grinned a toothy grin, then went back to rolling marbles.

"Hello," said Beckwith as he put his hands in his pockets. He never put his hands in his pockets.

"Hello," said the boy without looking up.

"Do you speak English?"

He looked up. "I am English."

"Oh, I see." It was uncommon to see black people in England but to see a black boy who was English was unheard of. "And you have a violin! Are you as clever on that as you are at marbles?" The boy looked at the battered, black case containing the child-sized instrument.

After considering the question for a moment, "I'm a bit better at that actually. Would you like to hear? You'll have to be the music stand as well if you don't mind."

Mr Beckwith said that he would very much like to hear him play and that he didn't mind holding the music in the slightest. He sat on his low wall and held the music. The boy stood and stuffed the marbles into his misshapen pockets. He unclipped the case, grabbed the little violin by the neck and propped it under his chin, squeezing his cheek against the black rest. He gave the music to Mr Beckwith who held it up for him. Then the boy started to play.

"You'll have to hold it still," the boy reprimanded.

"Righto," said Mr Beckwith.

His eyes followed the notes on the page in rapt concentration. Beckwith checked the page for his moment to turn. It was rather an advanced piece for a child of his age, Beckwith assessed, but he played flawlessly. His fingers darted about on the instrument's skinny neck. Mr Beckwith couldn't suppress his broadening grin. The bow was handled as lightly and as swiftly as the little chap had spoken. He was expressing himself through the piece. He brought an emotional depth to it that many adult learners never achieve but the piece was brief and ended too soon. The boy gave a well-rehearsed bow and Mr Beckwith clapped. The violin went straight back into its case.

"You are a clever boy, aren't you?"

"Not really," he said simply as the marbles came out of his pockets again.

"Yes you are," Beckwith enthused, "What's your name?"

"I'm Samuel.... Samuel Coleridge Taylor. What's yours?"

Samuel lived nearby in Waddon Road. Mrs Evans, the woman he called 'Mother', was Welsh and white – surprisingly. In fact the whole family were white. Mr Beckwith never asked into the boy's parentage or circumstances even though he was dying to. He visited the Evans' 'mend-and-make-do' household in order to introduce himself and to offer his services, free of charge of course, as music teacher. To have a student as engaged and talented as Samuel was, would be a joy. He was too talented, he told Mrs Evans, not to be nurtured. She insisted upon a fee and so a peppercorn one was agreed and hands were shaken.

Two months later, Mr Beckwith was enjoying a drink at the local watering hole with his friend, Herbert Walters and spoke of his outstanding new pupil and little else. Colonel Walters listened silently. How many black or mixed race boys of that age could there be in the local area, he asked himself. It must be – it simply had to be Dr Taylor's boy. The last time he had seen him was when he was a baby, a little over five years before. He had been friends with the newly qualified Dr Taylor and had been responsible for all the adoption arrangements following Taylor's decision to return to West Africa. The good people of Croydon had not been quite ready for a doctor of colour.

Despite being a retired Colonel of the Queens Royal West Surrey Regiment, Walters was only a year older than Beckwith. He was a well-born, handsome and highly entertaining man – knowing simply everyone. He was well known for his philanthropic ways and was musically gifted himself. Although not a professional, he was, at that time, organist and choirmaster at St George's and also at St Mary Magdalene's in Addiscombe.

One of the many that the well-connected Walters knew was Dr Drage, headmaster of the British School in Croydon. Within a few weeks of Mr Beckwith reacquainting the young Colonel with Mrs Evans, Walters found himself intervening once again in the boy's life and secured him a place at Drage's school. Mr Beckwith continued to tutor him once a week, Samuel excelled at school and in this way, and all too quickly, the years passed.

When Samuel was about eight, Herbert Walters made a place available in his choir and this proved a fertile ground for the lad to develop musically. He had a charming singing voice and was soon singing solo parts.

For the most part things went splendidly well, but just as in any child's life, the road wasn't entirely without its rocks.

Just before a rehearsal for that year's Christmas Carol Service, Colonel Walters learnt that one of the other boys had called the lad 'Sambo'.

Samuel hadn't been particularly bothered but Walters took him to one side nevertheless and explained that he didn't believe there was any malice in what had been said, just a lump of stupidity. He told him that it was probably because his name was 'Samuel' – and then a thought struck him. He asked if it might be alright if he called him 'Coleridge' instead – if they all called him Coleridge. Suddenly another thought flitted across his mind.

"I expect they might call you 'Coley' in that case. Would you mind that?"

"No, Sir. They call me 'Coley' at school. I like 'Coley'."

It was settled.

Colonel Walters was called upon to make three more interventions in the boy's life. The first was when Coleridge was pushed into the stream on his way to choir practice. Colonel Walters had had to walk his charge, looking more like a drowned rat, home. Mrs Evans laughed. She gave Coleridge a towel and a cuddle and told him that every boy under the age of twelve had ended up in that stream one way or another since time immemorial. The second event was more serious and warranted a 'bit of a chat' with both Coleridge's mother and with Kenneth's mother in attendance – Kenneth being the offending chorister.

During the Carol Service, Kenneth had used a candle to set Coleridge's hair alight, just as 'the little Lord Jesus lay down his sweet head'. Without negating the seriousness of the incident, Walters told Mrs Evans that it wasn't the first time a chorister had caught fire during the annual Carol Service and that he was almost sure it wouldn't be the last.

Mrs Evans nodded, sagely.

"I'm really sorry, Coley. I didn't mean to hurt you," Kenneth said. Coley hadn't been hurt. "I just wanted to see how it would burn."

The smell of candle wax and singed hair hung in the air of the then empty, austere and gothic suburban church. Kenneth's head hung low, weighted with leaden shame, but it was embarrassment that made Coleridge's head hang heavily. He hadn't even been aware of his head being on fire. One moment he was singing out, with all his heart, 'We love thee Lord Jesus', happily thinking about the donkeys and shepherds, when suddenly and without warning, about six of the surrounding choristers started to wildly thrash about his face and neck with their song sheets.

"Now, I think that you two should shake hands like proper gentlemen," said the Colonel. The boys shook hands as their mothers looked on. "There now, the matter is closed." Closed with a civilised, unequivocal and military handling.

Walters knew that there was only so far anyone could go in a small parish choir and all too quickly, Coleridge had turned from a little boy into a young man, and so – the final intervention. Walters and Beckwith had organised a number of concerts in the church hall over the preceding years, so that Coleridge could perform, thus enabling him to not only become a more confident solo performer, both at singing and on his violin, but also to broaden his repertoire into the more secular and popular music that he enjoyed so much. But in 1890, when Coleridge was 15, it was beginning to become clear that he was outgrowing these too and so a question arose as to a next step.

Colonel Walters had many friends in the City and often managed to secure his boys junior positions in London firms. Coleridge certainly had the schooling and the ability to make a career in the City, but Walters knew it would spell the end of the boy's first love. It was patently clear that the boy wanted to be a musician despite the well-worn fact that this was not normally considered a viable career option – especially for a boy from a family that was, to be frank, far from wealthy. Musical careers were the preserve of those with means, to whom any career was an undesirable option rather than a necessary evil. A musical career was not for boys like Coleridge who couldn't afford a violin larger than the child-sized one he had been playing for the past ten years.

There was always Sir George, an acquaintance of Walters' late father. Sir George had founded the Royal College of Music.

Walters had already broached his plan to Mrs Evans so as to take every precaution against unrealistically raising Coleridge's expectations but if he could arrange a meeting and if the boy could secure a place there, then, Walters had told Mrs Evans, Coleridge should surely apply for the scholarship. What was there to lose?

The church hall had all but emptied. Walters sat on the edge of the stage watching as Coleridge slowly walked towards the far end, to close the door behind the last to leave.

He was a thoughtful and modest boy; bright too. Perhaps a little small for his age. He was a good performer but somewhat awkward and gangly when he wasn't playing. He was always dressed in 'hand-me-downs' but clean and very neat and tidy. When his clothes needed mending they were repaired with the care and expertise of a very proud and loving mother.

As Coleridge closed the heavy door, the thought that he had successfully pushed from his mind all evening, gradually started to loom and demanded to be acknowledged. That concert was to be the last of his concerts in the church hall organised by his teacher Mr Beckwith and his protector Colonel Walters; his benefactor and friend. This was the step nearer the end of a chapter without any clue as to what might come next. Coleridge took his time before turning. This was a goodbye.

He turned and saw Walters sitting casually on the stage with the violin bow in his hand. Coleridge awkwardly walked back down through the lonely hall and sat next to him on the edge of the stage. He looked out at the rows of empty and upset chairs. He slowly swung his legs and looked at his shoes.

They sat in silence for a moment or two and then, as if reading the young man's mind and answering the unaskable question, Walters told him that his father would have been very proud had he been there.

"Will you tell me about him once more?" Coleridge asked.

Walters smiled.

"Well…. Dr Taylor, your father, was a charming man. Not very much taller than you. He was most fastidious in his appearance and quite the cleverest man I ever met. He was a very fine doctor. He was a very good friend to have."

"I can't picture him," Coleridge said. "I can't imagine his face. I try all the time.... I thought he might come back one day – if I could make him proud."

Walters clipped the bow into its clasp on the hinged lid.

"You need a bigger violin," he said. He couldn't think of what else to say. He collected his thoughts. He started to talk, then couldn't. He said, "Coleridge, everyone does the very best that they can with what they have at the time – with what they understand and know and think and believe... at the time. Does that make sense?" Coleridge nodded. "Mr and Mrs Evans are wonderful people...."

"Oh, I know," Coleridge said, suddenly feeling ungrateful – a feeling he hated. Words weren't coming very easily to him either. He knew what he wanted to say but didn't know what words to use to say it with. He knew at least that he had to try. He knew that there may not be another opportunity and so.... "Colonel Walters, I... I need to tell you that... Well, what I want to say, Sir is that I don't quite know how I will ever actually be able to thank you properly for all you've done for me."

Walters smiled as the warm light filled him.

"I just want you to be happy, Coleridge." The only thing Herbert Walters ever asked of those around him was that they be happy and for many this was simply too much to ask. Coleridge knew that this was the only thing that any truly good man ever asked. Walters smiled down at the young man but saw that his eyes were beginning to fill with tears and one sploshed out and fell on his trouser knee. Walters pretended he hadn't seen. He drummed his fingers on the violin case and changed key.

"So, the only question remaining is where to place you. You know I have many friends in the City?" Walters asked. He looked at the crooked rows of chairs, some with their programmes still on, still twisted from the boy's first standing ovation.

"You've done too much for me already." He couldn't take his eyes from his shoes.

"And you know I have found positions there, for those boys who have outgrown us here."

"Yes, Sir," Coleridge said.

"Well, I can't help wondering if you might be far happier elsewhere." Coleridge frowned in puzzlement. "Coleridge, I would like you to tell me... what do you really want?"

Coleridge thought.

"If I could, I'd like to work in the City."

"Fibber."

Coleridge sighed, "Alright, if I really could," he said, "I'd be a musician, but..."

"– a what... did you say?" Walters interrupted, playfully nudging Coleridge's shoulder with his own.

Coleridge smirked a little and he pinched his eyes drier. Walters was glad of the smirk. The last thing he wanted to do was overwhelm the boy.

"A musician," Coleridge repeated smiling at Walters who was still looking ahead, but nodding thoughtfully.

"Ah," he said as he passed the violin case to Coleridge, "then you might be pleasantly surprised to learn that I wrote to Sir George Grove at the Royal College of Music to arrange for you to see him there,"

Coleridge gasped as his jaw dropped and his eyes widened. "…and if you should be accepted there as a student in September, I shan't hear a word from either you or your parents worrying about the fees."

This was too much. Another thick, glassy tear rolled out of Coleridge's eye and down his cheek and then another. He threw his arms around Herbert Walters' neck.

"Thank you," he said. He squeezed him. "Thank you, Sir." He sniffed and squeezed him. He squeezed him and silently sobbed. There were no words that could say that particular 'goodbye'.

At last, he let go. He wiped his eye and blew his nose and became a gentleman again. He looked up at Colonel Walters. Walters had joy emblazoned upon his face. But it transcended joy and it wasn't on his face, it was coming from within. Joy was expressing itself through him.

He took his mentor's hand shook it. "Thank you, Sir."

Coleridge jumped down from the stage.

"I'd better go."

Colonel Walters nodded. "You better had."

"What can I do to…?"

"The only thing I want from you Coleridge is a promise. I want you to promise me that you'll always be happy. Can you do that? Will you promise me that you will always be happy?"

"I'll always work hard. I promise. I'll always do my best. I promise. Better than my best… I promise."

Chapter 2

It was only the second time that Coleridge had made this particular trip, the first being his interview with Sir George Grove. Colonel Walters had offered to accompany him but Coleridge had insisted that he go alone and so instead, Walters wrote a letter of introduction to Sir George.

Coleridge didn't like being scrutinised. He much preferred that his music speak for him but being interviewed and having to explain and justify his work in this way; for this to be his one opportunity and for so much to be riding upon it, it terrified him.

Sir George looked rather formidable behind his large, mahogany desk and splendid, grey moustache. The Principal must have been about seventy. His Royal College of Music was recognised as the finest establishment of its kind in the world. Sir George had gathered the greatest musicians together to lecture there and it seemed umbilically linked to the Royal Albert Hall. A magnificent stairway rose up from the entrance of the College taking one up to the magnificent Hall. This was the journey that the students were to aspire to. This, the hill to climb – this the goal, the challenge to all those who entered Sir George's Royal College of Music.

Coleridge had been told many times that he was a talented musician but this man, with an entire lifetime's skill and knowledge and experience and of such a breadth and depth – this old man with the contacts; musical, artistic, political and even Royal – a man such as this was sure to discover that Coleridge was a fraud, he thought to himself. The icy fingers of panic took hold and then tightened its grip.

By the time he had entered Sir George's study and saw the great and formidable walrus with those twinkling, beady eyes set in a face of primarily long grey whiskers, the boy could barely get his name out. It was morning but the stale smell of tobacco smoke from the night before, still hung in the study air. The desk was the size of a football pitch; the portraits, books and portfolios looking down, the musical parchment, the work of students – it was all so intimidating. Concertos and whole symphonies lay here and there – strewn, littered about on the desk and chairs.

The old man had called him, 'Mr Taylor' as Coleridge approached the desk and the door was closed behind him. It was the first time an adult had ever called him that before. Coleridge thought himself totally out of his depth. The panic smirked and gripped his throat, beginning to squeeze. He had never felt more like a little boy, never more so out of his league and never less like a 'Mr Taylor' than he did right then and there in that very mature room.

There was some handshaking, the letter of introduction was practically thrown at the old man and a chair was offered, but before Coleridge could answer he was being asked if he'd rather launch straight into some pieces and he sort of found himself nodding.

He dropped to the floor to open his violin case. Out of sight of the old man, he took a moment to himself.

The situation seemed so absurd. He took a breath and his instrument by the neck. He stood and placed it under his chin. Coleridge began to play.

Sir George listened.

He finished playing. He had done his best; he could do no more.

Coleridge held his violin by the neck like a throttled chicken as the old man read Colonel Walters' letter through pince-nez. A man came in and interrupted Sir George's reading. The walrus asked for a pot of tea to be sent up. He finished the letter and noticing that Coleridge had been standing all that time, asked him to sit.

They sat there in awkward silence. Sir George sat with his A-frame elbows on the desk; hands knotted together, the fingers holding his nose up, the eyes looking at the boy who didn't know where to look. The old man had white whiskers sprouting from his ears and his hands looked like they'd spent a lifetime chopping meat. He scrutinised the boy as Coleridge's eyes flitted about in acute embarrassment. At last, Sir George asked Coleridge where he lived and about his family. Coleridge managed to say, 'Croydon' and then couldn't think of anything else to say except that it was nice there and that it was handy for the train... and... anyway.... Thankfully, the tea arrived and both began to relax somewhat.

The old man started to ask about his time in the choir, about his lessons with Mr Beckwith and the concerts he had given and this got Coleridge talking. Coleridge began to relax more. He started to open up and soon, he found himself talking quite unreservedly, as if he were talking to a friend – as if he were talking to Colonel Walters. He spoke quickly and lightly, explaining this and that, likes and dislikes, influences and so forth.

The old fox was a very skilled interviewer and knew exactly how to get someone to present themselves as they really were, however shy and modest they might be at first. Once Coleridge had warmed up, Sir George asked him questions concerning the subject he most wanted to know about; the pieces the young man had composed and had just played.

Sir George's unconscious ear listened as Coleridge spoke but his conscious mind was watching, assessing. He considered Coleridge to be far too self-deprecating, but not to the point of self-loathing. The boy needed a little time invested in him in order to get him to open up. He was clearly sensitive and needed to be handled rather gently but he was engaging enough – quite an affable little chap. He could certainly play. He was very creative and passionate. He was young. It was difficult not to warm to him. He had been terribly nervous but a little bit of nerves is a good thing Sir George believed, as it shows that the boy really cared. A place at his College would mean so much more to this aspiring musician than to many of the other students there.

Coleridge clearly had a good knowledge of Classical literature and was keen on poetry, and that was always good. He was clearly very intelligent, artistically gifted and dedicated but Sir George was still concerned by his intense level of modesty. Coleridge was not good at blowing his own trumpet and had difficulty receiving praise and that could become a problem for him. It was as if he didn't quite believe that anyone should think any good of him. Sir George knew that these aspects of the boy's character would need to be worked upon but he was a musician, that was plain enough to see, and possibly – possibly even a composer too, albeit an embryonic one at that stage. A work in progress.

Coleridge was offered a place.

On the first day of term, Mr Taylor arrived early but still later than he had planned. His mother had discovered that his smart trousers had needed some mending and she was still finishing them off as he was pulling them on.

He had decided to arrive just a few minutes before his first lecture and to leave straight away at the end of the day. This way, he reasoned, he would avoid having to talk to anyone without appearing unfriendly.

He had waited outside, across the road at the top of the Royal Albert Hall's majestic stairway. He had watched as the students arrived and pretended to nonchalantly read his Musical Times as he trembled in his boots. The students all seemed to know each other and seemed to know what they were doing and where they should be going. Some were with their parents and nearly all were carrying their instruments – in new and rather splendid cases. It was then that he realised that he was going to be the only one with a child-sized violin. He was going to be the only one on his own and knowing no one; the only one who didn't know where he was meant to be or what he was meant to be doing, with what and when – the only one who felt sick. They would all see that he didn't know; that he was a fraud. He would be the only one with a large, circular patch on the knee of his best trousers and the only one who was of colour.

Soon, no one else was entering the building. He would be the last to arrive. He stood and walked towards the building. He decided that he should just throw himself into it. They were all sure to discover that he was mediocre at best so what did he have to lose, he thought, and so he bravely walked down the steps, across the road and into the Royal College of Music.

A very kind lady asked his name. He was convinced that he wouldn't be on her list and that this would be the moment where he would be told that someone had made an awful mistake and that he wasn't going to be a student there after all and that it was probably some regrettable mix up; an administrative error. He was convinced that she would be soon telling him how very sorry they were to have to disappoint him but that he could always apply again next year; and of course he knew that he could not. He would be very understanding when it happened, he decided, and would tell them not to worry, and apologise for any embarrassment he'd caused. He would reassure them that it was an easy mistake to make. He would be relieved. He heard some muffled instruments being tuned in distant, echoing rooms.

She found him on her list straightaway. He was startled. It would be somebody else's task to expose him. She ticked his name. He could see that there were other names that had yet to be ticked off meaning he wasn't quite the last to arrive. She told him the room to which he was to report to and gave him directions but he couldn't hear. He tried to concentrate on what she was saying so he wouldn't get lost but, not quite believing that he seemed to be getting away with it all, he had some difficulty. He convinced himself that he was bound to forget and get lost, or worse – end up in the wrong place and face that fresh hell. She smiled at him. He looked absolutely terrified. She squeezed his shoulder and told him he'd be just fine.

Now he sort of knew where he was meant to be going, he felt a little more confident. He walked down the marble corridor and pushed open a pair of heavy double doors into another, much longer corridor that was bustling with first and second year students and their lecturers. The sound of the chatter and of leather soles on the institution's cold floors filled the halls, and was mixed with the sounds of more instruments being tuned behind closed doors. Scales and arpeggios were played up and down and horns trumpeted as he walked the long corridor; echoing discordance, monstrous and magnificent – a musical Bedlam.

Scales on every type of instrument were played out, rising and falling, and keys were changed. There were pneumonics and sounds bending sharp and flat as strings were tightened and levelled off, in and out of tune. There were cymbals and piano chords and voices warming up as rhythms were clapped out by ratty professors in smoky practice room. Timpani keys were turned and the stretched skins thrummed like distant, rolling thunder. There were acidy sharps that suddenly fell limp and flaccid and flat but somehow, still fizzed. It was all things all at once. It was loud and messy. It was an assault on the ears and to Coleridge, it was probably the most perfect and exhilarating racket he had ever heard in his life. He tried to assess the talent behind particular doors as he passed but it all flooded over him and he had no choice but to give himself up to it. His skin prickled as the lunatic noise stroked his neck and nibbled his ears and set his teeth on edge. It drenched him – soaking him to the bone, and his toes curled. An ecstatic smile began to force its way out and he wanted to laugh. He was going to be lucky enough to hear this din every single day, he thought.

A clock on a stone arch spanning the corridor told him he should already be where he was meant to be but he didn't want to miss a thing. On a green baize notice board, he half saw information about additional classes and clubs and concerts and invitations to join quartets and people looking for rooms. He would look properly later, he thought as his heart punched at his chest and blood belted through his ears. He couldn't be late. He felt that he was nearly there and not one person – not one had told him he shouldn't be there; that he was a fraud and didn't belong there. Perhaps, he wondered, just perhaps he really did belong.

He arrived at the door. A large door with the name 'Dr Parratt' on it. He stopped outside. This was where he was meant to be. He had made it. Coleridge knocked.

His first day passed so quickly it blurred. Soon a whole week had gone in the same blur and a routine and normality had begun to establish itself. His weeks were disciplined but quite regular, and at the weekends he practiced. The journey from Waddon to Victoria soon became the norm and less of an adventure. He usually hailed an omnibus from Queen Victoria Station but occasionally, when he felt flush, he would take the brief underground steam train journey to South Kensington for the price of tuppence. Passing the splendid Royal Albert Hall on his way to college became routine but none of it was ever taken for granted by Coleridge and it never lost its thrill.

There was a boy there who seemed familiar. Coleridge realised at last that he recognised him from being out and about in Croydon, but more than that, he had seen the boy in one of the other choirs a year or so before. He thought that perhaps they had actually sung together in a joint choir once. The boy had introduced himself as William Hurlstone. He had recognised Coleridge too – a friendly face. He was a little taller than Coleridge but around the same age. His shoulders were narrow and his face pale. He had round, doe-like, brown eyes that peered out from large, lashy lids. His darker-than-chestnut hair gently curled at the ends. His fingers were long but he looked generally more like a poet than a pianist. He actually looked a little sickly. He had dry patches of skin and wheezed very slightly. He looked like Chatterton; like he belonged in a dusty garret somewhere, penning poems of love unrequited or spurned.

William Hurlstone was the first and best friend Coleridge made at the Royal College. Although they didn't share any classes together that first year, they often had their sandwiches together in Hyde Park and shared the journey to and from college. Not that they spoke much on the train, there were too many people for that. Apart from a polite 'good morning' to the other travellers already in the compartment when boarding the steam train, no one would speak until they alighted at London. William preferred to look out of the window to reading, as reading on the train made him feel queasy. Coleridge had requested that the paper stand at West Croydon take the Musical Times so that he could read that during his morning commute.

They soon became second years and Coleridge started to take a poetry book with him for the train, as a girl had started getting to the stand and buying his copy of the Musical Times before he could get there. He rather resented the fact that he had requested it and that she should buy it instead. She was a first year student. He made a real effort to get to the stand before her but he invariably ran late.

One morning, just as it did every morning, the train chuffed its way out of West Croydon Station. The carriage was full as normal and William looked out of the window. He closed his eyes. Coleridge had a piece of ribbon marking his place and opened his book. He was reading Longfellow's epic.

'...I should answer, I should tell you:
I repeat them as I heard them
From the lips of Nawadaha,
The musician, the sweet singer...'

Someone was approaching their compartment down the train corridor. Someone looked in the window and Coleridge looked up at the person looking in. He looked down. The girl sat opposite him. She had his Musical Times. She was late and she still managed to get to it before him somehow. She wasn't even going to read it. It just lay closed, flat across her lap. She was probably about the same age as William and he, about eighteen or nineteen. He was a bit bloody angry about it actually but she wasn't paying any attention to him. She wasn't what you would call pretty by any stretch. She had quite a long, oval face, a rather large and unfeminine jaw and a big, high forehead. The word 'oboe' sprung to mind for some reason. Her hair was the colour of an oboe and her eyes were.... She glanced across and caught his glance. He looked down. She looked out of the window again without exchanging her vacant expression for something a little more sentient.

Judging purely by physical appearance alone, Coleridge thought she looked clever; like an expert on birds or something. He wondered what her instrument was.

She was gazing out of the window so she wouldn't notice him looking. She didn't have a pianist's hands like William did and pity the poor violin that had to sit under that jaw. She didn't carry an instrument. It was probably the cello, he decided, on account of the sturdy knees she must surely have under her skirt. Suddenly appalled with himself, he looked away.

One of the other passengers stretched his legs out a little. Coleridge sat neatly. His shoes were polished and together, his hat was on the rack over his head with his violin and his gloves lay over his knee as he held his open book. Resting on her knee was his Musical Times. He couldn't distract himself from this fact and so he closed his eyes. He never saw the oboe opposite smile in victorious amusement as the train chuffed on.

As the rapidly dappling sunlight flicked and flashed across his closed eyelids, Coleridge began to drift off. The light flickered before him and a moving picture formed. He saw a prairie. There were mountains in the distance and a forest so large you could lose a cathedral in it – you could lose the Royal Albert Hall in it.

He loved the way the words of this place sounded – the way his mouth felt when he said the words, 'the Land of the Dakotahs'. The 'Dakotahs' – it wasn't like any English word. It was hot and dry. He could smell skins being tanned in the wigwam village, stretched over cut branch frames. He heard children giggling like the brook that bubbled along just a flat stone's throw from the village; it would never quench the great lake's insatiable thirst. Painted skins were slung over the cone-shaped frames with the stalks at the top poking out – pointing to different parts of the sky like the feathers in a warrior's hair.

You could see horizon all around you in that place and in the winter you would snuggle under buffalo blankets and be so hot your cheeks would turn pink. He saw a child, snug and bound, on her mother's shoulder as she ground herbs and the wild grass seeds she'd gathered. Daft barking dogs yapped around and played and the horses were all securely corralled and gently chomping on dried grass. People were gathering berries and other wild fruits and crunchy nuts. The men were away from the village hunting skittish deer and rabbits and Coleridge heard his own voice saying the words he loved as he dreamed on.

'...Ye whose hearts are fresh and simple,
...Who believe, that in all ages
Every human heart is human,
That in even savage bosoms
There are longings, yearnings, strivings,
...Listen to this simple story.'

A little way from the village, a great warrior stood, watching over his people. He was from this village but not of it. He had been put there by his father – left there by the Great Spirit to unite all the warring tribes. The warrior was handsome and strong. His long hair, black like a crow's feathers, was tied back and hung between his muscular, tanned shoulders. If you wanted to see his face, you could not. Coleridge wanted to but could not. The Indian raised his arms as he gazed into the morning sky. There was a breeze on his face and it ruffled his hair and startled his feathers but he was not moved. He raised his hands to the pale, morning sky and it watched him with love. His mother, the earth and his father, the sky watched over him. He raised his cupped palms to catch more life – as much of the life that was breathed into everything by his divine parents as he could catch in mortal hands.

The train clattered and Coleridge opened his eyes. The train had just passed Battersea. They were nearly there. Everyone in the carriage had been dozing and their heads had lolled about. All, that is, but for the girl with his Musical Times still closed on her lap. Coleridge's book was still open on his. He read again the words of the Great Spirit spoken to mankind.

'...I am weary of your quarrels,
Weary of your wars and bloodshed,
Weary of your prayers for vengeance.
I have sent a prophet to you
A Deliverer of the nations
Who shall toil and suffer with you
That the tribes of men might prosper,
That he might advance his people!'

Coleridge closed his book, The Song of Hiawatha. William gently elbowed Coleridge in the side and smiled at him as he stretched a little. The passengers started to ready themselves as they were entering Queen Victoria Station. The girl opposite moved out of the compartment and into the corridor.

"No Musical Times this morning?" William asked him with a knowing smirk.

"No, no Musical Times this morning."

As soon as the train began to slow and the platform raced to catch up, the man opposite William turned the handle of the compartment door in readiness. When the train had slowed to that safe-enough-to-jump speed, the man opened the door. A puff of steam and the door swung open hitting the side of the carriage. The man skipped out and the train slowly came to a standstill with a final sigh of steam and a heave on the heavy brakes.

The station smelt of coal smoke and oil and was full of commuters from those suburbs spreading all around the smoggy Capital. They poured out and flooded towards the station barriers at the far end of the grimy platforms.

So it had been every day since that terrifying first day in September over a year before.

William was studying composition and piano and the way he talked of composition had inspired Coleridge. He had always enjoyed composition but had never had the courage to invest all his study in it. It was harder to make a living as a composer than a musician, unless of course you were very talented and very lucky. But, performing was merely interpreting somebody else's work; composition was truly creative, William would say. As such, however, it was also truly terrifying. Coleridge had a talent for composition and William knew this. Coleridge already had two pieces published. He had given the money that Novello gave him for the pieces to his mother but he chose to dedicate them to someone else. Coleridge had sought advice on the composition question from his mentor, Colonel Walters who in turn arranged to meet with his late father's old friend to discuss the feasibility of a change of direction.

Colonel Herbert Walters sat across the mahogany desk in Sir George's office. After reading the two pieces, Sir George handed them back to Walters with poker face.

"And he dedicated them to you, Colonel!" said the old man.

"Indeed, Sir George. It means a great deal to me. But sentiment aside, I am sure you will agree, it is a careful setting of those words –"

"He's a clever lad," interrupted Sir George as he eyed Walters through the plume of aromatic pipe smoke. Walters had been slightly thrown but decide to persevere.

"He is sacrificing his melody to correct interpretation …rather than torture the words to fit a preconceived…."

Walters trailed off realising that 'sacrificing' was probably not what a composer ought to be doing to his own music – what was the word? He clawed at his mind for it.

"Quite," said Sir George. "He's had a productive first year."

He waited, rather sadistically. After all, he didn't really need convincing that Coleridge should change to composition but he didn't want to make it appear that easy to switch mid-term either. But enough was enough. He couldn't torture the young Colonel any further; he was far too much of a gentleman for that.

"I have arranged with Dr Stanford to take Taylor with composition as his first study."

"Thank you, Sir George."

"Both Dr Gladstone and Dr Stanford were very pleased with these two anthems. They show a great deal of feeling and aptness for that style of work. I have spoken with Mr Holmes, and he agrees it's best for him to drop the violin and take piano for the second study. I told Mr Holmes that I do not myself see where the violin is to lead, whereas the piano is all-important if he is to be a composer. Mr Holmes, I can tell you, didn't like that one little bit. But what do I care, it's my school and I can say what I damn well please."

"Quite," Walters chuckled.

"I have also excused him the class of Dr Parratt," Sir George continued handing a piece of paper to Walters. "The new time sheet, Colonel Walters. I do hope your wishes have been met."

The meeting was over. They had been.

Coleridge was over the moon to be taking composition. That first day on his new timetable, he had that familiar anxiety caused by unfamiliarity but it was more manageable this time – it being familiar.

Coleridge was in the corridor looking at the notice board when he heard a voice from behind him, over his shoulder. It was a voice that was hushed but very matter of fact.

"Brahms," William said.

Coleridge turned and looked at him, but William pretended to be interested in the notices. Coleridge smiled and stared back at the board. He had suspected that yesterday's, let's call it a discussion, had not quite been resolved.

"Dvorak," Coleridge replied in the same hushed voice, but with an adamantine unflinching. The gauntlets were down and this was now a duel. There was a silence then William cleared his throat.

"Brahms," he said with a sigh.

Coleridge wanted to laugh but would not allow himself to. He turned and looked at his friend with something akin to pity. He put his hand on William's shoulder.

"Dvorak," he whispered back with finality. William's laugh bubbled up from deep down. Coleridge giggled too. William put his arm around his best friend's shoulders and they set off to Dr Stanford's class.

"I know his influence on English music has not been great," Coleridge continued to reason from where the 'discussion' had left off.

"Is that a criticism?" asked William, ever the one to rise to an occasion and always looking for even the slightest chink in a foe's armour.

"No, it's just my personal predilection," Coleridge replied simply. William guffawed.

"And quite probably largely temperamental," William parried as they entered the already full lecture theatre. No one was ever late for Dr Stanford's class.

"Brahms," he said quickly as they entered the theatre.

"How utterly childish," Coleridge mocked, his tongue firmly planted in his cheek.

William and Coleridge took their seats and settled as Dr Stanford entered. Stanford was in his forties. He walked with a longer stride than you would think his rather stubby, Irish legs would allow. He spoke swiftly and loudly and once only – he never repeated himself without throwing chalk or board rubber or whatever else was within easy grabbing distance at the time. One would listen when he spoke not for fear of missiles but because the man was a genius and a wonderful teacher. His students stood when he entered the room.

Dr Stanford was also kind and very funny. These things made him the most popular lecturer at the Royal College of Music.

It was largely due to Dr Stanford that the generation of students he taught there, inevitably went on to become names because of their work. He was an inspiration and smelt of tobacco, though strangely, was never seen to smoke it. He could energise any flagging room.

He threw down his papers on the desk, slamming the door and ushering the young men to sit.

"Dvorak," William blurted out under the sound of students taking their seats, disguising, rather poorly, the great composer's name with a cough.

"Brahms," Coleridge whispered swiftly, managing to get the last word in before Stanford spoke.

"Good morning, gentlemen."

"Good morning, Sir," the young men answered.

Stanford suddenly stopped and just stood there. Arms straight, whitening knuckles on the desk in front of him. He looked livid. He was silent and his face was quite red. He raised his eyebrows and looked at them. He was waiting but for what? Someone was for the chop. He looked at one half of the room and then his head swung and looked at the other half of them with baleful eyes like Milton's new emperor of Pandemonium, surveying his kingdom for the first time.

He raised his eyebrows even higher than they had been before and his face grew redder still. It was clear to everyone that the mad Irishman was about to explode. His head suddenly swung again and he looked straight at William. Coleridge felt his friend's whole, skinny body suddenly prepare for impact – for fight or flight but probably flight.

"Mr Hurlstone!" Stanford growled fiercely. "Are you to insist – to insist, I say, that I introduce myself to our new student of classical composition?"

"Sir, I do apologise. Please forgive me. This is Samuel Coleridge Taylor."

"Thank you, Mr Hurlstone. And I," he said replacing the Satanic hiss with a purr and relaxing poor William and the rest of the room at a stroke, "I am Charles Villiers Stanford, Mr Taylor – known to some of my critics as the 'Irish problem'." The boys laughed, mostly in relief. Stanford winked a warm smile at Coleridge and William. "But you can call me Dr Stanford. Now gentlemen –"

That was Coleridge's introduction to Dr Stanford. He was a man who challenged his students and who demanded nothing but their best work and they idolised him for it. The stories about old Stanford became the stuff of legend. He was volatile but never rude or belittling – apart, perhaps, from that one time. He was very encouraging. He was emotional. One quickly learnt never to start a sentence with the words, 'with respect'. The word 'but' introduced instant conflict and so was to be struck from one's vocabulary when in the company of old Stanford. His eyes would well up when describing work that moved him. He would leap up and down and clap like a goon when something pleased him. He was the teacher that none of his pupils would ever forget. He appeared exasperated by the world and demanded that his pupils challenge it and change it for the better. He loved to ask them questions that he himself had no answers to; that no one knew the answers to, and he was always interested to see who would have the courage to take him up on his extra-curricular challenges.

"He wouldn't say something couldn't be done unless he wanted someone to try and do it," Coleridge excitedly said to William as they sat alone in the train carriage waiting for their homeward journey that evening.

"But a clarinet quintet with no Brahmsian influence? I think that he was simply saying it couldn't be done, Coleridge."

"Sir George must have told him how I feel about Brahms. This one was directed at someone. I know I can do it. You watch," Coleridge said with a surety rather than determination.

He knew Brahms well, not as well as William obviously, but well enough.

"And while we are on the subject of Brahms and Dvorak…" he went on, anticipating William's long overdue and no doubt, graceless concession.

"Alright," William said with a grace so cod you could almost smell the batter, "when both are truly inspired," he said carefully, "there is not much to choose between them and when uninspired, I concede that Brahms is …dull."

Coleridge tried not to smile too hard and so nodded rather too courteously.

"And… do you not have something…?" William didn't have to finish the question he couldn't finish. The duel was to end but could only do so through some sort of compromise on both sides. Coleridge sighed and spoke with an equal, forced nobility and ungenerosity of heart.

"When uninspired, Dvorak can be –"

"Can be?" William interrupted. There were to be no 'can be's' or 'may be's' if the war were to end; or perhaps this wasn't a war, perhaps this was just a battle.

"'Is', then, 'is'! Bloody hell, William! When uninspired Dvorak is commonplace."

William smirked. Coleridge smirked back.

"Thank you, Coleridge. 'Commonplace'!"

"'Dull'!"

They looked at each other but they couldn't hold back the grins. They laughed long and loud.

Once they had calmed down and felt really quite weary, Coleridge reached for his book and fished for the ribbon marking his place. The door to the compartment opened and the Musical Times thief entered. Coleridge and William stiffened. She sat next to William but left a narrow space between them so that they didn't actually touch.

It was then that William broke the first rule in the English Commuter's Rule Book. He broke the rule that says that friends must not, under any circumstances, talk when there is another commuter in the train compartment.

"And you agree, of course," he said archly, making Coleridge look up from his page, "that it is far worse to be considered 'commonplace' than it is to be considered 'dull'?"

Coleridge laughed out loud. He couldn't help himself and it went on too long. Eventually, he sighed to indicate to all that the laugh was spent except that it wasn't. He couldn't quite focus on his book. The silliness of it all and the wrongness of laughing drew the chuckle back up his throat again and his shoulders shuddered and heaved. William was enjoying his friend's pain immensely.

Coleridge giggled and knew it was wrong. He was afraid that the oboe girl would think he was laughing at her. He looked at his book. He had a huge grin on his face as he tried to read but his shoulders shook in occasional and silent, stifled spasms.

He looked up and over at his friend. William made his eyes go crossed and inflated his cheeks with the tip of his tongue sticking out. A rather high-pitched snorting burst out of Coleridge's face. The girl smiled awkwardly and looked at William who suddenly looked normal again – perhaps a little too innocent and nonchalant. The girl opened up her Musical Times and also pretended to read. William winked at Coleridge and let him get back to his book.

William was such a great chap and could be a total twit at times, Coleridge thought as he looked at the words on the page. He was great fun though and very bright.

During the course of the journey home, Coleridge found it increasingly difficult to concentrate on his book. Stanford's challenge tugged on his mind. He was determined that he was going to do it – or at least he would give it a go. He would dedicate his spare time to writing a clarinet quintet with no discernable Brahmsian influence. He would solve it for himself but he would do it for Stanford.

They were nearly back at Croydon; the nights, drawing in. Outside, the streetlamps were being lit and smoky chimneys reeked the chilled, late autumnal air. He looked across the compartment. William's head hung in front of him. He had his chin on his chest, his floppy hair flopping. He'd been dozing for most of the journey.

On the seat directly opposite Coleridge, was the girl. He could just see her eyes under the brim of her hat and over the top of her paper; over the top of his paper, and she wasn't even pretending to read anymore. She was looking directly at him. His stomach flipped. How long had she been watching him? He slowly looked down towards his book but his face was tingling with embarrassment. Without lifting his head, he slowly raised his eyelids to make sure she wasn't still looking at him but she was; all he could see was her eyes and she wouldn't look away, even knowing he now knew. She just stared at him with those oboe's eyes, and then, in that train compartment and over the top of the Musical Times she'd taken, her twinkling eyes smiled.

CHAPTER 3

"You've done if m'boy!" yelled Dr Stanford. "Not one ounce of Brahms!" Coleridge hung his head. To Dr Stanford, it was just he and Coleridge in the lecture theatre but to Coleridge, the room was painfully full of his peers and he was being singled out in front of them all. He hadn't done it for this; he had done it to see if it could be done; knowing he wouldn't stop until he'd done it. He hadn't stopped. It had taken him months. Stanford squeezed past the other students in the row and wildly shook Coleridge's hand with both of his, still clutching the Concerto.

"Wonderful!"

"Thank you, Sir. Thank you. Thank you."

"You have your programme!"

This was the programme for their Spring concert, which at that time, was still some months away. As the date of the concert drew nearer however, the student composers started to feel the mounting pressure – even Coleridge. He never quite believed the good things people said about his work and any criticism was always taken much too personally. It was brooded over for days. He was equally concerned that his own criticism of the work of others was taken in the same way and so he tended to over-enthuse when he liked someone's work and not to say anything when he didn't.

Wherever possible, he would leave William to speak that for him.

"So if Thomas Dunhill, Fritz Hart, Frank Bridge and John Ireland sit mine out, and we are all agreed that they should…?" The boys nodded.

The rehearsal room had seen some deliberation over who played what on whose piece in the concert. Each trod carefully to avoid giving rise to offence and each wanted to present themselves as best they could – in the best possible light without, ostentatiously, outshining one another. No one wished to be overlooked, but neither to be seen to promote themselves too heavily. They were gentlemen, after all.

The coal fire in the pokey rehearsal room did all the crackling and hissing and spitting for them. The boys nodded in agreement but poor Ralph's nod was a little weaker than the others. Coleridge glanced over at him being sure that it wouldn't be noticed. The others couldn't look. Poor Ralph, he thought. William was writing the final, final list and he summarised aloud what had needed to be seen as fairly debated and unanimously agreed.

"That will mean: Samuel Coleridge Taylor – violin, myself – piano, Gustav Von Holst – trombone …and Ralph Vaughan Williams …the triangle."

William looked up. They all gave considered nods of approval, even Ralph. He was desperately trying to look like he really did agree and really wasn't bothered but the mask was thin and slipping a bit. Poor Ralph. He wasn't there on merit as the scholar Coleridge Taylor was and he wasn't nearly as accomplished as Hurlstone, Stanford's clear favourite and besides, someone had to play the triangle.

Coleridge knew that as a student composer, Ralph could be a bit 'hit and miss' and hoped that he would be a little less so with his triangle playing. He hoped very much that one day Ralph would come into his own and have his day too.

The concert hall at the Royal College was much smaller than one of the commercial halls and a lot less ornate. It was very functional, however and comfortable and had been made to look rather jolly with the large daff and fern bunches in vases either side of the orchestra area.

Sir George followed the progress of all his pupils closely but he had a special interest in young Taylor. In addition to the Concerto, Coleridge had his Sonnet in F Minor performed. Unusually, however, he had chosen not to conduct it himself. Sir George sat next to Dr Stanford as the final bars of the piece were played to the packed hall.

"Very promising, Charles," Sir George said to Stanford as the enthusiastic applause started with the end of the piece.

"Of course he will never write a good slow movement until he has been in love," said Stanford. "Where is he anyway?"

The student orchestra stood and the applause swelled and grew a little wilder. Sir George looked around for Taylor in the crowded room as the shouts of 'Composer! Composer!' rang out. Members of the audience began to rise to their feet and the applause grew wilder still.

Sir George stood suddenly, rather angrily, and left the hall. The applause and whoops and whistling echoed down the corridors as Sir George briskly passed through them. He knew exactly where to look. Taylor would be in the organ loft. He marched right in and up to Coleridge who stood as soon as Sir George entered. There was barely room for one. Sir George grabbed him by the collar and dragged him from his hiding place.

"Oh, no. Please, Sir. I can't…" Coleridge pleaded weakly as he was manhandled from the room by the surprisingly strong old man and marched down the spiral stairs and towards the hall.

"You are here to learn to be a composer and part of that is learning to be gracious towards your audience," Sir George said firmly.

Sir George pushed the door of the Concert Hall open with the toe of his shoe and marched Coleridge down the aisle. He gave him a gentle shove and Coleridge stumbled out in front of the mob with half his collar sticking out after springing away from its stud. Everyone stood and cheered.

The old walrus stood in the side aisle and clapped his old, butcher's hands loud and deliberately. Coleridge was mortified and this just seemed to encourage them even more. They were whistling and clapping their hands over their heads and laughing. Sir George went back to his place next to the grinning Stanford.

At the very back of the hall Jessie, a first year with singing as her first, was clapping just as exuberantly as her fellows. She already knew of Coleridge Taylor, everybody did, although they had never formally met – Jessie and he had only ever shared a train carriage together and had competed for the only copy of the Musical Times that the paper stand outside West Croydon train station stocked.

The next morning, Jessie managed to catch up with Coleridge just as they approached the entrance to the College.

"I very much enjoyed your piece last night," she gushed. Coleridge stopped and turned. It was the oboe – the Musical Times thief from the train.

"Thank you," said Coleridge quickly. "Thank you. Thank you."

He started to turn but she stopped him by sticking her hand out to him, which he involuntarily took and shook.

"Jessie Fleetwood-Walmisely – Miss. You have, 'aroused quite exceptional interest'... in The Musical Times..." she added quickly holding up her paper. It was rolled up at the page but she knew the review almost by heart, "...to deliberately 'apply a different standard from that which pupils' compositions are generally judged'." She squinted in the sunlight and cupped her hand over her brows. Coleridge smiled. He was surprised and didn't really know what to say. He didn't have to say anything – her gushing continued.

"You live in Croydon, don't you? We get the same train. Buy the same Musical Times. I sing – and piano."

She looked over her shoulder, then at her sensible shoe which tipped to its side and tapped once or twice. She squinted back at the handsome silhouette in front of her. He stared at her. She was breathless and not knowing what to say.

"Anyway...all jolly good...." she said awkwardly. She smiled and shrugged. She had been determined to speak to him. She bounded up the steps, wondering whether she had made a total nitwit of herself or whether it was he who had. She ran through the College doors leaving Coleridge standing.

Just as Coleridge went in, he saw her disappear around the corner at the end of the corridor. He made his way towards his favourite rehearsal room. People were noticing him. They smiled as he passed them. William passed and mouthed, 'Well done' at him – patting his shoulder and giving it a gentle squeeze. He continued on down the corridor, approaching the turn at the end where a group of students were standing, chatting.

Coleridge passed the door to Dr Stanford's study and turned the corner where the group were to see Dr Stanford coming the other way. Just then, one of the gaggle of students at the corner, not noticing Stanford behind them but clearly noticing Coleridge, completed his sentence with a sneer.

"...after all, he's only a damned nigger," he said.

Stanford walked straight into Coleridge and took him by the elbow, walking him back the way he'd come and towards his study door. Still holding onto Coleridge's elbow, he dug into his pocket for the key and unlocked his room. He shot a glare at the student as they went in. He never liked that particular boy anyway but this, Stanford could not abide. He would deal with him later. He took Coleridge inside and closed the door.

"Sit down, please," he said firmly.

The room was warm but a mess, and dark – the curtains were still closed. Manuscripts were strewn everywhere, unread and ribbon-tied, on the desk, the chairs and the floor. Books lay open on top of other open books. A steaming teapot was precariously balanced on top of one of the smaller stacks on the desk – precarious but still the safest place for it. How could he operate in a room like this, Coleridge wondered. The shelves were packed with more books, some stuffed with papers – a great man's notes, thoughts, observations and comments. It was the room of an alchemist.

Coleridge sat down noticing the same day-old tobacco smell that Sir George's office always seemed to have but this aroma had an Irish malt aftertaste to it.

"Tea?" asked Stanford as he pulled back the curtains and opened the window a fraction. The inside panes were sepia-stained and unaccustomed to fresh, sunny, daylight air. Coleridge nodded. Stanford sat behind his desk and retrieved a couple of teacups from the second or third drawer down. He decided they would do another day but wiped around the inside of one with his finger as he had a guest. He began to pour.

"Of course you could be Irish too – and or Jewish!"

Coleridge smiled wondering where the milk would be coming from and where, for that matter, the tea had come from. The cup was handed to him. There wasn't to be any milk or lemon.

"Thank you," he said taking a sip. The teacup tasted of whisky. "Some of the boys in Croydon... they follow me along, laugh at my hair, tell me to go back to bongo-bongo land."

"They're jealous," Stanford said matter-of-factly.

He sat back and sipped his tea. A frown rippled across his forehead and he smiled at the boy with a friendly puzzlement.

"You know, you and your friend Mr Hurlstone are the strongest students the college has at present, or has seen for some time."

Coleridge looked down through the tea, down to the bottom of the cup and to the centre of the earth. He took another sip; the tea and stale whisky combination, at first surprising, was now beginning to please. Stanford felt an anger rise up in him. Anger at the boy outside and how it should have made Coleridge feel – at how Coleridge seemed to take the name calling as normal. His rage was fearful when the lid, that he normally kept on it, failed and it burst out all over everything. He managed to push it back down.

"Sir George agrees. We all do in fact. That's why you won the scholarship. On merit. Have you seen your reviews?"

"Someone told me about them…."

Coleridge suddenly remembered that strange, bounding girl; the Musical Times thief, the oboe – all 'jolly hockey-sticks'.

"I understand you have recently been asked to conduct at the Croydon Conservatoire?"

"Yes. That was because Mr Humphrey, the violin teacher there, was unable to do evenings and now, as their conductor isn't very well – unfortunately, actually they are not sure if…."

Coleridge trailed off. He was actually quite concerned about the Conservatoire's conductor and didn't want to be seen as too keen to take his place. Stanford felt that Coleridge was wilfully refusing to understand the point he was trying to make and so he decided to be blunt.

"Why do you think Novello publishes your work?" he asked, but Coleridge was not going to rise to it. It was Coleridge's turn to look puzzled. "Merit, my dear boy, merit! But, for the love of God, when you're not walking about saying, 'Sorry, sorry, sorry' you're saying, 'Thank you, thank you, thank you'. You can afford to be a little less grateful, Mr Taylor and a lot less sorry."

Stanford had been looking over Coleridge's Symphony with Sir George the previous evening with a number of shots of the Irish. He reached over and retrieved it.

"Now, this symphony of yours...." Stanford's anger at the abuse directed at Coleridge by that idiot outside was rising like red-hot magma but he just managed to maintain the thin veneer of normality. His hand shook.

"This symphony...." The anger was pushing at the crust. It was seeping through the cracks and he couldn't hold it back. It had passed the point of no return but he pressed stoically on.

"This symphony..." and then it came out.

Stanford was livid.

"You have no bloody concept of your own worth, Mr Taylor and it's high time you bloody did because you have more music in your little finger than that arse has in his whole body – Damn it!"

His fist came crashing down on the desk and caught the edge of the stack that supported the teapot he'd placed back on top of it. The force of the blow launched the hot teapot into the air and for a moment, time seemed to hang. Their stomachs churned as if it were they who were falling. The papers fell from the desk and slid in the air as the room was sprayed with steam and tea from the spout of the teapot, whirly-dervishing above the desk. Stanford threw the boy's opus back at the desk and lunged at the pot in an attempt to catch it but instead, he knocked the lid off with his thumb. Coleridge couldn't move. It would have been too late even if he had been able to. The lid flew someway off into the corner of the room and the sound of the knob cracking off was heard.

It all happened so quickly.

The teapot sat upside down in the centre of the paper-covered desktop. Stanford and Coleridge were spattered with tiny, light-brown liver spots; even their clothes, and the papers on the desk were soggying in the great pool of hot liquid as it started over the edge of the desk and trickled to the floor, that was papered with original manuscripts.

"Oh – my – bloody – God!" said Dr Stanford.

Coleridge had no breath left in his lungs to make sound and his eyebrows had all but disappeared into his hairline. He mouth hung open. The pot had landed upside down on top of his work. It had taken him days. The paper darkened as it drank and the notes on the pages were lost amongst the loose tealeaves. It was gone. The ink on his only copy of the piece, bled away and the work was drowned.

"Sorry Coleridge. ...I think I made an accident."

Stanford retrieved the least drenched page of the work and it hung like a filleted lettuce leaf from the dry corner he pinched. His anger, even when justified and well meaning, frequently seemed to lead to an accident being made, the impact of which he would attempt to dampen with humour – usually misplaced. Never more so than on this occasion.

"Symphony in T," he said.

The next two years passed very quickly. Coleridge went on to win the scholarship each year and in 1896, at the age of twenty-one, was nearing his graduation. He was now a composer to all that knew him or knew of him but to himself, he was still a bit of a fraud masquerading as a musician.

He had moved out of the family home but not too far away. He was, in fact, less than five minutes from his mother, in rooms on Waddon New Road. His rooms were right between the family home and the station. He paid the modest rent by selling anthems and quartets to the publishers, Novello. His was the ground floor room to the left of the front door, his window looking out onto the quiet road.

He had recently picked up his old copy of Longfellow's The Song of Hiawatha again, and all over again had been swept away by its eight syllable iambic, the exotic names and words and the vivid pictures that it painted in his mind. He couldn't read it this time though without hearing melody in his head and had, just for fun, just for himself, been working on a setting of a section of it. The entire poem was far too long, so he had chosen the part that celebrates the young Hiawatha's wedding to his love Minnehaha and the feast and festivities that followed. He loved the name, 'Minnehaha' but loved its meaning even more. It means 'Laughing Water'.

The 'Hiawatha's Wedding Feast' cantata was all but completed, but what on earth was he to do with it? There wasn't really a market for that kind of thing, it was too different. All choral music traditionally had a religious theme and this was clearly secular in nature although, you could argue that the poem itself contained a simple spirituality.

Coleridge was in his room, making some final amendments to his first draft when he heard a knock at the front door. He tidied his papers and put them on top of his cottage upright. Another rapid knock followed the first, a little too quickly. Impatient, he thought. He stopped and stood in the centre of the room and listened. He felt nervous but could think of no reason why he should. The knocking came again. He put on his jacket and hat. He would normally have arranged the curtains so that they fell in an appealing way in front of the windows but he didn't want the person outside, whoever it might be, to see the nets move. He heard his landlady coming down the stairs, grizzling as she slouched her way towards the front door.

He plumped up the cushions on the chair and placed them so as to make neat diamond shapes in the crooks of each armrest. He smoothed the covers on his already perfectly smoothed bed. You could have bounced a sixpence on it. There was a place for everything and everything was in it – the jug and washing bowl, shiny on the dressing table. The small oval rug by his bed was slightly off angle. He adjusted it and then adjusted it back again very slightly when he saw he'd moved it too far, making it not quite parallel with the bed frame and the line of the floor boards.

Coleridge never had visitors and so he rarely answered the front door but he had a strange feeling in his chest and wanted an excuse just in case the caller was calling for him. He breathed slowly so as not to make too much noise. He silently put on his gloves and carefully picked up his cane – all the time listening to the front door being opened. He heard voices at the front door. One voice was his grumpy landlady's and the other – the other was familiar also.

There was a knock on his door. He stood motionless for a moment and the knock came again. He opened the door expecting to see his landlady but she had already started back up the stairs weightily in her slippers.

"Someone to see you, Mr Taylor," she called out over her put-upon, chip-laden shoulder. He looked and saw that Miss Fleetwood-Walmisely was standing in the sun on the step.

"I went to the wrong house," she said. "But the people there told me you lived here, on Waddon New Road. You're clearly world famous in Croydon! By the way, they think you're from Calcutta."

Coleridge never knew what to say to this girl. What did she want?

"Do you mind?"

"Mind...?" Coleridge asked. Mind about what? What was she talking about? Mind?

"You're a scholar and I'm just...." She trailed off suddenly noticing his hat, gloves and cane. "But you're on your way out."

His plan had worked. He opened his mouth to speak but nothing came out.

"I forgot to mention," she went on. "I saw you at the pantomime last Christmas, at the Grand – and with my Musical Times...."

"I went to listen to the scoring. William Hurlstone told me it was beautiful. It was," he said, finding his voice. He had very much enjoyed the pantomime and especially enjoyed seeing his old music teacher, Mr Beck-with, there.

The door to Coleridge's room was still open and the girl was now looking past him, over his shoulder and peering in without any subtlety. This mare was a bull in a china shop, he thought. He was not going to invite her in.

She looked into his private room and saw his piano and the papers on top. She could see the pen and inkpot. She could see the spare nibs. She could tell he had been composing. Coleridge found her forwardness and familiarity disarming and a little rude.

"What are you working on?"

"It's nothing. It's about Hiawatha."

He was suddenly embarrassed of his personal work. It was a private matter. He hadn't even told William about it yet. "I'm also finishing another symphony for Dr Stanford."

He waited for her to speak but for a moment, she didn't. She just looked at him; her head at an angle like a puzzled dog, her wet eyes twinkling and squinting in the sun.

"I see...." she said at last. "Well, I'm looking for a partner and I wondered if.... I have some duets, I mean – Schubert," she added quickly feeling the need to clarify. "I put a notice up but haven't had much luck in finding someone to practise with yet." She looked at him. There was that silence again.

"I can help," he said chirpily and instantly hating himself. He knew she was trying to force his hand. Her manipulations were all too obvious and yet there he was, being manipulated. Fancy turning up on someone's doorstep out of the blue. Someone you don't even really know, unannounced and on a Saturday morning, he thought. But he smiled helpfully as he found himself commit to something that he couldn't have wanted to do less. He would rather have chewed off his own foot than spend too much time in the company of this pushy, manipulative, oboe-headed, Musical Times thief; a young lady with all the deportment of an albatross walking across hot coals.

"Would you?" she cooed. "I wouldn't ask, but…. Perhaps, I'll see you tomorrow, on the train, and…. arrange a time, maybe? When we're both in a little less of a hurry, a bit less busy?

"Yes of course," he said and she smiled and started down the pavement.

"I'll miss seeing you on the train each morning once you graduate," she called back as she walked away.

Coleridge closed the door to his room and then stepped out of the front door. He walked in the opposite direction to that taken by Miss Fleetwood-Walmisely.

Something was afoot, he mused, something was most definitely afoot. He walked around the block and, not more than ten minutes later was back at his piano finishing his cantata and the ending to that symphony that Stanford kept rejecting.

A few weeks and a few duets with Miss Fleetwood-Walmisely later, Coleridge graduated from the Royal College of Music. He and William disliked such affairs, both for very different reasons. Straight after the ceremony, Coleridge had asked his friend to keep him company in one of the practice rooms until most of the people had gone. William was all too happy to leave behind all those frauds who said things they didn't really mean to people they actually couldn't stand.

The air outside the room was oppressive. The smog that descended in the early evenings seemed to get worse each year, especially in the summer months. It smelt strongly of burnt coal dust. It was acrid and had a faint, yellow tinge to it – a real 'pea-souper'. It could give you a sore throat.

For some reason there had been a fire in the room but it was dying in the grate – just embers and ash. Although happy to leave the fakes to their fakery, William was rather hoping to get back to his parents and sister, Judith, who had all made the journey from Salisbury for his special day. He never felt he saw enough of them.

William was the first musician in the family although he did come with a distinguished artistic pedigree. His grandfather had been President of the Royal Society of British Arts and was known primarily for his portraiture. William's father was still horribly marked by the small-pox he suffered as a child and was almost completely blind. It was because of this that he had not been able to earn his own living and so his share of the family's substantial fortune had dwindled over the years to almost nothing.

William stood by the closed window to the practice room. He had been suffering slightly with his asthma all day. His breathing was growing shallow and a little faster than normal. It was harder to breathe than it should have been. He tried to sigh, but no sigh seemed to satisfy.

"You know, this is the sixth time he's sent it back," Coleridge said holding the final page of Dr Stanford's final assignment. To William, Coleridge had rather gone on about this. It was the closing movements of another symphony and no matter what Coleridge did to improve it, it never seemed to please the Irishman and so he kept rejecting it saying Coleridge could do better.

"Then stop re-doing it for him," William said.

"But he's right!"

"You can leave it now, Coley. We've graduated. It's done."

Coleridge screwed up the final page and tossed it at the fire, just missing. William retrieved the ball of parchment and unscrewed it. He ran a finger along the inside of his collar.

"Would you leave a finale unfinished?"

"It's not unfinished, it's just –" said William reading the sixth re-write for the first time.

"It's just wrong," interrupted Coleridge.

Coleridge turned in irritation. He couldn't bear something being left undone that could be done and he could do this. He just couldn't understand why it wasn't working – why he couldn't get it right. He didn't notice William.

William turned to the window as if looking out of it would help clear his lungs. Coleridge had seen him have attacks before but for some reason, he didn't seem to notice that one coming on. William looked at the crumpled page of music. He was finding it increasingly difficult to breath. He hated his condition. His attacks terrified him. There was nothing he could do to prevent them and nothing he could do about them once they were happening. He stretched the crumpled paper to read and tried to relax.

"We should go down," he said as pinheads of cold sweat started to appear on his lip and forehead.

"At least he didn't throw his tea at it this time!"

"Nobody's right all the time, Coley." William spoke in short breathy bursts, quietly gasping between times. "Personal taste can cloud objectivity. Why does everything have to be perfect with you? I think it's rather beautiful and dreadful that it should end up burnt. It's enough."

It was going to be a bad attack. His breathing started to rasp noisily. He tugged at his collar with his finger but the starch and the stud made undoing it difficult. He tried to open the window a little as the air, however warm and smoggy might help a bit, but the brass catch was stiff and awkward against the thickly-painted wood sash and he didn't have the strength in his slipping, sweaty fingers.

"Keep it if you like it so much," Coleridge said, still oblivious.

Coleridge turned to him. William's face was pasty and his eyes wide in panic, panting shallowly. He couldn't breathe and pressed his palm on the glass of the window, gasping. He struggled again with his collar stud. Suddenly, he hit the pane with his palm and started to rip and tear and tug in terror at the collar round his neck as he suffocated. He hit the glass again. He wheezed and gasped. He was pale and his face was wet, his mouth was open wide and his eyes rolled. His lips were turning blue and he croaked horribly. Coleridge went to him.

"William...?"

Sweat trickled down his cold white face like condensation on a tiled wall; his knees started to buckle and his eyes rolled back.

"Will be alright –" he said.

William wheezed and rasped and hit the window with his palm. Coleridge knew that panic only made things far worse for his friend. He put his hand under his armpit and supported him. William managed to pop half his collar off the stud. He undid the top of his shirt. His shirt was wet. With his other hand, Coleridge pinched the window lock apart and threw the sash open. The tepid air stung the back of William's throat but there was a breeze at least. He could taste metal. He took another breath.

Coleridge stood behind and popped the other end of the collar off the neck stud and put it in his own pocket. William could support himself. Coleridge put one hand on his friend's shoulder and with the other rubbed his back in gentle circles. William held onto the open window frame. The dark hair at the nape of his pale neck was tipped with sweat.

"You'll feel better in a minute."

In the quiet, Coleridge silently reprimanded himself for failing to notice the attack's onset. For being so wrapped up in himself. How could he have been so selfish? He had sounded like a spoiled child, he chided.

"I'm so sorry, William."

William's breathing was slowing. Coleridge stroked his back between the shoulder blades in steady, rhythmic, circular motions.

"What have you got to be sorry for?"

Feeling better, William turned to him, but Coleridge's hand remained resting on his friend's shoulder. Their faces had never been that close before.

Coleridge said, "We'll always be friends, you know."

"Well of course we will. What are you talking about?"

Coleridge recalled a line from the poem.

"'Most beloved by Hiawatha was the gentle Chibiabos, He was the best of all musicians…'."

William smiled.

Coleridge squeezed his shoulder then patted it. He pulled William's collar from his pocket and handed it to him. William offered the crumpled piece of music in exchange.

"You keep it," Coleridge said. "Happy Graduation Day."

The two young men started to move towards the door and the outside world. William took a breath. It was a long, deep breath that did at last satisfy him.

"Did you know that Stanford thinks you're the most promising of all of us?" Coleridge asked. William raised an eyebrow.

"I told you he wasn't always right."

CHAPTER 4

Coleridge had rather dreaded leaving college. He had produced some outstanding work whilst a student and received much praise but the anxiety caused by the fact that he would now be expected to operate commercially and earn a living at it, was almost too much to bear.

He continued to compose and publish small pieces here and there which he sold to Novello outright. Occasionally Mr Jaegar at Novello would reiterate that he would not receive any royalties through selling his pieces but Coleridge was just glad he was earning money at all and besides, he earned more by selling them outright than by accepting a lot less for them up front and then relying on royalty payments. The royalty payments, he had heard, would be minimal and the money he would receive through retaining the rights wouldn't have been enough to feed a church mouse. In addition to the money made from compositions, he was also in receipt of a small annuity from Novello. This was an investment in him, entitling them to first refusal on all pieces composed. Coleridge was also still conducting for the orchestra in Croydon and occasionally conducted his own compositions there.

Coleridge supplemented this income by teaching. He had a number of violin and piano students who he taught at his rooms on Waddon New Road. He had also started to teach at a new music college in Rochester.

William had taken rooms in Battersea and was living a life very similar to that of Coleridge. They frequently attended concerts together and always seemed to appreciate the same points in the works of other composers. They both shared the same opinion regarding pieces that failed to make the grade for them.

William had a low tolerance of work that was all show but of little substance. He hated the fakery of such work and to say that neither of them had a particular fondness for the Russian composers would be an understatement.

They walked together regularly, talked about music, life and everything and had even spent a weekend in Eastbourne together to attend a concert there; but later in that year of Her Majesty's Diamond Jubilee, 1897, William felt himself slightly side-lined by Coleridge's growing friendship with the oboe.

Jessie Fleetwood-Walmisely, or Jess as she had insisted Coleridge call her, was due to graduate later that year. She lived not five minutes from Coleridge so it was inevitable that they should see more of each other. But William found that Coleridge had started to talk of concerts and other performances that he had been to with Jess and to which he himself had not been invited. William knew that it would not have been his friend's decision to leave him out of such things. William hated a fraud when we saw one and had tried to give Jess the benefit of the doubt. He tried not to let the fact that he felt pushed away from Coleridge by her, affect his opinion, but he couldn't shake the unease he held about her. He found her ... 'manipulative' was perhaps too strong a word for it. It was as if she had an agenda. Time would tell; if indeed there was anything to tell. Until then,

William had decided to keep his opinions on the subject of Jess, and his growing unease, to himself.

Coleridge was English and always saw himself as English. What English people saw when they looked at him though, was different. He was one of what seemed to be only a handful of black people living in London and possibly the only one of mixed, Anglo-African parentage. Whenever two people of colour found each other, a bond was instantly forged – each having an unspoken knowledge of the experience of the other. Coleridge had struck up one such friendship with Kathleen Easmon, an African poet and painter residing in London. He had met her at a reading of her work about six months earlier and they had arranged to meet again a few days afterwards. Kathleen was beautiful and great fun.

One evening, Coleridge was invited by Kathleen to attend a poetry reading in a room in the British Library by the black American poet Paul Laurence Dunbar, who was on the London leg of a European tour. Kathleen and Coleridge had stayed behind after Dunbar's reading to meet him. When he introduced himself, Dunbar had shaken his hand so warmly. The two young men were about the same age and both lived in predominantly white countries but their life experiences could not have been more different.

Dunbar had heard of this young, black, English composer, as most black Americans had. In fact, he knew Coleridge's waltzes very well and had hoped the two would meet. Coleridge was amazed and flattered to find that the pieces he had been rattling off in Croydon and selling to Novello were known all the way across the Atlantic. He suspected that Dunbar had simply done his research before making the trip and perhaps didn't really know that much about his work after all. He told himself that Mr Dunbar was just being courteous. Nevertheless, they decided to meet the next day for tea.

"My father left me too, in a way," Dunbar told him as he tucked into his sandwich.

How extraordinary, Coleridge thought, that it was not considered impolite in America to speak when one had one's mouth full.

"He'd been a slave in Kentucky but escaped. Joined the army. Fought in the Civil War; 5th Massachusetts Coloured Cavalry Regiment. He died when I was 12."

"I'm very sorry to hear that," said Coleridge.

He had bought a copy of Dunbar's Lyrics of a Lowly Life at Paul's reading and it had already set his mind racing. He hoped that Dunbar wouldn't be offended but when he had arrived home late that evening, Coleridge sat at his piano and, touching the keys so softly that they did not make a sound, had already begun to start setting some of the poems.

"My mother had been a slave too," Dunbar went on. "Joshua and Matilda, both Kentucky slaves. She loved singing. I think she liked the words most. She got me reciting poetry when I was six. I worked my way through college and was heading towards a career in law but unfortunately, being…. Well, let's just say I only got as far as the elevator."

Coleridge looked puzzled so Dunbar clarified for him.

"I was elevator operator in the Callahan Building in Dayton. I used to pen verses between floors as I ferried the white folks up and down. Sold a few there too. Also wrote for an African-American newsletter." He took another bite of the dainty sandwich he was obviously enjoying.

"But things really took off for me when Frederick Douglass asked me to recite at the Chicago World's Fair. He called me 'the most promising young, coloured man in America'. What do you think of that, Coleridge?" he said slapping his leg and letting out a laugh in disbelief at his own good fortune.

"I er…" Coleridge hesitated as he dabbed the corners of his mouth with a folded napkin point. He had never met an American before, and this one seemed to Coleridge to be extraordinarily cheerful, to the point of childlike. Well, they were a very, young nation after all. But this one seemed almost entirely without inhibition. It really was most extraordinary, Coleridge thought.

"I have a confession to make," he said to Mr Dunbar at last, "and I do hope you won't be too offended but …I have started to set some or your work."

Dunbar tilted his head to one side with a genuinely puzzled look that broadened into a smile.

"I thought they might make rather splendid songs," Coleridge went on. "The rhythm… words. I do hope you don't mind."

Paul suddenly realised that he had done all the talking. He had so wanted to impress Coleridge, this true artist, that he hadn't let the poor fellow get a word in edgeways. He had wanted to impress Coleridge because he was such a devoted follower of his work, as were all of his friends back home. He loved Coleridge's music. He was fanatical. To him, this young English composer was a great man. He was a hero. He'd been so honoured that Coleridge had attended his reading and so nervous about meeting him for a proper English tea, and at his invitation, that his mouth had run away. The folks back home wouldn't believe that he had actually sat with the man. He suddenly felt a little ashamed of himself but deeply, deeply touched that this quiet and modest, though perhaps a little up-tight, composer thought his verses worthy of musical accompaniment.

"Mind? Really? Well, I'll be...." and then, in the middle of the teashop, Mr Dunbar stood up. Coleridge stood also, without understanding why – probably something American. Mr Dunbar took his hand and shook it. "Thank you, Sir. You do me a very, very great honour. Thank you."

Extraordinary, Coleridge thought as his hand was vigorously shaken.

Dunbar was in London for some months and during this time, Coleridge showed him the sights, some of which were left over from the Great Exhibition of 1851, such as the Crystal Palace. They visited the Royal Albert Hall, the Natural History Museum, British Museum, Science Museum and the galleries including the National Portrait Gallery. They even took time to organise a recital together in a room on Great Marlborough Street. Coleridge performed his 'Fantasiestucke' for string quartet and 'Seven African Romances' – the poems of Dunbar that Coleridge had set.

All too soon however, it was time for Paul Laurence Dunbar to return home. They had started collaboration on a short opera called 'Dream Lovers' but hadn't managed to finish it before Paul had to leave.

They struggled on, long distance, but the opera's completion, dragged; their collaboration greatly suffering at the hands of the Atlantic between them. Once it was completed, Mr Jaegar at Novello didn't want to buy it, which was a blow to Coleridge as this was the first time he had had his work rejected. Luckily, however, Boosey & Co did buy it. It was fortunate because Jess had decided that once Coleridge was more on top of his debt, the two of them should start saving.

The sound of horses clopping, trams and street vendors drifted up and through the window overlooking London's West End. Mr Auguste Jaegar was in his early forties as was the gentleman opposite him. Mr Edward Elgar had a large moustache and was greying slightly at the temples. His face was rather bony and sharp but he had a good sense of humour and was always taking up and then promptly abandoning fad after fad. His latest fads were the bicycle and his giant, white rabbit. He seemed to dote on the rabbit more than his young daughter for whom he had bought it.

Mr Elgar was a composer who was already very well established by 1898 although success had come to him rather later in life. His success however was mainly thanks to the tenacious drive of his single-minded wife, Alice. Mr Elgar's father had owned a musical instrument shop and it was in this environment that the young man grew. He was a self-taught musician and could play every instrument in his father's shop. He started teaching and Alice was one of his students. Her parents, stalwarts of the relatively new middle-classes, had not approved of their daughter's engagement to her music teacher, itself a rather unbecoming profession for a gentleman, and so had disowned her on the day of her marriage.

Alice believed in Edward's musical talent unreservedly and realised early on that she was not only to be a wife to this man but also to manage his commercial affairs. He was certainly no businessman. Mr Jaegar mused that Edward Elgar would probably not be sitting in front of him on that day, had it not been for his good lady's scrimping and saving, her drive and her unrelenting letter-writing to publishers such as he.

They were nearing the end of their meeting when Jaegar started to talk about another composer in Novello's stable, with whom he had been very impressed of late. Jaegar was a hard-nosed businessman and saw people only in terms of the return he could expect from his investment in them – be it an investment of time or of money or even cordiality. The composer he was talking of was Samuel Coleridge Taylor. He spoke as if a long-awaited bequest had finally arrived unexpectedly.

"I had, as you know, been looking for an English composer of real genius and since hearing his Ballade in D Minor, I believe I have found him. That boy, that very nice, dear boy, will do great things. His originality is astounding."

Jaegar stood and slowly moved around the desk. Mr Elgar knew this was his cue to start thinking about leaving. "When he grows older and develops beauty a little more – in his music I mean, he will be a power. He is the coming man."

Outside the door to Mr Jaegar's office sat 'the coming man', nervously clutching the leather bound cantata – or rather the final few pages of it that Mr Jaegar hadn't already seen. Mr Jaegar rather frightened him. He had finished his 'Hiawatha' piece and had wondered if it might be something that Novello would be interested in as he hadn't got as much for the Dunbar opera as he would have liked.

As he sat there, he began wondering why he had written the 'Hiawatha' thing at all. It didn't really fit into any category. Perhaps one or two of the choral societies would buy it. Every town and village in the Empire had at least one such society. Maybe, he wondered, a few of them would find a piece about Hiawatha's wedding feast an amusing and novel diversion from the Christian-themed works that they were so familiar with. He'd written it as an exercise to entertain himself, he recalled, but might get something for it. Besides, as Jess had pointed out, what did he have to lose?

There were two clerks outside who drafted the contracts, handled Mr Jaegar's accounts, liaised with the printers and publicised the works. Coleridge looked up and noticed one of them, the one with bad skin, looking at the threadbare trouser seam that hung over Coleridge's tatty shoe. He tucked his feet under the chair, crossing them at the ankle.

"Where are you from anyway?" the spotty clerk asked. The other clerk, the nice, German-sounding one, looked up from his work.

"From Croydon, actually."

"Croydon?" the spotty clerk asked.

"Yes, near.... Do you know Kingston?" Coleridge asked.

"Jamaica?"

"Kingston-Upon-Thames," Coleridge replied. "It's in Surrey. I live near there, in England."

The spotty clerk was terribly ignorant and rather rude with it. He went back to his work.

Coleridge thought the German-sounding one looked a little like he imagined Bob Cratchett would look. No – he had a Bob Cratchett personality, but looked more angelic than Bob. He was, perhaps rather unsurprisingly, called Fritz and was very handsome with impossibly blond hair, thick but chopped short at the back and sides like the feathers on a swan's neck. He had pale, blue eyes and his flushing skin was so smooth it was almost like a girl's. A couple of kiss-curls on his forehead, but a strong, square jaw line and broad shoulders for a young man – for a clerk.

Fritz looked at Coleridge with a 'just ignore him' kind of look. But there was more. He had an air of concern about him. He was just a clerk, that was true and was in the process of drafting the sale document, but he also knew music. He had stolen a few moments from Mr Ogre in order to read Coleridge's 'Hiawatha' cantata before even Jaegar had seen it.

Coleridge had dropped it off at the Royal College of Music for Dr Stanford the week before and had visited again a few days later to hear his views on the piece. It had been wonderful to see him again. Old Stanford had been rather enthusiastic about the piece and had asked Coleridge if he might conduct its premiere, suggesting that it should first be performed at the Royal College. A date was set there and then. Coleridge had then taken the piece with him and dropped it off at Novello with a note saying that he would return with the final pages, which still needed some re-working, at a later date.

Fritz liked Coleridge – it was hard not to. Mr Taylor was quite timid but was friendly enough. He was modest and didn't talk down to him like some of the others, being as he was, 'just' a clerk.

Fritz had been instructed to write out the contract for the piece and to leave a space for the price Novello would buy it for which had yet to be negotiated. Fritz had something he had to say to Mr Taylor but just couldn't in front of his colleague. He knew that if Old Jaegar heard what he wanted to say he would be for the high jump and most probably, looking for a new position.

The door handle to Mr Jaegar's office moved slightly. Someone the other side was resting a hand on it. Muffled voices could be heard from within but no actual words could be discerned.

Mr Elgar stood by the door inside the office but took his hand off the handle for another moment. Would he never leave, thought Jaegar.

"So I wrote to old Brewer at Gloucester," said Elgar in full flow, "and told him that I was far too busy to compose for the Three Choirs Festival this year."

Mr Jaegar gave him a quizzical look.

"Well of course I'm not but … Taylor needs the recognition and is far and away the cleverest fellow going amongst the young men. So I asked Brewer to see that his committee didn't throw away the chance of doing a good act."

Jaegar's look of utter bewilderment was almost comical. Mr Elgar felt the need for some sincere and heartfelt justification.

"You don't forget the struggle up that greasy pole and you don't forget the kindnesses shown to you from others a little further along, I certainly won't. And if one day you're fortunate enough to find yourself in a position to give another chap a leg up, well you do, don't you? It's rather churlish not to, I think."

Mr Jaegar smiled a smile with his face but not his eyes. His smiles were few and far between, even ones such as this. Smiles were reserved only for the higher performing beasts at his publishing house. His smiles normally flicked across his mouth and then they were gone before they ever managed to reach his eyes. They never started at his eyes.

He reached for the door handle, as Mr Elgar didn't seem able to anymore – he just stood there, rather sadly.

Outside, Fritz looked at Mr Taylor. He had decided to tell him even if it was in front of his colleague. He had to tell him that he shouldn't sign the contract. He had resigned himself to the dismissal that would inevitably follow such an indiscretion but some things had to be said. He wanted to tell him that for this piece, for this one piece, he should retain the rights and be paid the royalties on it.

"Excuse me, Mr Taylor," Fritz said softly. Coleridge looked up. Spotty clerk looked at Fritz but the door to Jaegar's office opened just an inch.

"And how is Alice?" they heard Mr Jaegar ask from within.

"Still formidable, sadly," Elgar replied.

"It is Mr Taylor, isn't it…?" Fritz bravely persisted in his beautiful German accent. "This piece, this piece ….wunderschon, you understand me?" but the door to the office opened a little further and then swung full open and Mr Edward Elgar came out followed by Jaegar.

"Hello, Coleridge."

"Good morning, Mr Jaegar, "he said, rising to his feet, "Hello Mr Elgar."

"What have you got for him, today?" Elgar asked noticing the manuscript he was clutching.

"It's the final part of a cantata, about Hiawatha," said Coleridge realising how dreadfully pathetic it all sounded.

"Is it really?" Mr Elgar exclaimed. "Well you stick to the Red Indians. And just so you know, I'm doing General Gordon. He's bagged. Just so you don't get any ideas, you understand.... You must come to dinner one evening. I shall speak to the battleship about it. And bring your.... You're probably too young to have a battleship of your own."

"I'm twenty-three actually and... well, she's more of a tug really." Elgar roared with laughter.

"Splendid! Then you shall bring your tug. But be warned – out of tiny tugboats great battleships shall grow!" He turned to Mr Jaegar and shook his hand. "Happy hunting, Nimrod."

"Come in, Coleridge," said Mr Jaegar as Elgar left.

Fritz had missed his chance.

Coleridge closed the door behind him, handing the completed cantata part to Mr Jaegar, and sat in the still warm chair that he was ushered to. Mr Jaegar tossed the leather cover to the side and put the final pages with the rest of the piece lying on the corner of his desk. He started thumbing through the piece a few pages at a time to remind himself. Then he slowed and read it one page at a time as he got to amended, new pages at the end.

"It's much better than 'Dream Lovers'" he said as he turned the final page. "Dunbar's vocal score was absurd! I hope that Mr Boosey does well out of it."

Jaegar scrutinised him. Coleridge had rather hoped that he would be in and out in a flash, as normal. Jess would be irritated for having to wait for him. He squirmed.

"You've built quite a portfolio of works with us now. Your chamber music is very well thought of and I am still convinced that you will one day show us a return on our not inconsiderable investment in you. And the premiere for this is…?"

"November. Nine months. At the Royal College under Dr Stanford's baton."

"Well, I can see that it's good. 'Onaway, awake' is a very fine love song."

He looked at Coleridge but it was impossible to tell quite what he was thinking or what was coming next. Coleridge knew that he had to take the lead but unfortunately it came out sounding rather more like an apology.

"I understand it's asking a lot to publish before it's been performed, Mr Jaegar."

Mr Jaegar clipped the end of his cigar and lit it – the smoke plumed, blue in the sunlight.

"This stuff seems to be striking a chord," Jaegar finally said with the cigar bitten between the front teeth of his open mouth. "Sitting Bull – that awful massacre at Wounded Knee, is it called? Funny names these Indians have. And the others all herded into reservations like so many cattle, all rather shocking really. Still, the music is good – worthy of Novello and it may be timely, as I say."

Coleridge judged his moment. He knew that he would never be respected unless on occasions he was seen to be firm and frank.

"I would very much like it… if Novello bought the cantata," he said.

"Outright you mean, for one immediate payment?"

"Yes, please, as normal."

Coleridge felt powerful. It didn't sit comfortably with him but Jess would be so proud; everyone would be. He felt a sudden urge to leap back in and make some excuse for his work or for himself but he rode out that uneasy wave and that eternal silence as Mr Jaegar, cigar in mouth and almost silhouetted against the window, looked at him. He took the cigar out of his mouth and leaned his elbows on the desk, the cigar gently swaying in the air like a cobra, scrutinising the wretch in front of its master.

"Novello will give you fifteen guineas for it," Mr Jaegar said with a hard-done-by sigh, so faux – as if he had been beaten into submission and then robbed of everything he had.

"Thank you, Mr Jaegar."

Jaegar stood at once and opened the door. He took the contract from Fritz who shot a look at Coleridge that Coleridge didn't quite understand before the door swung shut on him. Jaegar hastily wrote in the space left by the clerk and counted the fifteen guineas from a tin in his desk drawer.

Coleridge signed. He signed quickly before old Jaegar could change his mind. Mr Jaegar pushed the money towards Coleridge and put the cigar back between his teeth. Fifteen guineas was more than Coleridge could have hoped to earn in any number of months even if he had worked flat out for it.

"Just before you go, Coleridge I want to talk to you about Gloucester…"

In the street outside, Jess was pacing. Coleridge had been in there a lot longer than normal. Every time the door opened she expected to see him. Eventually the door opened again and it was him. He had a funny look on his face. He had the look of someone who had just robbed a bank. He was smirking. He trotted down the steps and, without stopping, took her by the arm. He actually wanted to run he was so excited but instead, he briskly walked her away.

"You will never guess," he said, getting her out of earshot of the building and bubbling over.

"Tell me."

"I have been recommended to do the Gloucester Three Choirs Festival commission."

"I wondered why you were taking so long," she said. "By whom?"

"None other than Mr Edward Elgar. Oh and he is going to talk to Alice about having us to dinner."

Jess gasped. She suddenly realised that that must have been the rather distinguished man she saw leaving Novello a while before.

"I was very firm with old Jaegar," Coleridge went on. "He wanted to pay less now and royalties later."

He suddenly stopped and turned her to him. He was so happy. She did love him, she really did, and her only pleasure was seeing him happy. This great happiness of his filled her with joy. He thought he would just burst with it. He could now give her something, something she wanted so much.

"Jess, with this commission –"

"It's only a recommendation," she pointed out not wanting to rain too heavily on his parade. It wasn't done and dusted yet and she wouldn't be able to stand the disappointment if it fell through. But what about the cantata, she wondered. That's what he had gone in there for. She was suddenly suspicious that he was softening the blow because they hadn't bought it. But he was too excited even for that.

"Yes, but if I do get it," he continued. "That, plus this year's annuity and the money from teaching at Rochester and conducting at Croydon…."

He paused for a moment to torture her as much as he could before continuing.

"All of that... plus the fifteen guineas in my pocket from the sale of 'Hiawatha's Wedding Feast'...!"

"No! Coleridge, you swine," she laughed, slapping his shoulder.

"He bought it!"

Coleridge patted the money in his pocket, the one without the hole. He spun his head to make sure no one had heard, and then turned back to her. She laughed and her eyes filled.

"Fifteen guineas, Jess. This means we can get married."

CHAPTER 5

The Jubilee Singers from America were touring Europe at that time in order to raise funds to found Fisk University. They were becoming so successful in their task that the funds were almost certainly secured at that time and they were becoming more popularly known as the Fisk Jubilee Singers. The singers, both male and female were all black and were credited for being the first to take the 'Negro Spiritual' music to the world.

Coleridge and Jess had been to one of their London performances and after the concert, Coleridge had introduced to himself Mr Frederick Loudin, the conductor. He soon found himself, much to his surprise, surrounded by the whole company. They were shaking his hand, clapping and patting him on the shoulders. He was surprised because in fact it should have been he congratulating them on their performance – that had been his sole reason for introducing himself.

Since meeting Paul Laurence Dunbar, Coleridge had become familiar with Les Chants et les contes de Ba-Ronga, Henri Junod's collection of authentic African music from that district on the borders of Deloga Bay in the southern part of Africa. He had read the music and had heard it in his mind but until he heard the Fisk Jubilee Singers, the music had not opened up to him.

The themes sung by Loudin's troupe were unmistakably African but they were different somehow. The words were primarily of a spiritual nature but the music and words combined created something of greater depth than the sum of its parts. It spoke. It spoke of men and women taken from their homes, from their parents, from their children, from their land and from their lives. It spoke of people taken to a far away and foreign place and of forced labour. This music was the music of slavery and was sung with the voice of the slaves.

Europe had never heard anything like this before. Europe had reinvented slavery and the voice of slavery had always been one-sided, but this response from the slaves themselves had travelled over time and sea to tell Europe how they felt about what had been done to them and it didn't sit comfortably.

Some who heard wept. Coleridge had been transfixed. He listened as a composer, as a musician. He listened as a man; a man with African blood in his veins, perceived as a foreigner in the country of his birth just as these people were; the children of an enslaved generation. Songs that were so beautiful. Songs that he had never heard before. Songs with beautiful names like 'Roll, Jordan, Roll', 'Been a-listening', 'The Wings of Atlanta' and perhaps the most beautiful of all those never heard in Europe before, 'Swing Low Sweet Chariot'.

A couple of days later, Coleridge and Jess met with Mr Loudin and a few of the singers at a tearoom not too far from the group's lodgings on the Vauxhall Bridge Road.

To see one black person in London was unusual but to see a group and a group that was so exuberant was extraordinary. The others in the tearoom couldn't help but stare at the happy group. Their dress looked the same as their own but their colour and accents were strange. Although Americans spoke 'English' and to the English therefore, should be no different to the English, they were a world apart in how they spoke and acted. They watched over teacup brims at Coleridge and Jess and the black Americans, with a warm and amused curiosity.

"Mr Loudin, to hear the music of my race," said Coleridge at a loss, "and to witness the service you are doing to make it known....! I don't know what to say. And all the funds...?" Coleridge enquired. He always spoke lightly and swiftly but the excitement he felt made him almost incomprehensible to his new friends. The Americans spoke loudly and languidly, as if they were still in the humidity of the Deep South and had to be heard over a distance. They spoke as if their lives were without any complication but Coleridge knew that this was not the case at all.

"All for our new university, yes Sir," Mr Loudin drawled.

"I am terribly keen on America," Coleridge said.

"America is learning about you too and not just the black folks neither."

"He keeps trying to go to Berlin as well but only ever gets as far as Eastbourne, don't you Coleridge?" said Jess chiming in, but no one really heard. It was a new and uncomfortable experience for her to be the odd one out in a group.

"There are some people in Washington you should meet – the Hilyers."

"Mamie will just love you," said one of the singers, a girl called Kitty. "She'll just want to gobble you right up."

"Well, I have to visit Jessie's parents first," said Coleridge.

Jess had spoken of little other than this painful meeting that Coleridge was to have with his future in-laws, to discuss his intentions towards their only daughter.

"And once the Gloucester festival and "Hiawatha" premiere are over…." Coleridge trailed off then suddenly changed track as he often did. His mind raced and the words couldn't keep up. His eyes had been opened and he was terribly excited.

"The classical potential here is enormous. Brahms did it for Hungarian folk music, Grieg did it for Norwegian, Dvorak for the Bohemian…."

"And I dare say that you are the best placed to do it for the music of black folks," Loudin told him.

They shared a wonderful afternoon with the visitors but all too soon it was over and the excitement of it dissolved in abject dread because a few days after their tea with the Fisk Jubilee Singers, Coleridge was to pay his visit to Mr & Mrs Fleetwood-Walmisely's on Belmont Road in Croydon.

This was a twenty or so minute walk from his home. Belmont Road was more towards Wallington, just the other side of a pretty piece of common land called Bandon Hill. He loved walking there in the spring, as Bandon Hill was clear and woody and always covered with bluebells in their season.

The meeting with Mr & Mrs Fleetwood-Walmisely had started well but deteriorated rapidly and rather spectacularly. Coleridge had been very respectful and cordial. He was after all an Englishman and although not born into the upper middle-classes as Jessie was, he didn't think that his behaviour or intentions warranted the actions that Mr Fleetwood-Walmisely had taken upon his person.

Jess had warned Coleridge that her father was prone to act first, out of extremes of emotion, and think later. She had also told him that the favoured emotion acted from could best be described as incandescent rage.

The cake trolley had just been wheeled in with a gentle tinkling and chinking of the china. The niceties were all but over and so down to business, Coleridge thought. Mrs Fleetwood-Walmisely took a sip of fresh, hot tea. Coleridge took a deep breath and then asked Mr Fleetwood-Walmisely's permission to marry his absent daughter.

Mrs Fleetwood-Walmisely spat the tea back into the cup and saucer and started dabbing at her chin with her napkin like a maniac restrained by primness. Mr Fleetwood-Walmisely didn't say a word. He looked at Coleridge in silence as the colour in his face slowly changed from red to redder, to very red and then to purple.

In an instant, he lunged at Coleridge and lifted him out of his seat by the lapels. Coleridge struggled, but only to put his own cup and saucer down without making a mess. He was frog-marched to the front door, his feet barely skimming the floor. The door was thrown open and he was pushed through it. Before he could turn to protest, Mr Fleetwood-Walmisely had kicked him quite hard in the bottom and slammed the door.

Coleridge had never, ever been so humiliated in his life and he rubbed his shamed and sore backside in the quiet, suburban street. He went straight home and packed an overnight bag. He sent Jess a telegram the next day asking her to meet him in Eastbourne at eleven where he would report back. He would meet her in the small public gardens near the train station.

It was a beautiful summer morning. It was wonderful to get away from the smoke and noise of London every so often and get to a place where you could see the horizon. It almost instantly brought on a deep sigh as the weeks of London and thick, London air, were expelled from the body and mind and soul. He found the sight of the expanse of the ocean and skies a real tonic.

On this particular day, however, Coleridge paced in the gardens, oblivious to the crisp, beautifully floral-scented sea air. He was unaware of the fresh and heady roses that graced the verges around the bubbling, ornamental fountain and lily pond where fat goldfish basked. Ladies in white kept the sun off their faces with large, white hats and lacy parasols and gentlemen in boaters and blazers strolled with their canes. But Coleridge paced.

"I got your telegram," said Jess and she approached him.

"Is there a quiet corner for a chat?" Coleridge wondered aloud as he took her elbow, his face buckling with quiet but frenzied intensity. There was a narrow bench behind a beautifully groomed hedge and they both sat.

"What did they say?"

Coleridge took out his cigarettes, his hand still shaking with the indignity of it all. He patted his jacket for matches. He couldn't find them. It was then that he noticed that they weren't quite as alone as he would have liked. A couple with a little girl of about six sat a little further along and slightly round the corner. The girl had been providing her parents with a commentary on the strange, black man pacing up and down and reported in a whisper how he had taken the lady, with the face like a cow's, behind the hedge. This had piqued the child's curiosity. She had recently been told what the word 'murder' meant and wondered if the cow-faced lady was about to get murdered and so she peered round at them, staring unashamedly.

"No match," he said in frustration. Indignity piled on indignity and now frustration to boot. He looked at the girl staring at him and softened. He smiled. The little girl returned his smile realising that the man was far too nice to murder someone and not a bit nasty.

"I'll get you one," the child said as she trotted over, wanting to be his friend. She was from Liverpool. The old gardener was having a smoke by the grass-cuttings compost heap and she ran straight to him. She had made friends with the gardener on the first day of their holidays and now, three days later, they were firm old friends.

Coleridge looked at his shoes and chewed the inside of his mouth. He looked up and away and shook his head. He was upset that things were not going to go the way he wanted them to – the way Jess had so wanted them to.

"I was kicked out of the house," he said at last.

"You're speaking figuratively, I suppose?" she asked nervously.

"No, he literally kicked me – out of the house."

Coleridge waited for the news to sink in. "So what do you want me to do now?"

Jess could twist her father around her little finger. It wouldn't end there. She paused for a moment then took Coleridge's hand. He looked at her for the first time since she'd arrived. She looked inside him. She wasn't a great beauty but she was a good friend and a talented singer. She was good for him. Too good, he suspected. He hoped she couldn't read his thoughts so that he wouldn't have to excuse them. She smiled at him kindly.

"So what do you want me to do?"

"Just marry me," she said simply. Coleridge didn't understand so she went on. "I thought this might happen so I went to the priest. I told him everything. Do you know what he said?" Coleridge shook his head sadly. "He said I had to follow the dictates of my own conscience before considering my parents' feelings."

"Really? He said that?"

Jess nodded. The little girl ran back to them and handed him the box of matches. She smiled a toothy grin and squinted in the sunlight.

"You may take only one!" she ordered dictatorially, holding up a sticky finger, making Coleridge and Jess laugh. He lit his cigarette and handed the box back to the child who ran away, giggling happily.

"Thank you, Miss Sunshine," Coleridge called after her. Some distance away, the child's parents turned to Jess and Coleridge and smiled over at them.

He turned to Jess, very seriously again for a moment. He needed her to understand him. He needed her to understand what she was taking on in marrying him but he hated having to say how he felt – he considered himself much more eloquent when his music spoke for him.

"Music will always be my first love, you know," he said to her at last. She nodded. She understood this and wanted him anyway. "You don't know how gentle a black man can be."

She squeezed his hand.

Jess spoke to her parents and gradually, they came around to the idea of a struggling, black composer as a son-in-law. This was fairly remarkable as their initial and immovable response had been that it was unacceptable; unacceptable on every level and it would be seen so not just by Mr & Mrs Fleetwood-Walmisely but also by all of Croydon society. However, they also knew that their only daughter knew her own mind, that they loved her and that they didn't want to lose her.

Her parents, to put it very simply, were embarrassed. They had no idea what they would tell their friends and neighbours. To marry beneath one! How could they possibly justify their daughter's actions to everyone? Well Jess provided them with an answer.

Jess had told her parents about Mr Elgar; about his father being a shopkeeper, a tradesman, and Mr Elgar himself being a music teacher to Miss Caroline Alice Roberts, the daughter of General Sir Henry Roberts. She told them how the teacher and student fell in love but that her parents couldn't accept the marriage. The marriage went ahead but the opposition was steadfast and so the parents lost the thing they sought to keep the most. They lost their daughter through their intransigence.

Elgar had just had his enigma variations performed and published to huge international acclaim. Jessie told them how Alice was the driving force in Mr Elgar's career, that it was she who pushed him to the success that he enjoyed. Well, Jess had told her parents, she could do the same for Coleridge.

Mr & Mrs Fleetwood-Walmisely knew that what Jessie wanted Jessie invariably got and that where she aimed herself, she would most certainly arrive. It wasn't that she was spoiled, it was just that they had long ago realised how unwise it was to stand in her way, unless of course one was particularly keen to be steamrolled as flat as a pancake.

Jessie was bright and had an answer for everything. To her, for example, the 'Negro issue' was irrelevant. Coleridge himself was of mixed parentage but being a mulatto hadn't hampered his progress so far, so why should it do so for her own offspring? They couldn't argue with that, nor with her for that matter, and so they eventually and rather wearily agreed to the marriage.

The summer rolled by and in October Coleridge conducted his Ballade in A Minor at the Three Choirs Festival in Gloucester. The piece had been commissioned as the centrepiece of the festival. This festival was for Coleridge what it had been to Mr Elgar a number of years earlier. It was the bed, from which a great career could grow and Mr Elgar took huge pride in the fact that he had given up his place at this prominent event in order that Coleridge might have a bite of the cherry. Later that same month, Coleridge had conducted the same piece at its London premiere at the magnificent Crystal Palace.

The Crystal Palace was one of many leftovers from the Great Exhibition. As if building the magnificent structure wasn't triumph enough, following the exhibition the Palace had been totally dismantled and was rebuilt near Sydenham Hill in what was at that time a vast themed park, itself also a left over from the Great Exhibition, and full of life-sized model dinosaurs.

The 13,000 exhibits in the Crystal Palace came from all over the world with art from ancient Egypt right up to the Renaissance. It also included art that was modern and technology that was going to change the lives of all in the Empire for the better and for good.

Inside the vast, glass cathedral were statues and sphinxes, fully grown trees, elevators to the three levels from which flags and banners from all around the world were hung.

In front of the Crystal Palace fountains, the like of which had never before been seen in England, threw one hundred and twenty thousand gallons of water one hundred feet into the air every day. Such was that marvel of glass and iron; such was the modern wonder of the Crystal Palace.

William had arrived early for Coleridge's big concert there and so they walked in the park amongst the dinosaurs for an hour or so beforehand. He hadn't seen as much of William that year as he would have liked and didn't quite know how William would react to his news. There seemed to be little love lost between William and Jess at the best of times and so he decided to be rather matter-of-fact about it all. William hid his true feelings well. Coleridge showed him the ring Jess had chosen and that he had bought with the money earned from the Gloucester Festival. The ring had also made a significant dent in the fifteen guineas.

"It's very beautiful, Coley. Many congratulations."

Coleridge asked if he would do him the honour of being his best man. He told him that the wedding date was set for 31st December the following year and that there was plenty of time and so no excuse not to say 'yes'. William wouldn't have dreamt of not saying 'yes'. They would 'see in' the turn of the next great century with the celebration of Coleridge's marriage to

Jessie. William joked that it would be an easy date to remember.

Coleridge had said his piece and William had heard it. They moved on to talk of other things – of anything other than the wedding or of Jessie.

In the Centre Trancept of the Crystal Palace there were daily performances from the in-house circus involving all the usual acts: high wire, trapeze, and the clowns that Coleridge always found rather disturbing and never very funny. The circus ring had been adapted for the concert with musicians taking up about three-fifths of the ring seating and the audience making up the rest.

William had to leave early for some reason and so unfortunately couldn't stay behind after the concert to chat to Coleridge and Jessie. But he did stay long enough to see the ovation and just how exuberantly the piece was received and that at least brought some warmth to his heart.

The combination of the Three Choirs Festival and the London Premiere at such a prestigious and unusual venue, had moved Coleridge Taylor from the critics' columns of the Musical Times and into the national newspapers overnight. Word was also getting around that the premiere of his choral work, 'Hiawatha's Wedding Feast' would be something very special indeed and that tickets at the Royal College of Music were selling fast. This prompted an unprecedented rush on his old college's box office the next morning, even though the premiere was a whole month away. It was a month that flashed passed.

It was early November and bitterly cold outside, something had gone wrong with the heating inside the Royal College of Music's Concert Hall and the heat inside was stiflingly oppressive. All the windows in the corridor were open, which was a very good thing as a great many people had not been able to secure seats and so stood outside. The corridors were also jammed with people listening to Stanford's orchestra playing and the choir singing 'Hiawatha's Wedding Feast'.

Critics from the national newspapers where there. There were even some American critics present. There had been such buzz in the build up but no one was disappointed. Quite the contrary, there was an instant standing ovation at the end of the celebratory piece and Coleridge was dragged up on stage once again by a very jovial Sir George Grove.

Coleridge was overjoyed too but a little surprised that the piece was quite such a success. It hadn't been a college task or commission, but rather written because he wanted to – because it was a challenge, it was fun and because it was all about love and celebrating that love.

At the reception following the performance, lavish by the Royal College's standards, Coleridge stood with Dr Stanford, William, Mr Jaegar from Novello and Sir Arthur Sullivan who had not yet fully recovered from a serious bout of his unnamed but on-going medical complaint. A very handsome American lady called Mrs Ronalds accompanied him. They all nursed their glasses in a large and rather unwieldy circle, the like of which always forms around the 'man of the moment' at such functions.

"I'm always ill now," said Sir Arthur, "but I decided to come tonight even if I had to be carried here. And very beautifully conducted it was too, Charles, if I may say so."

"Thank you, Sir Arthur," Dr Stanford said just as Jess returned to the group.

A space in the circle politely opened up for her and was joined once more by her stepping in opposite Coleridge, making it a little more warped and unwieldy than it had been before.

She was brimming as she had just overheard two people talking. They were clearly critics. One had said that it had been 'wonderfully buoyant and vigorous' and was amazed, as it was Coleridge's 'first piece'! If only they knew, she thought as she passed by anonymously and overheard the other critic's gushing response – that the performance was 'one of the most remarkable events in modern English musical history'.

She had met or already knew the others in the circle – except for the two who had joined them shortly after she had excused herself.

"May I introduce Miss Fleetwood-Walmisely, my fiancée," said Coleridge. "Jessie, this is Sir Arthur Sullivan and Mrs Ronalds."

"My muse," said Sir Arthur feeling the need to explain away Mrs Ronalds.

"Would you excuse me," said Mr Jaegar as he moved away from the group to talk to Sir George at the other end the happy, crowded room.

Mr Jaegar had been surprisingly cheerful all evening, Coleridge thought. Quite unlike his normal grumpy, frightening old self. The gap in the circle closed up again.

Sir Arthur Sullivan and Mrs Ronalds fascinated William. She was obviously his mistress and everyone knew it, but they looked more like great friends than lovers; almost naughty. They acted as if they shared a private joke between them.

Sir Arthur and Mrs Ronalds were indeed playing a game, the aim of which was to expose the dirty little mind of the other without raising an eyebrow of suspicion in polite company. William couldn't believe that this thin enamel of innocence was genuine and although he normally detested fakery and humbug, he was thoroughly enjoying this legendary showman and his bright, buxom and independently wealthy 'muse'. However, if they had ever been in one of his classes, he concluded, he would have had to separate them.

"It's a great honour, Sir Arthur," gushed Jess shaking his hand and totally ignoring Mrs Ronalds. This wasn't lost on William, nor on Mrs Ronalds. She and William exchanged eye contact in a flash but neither Mrs Ronald's facial expression, nor his, changed for one instant. They had bonded in a glance and had bonded, one could say rather unkindly, against Jess. They both knew what the other had thought and that was enough.

"The honour was ours, I think," Sir Arthur replied sounding a bit merry. Jessie flushed pink but she didn't know why. Sir Arthur looked at Coleridge and raised his glass. The room was jam-packed with people and some turned to enjoy the great man's admiration of the bright, new star.

"Tonight, young man, we heard melody and harmony in abundance. The scoring was quite, quite brilliant. It was full of colour. So luscious," he said now looking directly at Mrs Ronalds, his voice deepening, daring her not to laugh, "so rich and... sensual. This work will put you on the map internationally, Mr Taylor."

"I don't know what to say," Coleridge said. "I do hope you don't expect a speech from me, Sir Arthur. I'll do anything but that."

"Are you hyphenated Mr Coleridge Taylor?" asked Mrs Ronalds innocently. She could always beat Arthur at this game and she wasn't planning on losing a set this time. She prepared the court.

"Er – no," said Coleridge, sounding a little unsure.

"Good heavens, then you should be," she said.

If Mrs Elgar were a battleship, Coleridge thought, this wonderful, beautiful and gracious lady was certainly a most stately, transatlantic liner.

"After tonight you will be a national figure," she went on. The trap was laid. She turned to Jess but before she could spring it, Sir Arthur seeing an opportunity, leapt gladiatorially into the ring to steal the thunder from under his muse with all the innocence of a drunken cherub.

"I am quite sure that Miss Fleetwood-Walmisely, will survive married life perfectly well without her hyphen intact, my dear."

William nearly dropped his glass. The group was silent. They looked at Sir Arthur who sipped. Jess's smile froze to her face. No one dared speak. Her smile still frozen, started to ache. Sir Arthur looked across at Mrs Ronalds.

"Poor Mrs Ronalds over here," he went on, "she lost her hyphen at a very tender age, at a very tender age indeed, and now I'm afraid she rather covets yours just as I covet this young fellow's genius."

Sir Arthur sidestepped his over-stepping of the mark more through tipsy teetering than any skill. The others were statues. For a second, William had seen Mrs Ronalds smirk at Sir Arthur but it was gone in the blink of an eye. She had noticed him notice this and for being such a clever boy in cottoning on to their private impropriety and for not telling, she rewarded William with a wink, again unseen by the others. She liked William. She didn't know him personally but she suspected that he might be musical and she always very much liked a young man who was.

"Hardly, Sir," said Coleridge.

Mrs Ronalds turned to Jess and took her hand.

"And this is the ring! You must be so very happy."

"I am a music maker," Sir Arthur said raising both his glass and, more unusually for him, the tone. He wanted to make a serious point for a change but the alcohol cruelly hampered him. Young Taylor should be toasted. "Just a humble music maker. I put on shows. Frivolous, frivolous shows! And do you know why? Do you know why I do it, Mr Taylor? I'll tell you why. I do it all… for the money. But you, Sir," he said looking at Coleridge, "you, Sir are not a music maker, like me. You, Sir, are a composer."

He pointed the finger of the hand with the glass in it at Coleridge and drank deeply. Someone jostled Sir Arthur slightly as they passed. A trickle ran down his chin. Coleridge was deeply touched. William was so proud of him. Jessie's face still ached.

"Thank you, Sir Arthur."

"My God but he's clever," Sir Arthur said suddenly thinking he had heard a penny drop somewhere. "Every town, every bloody village in the land, every street in the whole Empire practically, has a choral society. There must be thousands of them – hundreds of thousands of people and every one of them sick to the back teeth of 'The Messiah'. How utterly fed up they must all be of bloody 'Elijah' by bloody Mental – by Mentalson. These choral groups all over the land, they'll all be falling over themselves to get to 'Hiawatha's Wedding Feast', you young fox. I don't mind telling you that my only wish is that I had thought of it first and had the ability to write the damned thing like that! You won't ever have to work again, my boy," he said as he rapidly calculated how many copies might get bought per society and the price per copy. Every singer would need one, of course, and if it was to be as successful in places like America as everyone believed it would be....

Coleridge suddenly felt a chill in his bones as he made the same mental calculations. William felt the chill too, and Jessie, but Sir Arthur couldn't stop himself. "This piece will make you an absolute fortune! You hadn't even thought of that, had you?"

The room was full of people – chatting, smiling, laughing. One laugh though, suddenly coming from somewhere, was louder than the others. Everyone seemed to be laughing – all except for Coleridge and the two who knew the sickening realisation that was dawning on him.

"Honestly! You are a common piece at times," interjected Mrs Ronalds airily. "How vulgar to talk about money!" Coleridge looked across at Jess. Her lips parted to speak and she turned the ring on her finger but there was nothing to say.

There was that laugh again, male but highly-pitched. Coleridge turned but the laugh had already stopped. It wasn't anyone he knew, he was sure of that.

"Think of the royalties on each copy sold!" Sir Arthur went on. "Hundreds of copies. Thousands! Hundreds of hundreds of thousands! Who are you thinking of getting to publish it?"

Coleridge couldn't answer. It was already printed. He was sick to the pit of his stomach. That laugh! He looked across the room to see where that absurdly loud and annoying laugh had come from again. He looked across the room but instead, his eye rested on by Mr Jaegar. Old Jaegar was actually smiling. Jaegar returned the glance and lifted his glass to him. Coleridge had never seen him smile like that before, right up to those twinkling eyes – a true smile. He nodded a smile back. Mr Jaegar returned to his conversation.

Coleridge turned back and straight away heard the laugh again, piercingly shrill. He looked across and saw, this time, who it was coming from. It was him.

It was Mr Jaegar's laugh.

CHAPTER 6

The chorus had been asked to take their positions and were chattering excitedly under the huge backdrop within the great, circular Hall. One of the girls, a girl called Bunty was listening in to a conversation happening a little way behind her; a very one-sided conversation. A woman in her early forties was chattering away, nine to the dozen. You could tell she was from Liverpool despite her accent being weathered by many years in the South East.

"So I gave the box of matches back to the old gardener," she said with a happy sigh of reminiscence "but that wasn't the last I saw of them. I was probably a bit of a pest actually; for not leaving them alone, following them along the promenade. I have such wonderful memories of Eastbourne. They were clearly very much in love. That summer he wrote the 'Bon-Bon Suite' and 'Mistress Sunshine' for me. He was such a lovely, lovely man. We always kept in touch – right up until…. Well, right up until the end in 1912."

She could have gone on but Dr Sargent had appeared at the end of the hall for the start of the rehearsals. He cut a rather dashing figure, Avril thought. The chorus broke into a spontaneous round of applause for him. It sounded rather thin in the great Hall. He gave a cheery wave and took fast strides across the narrow footbridge until he was standing in front of the vast chorus and orchestra.

"Let's hope I don't get carried away tonight and end up in there," he said pointing his baton at the artificial lake that surrounded his stand. The chorus laughed. They were revved up and ready to go.

"Good morning," he called out. "ladies and gentlemen of the chorus, ladies and gentlemen of the orchestra, crew and of front of house. We number over two and a half thousand here today in the Royal Albert Hall." They applauded again.

"We have come from all parts of the country and for one reason only. In each of our separate corners, over the past few months, we have all been practising hard for tonight, because tonight is a very special night indeed. Tonight's performance marks the twentieth anniversary of our composer's passing to the 'Islands of the Blessed', the 'Kingdom of Ponemah' – the 'Land of the Hereafter' and we have to do the great man justice."

"We have just a few short hours to pull this thing together before this evening's performance. So I want everyone to work very, very hard for me today – and also for him. We will have plenty of breaks during the course of the day and a longer break before this evening's performance as I know that many will need to get back to their hotels to collect costumes and whatnot. I will introduce those who will be organising us all later on but I think that it is high time we started, don't you? We start at the beginning – with, 'Hiawatha's Wedding Feast'!"

They opened their scores. He tapped his baton.
Silence.

The eyes of everyone were on the tip of Dr Sargent's baton as if it were prey they were stalking. The orchestra was primed. He lifted his arms. A fast and circular sweep of both arms brought the silent multitude to their feet as one. They stood in silence, not daring to breathe.

The conductor brought in the opening bars of the soft and simple fanfare on lone trumpet. The horns responded. A pause and then the same fanfare, this time shadowed by the flutes and a little louder than before. The response to that came from the strings and then suddenly it all changed. The strings descended and twisted the piece into a deep, guttural and very rhythmic sound that, over the years, had become synonymous with Red Indian encampments at picture palace, main feature presentations. Then the whole orchestra joined in a joyous call to the celebrations. The deep, string rhythm formed the backdrop to the female voices of the chorus that introduced this section of Longfellow's wonderful epic tale.

The piece went on and built. The echoes of the voices, sung perfectly as one, reverberated through all. Bunty and the rest of her choral society had indeed been rehearsing the piece religiously for some months but to sing with so many other accomplished choral societies – to sing with hundreds of others was awe-inspiring.

"'…How the gentle Chibiabos,
He the sweetest of musicians,
Sang his songs of love and longing;
How Iagoo, the great boaster,
He the marvellous storyteller,
Told his tales of strange adventure.
That the feast might be more joyous,
That the time might pass more gaily,
And the guests be more contented.
Sumptuous was the feast Nokomis
Made at Hiawatha's Wedding…'."

The members of each society were strewn and mixed throughout the choir. Everyone was alone and yet they were one body. Singing on this scale was a physical experience and the sound of the voices vibrated the bones, sending chills up the spine and pimple-bumps across the skin, like a dentist's drill.

"'...How the handsome Yenadizze
Danced at Hiawatha's wedding';"

As Bunty sang, she thought of that woman she'd overheard meeting Coleridge and Jess all those years before, when she was just a child – how in love they were. Instead of Hiawatha's wedding, Bunty imagined the excitement in the homes of Coleridge and Jess on the morning of their own wedding. Their wedding day thirty-three years ago on 31st December 1899; the dawn of a bright new century and a brave new future for Jess and for Coleridge.

The house of the Fleetwood-Walmisely's was bustling with activity that morning. Jess's parents were having breakfast whilst all around was chaos. A maid had answered the door to yet another telegraph boy and on her way to the breakfast room, passed a huge bunch of yellow chrysanthemums in the hallway. Jess galloped down the stairs. She was singing at the top of her voice. She held a letter she was simply bursting to read aloud to her parents.

"Unlucky to sing before breakfast, Sweetpea," said her father as she entered and sat down at the table, flicking out a napkin and smoothing it on her knees.

"Never unlucky to sing," she said as she reached for some toast. "It's from Fritz at Novello. I found a mistake he'd not spotted in one of Coleridge's orchestral proofs. He thought it was a Soprano clef but it should have been alto. Anyway, listen," she said as she unfolded the letter and started to read.

"'There was a young lady called Jessie,

Perused CT's proofs rather messy,

Poking fun at old Jaegar,

Which his knowledge is rather meagre'," they all winced at the poor scanning of the limerick, "This sharp-eyed young lady called Jessie'."

The doorbell rang for the umpteenth time.

"I'm not sure that it's seemly to be receiving bad poetry from gentlemen today – German or otherwise," said Mrs Fleetwood-Walmisely with all the warmth of a wasp.

"And we found out who was responsible for the deluge of postcards," said Jessie. "A very contrite Mr William Hurlstone finally owned up to asking every conductor in the land to send us their best wishes."

"He should apologise to the post boy," said her mother.

"One was even written in the metre of Hiawatha. That one might have been William's actually, he's very clever…" said Jessie. The maid entered the room, handing her another telegram.

"For you, Miss."

"You're not even changed," Mrs Fleetwood-Walmisely continued.

"Mother, I've only just got dressed."

"And who goes shopping the whole day before their wedding, I ask you?"

But Jess wasn't listening. She was already reading the latest telegram. She read it aloud.

"'You shall enter my wigwam for the heart's right hand I gave you'."

"Who's that one from then?" asked Mr Fleetwood-Walmisely dryly.

'Hiawatha's Wedding Feast' had been the overnight success that Sir Arthur Sullivan had predicted it would be. Demand had outstripped supply within twenty-four hours of the premiere. Vast quantities of copies of the piece had been sent out all over the world, but sending copies to America and across the Empire was like trying to fill a bottomless hole. It had even gone out to Africa despite the second terrible war being waged in the Transvaal.

Samuel Coleridge Taylor was now very much a household name both at home and overseas and everyone close to him basked in the reflected glory of his success. Those who knew, never spoke of the terrible mistake that had been made in selling the piece outright. All Coleridge had said on the matter was that he had written something the public loved once and that he was almost sure he could do it again.

Mrs Fleetwood-Walmisely could never forget the day the shock of hearing Coleridge's intentions towards her daughter had caused her to spit hot tea back into her teacup. Some tea, to her astonishment, had also come out of her nose through one nostril. But her feelings about the wedding had mellowed in the light of Coleridge's explosive success.

She couldn't abide syrupy, emotional displays of affection and so any real expression of feeling was always delivered with the requisite, twist of something lemony – for piquancy and added to taste.

"Jessie," she said after a considered pause. "Your father and I would very much like to shake hands with Coleridge before you are married."

The Holy Trinity Church in South Norwood was flooded with winter sunlight. The church was full of joyous, expectant friends. Garlands of green and crimson and white were strewn over the choir stall's front and pew ends. Flowers erupted lavishly around the font and lectern. At the front of the church, the kindly vicar ushered William and Coleridge to stand as the organ started. The congregation stood.

At the far end of the church behind them, Jess and her father walked slowly down the aisle. Coleridge could hear the heads of their friends and relatives turning and the gentle coos and smiles of admiration as she made her way towards him. He wouldn't look until the last minute. Coleridge glanced at his best man who gave him an encouraging smile and nod.

Coleridge heard a rustling and Jess stopped at his left side. She was lifting her veil, very regally, as he turned to her. She looked like a meringue. But he could see how happy this was making her. A moment's panic glinted in her eye as she found she couldn't lift her veil all the way as it was tugging at her hairpiece pin. He adjusted it for her and straightened it so that it looked nice and symmetrical and flat at the sides, then he tucked a wayward lock under her satin headband, or 'tiara' as she had referred to it.

Coleridge's obsession with order and symmetry, especially where fabrics and soft furnishings were concerned, always amused William. The vicar gave a gentle instruction for the congregation to sit, leaving only Coleridge, Jess and William standing at the altar.

"Ladies and gentlemen," the vicar announced. "Today is the 31st December 1899! It is the cusp of a new century and the dawn of a new life for two special, young people. To our many distinguished and foreign visitors, welcome to London, South Norwood and to all, welcome to Holy Trinity Church. We are here to witness the union by God of Miss Jessie Fleetwood-Walmisely and Mr Samuel Coleridge-Taylor...."

Coleridge had started using a hyphen in his name and all his published pieces now carried it. He had joked that this was to be his wedding gift to Jess.

The day seemed to pass all too quickly but was peppered with special moments that would live long in everyone's memory. For example, there was the moment that Coleridge struggled to get the ring onto Jess's finger; there was the beautiful moment that the register was signed as the choir sang his Christmas anthem 'Break Forth into Joy'; there was the pealing of the bells as they came out of the church into a light snow as if the heavens were joining in by tossing confetti blessings down on the happy couple.

They took a ride in the oldest hansom cab in Croydon back to Jess's home where they changed and collected their luggage. That evening, they stayed over in the opulent Grosvenor Hotel – arriving to the sound of fireworks that popped and fizzed and crackled through the early evening sky, lighting their happy faces with pink and gold.

The next morning, they arose and made ready at a leisurely pace, enjoying a sumptuous wedding breakfast at the hotel before their journey; first by train and then by boat, to Shanklin on the Isle of Wight where they were to honeymoon.

The weather was bright and crisp during their time in Shanklin. Their days were spent ambling through the town, picking up décor ideas for their new home. Every-one smiled at the newly-weds and nobody seemed to be able to do enough for them. The pair made up silly private stories and limericks to amuse themselves and spent so much time giggling that it almost seemed that they were enjoying life too much. They were both so glad to have found each other.

They enjoyed delicious teas with dainty, crustless sandwiches cut into triangles, cakes on doilies on silver, tiered stands, butter-yellow scones with homemade raspberry jam and real Devonshire clotted cream.

In the evenings, with their arms aching from holding onto their hats in the gusts and with their faces still glowing from the days' adventures and with their eyes sleepy from drinking in so much ozone-rich and fortifying fresh, sea air, they would wash and rest and then dress and go down for dinner.

Afterwards, perhaps they might play cards with some of the other guests or enjoy a nightcap and each other's company in a quiet corner before it was time for bed.

Their modest room at bedtime was very cosy. The coal fire gave off a rosy glow that seemed to animate the pale, pink curtains and bed linen with phosphorescence. The walls were warmly papered with a criss-cross lattice of coral rosebuds with short, bright green stems and pairs of heart-shaped leaves. The fire warmed the wooden fittings of the room and outside the wind whistled and sea-spray spattered the thick, glass sashes.

Coleridge had kicked off his shoes and lay on the bed with his ankles crossed and his hands behind his head. He was watching Jess in her nightgown and bed-jacket, slowly brushing her hair.

She caught his eye through the mirror. He had a funny, knowing smile on his face. He's up to no good, she thought.

"I wouldn't have married you if you had no sense of humour, you know," he said. "If you ever lost it I'd simply have to divorce you."

She smirked and raised an eyebrow as she continued to brush, refusing to rise to his deliciously childlike sense of humour.

"It's as simple as that," he went on with a sigh.

She continued to ignore him and to act aloof and unamused.

"By the way, your hats, Mrs Coleridge-hyphen-Taylor, should always be chosen by your husband from now on, I think. He has such exquisite taste and you, poor thing, have no powers of discernment."

"True," she said plainly. "Look whom I married."

"You wretch!" Coleridge complained laughingly as he launched a pillow at the back of her head. It hit her quite hard but she didn't say, 'ow'. She took the pillow and went to him. She lay next to him. He wriggled around and rested his head on her breast. She poked his nose and stroked his head. His head moved slightly when she breathed. He stared intently in the direction of the window. They enjoyed the quiet of the room and had long given themselves up to the 'nothing to do'.

"I do like those curtains," he said at last. "Something like those would be just perfect."

"Oh," she said suddenly remembering and jumping up. "I packed you a book." She rummaged through the half-unpacked trunk at her side of their bed.

"Did you now?" Coleridge said, sensing mischief.

She climbed back onto the downy bed being sure to hide the cover. He put his head on her belly and she handed him the book.

"You were so generous in your wedding gift to me...." she continued.

"Now, what has my wife...? Oh, I see..." he said knowingly.

She waited with her hand over her nose to stop herself from laughing as he played along.

"'Mrs Caudle's Curtain Lectures'!" he read. Jess's attempts might have stifled an audible laugh but her stomach started to convulse with the daftness of the book's title, making his head bob up and down.

"It's a family heirloom," she said. "It's for our heirs now." She snorted and started to laugh; laughing more at his head bobbing up and down and the snort than the ridiculous book she had found on a shelf at her parents' house.

"You never mentioned anything about heirs. Anyway, lucky heirs!" Coleridge said – his wife's snorting making him giggle. "You and your family really are the most generous.... Now, why haven't I read this before?"

"I know you have a fondness for...soft furnishings... and it's only fair that our offspring..."

Their giggles were beginning to bloom into hysteria, his head now bobbing up and down on her stomach with each laugh she made. The more it bobbed the more she laughed, the more she laughed the more she snorted, the more she snorted the more he giggled and chuckled and the harder he found it to get words out.

"Just what I need," he said as his head wildly bounced about on her belly as she snorted and squealed. "'Mrs Caudle's Curtain Lectures'. Curtain Lectures! Lectures... about curtains!"

They gave themselves up to it and rolled over giggling hysterically. He kissed his new wife on the cheek.

They lay there smiling contentedly – the odd chuckle bubbling up again here and there as they got their breath back. He closed his eyes, just breathing, just being. No beginning of one and no end to the other. Beginning to drift off, all arms and legs, like a pile of puppies. His eyes closed.

He saw the warrior, brave Hiawatha, handsome and bare-chested but for his porcupine-quill breastplate. He was inside his wigwam as a light snow fell outside. Coleridge smelt the scent of juniper and pine, of pipe smoke. He saw the beautiful young squaw on a bed of thick, woolly buffalo hides; both of them contentedly full from the wedding feast.

Outside, the last to leave was Chibiabos, Hiawatha's childhood friend. He saw Hiawatha and acknowledged him with a wave as the young Chief undid the tie to close the wigwam flap. Chibiabos saw his friend catch a diamond, filigree flake before closing the tent for the night. It melted in the warmth of Hiawatha's hand and Coleridge heard the words – the words of Longfellow's 'Wedding Feast'.

'...Such was Hiawatha's wedding,
Thus the wedding banquet ended,
And the wedding guests departed,
Leaving Hiawatha happy
With the night... and Minnehaha.'

In his apartment in Battersea, William too lay on his bed. The fire was dying in the grate and the silence in his room was disturbed only by the wind whistling around ferociously outside. It was going to be a very cold winter, he thought, but at least that meant he wouldn't suffer quite so much with his asthma for a few months.

He gazed at the ceiling. He couldn't sleep. His mind raced. Someone had burrowed into his life. Someone had come in, uninvited and had started to push him out of his own life. Someone had stolen his happiness.

How could Coleridge be so blinded by her? What on earth was he doing? William raged inside his head. It was because of her that all the money that Coleridge had in the world had now been spent ten times over on a wedding and a house he couldn't possibly afford. It was because of her that Coleridge would now have to work all the hours he was sent, to keep her in the manner to which she was accustomed. It was because of her that Coleridge had abandoned him just as Hiawatha himself had been abandoned by his father.

William rolled over onto his side and curled up. Alone. His anger turned in on himself. He rebuked himself for being so selfish. He should just let Coleridge get on with his life and be adult and gentlemanly about it all. But why was he still so angry?

Coleridge was his oldest and greatest friend. He had enormous respect for him. He cherished their friendship. Coleridge was only person he could ever really talk to about anything and everything and he knew that Coleridge felt the same way about him. The trust was implicit, unspoken and without question. The friendship was boundless, profound and without condition. Each one knew the thoughts of the other and so silences between them only brought comfort and never one ounce of awkwardness.

He reprimanded himself for being irrational and over-sensitive and over-emotional, but still, he couldn't quite shake the nagging doubt that it may not be quite as irrational as all that. His very deep misgivings, although not based on anything tangible or conscious, might not be all that imagined. The concern he felt about the future that she was leading his only friend towards, was real, whatever it was based on. But the truth was, without risking losing that friend, there was nothing he could do about it. He was in pain and struggling but was powerless. He detested dishonesty, so how could he say nothing and pretend to like her, just to please Coleridge, and when he just didn't?

He closed his eyes. He couldn't wrestle with it any longer. He was tired and there was only one path to take. It was obvious. He knew what he had to do and he hated himself for it. He simply couldn't tolerate the thought of Coleridge being upset with him over this or to jeopardise their friendship. He didn't trust her with his friend's life or happiness but he would simply have to live with that and say nothing. He would have to pretend to be happy with Coleridge's choice of wife and say nothing. And in the end, when it all went wrong for Coleridge as he truly hoped against hope that it wouldn't, it would be he who would be there to provide his friend with the shoulder and to pick up the pieces.

CHAPTER 7

Sargent ushered them to sit and excited chatter ensued. It had been a remarkable morning. It had exceeded everyone's impossible expectations and had been so much more than wonderful. They all knew that that evening's audience would not be able to restrain themselves at the end. It couldn't be anything other than an ovation.

"We shall break there," Dr Sargent called rather seriously considering how well the rehearsal had gone. "Meeting back here please, to start at ten-thirty for the second part of the trilogy 'The Death of Minnehaha' through to the final act, 'Hiawatha's Departure'. We shall wrap up at one. Oh and please remember where you are sitting, everyone. Thank you."

He started to stand down and there was an uneven clatter of applause and then, as an afterthought –

"One more thing. This afternoon, the Hall is Mr Fairbaird's for the 'tech'. The call this evening will be six p.m. for seven-thirty."

The mass of people started to stand and pick up coats, hats and bags. They patted pockets for packs of cigarettes, starting to make new friends of their neighbours, marking mental notes so that they would recognise their place in the arena and most importantly of all, wondering where a cup of tea was to be had.

"Dr Sargent, I presume," said a voice as the conductor started to walk back to his room deep in the hidden bowels of the great Hall. Dr Sargent could recognise Havergal Brian's voice anywhere.

"Havergal!" he said turning and shaking his hand.

"How are you, Malcolm?"

In the violin section, the first violin, a Welsh woman in her forties, was continuing a heated debate with another violin – a rather pompous and arrogant man.

"What do you mean?" said the arrogant violin. "The Performing Rights Society was established in the wake of the 1911 Copyright Act and nothing to do with Coleridge-Taylor."

"Yes but all those letters to The Times," she said in her melodic Welsh accent. "The constant source of embarrassment. You're not going to tell me that none of that had anything to do with its formation. I'm telling you, if it hadn't been for him –"

"It was a legitimate business deal, a contract. Look, I'm not saying anything bad about him. There's nothing bad to say, but no one could predict how well the 'Wedding Feast' would do."

"I think Novello could," she said.

She had met Coleridge-Taylor once. It had been in Wales more than thirty years before. He had been so encouraging to her and since then she had never let anyone say a bad word against him especially with regard to his influence on the lives of modern musicians.

She looked around the magnificent Hall. She watched as the people slowly streamed out into the August sunshine. She looked up at the sky-painted sails that swathed the great domed ceiling, at the spectacular and awe-inspiring backdrop, at the lake and indoor streams that flowed down the rocky, loggy chutes between the sopranos and tenors ending in waterfalls that would cascade into the otherwise still and silent pool. She smiled to herself. What on earth would he have made of all this, she wondered. Where was he now? Could he be listening? Could he be watching?

Outside the Royal Albert Hall, Avril sat on a step. Bunty walked over to her thinking about how pleased with herself that Liverpool lady had sounded, talking about her childhood meeting with Coleridge-Taylor in Eastbourne. Bunty was about the same age as Avril; late-twenties, early thirties perhaps. Bunty had thick, black hair, chopped short and set in perfect, marcel waves. Her eyes were so brown that they were almost black. She lit a cigarette as she perched next to Avril on the step even though the two had never met.

"I don't suppose we have time for a cup of tea somewhere?"

"I'm not sure what's around here actually," said Avril.

"He's very good isn't he – Dr Sargent? A wonderful conductor and rather a fine figure of a man, don't you think?" Avril smiled. "Where are you from?"

"London."

"Me too. Don't know round here though. I'm Bunty, by the way. Gwendolen, actually but everyone calls me Bunty. It's a lot less – thing, you know."

"Avril," she said introducing herself and declining the cigarette offered with another smile.

Just the other side of the road, quite far off in the park near the Albert Memorial an old lady was watching them. They both saw her. The old lady in the distance took a couple of steps forward and reached into her bag. She was looking across. She appeared to be looking at them, appeared to be saying something. Avril and Bunty were transfixed.

They saw the old lady take a piece of paper from her bag. She seemed to hesitate but took another step forward. She was well dressed and a long way off but it was clear, patently clear that she was looking directly at the two of them. She had a look on her face, anxious, a strange look. Not malevolent – more curious or questioning. She was holding a piece of paper. The edges of the folded square were blowing in the gentle August breeze or perhaps it was her hand that was shaking. The old lady hesitated. She held the paper out as she looked at them.

"What the hell does she want?" Bunty asked at last, under her breath, but there was no reply.

Avril looked at her companion. A cloud of concern had fallen over Bunty's face. Suddenly, an open-topped, double-decker bus passed in front of the old lady and stopped, breaking the strange connection. When eventually the bus pulled away, the woman had gone.

The two began to relax again slightly. Bunty took a drag on her cigarette and opened her mouth, turning her head so that the smoke just fell out and upwards and then just hung there as no breeze claimed it. Why would she hold that piece of paper in such a tight grip? No, Avril thought, the old woman was probably just a little 'do-lally', poor old soul. She had just been waiting for the bus. But Avril couldn't help wondering what had made the old lady stare so intently at the two of them; or perhaps she had only been staring at one of them. Avril turned to Bunty, who had relaxed again. Bunty blew another lungful of smoke into the summer heat.

Cigarettes lit, Dr Sargent and Havergal Brian had descended the steps beneath the Hall and continued through the spiral labyrinth as Dr Sargent finished off his own 'Coleridge' anecdote.

The underside of the Royal Albert Hall was like the inside of a giant snail shell, spiralling ever deeper back on itself, with the rooms off the corridors diminishing in size as you went.

Following the unprecedented success of 'Hiawatha's Wedding Feast', Coleridge had gone on to set another part of Longfellow's poem and called it 'The Death of Minnehaha'. Brian had heard Dr Sargent's telling of the 'Minnehaha' premiere before but he didn't interrupt. It was still touching on the second or possibly even third hearing.

"Anyway, Bennett's notice for 'Minnehaha' had not been at all encouraging to say the very least, as you probably know," Sargent said. "Such an old bugger and a vicious critic. So, the theatre manager says to poor old Coleridge, 'Oh, here comes Sir Joseph Bennett now, have you met him?' and dear Coleridge, bless him, says 'No, I haven't but I should very much like to,' in that earnest way he had but knowing full well the old bastard had just slated his new work. That's the kind of man he was – a lovely, generous man." The two men smiled. "'I'm very pleased to meet you,' Coleridge says to him and Sir Joseph said, apparently any-way, 'Are you ...are you really, Mr Taylor?' in that bloody old voice of his."

Havergal laughed as they approached the door. Sargent, smiling, his cigarette now clenched between his teeth, opened the door and entered his dressing room.

"I was in Hanley for that Festival, funnily enough," said Havergal as he followed Sargent into the room. "The Royal Choral Society had commissioned it. I was deputising cellist in 'Utopia' while my friend had the greater honour of playing in 'Minnehaha'. They can't have been married that long. She was pregnant, I remember, with her baby-bump. Poor Coleridge. He was treated rather badly there too, I'm afraid. Someone had plotted so that he had hardly any rehearsal time with his orchestra. People can be such swine. But he was always cheerful. Of course, everyone who was anyone knew about the fifteen guineas and Novello by then but he held his head up high, despite all that and the treatment he got there that year. In fact, I would say that he was the very image of the hero of his piece."

The premiere of 'The Death of Minnehaha' was in North Staffordshire for the music festival that had commissioned the work. It was 1900. Coleridge had been sitting at the back of the concert hall waiting with Jess for their own rehearsal to start. They had been waiting an eternity. The piece being rehearsed was Handel's 'Messiah' and the conductor had run well over his own time and was now greedily eating away at Coleridge's. It was no accident. It was a plot.

"He's doing this on purpose," said Coleridge through gritted teeth. "He's an hour and forty-five minutes late! We're not going to have enough time....They could perform this in their sleep!" Jess ignored him, trying to suppress her own rage.

A full twenty-five minutes later, the 'Messiah' rehearsal eventually ended and the conductor addressed the orchestra, some members of which occasionally glanced across at Coleridge-Taylor in sympathy and some considerable embarrassment.

"Thank you all. Unfortunately, the gentlemen of the orchestra will be too tired to stay any longer. Therefore the run through of 'The Death of Minnehaha' will not commence until two."

"It's not enough time," Coleridge whispered to Jess so that the young man sitting a few seats in front of them wouldn't hear. The orchestra began to pack away their instruments as instructed.

"Coleridge, this will quickly pass," Jess whispered. "The Royal Albert Hall is next, remember. And very soon…" she said patting her belly, "Barbara! For now, chin up."

Jess followed Coleridge down the aisle of the auditorium towards the stand, so that he could set up. Despite talking quietly, the young man sitting a few rows in front, had overheard them. Havergal Brian watched as the two of them proudly passed down the aisle like Hiawatha and his bride on their way to the wedding feast.

The piece had gone down extraordinarily well at Hanley, despite one particularly venomous review, which had come, strangely enough from the pen of an old friend of Mr Jaegar's. The second performance, and the first in London, was at the Royal Albert Hall with the Royal Choral Society. None other than the Duchess of Sutherland herself attended the performance. Towards the end of the piece, even the most hardened critics were seen to sniffle and dab at their eyes as the Royal Choral Society sang the closing bars.

"'Soon my task will be completed,
Soon your footsteps I shall follow

To the Islands of the Blessed,
To the Kingdom of Ponemah!
To the land... of the Hereafter'!"
The ovation was deafening as the audience leapt to their feet.

Only two of those who heard the performance rose to their feet with any reluctance, Mr Auguste Jaegar and Mr Edward Elgar.

"So this is what it looks like, when one writes for the market and not for Art," said Elgar to Mr Jaegar whose own face was blacker than thunder.

"Rot," Jaegar spat. "Utter rot."

Coleridge composed in the shed in his garden with a cigarette and a cup of tea. There was an upright piano, in front of which he would stand and notate, and a kitchen table that was always covered with notes and manuscripts; some finished, some ripe for review and some just sketches. Coleridge always composed standing. On the piano stood a picture of Dr Stanford, or rather, it hung from a candle sconce in a velvet, horse-shoe-shaped frame.

It wasn't quite Spring and Coleridge was finishing a third part to Hiawatha, called, 'Hiawatha's Departure'. Since the success of 'Hiawatha's Wedding Feast', he had tried to replicate that monumental success but perhaps just falling short. Not that it wasn't wonderful – 'Minnehaha' was wonderful, and nearly everyone had said so, but expectations of him had been so high following that first, fantastic success.

He was still struggling financially and seemed trapped in a cycle of having to sell works outright in order to cover the debt that had accrued since the last big

sale and composing was so all-consuming – so time-con-
suming. There was still the Novello annuity, depreciat-
ing a little year on year, and the teaching too but his
incomings never seemed to be enough to adequately
cover the outgoings and each month he inched a little
further into debt. Saving never seemed to be an option
and so neither was retaining the rights to the works he
penned. He needed the money up front to pay the overdue bills. He knew he had made a mistake in selling the
rights to 'Hiawatha' but he never seemed to be in a position to afford to change this habit. Jaegar's financial
incentives to sell outright, relinquishing all rights to future royalties, were generous and hard to refuse. So he
worked to churn out more and wrote what he was almost sure the public would like even if Mr Jaegar
seemed harder to convince. He couldn't risk the public
not liking what he composed but luckily they still
seemed to. Their love of his music enabled him to keep
his head just above water.

Normally he would lose himself in his work but that
particular day in his shed, he struggled to concentrate –
because inside his house, Jess was screaming. He tried
not to listen. He looked at the blank paper in front of
him as another swelling wave of harrowing screams
came from their bedroom window. He couldn't bear it.
How much longer would it go on? He put down his pen
and pinched the bridge of his nose. He looked out of the
window and across the road at the house opposite. They
would be able to hear everything but nothing stirred and
no nets twitched. The shed windows were dusty. There
was a web in the corner. After working, he always smelt
woody and of lacquered, piano dust. He doubted that
Mr Elgar composed in a shed.

The screaming stopped. There was a silence. Apart from the sound of a pigeon on the roof of the house, there was silence, a silence that went on too long. He bit his lip. That awful silence was going on far, far too long. But then, it was broken, quite suddenly and he stopped biting his lip and breathed out, closing his eyes to the sound of his baby's first cry.

"Are you sure she's alright?" Jess asked the doctor from the hot and wet, crumpled bed sheets. Condensation covered the inside window glass.

"Will you go and tell, Mr Taylor please?" Dr Collard said to the midwife as he finished up.

"Yes, Doctor."

"Is she black, white, red or yellow?" Jess asked as the midwife left the bedroom.

"He's a beautiful boy," Dr Collard answered, "and a first in the Taylor household, arriving early!"

Jess's eyes closed in relief.

"To bring it on, Coleridge and I have been playing Brahms Hungarian dance duets as fast as we can all week," she sighed.

"I see," said Dr Collard chuckling to himself as he held the baby and went to the window, wiping a foggy patch clear so that he could see out. He saw the midwife cross the meagre, front garden and knock on the door of Coleridge's Music Shed.

"Did you say a 'boy'?" Jess asked with a frown as the young doctor placed the gurgling bundle in her arms. "And we were going to call you Barbara. I was so sure."

From the upstairs window, Dr Collard watched as Coleridge came out of his shed where he had been hiding. He saw the midwife speaking to Coleridge, telling him he was a father, telling him it was a boy. He saw Coleridge drop to his knees in the centre of the patch of green, damp grass and Dr Collard smiled down.

"He'd hate me telling you this, Dr Collard," Jessie said, her eyes still closed in exhaustion, "but Coleridge thinks that you have the most perfect speaking voice."

"Really?" Dr Collard said, turning to her.

"Yes. He said that he hoped yours was the last doctor's voice he heard on earth."

A few weeks later, Coleridge was back in Mr Jaegar's office at Novello. Jaegar was amending Coleridge's folios. He always seemed angry and needlessly rough with his work as he fumed and fault-found. He was a brusque man at the best of times and whenever Coleridge saw him, he seemed to be annoyed about something. Coleridge could never really understand why people chose to be angry when they could just as easily choose to be happy and he had only ever seen Mr Jaegar really happy once – just that one time.

"We should change this – 'Came the Spring with all its fullness'," Mr Jaegar said as he scored it out. "...with all its 'splendour'. Easier to sing 'splendour' than 'fullness'."

He looked at Coleridge.

"Don't you have a view?" he said, irritated by the silence and Coleridge's placid, passive nature.

"I agree, Mr Jaegar."

There was an uneasy silence and Jaegar continued to read and amend and flick folios.

"I received a very encouraging letter today from a man in Boston," Coleridge said as he waited. "It seems 'Hiawatha's Wedding Feast' is as popular there as here."

"But why make it a trilogy? 'Came a hundred warriors'. I thought we'd agreed only two syllables in the word 'warriors'?"

"It's practically only two, the F being so short."

Mr Jaegar looked at him.

"You should leave them wanting more, not less," Jaegar said as he continued to read and scrawl and cross out and scribble in. He suddenly grimaced.

"What the hell is this F sharp doing against the G of the voice? Did you mean to do that?"

"Yes."

"I don't like it at all," he said as he changed it.

Mr Jaegar turned the final few pages very quickly. He had already nit-picked and criticised and corrected those and he couldn't bring himself to look at them again.

He gathered the papers together and sat back in his chair scrutinising the man in front of him. Coleridge felt uncomfortable, crushed. Mr Jaegar seemed to be confirming what he had never quite stopped fearing – that he was a fraud and not a real musician at all. That he was not a proper composer. That he was a sham. He had put his all into that piece. He was drained.

"You know this really won't do?" Jaegar said at last. "The public expects to see you progress, to do better work than before, but this – this is your worst."

He shoved the music across the desk in one dismissive movement. Coleridge looked at the floor and concentrated on not allowing his eyes to fill. He had lived and breathed that piece and managed to meet Novello's unrealistic deadline. Mr Jaegar stood and went to the door and opened it. Outside, Fritz stood and handed the contract to Mr Jaegar. Fritz glanced at the hunched, condemned figure of Coleridge and smiled at him, just with his eyes, as the door swung shut on him.

Mr Jaegar scribbled in the sum that was to be paid for the piece and started to count out Coleridge's money. He couldn't wait to get him out of his office.

"I hear you are to judge at the Welsh Eisteddfod this year."

"We're very much looking forward to it," Coleridge said with some semblance of salvaged cheerfulness and optimism.

"Dr Turpin did that last year. The Welsh threw flour and rotten eggs at him. If they can do that to the warden of Trinity College of Music, what do you think they'll do to you?" Coleridge's face fell again – a little further than it had been before.

"I have already written and confirmed it now," he said. "Their invitation seemed very kind."

Coleridge collected up the money that was left for him on the table and put it into his pocket. Mr Jaegar went to the door. Their meeting was over.

"Have you decided on a name, yet?" Jaegar asked. "Congratulations by the way."

"Thank you. Yes.... er...Hiawatha."

"No, for the child I mean," Mr Jaegar quickly said.

Coleridge's silence led Jaegar to a realisation that both embarrassed and appalled him.

"Oh I see.... How charming."

"Thank you, Mr Jaegar. Thank you," Coleridge said as the office door was closed on him.

Coleridge was so warmly received wherever he went that he never quite understood Mr Jaegar's attitude towards him. He was still frightened of him but respected the senior man's experience and views. Coleridge just tried to tell himself that Mr Jaegar was a bully because that was just the way he was and that it shouldn't be taken personally. He was, after all, pretty much like that with everyone, even Mr Elgar to a degree. Normally he would have stopped to chat to Fritz, but not that day – there was somewhere he pretended he needed to be.

Coleridge could never quite shake the suspicion that haunted him, just as his mistake with 'Hiawatha' still haunted him, the suspicion that further undermined the pitiful confidence that he had in his competence, the suspicion that he was mediocre at best. That unreasonable shadow of doubt was always there, just beneath the surface, malevolently waiting for a pinprick to release it – waiting for a veil to be drawn so that it could play in and play on the injured corners of his mind, prodding and poking in uninterrupted glee. When it happened, it was better that he was on his own.

It was a beautiful afternoon in South Wales and Coleridge had just completed the presentations at the Eisteddfod. Jess pushed baby Watha in the pram to meet Coleridge as he stepped down from the podium. A local dignitary had been wonderfully hospitable to the young Coleridge-Taylor family.

"I have had a marvellous time," he said to their host as Jess drew close. "Not the welcome I was told I should expect."

"Ah!" said the dignitary, in some embarrassment. "Dr Turpin! This doesn't make it right of course, but you greeted them in Welsh and he took ten minutes where you only took two. We Welsh folk get restless rather quickly."

"Maybe that's where I get it from. My mother – my adopted mother – is Welsh."

"Well, I didn't know that."

"Extraordinary that people should feel it prudent to take rotten eggs and flour with them to a concert," Coleridge said with a genuine curiosity that tickled the dignitary. "It sounds a little premeditated, to me."

A girl approached them with a violin case. She was holding her mother's hand. Coleridge recognised the child straightaway as being one of those he had adjudicated earlier.

"Excuse me, Mr Coleridge-Taylor," the girl's mother said. "I am so sorry to bother you."

"Not at all," Coleridge said, noticing Jess glance at her watch.

"Is there any encouragement you could offer her? She so wanted to win. Coming from her favourite composer, it would mean so much," the lady said.

Coleridge smiled at the child. He reached into his pocket and took the girl to one side and out of earshot of the adults. He pressed some coins into her hand, closing her fingers around them. Still holding her hand, he wormed his finger at her to come close enough to whisper. He cupped her ear with his hand and whispered something. She listened and the adults watched. When he had said what he needed to say, he walked the happy child back to her mother.

"Thank you, so much," said the lady.

Coleridge and the group of important people walked away.

"There you are," she said turning to the girl. "What did he say?"

The girl looked up at her mother. She was overwhelmed at meeting her hero. She watched as Coleridge and his wife and baby and the dignitary disappeared.

"He said to make my parents proud of me and 'To strive, to seek, to find and not to yield'."

She opened her hand and gasped in surprised delight. He had given her ten shillings.

"He said that he looked forward to hearing me play first violin in 'Hiawatha' at the Royal Albert Hall."

A little way off, and now alone with her husband, Jess asked how much he had given her. He couldn't lie to Jess.

"Ten shillings," she whispered furiously in disbelief. "Ten shillings!"

'Hiawatha's Departure' was the final part of 'The Song of Hiawatha' trilogy. It too was premiered in Birmingham and was really the piece that everyone had been waiting for since 'Minnehaha'. This was the concluding part of the epic trilogy. The first part was the joyous wedding of Hiawatha to his love. The second described the cruel winter that led to the famine and disease that took his love from him and of visits by mischievous spirits. It also spoke of how Hiawatha's mission, to unite the many warring tribes as one great people, was concluded and foretold of his own journey to the 'Islands of the Blessed'.

The final part, 'Hiawatha's Departure', described a continent's outpouring of grief as Hiawatha left his beloved people on the margin of that great inland sea. He crossed on his enchanted bark into the emblazoning sunset to return to his love and to his father in the 'Kingdom of Ponemah'. Without a departure, there can be no arrival and for every leaving, there is always a far greater reuniting. It was a fitting end to the trilogy and both the audience and the critics loved it.

At Birmingham, at that same festival, another piece was also premiered. This piece, however was somewhat overshadowed by the tumultuous reception that 'Hiawatha's Departure' received, much to that particular composer's vexation.

"Real music should never have been pitched against that," Mr Jaegar said to Elgar in his smoky, London office.

"And my rehearsal time was woefully inadequate," complained Mr Elgar.

"'Gerontius' is a great piece!" Jaegar enthused.

"But the orchestra was totally indifferent and the audience couldn't understand it," Elgar went on. "All Birmingham wanted to hear was his blasted trilogy. Standing ovation of course – mine raising barely a ripple. I was cruelly disillusioned by his 'Overture to Hiawatha', which I think is...really only...rot. This isn't sour grapes, Auguste, honestly it isn't. He's spreading himself too thin – appealing to the masses like that. Who said that thing about glory and ripples and ever-diminishing circles?"

"The lesson is a simple one. You should never sell Art by the yard and nor should it be written for that purpose."

Elgar nodded. He had once been so encouraging to the young composer but now saw him as competition and competition that was unfair considering his popular appeal. Both despised any composer who, in their opinion, peddled pulp for the market.

"If this is the way things are going...." Elgar said; but Mr Jaegar had stopped listening – he was raging inside. Despite the vast sums he would make from the works that he continued to buy outright from the young fool, he simply couldn't bear him. All the things he once liked Coleridge for, he now despised. He loathed his modesty. He loathed his shyness and his eagerness to please. He loathed his cheerfulness. He loathed his popularity and he loathed his bloody awful music. It was a love affair gone bad, extreme and unjustified. Whenever Coleridge visited Novello, Jaegar couldn't wait to get him out of his office.

Everyone known to Jaegar knew of his feelings towards Coleridge. They all heard the negating tone of contempt smouldering behind ineffectual words or if there were none, noticed the crucifying rise of that eyebrow. His contempt was no secret to anyone and nor was his desire to bring the upstart down, even if it did come at Novello's expense. His hatred was no secret to anyone except perhaps to those closest to Coleridge – and to Coleridge himself, of course.

CHAPTER 8

Coleridge felt that he was trespassing in alien territory as he was led up the narrow and deep, green, gloss-painted staircase. He could hear a voice shouting in the dark some distance off. Heavy black curtains covered any doors they passed and the smell of dust and 'size', used to stretch the calico over the flats, filled his nostrils. Flat-props and weights were left on the corners of the stairs, as they spiralled up towards the stage, with other pieces of theatrical flotsam; a button, faded strands of dyed ostrich feather, a dog-end of crimson lake greasepaint trodden in to the steps.

The stagehand turned and put his finger to his lips as they reached the top of the stairs and yet another door-way. The stagehand found the handle behind the blacks and opened the door silently. They crept through into the wings of the Theatre Royal, Drury Lane.

The expansive stage was a shock after the narrow maze of tunnels that they had passed through. It was a new perspective for Coleridge, that side of the prosce-nium arch. Things were unspeakably tatty – durable and workaday but the whole thing was not altogether honest. The view from the front was magical with its gold and red splendour and glamour but from this new and close-up viewpoint, Coleridge could see where tricks of the trade were used to create the illusion of grandeur and where the corners had been cut.

On the stage a man in his late twenties was bellowing out a speech. Coleridge was left by the stagehand in the wings to watch until the rehearsal ended. The actor had thick, wavy hair and handsome, brooding eyes. He was in trousers and a shirt with the collar unbuttoned. He was holding a half-smoked cigarette in one hand and a bejewelled goblet in the other. He paused dramatically, then shook his head as he sank back into his throne. He looked up, torn and despondent, a king losing his kingdom perhaps?

"Let her be given what she asks!" he at last projected to the Gods. "Of a truth she is her mother's child! ...Who has taken my ring? There was a ring on my right hand. ...Who has drunk my wine? There was wine in my cup. It was full of wine. Someone has drunk it? ...Ah! Wherefore did I give my oath? Kings ought never to pledge their word. If they keep it not, it is terrible, and if they keep it, it is terrible also."

"My daughter has done well," said a male voice from nowhere, flatly reading in the other character's part, devoid of emotion.

"I am sure that some misfortune will happen," the King responded. Suddenly his hands flew to his face as if driven mad with remorse and his fingers sunk deep into his hair in despair.

"Then Salome leans over the pit," the voice from nowhere said, "and listens and so on. Do we know if he's here yet anyone?"

The man on stage dropped the persona of Herod as if he were tossing his hat on the table and stood nonchalantly. He walked towards the footlights and shielded his eyes to try and see his brother in the audi-torium.

"How the hell should I know!" he said drawing on his cigarette. "I've been busy with the whore of Babylon in case you hadn't noticed – the 'daughter of Sodom!'" he boomed suddenly flinging his arms to the side.

Coleridge craned to see if he could see who the other voice was. He peered round the curtain; a little afraid, as the lay of the land was so foreign and the theatre so dark. Although terribly exciting, these people were a very different breed to him.

Stepping from the dark auditorium and into the light flooding from the stage came a man in his late forties. Mr Herbert Beerbohm Tree, the great actor-manager had put on a little weight. Coleridge had never met him, but had seen portraits of him in some of the finest roles of his early days. This was the man Coleridge was there to meet. Suddenly he was spotted.

"Mr Coleridge-Taylor? How wonderful!" Tree shouted. He clapped his hands and ran round to the blacked steps that ran from the stalls to the corner of the stage. The handsome actor on the stage turned and beamed at Coleridge. He had the most beautiful, pearly-white teeth and steely-blue eyes. Coleridge stepped out of the shadows and very uncomfortably stepped onto the stage. He had kept his hat on until then. He took off his white gloves in anticipation of a handshake and popped them in his hat. The actor wiped his hands on his trousers and all three met down stage centre.

"Thank you, Sir. It's a very great honour to meet you, Mr Beerbohm Tree if I may say so."

"Max, meet the music," said Tree, introducing the actor to Coleridge.

"Hiawatha himself!" Max said. If Max had had a tail it would then have been wagging vigorously.

"My step-brother, Max," Tree said.

"We love you! You'll be bloody perfect for this," Max said as he shook and then held Coleridge's hand in both of his.

"Of course he will, and 'Herod' is just the beginning, Mr Coleridge-Taylor. 'Ulysses' next then 'Nero', 'Faust', 'Othello' – we shall do them all; your music and my... my... whatever it is I do...."

"What you do," Max explained, "is to make it up as you go along and for some reason it bloody-well works! It's not everybody's way of working, I suppose," he said turning warmly to Coleridge.

"It will be good for me," said Coleridge. "I am rather too systematic I'm afraid. Composition from nine until twelve..." Max and Tree nodded encouragingly even though it was clear to Coleridge he was speaking a different language. "Then I normally take a book of poems and go out for a walk."

"I have never once in my life gone out for a walk, have I Herbert?"

"No, but you've been taken out for walks though, haven't you!"

"That is another matter entirely," Max replied wickedly. He winked at Coleridge. Max's eyes sparkled bright with a crackling energy that projected out of him as if he were a lighthouse.

"Have you heard the sad news from Paris?" asked Tree.

"No...?"

"The creator of our piece, Mr Wilde, has died. A great man. A very sad day. Dead... dead... dead.

Anyway...!" he said impatiently returning to his bubbling, former self. Tree grabbed Coleridge by the elbow and started to walk him to the corner of the stage. He fished in his pocket and pulled out a small Bible.

"You'll forgive me if we walk, Mr Taylor, but I have a cab waiting to take me home. I wanted to read you something. 'Chronicles'. Poetry, Mr Taylor," Tree said raising a finger in respect of words, "I understand we share a mutual love of poetry."

"Well, yes..."

"It was very nice to meet you," Max said with a wave as Coleridge and Tree descended the blacked steps.

"Yes," Coleridge said as he tried both to turn and to put his gloves and hat back on. The stagehand reappeared in the auditorium with Tree's hat and cape. Tree read loudly from the tiny Bible as they walked.

"'...and all the Levitical singers, Asaph, Heman and Judu'thun...'," Tree grabbed his hat from the stagehand without slowing his pace as they marched up the aisle of the theatre. The stagehand, tripping to catch up, fastened the cape over Mr Tree's shoulders as he continued proclaiming in a dramatic, booming voice. "'...their sons and kinsmen, arrayed in fine linen, with cymbals, harps and lyres, stood east of the altar with a hundred and twenty priests who were trumpeters and singers to make themselves heard in unison in praise and thanksgiving to the Lord...', do you see?" Tree said turning to Coleridge with a mad grin as they burst through the doors and into the lavish foyer, heading towards the front entrance. Tree had his cane thrust into his open palm and continued to read with a widening, rolling-eyed drama. "'... and when the song was raised, with trumpets and cymbals and other instruments of music, in praise of the Lord – for he is good, for his steadfast love endures forever – the house…' listen to this bit," he said suddenly dropping the drama for a moment only to pick it up again, an intense semi-tone higher, "'…the house, the house of the Lord…'."

Tree flung open the heavy theatre doors, startling pedestrians and the cab driver's horse. They stepped out into the overcast and brooding day and he threw his arms apart like Prospero, his cloak billowing like mad King Lear on the blasted heath, his wide conjuring eyes burning out from under his topper and over the Covent Garden rooftops, he yelled to summon the darkening heavens.

"'…The house of the Lord was filled with a cloud so that the priests could not stand to minister because of the cloud, for the glory… the glory of the Lord…! It – filled – the – house – of – God'!"

A flash of lightning split the leaden sky apart and it cried out in anguish with a guttural roll of thunder. The wildly clopping cab horse reared up. The top-hatted cabman held on to the reins and whip for dear life as the wheels rolled back and forward, struggling to stay standing on the slippery, foot-plate at the back, his ankle-length, black rubberised mackintosh flapping in the building and eddying wind.

Tree climbed onto the cab and sat down, and suddenly turned to Coleridge like a man possessed. The horse's eyes bulged and rolled behind the thick, black leather blinkers.

"That's what I want, Mr Coleridge-Taylor. That's what I want. I want the 'Glory of the Lord' …in there," he said pointing at the theatre with the silver head of his ebony cane. "Can you write music that will do that?"

"I promise I shall try."

Tree smiled as large sploshes of rain started down.

"Splendid! Then bravo to you, Sir!"

The cabman shrank into his high coat collar as his topper was pelted with a thrashing of tiny, icy and stinging hailstones. People darted for cover. Skirts were lifted over puddles and stair-rods plundered the flags and splattered on steps.

Coleridge pinched his jacket lapels together under his neck and stepped back under the cover of the theatre's awnings. He held his hand up to wave Mr Beerbohm Tree off. The sound of the hail and rain thrashed on the awnings making it difficult for him to hear the cabman calling to Tree.

"You gonna tell me where to then, Guv or what?" The horse impatiently stamped its great, maney feet in the cobbley puddles.

"And what on earth makes you think that I would ever tell the likes of you my address!" an affronted Mr Tree bellowed back in a voice so loud that the chomping horse reared again and whinnied in panic.

Another blast of thunder and lightning smashed the sky apart like a china plate hitting the floor; like a plaster ceiling that had buckled and given way under the weight of a flood above.

The horse suddenly reared and with a ghastly shriek cantered off towards Covent Garden, randomly and at a perilous speed. Lightning forked across the blackening skies as the flood emptied itself in bucketfuls onto the London streets below.

Over the sound of hooves and rain, Coleridge heard Tree's cheery voice diminishing with the growing distance between them.

"Goodbye, Mr Taylor! Goodbye!"

Coleridge could just see Tree's hand waving as the cab faded away into the thick veil of downpour. The rain this magician had summoned was torrential.

Coleridge stood there for a moment under the awnings in that stair-rod rain, assessing what had just happened. Water drained noisily down the gutters and the pavements were awash with splashing puddles. He couldn't afford to turn anything down just now. Not that he would have turned down a commission to write some incidental music for Mr Tree's production. Herbert Beerbohm Tree was a legend – he himself was the London West End. But no contract between them had been signed and no fee determined. Coleridge wondered what Mr Jaegar would say. Coleridge was almost, but not entirely sure, that he had been offered a job but he thought it best to write to Mr Beerbohm Tree the next day, just to confirm.

In addition to his composing and commissions, which indeed included Mr Tree's, Coleridge had been asked by some friends of friends to join their work in representing those of African descent now residing out of Africa. Jess had been resistant because, as Coleridge had initially surmised, there was not to be any money in it. This was a factor; however, her resistance was much more to do with Kathleen Easmon's involvement in it.

Kathleen was a beautiful woman, a few years older than Coleridge. Coleridge had been convinced by her that with his world fame as a black English composer he was ideally placed to figurehead the Pan-African movement, but it transpired that his involvement was to be more than that of merely patron and he had become increasingly involved in their meetings. He also wrote some articles for them and was in discussion about establishing a periodical. This, on top of the Coleridge's teaching, composing and conducting engagements, was a strain but he justified his commitment to the movement by telling Jess that he always worked on more than one project at a time and thrived on that. The truth was, that he did so more out of necessity than choice but how could he say no to Kathleen and to the Pan-African movement, he reasoned. How could he say 'no' to anything he was offered?

Coleridge sent a telegram asking to meet with William. He had seen less and less of his best friend over the intervening years but William was a great sounding board for new ideas, and the fact that they had known each other for such a long time led Coleridge to believe that William would keep him grounded in a world that seemed to be changing so rapidly. He needed to be grounded. William would be honest with him. He always had been.

They met at Crystal Palace Station and walked up the steep hill to the park – the great, glass Palace construction looming over their shoulders on the right.

As they walked, Coleridge described a poem to William, which he had recently been rather taken with. The poem had got under his skin, just as 'Hiawatha' once had. It was to be another cantata to rival 'Hiawatha'. It was inspiring his unconscious mind. William was sure to tell him if there was any mileage in the idea or not. William, however had other concerns on his mind. This piece, Coleridge enthusiastically told William as they walked, was to be another great choral work, but instead of the paradise of the Land of the Dakotahs, this one was set on a dark and remote Scottish beach surrounded by black, granite cliffs.

In this nightmarish world the sea crashed with violent and cold bitterness. Coleridge could see Meg Blane clearly in his mind's eye. A large woman in her dark, tartan rags soaked to her frozen skin and stained with salt and sand. Hers was a strong but beautiful face that had been exposed to the elements all her life. She looked out from her shack on the shingle at the ship tossed perilously on the icy and ferocious, rocky and unforgiving seas.

"She has been waiting by the water's edge for twenty years," Coleridge explained. "He promised he'd return to her. It's a terrible night and a ship is being wrecked on the rocks but she has to save them. So she risks her life and rows out alone but she is too late and they are all lost, all of them drowned, all that is, but one. He is pulled from the surface of the deep by fishermen and it turns out that this is the man she has been waiting for; the man who promised to return to her. He doesn't recognise her at first but when he does, he tells her he has long since married someone else. Then he discovers he is the father of her dim-witted son, the son he has never met. It's by Robert Buchanan."

"Abandonment again," said William, "like 'Hiawatha'."

Coleridge thought for a moment.

"It's different though," he said thoughtfully. "Hiawatha was sent on a mission to bring wisdom and peace, to deliver his people. Meg Blane is abandoned by her lover, by her son's father."

They continued to walk in silence until they arrived by the life-sized, model dinosaurs and sat on the bench looking at the fabulous creatures.

"If I had it in me to do it once, William, surely I can do it again. I must just try a little harder with this one, that's all."

William was silent.

"How's Jessie?" he asked at last, not because he was interested but because he felt he had to. It was Coleridge's turn to be silent for a moment. Only friends can be silent together and for there to be no awkwardness.

"It's not what I thought it would be," Coleridge confided. "Sometimes, there may as well be an ocean between the two of us. I spend too much time with Kathleen apparently. I think you've met my friend Kathleen Easmon, the poet. I set some of her works. But Jess.... I mean it's not as if Kathleen and I were ever alone but Jess seems so protective – so suspicious all the time. And whatever I do, it never seems to be enough. Whatever I do, it never seems to be quite right or quite good enough and I'm not just talking about her now. But the Pan-African Movement is not Just Kathleen and I, for goodness sake."

"I don't know how you do it all, Coley. It's too much for one person." William was right.

Rather than take the train back to West Croydon. Coleridge decided to take a series of omnibuses and trams until he reached home. The old, garden-seat horse omnibuses were his favourite. They reminded him of his childhood when he would see the Shillibeer buses, which were unaffordable to his family then at a shilling a throw.

He had hailed the omnibus and climbed the little staircase to the top deck where he sat alone at the front. Once he had settled, the driver bade his horses, 'walk on'.

It turned out that the omnibus was going all the way into the centre of town to change horses before heading for West Croydon. Coleridge never had time to waste but decided to stay on the bus until the end nevertheless.

The roads of central London were always full of traffic but it was getting much worse lately. Cabs and omnibuses dominated London but the horse-drawn trams, which ran on metal wheels, were becoming more and more common; and then there were all the trade carts and pedestrians. The ride was much smoother on the trams than the omnibuses but the routes taken were much less flexible on account of the rails that they ran on. The trams only needed two horses to pull them and could carry fifty people whereas the omnibuses could carry about twenty and needed three. Times were changing. Even though the trams were relatively new, there was talk of some of these trams being run by electricity, which at least would mean that the roads would be less full of dung.

Coleridge's omnibus clopped and rocked its way through the busy streets. Hardly any of his time was his own anymore, he thought. Barely even a fragment could be said to be his own. In fact, he concluded that the only time that he did have to himself, was when he was travelling from one place to another on a train, tram or omnibus.

He suddenly felt quite alone. So many people wanted a piece of him, it seemed. So many people wanted him to do things for them; to attend this, to judge that, to compose, to write, to teach, to conduct and saying 'no' was not possible, even if he could afford to, which he couldn't – even if there seemed to be nothing in it for him, it was still difficult.

The London streets bustled away as he looked down from his bench on the top deck. People were shopping. Life went on. Children played and men... men coped. Men were doing what they were expected to do and handling everything that was expected of them without raising an eyebrow. If they could handle it, if they could cope, why on earth was he finding it all so difficult, so relentless?

To have a finger in many pies seemed a sound investment, he'd thought, as nothing was ever forever. But, it was as if none of the people he did things for, could see anything else except for what he happened to be doing for them. None of them could see the whole picture and so they pushed and demanded and chased and asked and expected, then complained and criticised and picked bloody holes in everything. Each one was responsible for a small part of his burden but totally unaware of the total load he shouldered. No one could see things from his point of view on his bench on that open-topped, double-decked omnibus, going wherever it was he was going. No one knew except perhaps William. William never asked anything of him. William was the only one who never harboured any expectation of him. William had always been there when he needed him and always listened when he needed to be heard and never asked for anything. He would listen without judging. He would listen without thinking about what he was going to say next. He would listen without having to talk about himself or say what he had done in a similar, or worse, situation.

William was the only one. He was always there when he needed him. He had been there that day. But, that day Coleridge hadn't heard anything about what William had been up to, he suddenly realised. He hadn't asked. In fact, William had seemed a little distant and he had never felt that from him before. The circles they moved in had remained much the same for such a long time but things had changed. The cogs they travelled on had somehow become different. Occasionally they met and instantly gelled but then, with a swing of the pendulum and a small ticking rotation, were moved on again; further and further away from each other; carried off to opposite ends of the mechanism until next time they met and were parted again.

He looked down into the street from the omnibus as it stopped at a crossing. The crossing sweepers, always old men it seemed, swept and shovelled the dung into piles at the roadsides for collection that night to be spread on the parks and gardens the following morning. Old men, in the autumn of their lives, sweeping mountains of dung at crossings. Is that where it all ended up? Sweeping away the dung from the path of the thoughtless, ignorant young?

It was then that Coleridge noticed him. Down in the road, in the centre of the crossing directing the traffic was a policeman beckoning forward and holding back the omnibuses, traps, cabs and carts. Coleridge couldn't quite believe his eyes. The policeman was black. Where had he come from? Was he English too? Coleridge wanted to call out to the man, to shout out. He had never seen a black policeman before. He wanted to wave at him but the policeman was too deeply engrossed in his duties. The policeman beckoned the omnibus to move forward across the busy intersection and the bus was on its way again. He hadn't noticed Coleridge on the top deck.

The sight of the black policeman directing the traffic in the centre of London had yanked Coleridge up from his dark, private thoughts by the bootstraps, in a way that he found surprising and for the rest of his journey, he didn't feel quite so alone.

That evening, Coleridge sat in bed eating an apple. He was reading a book that professed to teach you German in fourteen days. He crunched and read as Jess brushed her hair. She was annoyed with him again for some reason or other, there was usually something, but he had decided not to let her frustration or irritation touch him.

"Three farthings! If you had just one farthing royalty on every one sold we would be wealthy now," she said.

"If I had ever dreamt that they would invent gramophones, Jess, then I would have been their inventor, wouldn't I?"

"But surely they owe us more than three farthings for the sale of all the records now? And what little is left at the end of the week, you use to keep that hopeless Croydon Symphony of yours from sinking without a trace."

He didn't want her to know that she was distracting him.

"Jess, say this word for me."

She put down the brush with a sigh and stood. She walked over to the bed and took the book from him, his finger still pointing to the word on the page.

"Wunderschon, is it?" she read quickly.

She let go of the book and went to her side of the bed. She got in.

"Doesn't that word just have everything in it!"

He smiled cheerfully, saying the word over and over in his mind and thinking of all the sentences he could use it in when he got to Berlin.

"So you're actually going, this time?" she asked as she moved down under the covers.

"Naturlich," he replied. She turned onto her side and blew out the candle. He couldn't read in that light. He closed his book in the dark and let it and the half-eaten apple drop gently to the floor. She moved further down the bed with a rustle of the cosy covers. In the dark, there was a moment of silence.

"Send me a postcard from Eastbourne," she said.

Coleridge sat in the shelter looking out to sea; salt spray in his nostrils, ozone filling his lungs. It was cold and windy. The sea was choppy but the expanse was invigorating. To be able to see the horizon and drink it in replenished him somehow. He put his book down and reached for the newspaper to see the article again. 'Mr Samuel Coleridge-Taylor was recalled three times and the audience clapped for five minutes. In gorgeous imagination he is another Tchaikovsky, in economy of thematic material another Dvorak...' he read but couldn't read anymore.

He looked out at the horizon and the tiny ships moving along it. All he had ever wanted was to be a musician, a composer, and here he was, a world famous composer.

He had been very successful. His works were played and sung by millions of people in the furthest corners of England, the Empire and beyond, in America even. Mr Herbert Beerbohm Tree himself had invited him to compose for his theatrical productions. He had commissions to conduct all over the country. He had even managed to keep up his students and the Croydon symphony, more out of his loyalty to them than any return.

Yes, he thought, he had arrived. He had achieved his goal and this is what it felt like. This was what it felt like to have arrived at your destination. You know you have been successful, he concluded, when there is nothing left for you to do; and you know you have arrived when there is nowhere left for you to go, except perhaps Eastbourne; that wind shelter on the front in out-of-season Eastbourne, to be specific.

He hadn't imagined that once he had arrived he would still be struggling to pay his bills, though. He smiled to himself. He had assumed that with success would come money. He hadn't thought that success would mean his wife would turn from him or that he would turn from her. This wasn't how he had imagined it at all. He had never considered that absolute success would have come with absolute loneliness – to poverty. Even William, he thought, even William didn't really seem to be there for him anymore like he used to be. William had barely said a word that day in Crystal Palace.

Coleridge looked down at his book's cover – Meg Blane & Other Poems by Robert Buchanan. It could work, he thought. He disagreed with William, that the theme was similar to Hiawatha, not that he had really said so. But even so, he had been a little hurt. He had never disagreed with William before, they always agreed on everything. That was why they were such great friends. How lucky he had been to find someone with whom he was in total agreement. How miraculous that had been.

He opened the book. He was successful, he told himself, but he refused to listen because it just didn't seem to be enough. How could he be a success if he still had to work his fingers to the bone?

He was suddenly irritated with himself. Here he was, in ropey shoes in Eastbourne, on a trip he couldn't afford to take and without enough money, in the pocket without the hole, for a proper dinner that evening.

He read the words of the poem facing the illustration.
"'Oh mother, it is like the sark folk wear
When they are drowned and dead!"
And Meg said nought, but kissed him on the lips,
And looked with dull eye seaward, where the moon
Silvered the white sails of the passing ships,
Into the land where she was going so soon.'

His eyes moved to the illustration. Meg was sitting outside her shack on the beach under a predatory sky, deserted by the only man she ever loved and who ever loved her. At her bare feet, on the cold and broken slate and granite shingle, lay her dim-witted, bastard son and on her lap, she held the shroud she had sewn for her body to be wrapped up in once she was dead.

Oh, for crying out loud, Coleridge thought, a smirk flicking across his face. For crying out loud! Things could be so much worse; things could be better but they could always be worse.

A single drop of water fell on the page. Coleridge slammed shut the book and wiped his treacherous eye. He stood, quite cross with himself for permitting the slide into such a pathetic self-pitying. How bloody selfish he had been, he laughed inside his head, how utterly self-obsessed. Feeling so maudlin and so sorry for himself.

He was choosing to feel as low as he possibly could, he believed, in order to satisfy some deep down lack in him; he was stitching his own shroud with his mind. He would simply have to choose other feelings – more productive, more resourceful feelings.

He would start by resolving to honour his wife as he had promised to do twelve months ago. He should just get on with his life and serve the people who had so generously favoured his work and put him where he was. He would be a man about it all and start really providing for his wife and son. As for money; well, he thought, he would simply have to work harder in order to make ends meet. He would just have to really knuckle down this time, and stop whining on. Give it some real elbow grease and stop that incessant whining that there was no one there prepared to listen to him whine on anymore. He would start to really put his back into it and make some real money for a change.

Perhaps it wasn't about arriving and leaving, after all – perhaps instead it was all about the journey. He had to get out of that place and get back to his wife and son and his work. He had to get away and back home to Croydon as quickly as he could. 'Wunderschon', he thought as he briskly walked back towards the train station.

Eastbourne had once again worked its magic.

CHAPTER 9

Coleridge threw himself into work with the same sense of diminished responsibility that leads men and women to leap to their death from Waterloo Bridge. Such actions were never selfish, he knew. Most of us are responsible for our own ends in one way or another. Leaping from a bridge is just a lot more instant and a lot less socially acceptable than say, eating and drinking too much for a lifetime. Leaping off bridges is the result of a fatal illness just as any other fatal disease ends in death. In fact, such actions were an act of absolute selflessness, understood only by the person leaping into the dark void at that moment. It was with that same absolute selflessness that Coleridge threw himself into work.

He seemed to spend his life on trams, trains, omnibuses and Shanks's Pony, going from one place to another. It gave him time to think, or rather to dwell, perhaps not altogether a helpful thing.

It was on one such train journey, going to a conference, that for some reason he started to think about his father. He remembered how Colonel Walters had described him but Coleridge had never quite been able to imagine his father's face. As a boy he had looked at his reflection in the mirror and tried to see his father's signature in it. But never having seen his birth mother either, it was difficult to pick out the mother's physical attributes from the father's.

He had thought about trying to trace his father but had decided against it. All he knew was that his father, Dr Taylor had returned to Sierra Leone shortly after his birth. Now that he had a son of his own, Coleridge found it harder to fathom how anyone could leave their only child.

Coleridge had decided that it would be far easier for his father to find him, if he ever wanted to, than it would be for him to find his father. He was famous. He had made himself a beacon to guide his father to him if he had wanted to come but so far, he clearly hadn't. He had made himself something his father could be proud of, to draw him back to England again, and if he never followed that beacon, the light from which reached into the darkest corners of the earth, then this would have to mean that he didn't want his son and Coleridge would have to accept that. Why would a son long for an embrace from a father who did not want him?

Coleridge opened the first Pan-African Conference in London, a conference that he had also helped to organise. The turn-out had been disappointing but it was the first time such an event had ever been held anywhere and those who did attend gave him a rapturous reception as he stood and addressed them holding a copy of the new African and Orient Review – a periodical that was Coleridge's own brainchild and for which he provided most of the editorial.

Coleridge still kept up his old students and still conducted the Croydon Symphony in rehearsal once a week. He still believed in the Croydon Symphony and it was this faith that had led him to invest some of his own money in it, so that it should continue and one day enjoy the success it deserved.

Coleridge hadn't seen enough of his friends and so made a point of seeing William conducting his new piece, 'The Magic Mirror', based on the fairytale of Snow White. At the end of the story, some shoes of iron are heated in a fire and then strapped to the wicked, witch-queen's feet. Not very forgiving of the handsome prince and Snow White, Coleridge and William had joked after-wards. William beautifully captured the macabre and terrifying dance to her death in that maniacal final move-ment. The whole piece was only twenty minutes long but if William's plan came to fruition, it would make a rather spectacular ballet.

A chair had been set next to the conductor's stand and at the end of the piece William collapsed into it sweating and breathing deeply, in a state perhaps not dissimilar to the agonising and fatal exhaustion Snow White's mother experienced. William wheezed as the audience applauded him. Coleridge applauded too but recognised William's breathing for what it was. He was having another attack, a milder one but it hurt Co-leridge that he felt unable to rush to his friend's side. Instead he rose to his feet with the rest of the audience and gave the man his ovation as he struggled for breath. Coleridge tried to catch William's eye. William looked across and smiled at him through the gasps and waved the baton in Coleridge's direction to say he was not quite at death's door and not to fuss.

Mr and Mrs Elgar did eventually make the formal dinner invitation to Mr and Mrs Samuel Coleridge-Taylor but the occasion had the trappings of a rather more sombre affair due to the sad circumstances that gripped the Empire at that time. Above the mantle, in the crimson dining room of the Elgars' London residence, where a gold rococo mirror would normally have hung, stood instead a portrait of Her Majesty, the late Queen Victoria with a broad, black ribbon checking the corner and then running, ruffled but languid, across the cold marble. Vases filled with lilies stood either side of the late Queen's portrait.

Coleridge was seated to the left of the twenty-year-old son of one of the many guests around the table and was listening intently to what he had to say. The young man was an enthusiastic, amateur musician. Like many people his age, he had very strongly held beliefs about this and that and this amused Coleridge slightly, as it made him recognise that the days of his own strongly held beliefs were well on the wane as this young man's would be too one day. Coleridge listened intently and decided not to shoot down the young man's views one by one as they flew with such youthful abandon. They would surely come down in their own time.

Jess watched Mrs Elgar as if the hostess were a specimen under a microscope. Mrs Elgar let her head tilt to the side when she was listening. It made a hostess look both interested and becoming. Jess's head tilted slightly as she watched. She too was listening to the man next to her but not really hearing. He was talking about pheasants and venison.

Mrs Elgar rested her hands in her lap in intense and practised repose. She listened to the man politely but her eyes were everywhere, Jess noticed. This was what made Mrs Elgar a great hostess. Her eyes darted around in unspoken enquiry. Did anyone have an empty glass? Would the sorbet be of the right consistency by the time

the fish course had been completed, between frozen and
semi-freddo? Was anyone bored with the person they
were placed with? Was the Negro composer's wife really
studying her every move?

No reaction flicked across Mrs Elgar's alabaster face
as she quizzed her own mind. No eye contact was made
with Mrs Coleridge-Taylor although Mrs Elgar was
amused that her social graces were being scrutinised so
intently and without any fan or cloak of seemliness or
subtlety.

Mr Auguste Jaegar whispered unkind comments to
Mr Elgar about Coleridge, and Elgar chuckled. The
words were inaudible but the whispering behind the
napkins and the surreptitious glances to see if the man
could hear them, was unmistakable. Coleridge knew
they were being unkind to someone but told himself it
was unlikely to be him; after all, both Mr Jaegar and Mr
Elgar had always been very encouraging. Indeed without
them, he wouldn't be where he was, professionally that
is, and for this Coleridge knew that he would always be
indebted to the both of them. Coleridge grew up with the
occasional, childish sniggering behind him in the street
but he knew that these two men would not now be
unkind to him because of his race. Both men, being
Roman Catholics, had probably experienced prejudice
themselves and so it was not conceivable that they could
be prejudiced against him on such similarly baseless
grounds.

Without moving his head, Coleridge glanced at Mr
Jaegar. Mr Jaegar glanced up at Coleridge – his twinkling
eye laughing over the starched napkin held to hide his
mouth. Jaegar quickly cleared his throat – a warning
signal to Elgar. The two men's heads had been conjoined

and Elgar had been mirroring Jaegar in every way, but the two men split away with schoolboy smirks. Elgar then glanced at Coleridge and away again at once just as Jaegar had done. Coleridge went back to listening to the young man on his right, envious of his innocence.

After a day of adjudicating some student musicians at the new music school in Crystal Palace, Coleridge had returned home to make the final amendments to his latest cantata, 'Meg Blane – A Seaside Rhapsody'. He stood at the Broadwood Grand in his upstairs study. He composed there, rather than in the Music Shed, in the evenings and during the chillier weather just as long as Watha was not yelling his gorgeous, little, berry head off.

Watha was then three and played happily on the floor with the wooden farmyard set given to him by his parents the previous Christmas. Coleridge looked down at the boy. He couldn't resist him. He picked him up under his warm, little armpits. He was getting heavy. He sat him on his knee at the piano, Watha's chubby legs sticking out sideways. Coleridge played a one finger version of 'Three Blind Mice'. Watha laughed and bashed the keys with his pudgey, open palm. He kissed his boy's head. It was finished.

At its premiere, later that year, at the Sheffield Music Festival, 'Meg Blane' received a polite public reception and a measured response from the critics.

Coleridge also wrote 'The Blind Girl of Caste-Cuille' that year and was appointed conductor to the Handel Society and to the Rochester Choral Society as well as professor of composition at Trinity College of Music. This was all in addition to everything else he was already doing. But there were two special highlights for which he would always remember 1903.

The first was the third Pan-African Conference, attended this time by more than two hundred people. This turnout really warmed the hearts of Kathleen, Coleridge and the other organisers. The other highlight was the evening he stood next to the wonderful Mr Herbert Beerbohm Tree and the rest of the cast behind the heavy, velvet drapes at Drury Lane to meet the Duchess of Sutherland, His Royal Highness Edward VII, his beautiful Danish wife Queen Alexandra and Mrs George Keppel, one of the royal entourage.

Coleridge had had quite a chat with the King who didn't seem to want to let go of Coleridge's hand at all after shaking it. The King had just returned from a trip to France, a visit on which the Entente Cordiale between Britain and France was founded. The trip was well reported in the newspapers but the King didn't want to talk to Coleridge about that.

The King had been very natural and kind. He had a warm, generous smile and seemed genuinely pleased to meet Coleridge who noticed him wheeze a little when he spoke, just as William often did. He seemed to be very human for a King. After their chat, the King made a fist and crooked his elbow proudly to beat out the opening bars of, 'Hiawatha's Wedding Feast' as he grinned and sang.

"Pom-pom, pom! Tud-um tum, tum-tum!" The royal party and the beaming line-up laughed. The King patted Coleridge's shoulder as he moved on. Mr Tree elbowed Coleridge in the ribs with a wink once the King, Queen, the Duchess and the rest of the royal party had moved on. Coleridge had been left breathless by the honour.

Even after such auspicious occasions as these, Coleridge always left a little early. Most assumed, and he chose not to correct them, that this was because he liked to avoid the people who gathered after such events and they were partly right. People waited so that they might catch him, talk to him and get him to sign programmes for them and so forth and occasionally, when the crowd was very large and a little unwieldy, he would in all honesty have preferred to avoid them. But the principle reason he left early after a performance was so that he didn't have to explain why he didn't have a cab to take him home. He didn't want people to see him walking, or taking Shanks's Pony as he called it, towards a place where he could hail a passing bus.

In addition to his composing, Coleridge frequently had more than three or four engagements per day – one of these would be in the evening and usually ending late at night. After his daytime engagements, he would often arrive home just in time. Jess would be standing at the bottom of the stairs with a change of clothes – black tie, conductor's jacket and the rest and he would change in the hallway to save time. He preferred this to carrying a change of clothes with him.

There was one particular evening when Watha was feeling under the weather and so Jess had called upon Coleridge's mother to sit with the boy while they were out. Jess always joined Coleridge on these evening trips into town and normally brought Watha with them too. Once, in the intense silence the moment before he was about to start conducting, his toddler shouted out, 'Coleridge'. Everyone collapsed in laughter. Coleridge dropped his arms, turned with a smile at his boy, blew him kiss and then comically shrugged his resigned shoulders to the people, and they loved him all the more. But that one particular night it was just Jess and Coleridge. They were late and standing outside St James's Hall, in the dark as Jess straightened his tie.

"I won't be waiting at the end," she said. "I need to get back to Watha. Don't be too late, will you."

He was tired and not feeling terribly well himself. He had felt light-headed most of the day, as if he were on a merry-go-round that was spinning, increasingly fast.

No matter how hard he tried, he never seemed to be able to arrive on time. People always joked that he would be late for his own funeral. He looked at Jess as she waddled her way up the stairs and into the hall. How was he going to afford to support another child, he wondered as he started up the steps himself and into hall.

"And where do you think you're going?" asked a voice from the shadows. Coleridge turned to see a policeman emerge.

"I'm accompanying Madame Crossley and Madame Albani. Here's my card."

The policeman took an inordinately long time to look at the card. He looked at Coleridge.

"I'm terribly sorry but I'm late...," he told the policeman.

"I do apologise, Sir," said the policeman as he touched the brim of his hat and handed Coleridge's card back to him. The policeman turned and walked back into the smoggy shadows from which he had silently emerged. Coleridge thanked him and hurried into the hall.

As usual, it had been a very well-received recital. Jess watched as Coleridge and Madame Albani took their applause and she readied herself to leave when from behind her, she heard the voice of a young woman.

"What a killing little nigger," the woman said. Jess prickled.

"I think every home should have one," her male companion replied. Jess's mood darkened. She had heard people talk about her husband like this before and had told people off in the street, for far less, more than once. Coleridge always found it rather embarrassing as Jess always did it quite loudly so as to cause the bigots as much embarrassment as possible. Coleridge just thought such individuals were ignorant and were best ignored.

"I wonder if he would be quite so accepted if he had taken a Negro wife," the woman behind her went on.

Jess was incensed and started to round on them but unfortunately a joyful encore began and stole her thunder. Madame Albani sang 'Big Lady Moon'. The words of the song were by Kathleen Easmon; it was one of her 'Five Fairy Ballads', every child's favourite. Jess waited for it to end and then, during the ovation that followed, left the hall and London to return to her poorly toddler.

By the time Coleridge emerged from the hall, Jess was already well on her way home. Madame Albani and Madame Crossley had insisted that he stay behind for a glass. The divas were hard to refuse and so he decided that if he couldn't be the first to leave as planned, he would be sure to be the last.

After seeing Madame Albani and Madame Crossley to their carriages from the steps of the hall, he started to make his own way into the London night, when for the second time that evening, he heard a voice from the dark behind him.

"Excuse me, Sir."

It wasn't the policeman.

"Yes?" said Coleridge as he turned. He stopped. There was nothing but silence. He was a little afraid and the smog was thick and cold. Somewhere in the dark, someone he couldn't see was watching him. "Where are you?"

"I waited for you," said the voice from the dark.

The voice was a man's, an African man's but with a slight, yet clearly discernable American twang. Coleridge listened to the sound of footsteps approaching him from the dark and then the man stepped into the lamplight.

He was a short, black man about the same height as Coleridge but rather portly, almost round. He was, rather unusually for that time of day, dressed in tweeds. In one hand, the man held a rolled up programme from the evening's recital. He looked at Coleridge and nervously, took off his tweed hat. The two men faced each other in the London night.

"Hello, Samuel," the man said.

CHAPTER 10

The man tapped the programme against his leg in hesitation then warmly reached out with his other hand. Coleridge instinctively took it to shake but just held it. His stomach flipped over and a cold judder moved down his spine. He let the man's hand go. The man was certainly about the right age, he thought in an instant. The man smiled at Coleridge. There was such warmth from the little man. Coleridge looked into his eyes. He hadn't seen him in the audience but the man had a familiarity about him that Coleridge couldn't place.

"My name... is Miller," the African American said with an uncertainty, as if he were thinking on the hoof. "They wouldn't give me your address at the door but said that if I waited here.... You were a long time."

"Have we met?" Coleridge asked.

The man suddenly looked concerned.

"Let me look at you," he said as he stepped towards Coleridge and gently moved him into a fuller light. "But you're ill, I was going to ask if ... if you wouldn't mind signing this for my wife but I can see now that you're not very well."

"No. I am just a little tired."

The man nodded quickly and reached into his jacket pocket, pulling out a large but thin, paper pad. He licked the end of a pencil and began to write.

"You must let me prescribe for you."

"You're a doctor?"

"Well, we can't have you succumbing to the influenza," the man said as he scribbled. "That will never do, Samuel, will it?"

"It's very kind of you but I really ought to be going. My boy isn't very well."

The man stopped writing and handed his pencil to Coleridge. He smiled at Coleridge and put his pudgey, childlike hand on Coleridge's shoulder.

"I too have a son," said the man. "Then you should both take this. If you will just write your address here...."

He handed the pad to Coleridge who wrote his address, "Aldwick', St Leonard's Road, Waddon, Croydon'. Dr Miller took the pencil and pad and tore off the top sheet, folding it single-handedly and popping it in Coleridge's breast pocket with a pat.

"Take this to your pharmacy," he said, "and have it made up. I keep this part – for my records you understand...."

The man put his prescription book back inside his jacket and stopped short after turning to go. He looked at Coleridge.

"Good evening, Samuel, and thank you so much. I hope you and your boy feel better soon."

He was gone.

Coleridge's last student of the day left his room at the Crystal Palace School of Art and Music. Coleridge hurriedly put his things away and put on his hat, coat and white gloves. He opened the door just as the Principal, Mrs Watson was passing.

"And where are we off to now, Mr Taylor?" she asked.

"Rochester. Actually, home first then Rochester."

"I have never known a man who was so careless of the value of time or of money," she said fondly as she brushed passed him.

She was an affable woman and a very good leader but he always seemed to bump into her when he was in a hurry – usually late in coming from or going to a class.

"Not, indeed that you waste either, you understand," she said over her shoulder, "but in giving your lessons, Mr Taylor, you linger far longer than perhaps you ought...?"

"Sorry," he said. "Sorry... sorry."

Coleridge went home and managed to get a couple of hours composing in before he had to leave again. Jess, looking very pregnant, had brought a cup of tea to his Music Shed knowing he wouldn't have time to drink it and very soon he was on the train again, from Bromley South to Rochester where he was to conduct the Rochester Choral Society in his work, 'The Atonement'. It was being tried at the Cathedral there prior to a performance at the Three Choirs Festival. This was to be followed by its London premiere at the Royal Albert Hall the following September.

His book, William Dubois' Souls of Black Folk was open on his lap. It had recently been sent to him from America by some friends of Frederick Loudin's called the Hilyers, with whom he had recently entered into a correspondence. In their letter accompanying the gift, which he was using as a bookmark, the Hilyers referred to their previous letter, in which they had invited him to conduct 'Hiawatha' in America. He had had to decline because of work commitments and also because they were not able to muster a professional orchestra. He had been some-what reluctant to refuse however, as their enthusiasm and kindness in the letter had been marked.

The letter that brought their gift had said that they were to be staying in London in a few months' time and that they should very much like to meet with him. Coleridge had sent them a telegram to say that he would be honoured and the meeting had been arranged. Coleridge had deliberately kept that particular week free anyway as he would have a commission to complete, but he was sure he could spare an afternoon. Besides, he couldn't have said 'no' to people whose flattering invitation he had had to decline previously, and who so wanted to meet him.

As the train puffed and shunted its way through 'The Garden of England', his eyes grew heavy. The only other person in the carriage with him was a vicar. Coleridge's eyes closed and it wasn't long before his head was lolling about sleepily and he drifted off. The light flashed across his eyelids like a magic lantern show.

He found himself looking over the shoulder of Hiawatha and the sun-baked prairies. The Red Indian Chief was standing on a mountaintop looking at his people, the Iroquois, below – at their encampment by the edge of a great expanse of water, more like a sea than a lake. On the lake was a boat and in the boat were white men heading towards the village of wigwams.

'... And the noble Hiawatha,
With his hands aloft extended,
Waited, full of exultation,
Till the birch-canoe, with paddles
Brated on the shining pebbles,

Till the Black-Robe Chief, the Pale-face,
With the cross upon his bosom,
Landed on the sandy margin....'

The train clattered over the iron bridge built across the River Medway and Coleridge awoke. The vicar opposite was smiling at him.

"Just a few more minutes until Rochester," he said.

Coleridge smiled and nodded. He closed his book and looked out of the window. He loved the view of the Cathedral and Castle as the train approached Rochester. He loved the lurid green of the ridiculously tall hops fields of Kent. The vicar looked at Coleridge as if he were burning to ask him something.

"Acre after acre of wonderful hops!" the vicar continued. "One shouldn't really approve. Do you grow hops in Japan?"

Coleridge was bemused. No one had ever thought him Japanese before.

The day after the Cathedral concert, which had been received without any particular warmth, Coleridge made his way back to London. When he arrived home, Dr Collard was making a house call to see how Watha was. He was just about to leave as Coleridge arrived.

Once the boy had been checked over and Dr Collard was about to make his way, he quietly took Coleridge to one side and out of earshot of the boy and Mrs Coleridge-Taylor. He was holding the prescription that Dr Miller had given him and that he in turn had given to Jess to have made up.

"Are you in the habit of taking this drug, Coleridge?" Dr Collard asked.

"No. I met someone and he said that we both ought to take it. I never normally take medicine."

Coleridge recognised his case of the sniffles as the beginning of a nasty cold, a cold he couldn't really afford to have.

"Well I would advise," said Dr Collard rather sternly, "that you leave this particular drug well alone. I'll give you both something for influenza."

Before Coleridge could say a word the doctor tore the prescription to shreds and put the pieces in his pocket.

Thankfully Coleridge had no evening engagements that day and so he and Jess had spent a quiet evening in front of the fire, the first for quite some time. He couldn't put down the book the Hilyers had kindly sent him. Jess sat gazing at the fire as it munched at the snapping fir-cones she had tossed upon it.

A good few hours later, Jess went up and when he couldn't keep his eyes open any longer, and the fire had died, Coleridge closed his book and prepared the house for the night. He made sure none of the still glowing embers could roll out onto the mat and he put out the lights.

The book had successfully staved off sleep but without it, he soon became all too aware of just how exhausted he was. His cold had really begun to take a grip. He felt lousy. Watha had been asleep for some hours and Jess was waiting for him in their bedroom. He turned to the stairs and started to put out the last light in the hall, when there was a knock on the front door.

The knock startled him and suddenly he was wide awake and alert again. He hadn't heard anyone making the short walk up the steps to the front door from the road. He stood there for a moment. The knock had come from nowhere and then from nowhere, it came again. He opened the door, suddenly worried that something awful must have happened to his mother. But he couldn't quite believe his eyes when he saw who stood in his porch.

"Dr Miller?"

"I am so sorry to disturb you this late, Samuel but I just happened to be passing. Have you had a dose of the medicine I prescribed?" he asked.

"Yes," Coleridge lied. "Yes, thank you and I feel so much better. Thank you."

The strange American just stood there smiling at him, perhaps awaiting a request for a repeat prescription.

"I have a rather long day …" Coleridge said politely only to be interrupted.

"And I won't keep you. I also have a difficult day tomorrow. I should have received a draft from my New York office this morning for some medicines for a poor lady – a neighbour of yours in fact," he said, waving his finger in an indeterminate direction, "and now I don't know what I will tell her."

"…Medicines can be very expensive."

"Five pounds actually!" said Dr Miller, nodding. "Still, we struggle on somehow…."

He smiled and looked away.

"It must be very serious indeed for that amount. I could write you a cheque – make you a loan, if that would help her," Coleridge offered.

"I am most dreadfully embarrassed. I was only passing and thought that I… I certainly wasn't asking you…." Coleridge picked up his book of cheques from the bureau.

"It's no trouble. She is a neighbour after all."

Coleridge wrote out a cheque for five pounds payable to Dr Miller. Dr Miller stood in silence with his hand on his heart as Coleridge wrote. The man was clearly deeply touched.

"I don't know what to say. ...Thank you."

He took the cheque and then as an afterthought tore off a page from his prescription pad scoring through the form side of the paper and writing on the back.

"I shall write you an I.O.U. I simply must insist upon that."

"Thank you," Coleridge said as he accepted the man's note.

"God bless you," said the doctor with a little bow of rather emotional gratitude.

"Goodnight," Coleridge said as he closed the door and drew the bolt across.

He listened as Dr Miller walked down the steps and away into the night. Coleridge turned. Jess was standing at the top of the stairs with one hand resting lightly on her bump. No address was printed on the page of prescription pad, on which Dr Miller had written out his I.O.U., and Jess looked at Coleridge accusingly. He started up the stairs. He didn't have the energy to discuss, explain or justify anything to her. He was tired and not very well and just needed to get to bed.

Coleridge's visitors arrived just a matter of weeks after the birth of his daughter. They had arrived at Coleridge's modest home in Croydon promptly at three, about an hour or so after Kathleen. Jess had arranged for tea to be served by a local girl called Elsie who occasionally did odd jobs around the house for Mrs Coleridge-Taylor.

Andrew Hilyer was a wealthy, black accountant from Washington. He was a quiet man, but this was more than compensated for by his ample and jolly wife, Mamie.

Mr and Mrs Hilyer were visiting Europe with their friends Dr and Mrs Cabaniss and the well-known American baritone, Mr Henry Burleigh. Burleigh was a strong and very handsome man in his late thirties. Coleridge had not been surrounded by so many black Americans since his tea with Loudin's Fisk Jubilee Singers six years earlier and this was the long awaited fruit of that initial meeting. Watha played on the floor and the new baby gurgled contentedly on Jess's proud knee.

"I used to stand hungry in front of one of Dennett's downtown restaurants," Mr Burleigh recounted, "and watched the man in the window cook cakes. Then I would take a toothpick from my pocket and use it as if I had just eaten one. I'd draw on my imagination rather than my pocket, you understand and then walk off down the street singing to myself." Jess laughed politely.

"No imaginary cakes here," she said.

"Hello baby Gwendolen," Kathleen cooed as the infant reached out for and gripped her little finger.

"Coleridge was adjudicating in South Wales," Jess said to Mr Burleigh. She had been waiting for a cue to begin one of the anecdotes she had prepared. "We were there at the invitation of our dear friend Lady Williams, the wife of the late Queen's physician, and she actually suggested the name to me."

"My, my, the Queen!" said Mrs Cabaniss.

"It's a lovely name," Burleigh agreed.

Coleridge sat across the room by the door and was deep in conversation with the Hilyers who were sitting on, and full of admiration for, his beautiful new settee in front of the window.

"Mr Dubois' book is about the finest book I have ever read by a coloured man and one of the best by any author, white or black," he told them. "Thank you over and over again for so kindly sending it to me."

Elsie rattled the tea things in on the trolley.

"Tea!" Jess announced. "And real cakes, Mr Burleigh, English cakes!"

The conversation inevitably turned from baby names and toddlers and from tea and cake to Coleridge's first love. Coleridge's latest pieces had been receiving very lukewarm responses but the African influences that had started to manifest in his work greatly interested Mr Burleigh who was very knowledgeable about African American folk music.

"All are distinguished by unusual and subtle harmonies," he told Coleridge from his side of the room, with Kathleen, Jess and the doctor and his wife, "the like of which I have found in no other songs but those of old Scotland and Ireland. In Negro Spirituals my race has pure gold – our contribution to America's artistic possessions!"

Later, Jess poured a second cup of tea for each from the replenished pot.

"I just love your English tea," Mrs Hilyer said reaching for another slice of Jess's Victoria sponge without being offered and as the others were barely through their first piece. "You know, we were most disappointed not to be here for 'The Atonement'. How did it go?"

The Three Choirs Festival had rejected the piece despite commissioning it.

"The fact is," Coleridge said with a response well-rehearsed, "the fact is that there has never been a religious work written by a coloured man before. They, I'm afraid to say, decided to revert to Gounod's 'Redemption'. They thought my portrayal of Christ by a baritone might offend. But I have to say that it held the people well at the Royal Albert Hall."

"Well, that's something at least," said Mr Burleigh encouragingly. Sensing his unease, Mr Burleigh skilfully changed the subject to one that he knew Coleridge would be interested in hearing about and it worked. Coleridge sparkled back into life and listened intently as Mr Burleigh recounted his experience of working with Dvorak.

"I am very proud of my association with him," Mr Burleigh concluded.

"Coleridge loves the open-air sound his music has, don't you?" Jess chimed in as she handed Mr Burleigh his second cup. "Coleridge and I believe our modern music lacks Dvorak's genuine simplicity." Coleridge nodded silently. Of course he agreed – he had said exactly those words to Jess less than a week before. She hadn't said anything at the time. He returned to brooding over 'Atonement'.

"Coleridge, tell us about this mysterious Dr Miller?" Kathleen asked in an attempt to dispel the inclement weather front that seemed to be drifting into the conversation.

Jess had mentioned the story to them when he had popped out of the room. He hid the irritation he felt that she had shared this embarrassing story with his guests in his absence. Dr Miller had called on two more occasions and Coleridge had made a total of three loans to him amounting to thirteen pounds. Dr Miller never returned as promised to honour his I.O.U.'s. Coleridge told them all about it with his usual self-deprecating humour.

"I felt such a fool," he laughed.

"Stitched up like a kipper, eh?" said Mr Burleigh in a poor English accent.

It was very funny to hear an American use such an English phrase. Coleridge's chuckle was genuine that time and at last he began to relax. He liked Henry Burleigh very much.

"Well isn't that what you English say? Eh, Coleridge?" Mr Burleigh teased, his grin broadening as Coleridge's giggles increased. To explain would be far too involved, Coleridge thought and to submit to the giggles far more pleasant.

"Yes Mr Burleigh, that's what we English say."

Americans really were extraordinary, he thought, but he was interested to hear the purpose of the Hilyers' visit to Europe. It seemed to him that everyone was talking of everything except why they were actually there. It was all too apparent that there was something that was waiting to be said. Everyone knew it. Coleridge wasn't the only one wanting whatever it was to be out in the open. Mr Hilyer had said very little but had been eyeing Coleridge over the brim of his teacup, waiting for his moment.

"He still keeps the I.O.U.'s though, don't you Coleridge – just in case!"

"Mrs Hilyer?" Coleridge cautiously asked choosing to ignore Jess's jibes.

"Goodness! Call me Mamie. After all our correspondence, surely we're old friends now, Coleridge…"

"Mamie then, thank you –" he said rather uncomfortably, realising that he couldn't possibly ask if there was something that they wanted from him – it would be like asking, 'why are you here?' He quickly thought of something else to say and although it was said to pull him from the hole he had stumbled into, it nevertheless came from the heart.

"Mamie, your remarkable compilation of the doings of the coloured race makes me wish I was doing my share. But perhaps in matters of art, it is better for a coloured individual to live in my country? Though all the people I've met from America seem to be extraordinarily cheerful. Perhaps it's because you are all so very philosophical about it and I am not so, I'm afraid. But all this earnest work you do – that you all do, surely this does something to leaven the prejudice?"

Mamie smiled at him but didn't say a word. Dr & Mrs Cabaniss smiled at him but didn't say a word.

"'Have I ...said something?"

"Coleridge, I'm going to cut to the chase, here if I may, as we Americans like to call it," said Mr Hilyer breaking his silence. "The fact is my wife here, Dr and Mrs Cabaniss and Mr Burleigh – we've come to England for a purpose."

"'The 'Passion Play' in Oberammergau was a ruse," Mrs Cabaniss added gleefully. "We weren't interested in that at all."

Then, as before, no one spoke. No one was drinking their tea either. The Americans smiled at him and he smiled back. He looked to Kathleen and to Jess for some clue but neither of them looked like they knew quite what was coming either. Whatever it was that needed to be said, was waiting for the silence to end first. Had he done something wrong, he wondered. Had he made some sort of American etiquette faux pas and they were waiting for an apology? Were they laughing at him? The smile on his face started to ache.

"Mamie was a founder member of Washington's women's vocal group –" said Dr Cabaniss, starting at the beginning.

"We called ourselves The Treble Clef Club," his wife interrupted, taking up the baton and flourishing her hand to express her dismissive attitude towards the old name. "But now, we're the Samuel Coleridge-Taylor Choral Society."

She clapped her hands together. She waited for his reaction and Coleridge was deeply flattered, but was that it? They could have told him that in a letter.

"We have Mr Loudin to thank for introducing your work to us," Mr Hilyer said, "and Mr Burleigh here for leading us to you personally."

"Everyone agrees that you are a splendid singer, Mr Burleigh," Coleridge said, "and also – more rare – a splendid musician. ...The two things do not always go together, I find."

"We know that you had other work commitments when we wrote you that first time," said Mr Hilyer "and totally understand your concerns about our orchestra –"

"Yes, about that. I have to say how sorry –" he began.

"Coleridge, –" Mrs Cabaniss jumped in again but she didn't go on. Her frivolous nature slid from her face.

She put down her cup and walked over to him and then, most disarmingly, knelt at the side of his chair. She suddenly looked rather sad. She sandwiched his hand between hers and he put down the teacup and saucer held in the hand she didn't have – he knew that if tea got spilt on his cushion covers it would be merry hell to get out.

His other hand free, she took that one too and sandwiched it also. He was going nowhere. She looked him in the eyes and spoke softly and with a heartfelt affection.

"Coleridge, I don't believe that you understand what you mean to us in America?"

He looked at her, then to them. He didn't understand.

"I know it is different here," Mrs Cabaniss said slowly, "but – and the others will back me up, you have inspired African Americans... but you won't come see us. Everyone's heard of you there and everyone wants you there and we've invited you but you won't come."

He couldn't draw his eyes away from hers.

"Our parents, Coleridge, our parents were slaves. Look at us. Coloured folks there have to struggle every day and I mean really struggle and you know, oftentimes it does feel hopeless, I'll admit it. Sometimes we may even want to give up, but we all still struggle on regardless. Now, in England you are a great musician but you ...you are so much more than just a musician over there, Coleridge. You are a cultural hero."

She saw his eyes mist over. He wanted his hands back. She rubbed them between hers and squeezed.

"You have done something wonderful for the African American spirit just by being you and you... you don't even know it. We... well I guess we hadn't realised we'd been crying out for a figurehead so never considered what form such a thing might take. But then you came along and... got chosen, I'm afraid. African Americans have chosen you, Coleridge, an English composer, as their inspiration and they need you there so that they can go on – they really need to see you there. Our people don't often get the success you have achieved and they want to embrace you, Coleridge. Would you deny them that? You fire our spirits. You inspire African Americans to keep on struggling."

He couldn't speak.

"So," she said, in conclusion, "please don't say to us you won't come. We came all this way especially to ask you. So, will you? Will you please come?"

She let go of his hand. He couldn't answer. Mrs Cabaniss stood and went back to her seat. He sniffed. Watha gazed up at him from the floor. They all looked at him and he opened his mouth to speak but nothing came out. He had no idea that that was how people there felt. It had never crossed his mind. Dr Cabaniss spoke.

"You know how many people we had crowded into the Metropolitan Methodist Episcopal Church to hear 'Hiawatha' last year when you wouldn't come?"

Coleridge shook his head weakly.

"Two thousand. All the rest had to stand outside to listen. At the public rehearsal nearly three thousand people had to be turned away."

Coleridge was overwhelmed by this wave from across the Atlantic Ocean. The thought of actually visiting America had never been seriously entertained. He'd taken the ferry to the Isle of Wight for his honeymoon, but all that way across the Atlantic?

He thought of his old friend Paul Laurence Dunbar. It would be wonderful to see him again. He thought of the Pan-African movement. He thought of Frederick Loudin and the Jubilee Singers.

"Come. ...Please," said Mr Burleigh.

The mood was far too intense for poor Coleridge, so Mamie cleared her throat and with a grin, put down her teacup noisily.

"Now, take your time over this, Coleridge," she blustered playfully.

Kathleen couldn't believe that her gentle, modest friend would pass up such an invitation after what had been said.

"Coleridge…!" she said prompting him to speak.

"We Hilyers are not used to being turned down twice," Mamie went on with a twinkle that made Coleridge smile at last. But the smile forced a tear from the corner of his eye and it rolled down his cheek.

"Let me spell it out for you. We have two hundred African American singers who have been rehearsing 'Hiawatha' for well over a year. We have Mr Burleigh here, we have Convention Hall and we want you there to conduct it for us and my husband here is paying. Now I understand that you were concerned about our little orchestra last time, weren't you, Mr T?" Coleridge giggled again.

"Well we got you the United States Marine Band, this time, Mister. Will that do you?" Her eyes rolled as she spoke and her head swayed like a beautiful, big, black cobra.

Mr Hilyer spoke. "This'll be the first time that a man with African blood in his veins ever held a baton over the heads of a white orchestra in the United States of America and you know what that means? Coleridge, you will be making American history."

He couldn't talk.

"Is it the prejudice…?" Mrs Cabaniss asked.

"Oh no," said Coleridge, at last finding his voice. Mrs Cabaniss was very crafty indeed – she knew exactly what to say to get him talking again.

"No. I am well prepared for it. Surely that which you and so many others have lived in for so many years will not quite kill me. I am English and I am a great believer in the coloured race. I never lose an opportunity of letting my white friends know it, do I?" Kathleen smiled at him. This was more like her Coleridge. "But if you make any arrangements to wrap me in cotton-wool, I promise I shall run a mile."

"Am I correct in understanding then, Mr Coleridge-Taylor," asked Hilyer, "that you will come to Washington as our guest and conduct us in your 'Hiawatha' trilogy there?"

"It sounds to me like this visit has already been deferred far too long," Coleridge said. "I can see that now. I don't think that anything else would have induced me to visit America, other than an established society of coloured singers such as yourselves, and what this dear lady, Mrs Cabaniss said to me just now. It is for this reason, first and foremost, that I shall be most honoured to come and all my other engagements are secondary."

They were overjoyed. Mamie and Mrs Cabaniss shrieked and clapped and danced about and the others laughed and shook his hand.

Coleridge looked at Jess. There was to be no discussion this time. It was to be his decision and his alone. He was not a spontaneous person but he had decided this and he would not be moved. Of course, old Jaegar would see no value in the trip either but Coleridge didn't care. He would cancel everything. He would be the guest of these wonderful, wonderful people. He would visit their great country and he would conduct their society named in his honour.

CHAPTER 11

Coleridge had watched the approach to Boston Harbour from the deck of the great liner. The crisp sea air filled his lungs. Excitement had roused him from sleep even earlier than normal that morning and the salty dew refreshed him as it blew on his face.

He had overheard that Mr Roosevelt had been re-elected for a second term some days before. Apparently, he had had a huge majority and remnants of the celebrations, banners and flags could just be seen lining the distant docks from his vantage point. The re-election of Mr Roosevelt had pleased Coleridge. He had written to the Hilyers expressing his hope that Mr Roosevelt would be successful.

Coleridge stood in his hat, coat and white gloves as the great liner approached American soil after its eight day voyage. As Boston came clearer into view, he saw people lining the dock, looking expectantly to catch a first glimpse of their loved ones from the old world. He rapped his cane on the deck boards, his excitement needing some outlet and his heart pounded under his dapper suit. He couldn't wait to arrive.

Eventually, the liner docked and the gangplanks were lowered. He took a breath and couldn't help smiling like a goon as he waited his turn to leave the ship. He couldn't look at the people on shore but was aware of the noise they were making. Trunks and crates were unloaded and loaded for the next part of their journey. Carriage horses clopped and whinnied, ladies waved lace handkerchiefs, the men waved their hats and the liner let out a great foghorn sigh that made everyone jump, then laugh.

He waited patiently in the queue that had formed on deck in front of one of the gangplanks and his papers were checked. He couldn't look to see Dr & Mrs Cabaniss since glancing down and seeing a small group of hard-nosed looking men. He had been almost sure that one had pointed at him and said, 'there he is'. The small group had pushed rather rudely to be near the end of the gangplank as Coleridge neared the on-board end.

The steward smiled at Coleridge as he set foot on the gangplank. The steward bade him enjoy his stay in the United States and Coleridge thanked him very much and then thanked him again.

Coleridge was then off the ship that had been his home for eight days and walking over the water, holding onto the rail to steady himself as the plank gently moved from left and to right. After just a few more steps he would be on American soil. He could barely contain his excitement but it was mixed with some trepidation as the jostling group of men at the bottom were clearly waiting for him.

"Mr Coleridge-Taylor!" Mrs Cabaniss shouted as she waved frantically, struggling through the people with the doctor to meet him. Coleridge's step quickened and he had truly arrived in America. Mrs Cabaniss pushed through the men and shook his hand and then suddenly threw her hands around his neck.

"Come with me," she said urgently as she tried to pull him through the crowd.

He was in the thick of it. People all around suddenly started calling for him, all at once, firing questions at him, pushing, shoving.

"Mr Coleridge-Taylor, are you happy to be in America?"

"Was your journey good, Sir?"

"Is it true you are to meet the President?"

"Sir, where will you be staying?"

Mrs Cabaniss and the doctor pulled Coleridge through the group of newspaper reporters. Coleridge had never seen anything like it. All he could do was laugh and say how 'extraordinary' everything was. He tried to answer as many of the questions as he could.

"Mr Coleridge-Taylor!" a man called. Coleridge turned and saw a number of photographers with their box cameras set up on tripods, flash bulbs held over their heads.

"Mr Samuel Coleridge-Taylor please, Sir."

Coleridge stood for them but Dr and Mrs Cabaniss tried to get away. He grabbed them, laughing and pulled them into the frame with him.

People started clapping when they managed to see who the special visitor was and the cameras went off in a blaze of bangs, fizzes and flashes that seemed to go on for an eternity. Coleridge's modest smile grew broader and broader. Why had he even thought twice about visiting America, he wondered. If he had ever imagined his reception would be half as warm, he never would have.

After stepping through Boston's clearance area, and just before stepping out into the street, Mrs Cabaniss turned to Coleridge.

"Ready?" she asked.

"Ready for what?"

She smiled at him and opened the door. He stepped through and heard a crowd's roar. Mrs Cabaniss held his hand as they made their way to the carriage. There must have been a thousand people, nearly all black, lining the sidewalks, four or five deep and being held back by policemen. They had come from all over to welcome him to their country. The trio made their way to the waiting cab. Coleridge looked around not quite believing what he was seeing. They were all shouting and waving the Union flag and clapping. He waved his hat and thought he had never been happier.

During their cab ride through Boston, it was difficult to know who was more excited, Dr and Mrs Cabaniss or Coleridge. Once on their way, and once the sound of the cheering had faded into the distance, he breathed out a heartfelt sigh. He looked at his travelling companions and burst out laughing. They laughed back and hysteria took over.

They travelled by train to Washington and on arrival there, they took another carriage towards the Hilyers'. Mrs Cabaniss had asked if he would first like to see a little of Washington from the carriage rather than going direct to his hosts'. He had thought this a wonderful idea, as he would be able to get his bearings. All that travel, all that excitement, different places, the ship, cabs, trains; he needed to settle a bit, he felt.

He was physically tired but mentally, too keen to succumb to tiredness for a while. He soaked everything up. He listened attentively as Dr Cabaniss told him some of the history of the great seat of American government.

From the cab, Coleridge was shown both the slums and the affluent shopping districts. He saw the starving and the well fed. He saw the stark contrast between how the black people lived against the white experience. Segregation was a totally alien concept to him and yet here it was, streets suddenly demarcated off as if a great, unseen line had been drawn straight through the city; along or across roads, through homes and businesses, cutting through parks and other public spaces. There were 'white only' seating areas on the omnibuses and some shops had signs in the windows saying that they would serve 'whites only'.

Here it was, being lived out in that otherwise great and civilised city. He saw the poverty that African Americans suffered. The difference was staggering. In some areas, the blacks and the whites lived side-by-side and yet the worlds they both inhabited were an ocean apart.

Washington was actually three cities; a black city, a white city and a city where the other two uncomfortably mixed, a place where blacks were 'tolerated'; a tense place. Subservience. 'Tolerance' was a far cry from 'acceptance'. The only people who should be denied the right to freedom of speech are those who would deny others that freedom. The only people who should not be tolerated are those who are intolerant of others. To be a person who accepted all others and yet who, by all others was either unacceptable or at best, 'tolerated' – this was not acceptable. To dream of acceptance but have to struggle in order to be at best, 'tolerated' – this was not acceptable. It was all too shameful – all too shocking.

Coleridge's arrival was reported in all the American newspapers and the keen coverage of his visit was almost diarised in the dailies. The Hilyers were very charming hosts. The chorus and the United States Marine Band were very well rehearsed for the three day festival, which started just a few days after his arrival.

On 16th November 1904, the President himself had been scheduled to attend the festival's centrepiece, 'The Song of Hiawatha' trilogy, but unfortunately was unable to attend at the last minute because of affairs of state. However, a posse of his dignitaries from the White House attended in his absence.

Three thousand, about one third white, also attended the performance that was as historic for the American nation as Coleridge had been told it would be. Mr Burleigh and the other soloists had been in fine voice. The audience had been ecstatic and the success of the festival resounded across the American continent. The morning following the performance, one of the newspapers observed that, 'the event marked an epoch in the history of the Negro race of the world' – the 'Negro race of the world' no less.

Coleridge had been a little disappointed that the President was unable to attend the performance, but as is often the way, this let-down was necessary as something much more splendid was trying to manifest in its place. Because the President had been so sorry that he was unable to attend, he sent Coleridge an invitation to meet with him, personally, at the White House – an invitation that could not be refused. Coleridge was collected in the presidential carriage and had a private meeting with the great man. The President told him of his admiration for both Coleridge's political and artistic works and of his hopes for the liberalisation of attitudes towards America's black and other marginalised citizens. He honoured Coleridge by presenting him with a fine portrait of himself that he had signed and dated for the occasion.

This meeting was also described in the newspapers. They said that it was 'unprecedented and history-making that a man of colour should receive such an honour'. There were so many events that made the trip unforgettable and all were widely reported and camera bulbs flashed wherever he went.

Coleridge visited the M Street School for Girls where he was very touched to be presented with a gold-tipped baton made from cedar wood taken from the estate of the Negro leader and the father of resistance to white supremacy, Frederick Douglass. Coleridge met the Dean at Howard University and also visited the Armstrong Training School, which provided higher education for young black people. He met the son of a real Red Indian Chief, in his full regalia, a handsome and wise young man called Oske-Non-Ton.

"But you can call me Oscar."

At a 'real English tea party', held after the second concert, where Coleridge conducted his settings of Longfellow's 'Songs of Slavery' and his 24 Negro Melodies, Coleridge had been introduced by the Hilyers to a gentleman called Mr Booker T Washington, a black writer and reformer who had himself been born into slavery. Coleridge was honoured to meet the great man but felt more in tune with Mr Dubois' rather more radical view that everyone should have equal access to everything. Dubois believed that, 'Through helplessness we may submit but the voice of protest of ten million Americans must never cease to assail the ears of their fellows, as long as America is unjust'. Mr Washington however, believed in a more conservative, emergent, 'baby steps' approach to change. Coleridge listened carefully to Mr Washington's view, that a modest start for the Negro race would be more successful in the long-term than one as radical as that espoused by Mr Dubois.

Whilst Coleridge was keen to learn as much about the life of black Americans as he could, those he met generally seemed more interested in talking to him about his music and England. Mr Washington however, was more than happy to tell Coleridge all he could about African America and was honoured to accept Coleridge's invitation to preface the 24 Negro Melodies, which although rejected by Mr Jaegar at Novello, had been taken up by a Boston firm for publication.

The discussion went on well past the end of the tea party and later became rather oiled thanks to Mr Hilyer's generously stocked cabinet.

As Coleridge put out his cigarette, Mr Washington said, "It's especially gratifying to me, that just when interest in the plantation songs seems to be dying out with the generation that gave them birth – when the Negro song is in too many minds associated with rag music and more reprehensible yet, the 'Coon Song', that the most cultivated musician of his race, that you Coleridge, a man of the highest aesthetic ideals should seek to give permanence to the folk songs of our people by giving them a new interpretation and an added dignity, well I think that that's just –"

"– Coleridge," Mamie cooed from the door to the smoky room. "I'm sorry to interrupt but there's someone here to see you."

Puzzled, Coleridge stood and around the corner of the doorframe where Mamie stood appeared the face of an old friend.

"Paul!"

"Hello Coleridge."

Coleridge ran and embraced his first collaborator.

"It's been such a long time," Paul said.

Leaving his hands on Paul Laurence Dunbar's shoulders, he stood back to take a good look. Something was wrong but Coleridge didn't let it show. He couldn't tell him how well he looked; it would be a lie. Paul was a thinner and seemed slightly weak – he had aged more years than had actually passed. His manner was warm towards Coleridge but perhaps, distant. Coleridge could smell stale alcohol. Paul had been so cheerful and ambitious, so optimistic, so full of life. He wasn't quite himself. But they hadn't seen each other in – how long had it been? Could it really be six years? It was still wonderful to see him.

Paul had married shortly after returning from England. Alice had a degree from Cornell and was a teacher and writer on racial and gender equality issues but she and Paul had been separated for two years, since 1902. Coleridge said he was very sorry to hear this. Paul was slurring his words a little and the alcohol made it hard for him to focus his eyes. He was still writing though, he said and reciting too. He was also working in the Library of Congress. In fact he had just come straight from there. He enjoyed his job, he said, but was planning to give it up and move back to Dayton to be nearer his mother. Paul said he thought that the dust in the library was maybe making his tuberculosis worse.

On his final evening, Coleridge's hosts held a sumptuous banquet, in his honour. It had been a wonderful trip and a most wonderful and enlightening experience but it had passed all too quickly. Just before the gentlemen left the table to retire for a smoke and cards, Mr Hilyer made a toast to their guest of honour. Coleridge hung his head as Andrew concluded his speech.

"...In composing 'Hiawatha', Coleridge, you have done the coloured people of the United States a service, which I am sure you never dreamed of when composing it. It is a source of inspiration for us, not only musically but... in the way it unites people. It lifts us above the clouds of prejudice to live wholly oblivious of its disadvantages and indeed all of our other troubles too. So I would like to ask us all to be upstanding and to raise our glasses to our friend and guest here tonight, the composer of 'The Song of Hiawatha', Mr Samuel Coleridge-Taylor."

"Samuel Coleridge-Taylor," the guests chimed.

It had all been too much for Coleridge but he forbade himself to cry. He looked up at the faces smiling down at him from around the table, their glasses raised, all of them standing. There was a silence as they sipped. He nodded and thanked them all almost inaudibly. Mamie came to his rescue as a large dark-wood case was brought into the room and they all returned to their seats.

"Coleridge?" she said moving around to him with the stealth of a mountain lioness. It was now his turn to stand. He stood by her and she held the case out to him. She undid the clasp, opening the box to reveal a huge, silver Loving Cup.

"Now I know that not all of you will have seen this," she said, "so if you will permit me, I should like to read the inscription to you all. It says, 'a token of love and esteem to Mr Samuel Coleridge-Taylor of London, England in appreciation of his achievements in the realm of music – presented by The Samuel Coleridge-Taylor Choral Society of Washington DC to their distinguished guest on the occasion of his first visit to America to conduct 'Hiawatha' and 'Songs of Slavery', November

16th, 17th and 18th 1904. It is well for us, O brother, that you come so far to see us'."

Coleridge's lip quivered as he took the cup. The guests clapped.

"Thank you. I don't know what to say. Thank you. I don't really make speeches, I'm afraid…"

"We know that and so we won't ask you," Mamie said as she put her arm around his waist and gave him a motherly squeeze. "We have one more surprise for you. Our soloist, Mrs Skeene-Mitchell of Cleveland would like to sing something."

Coleridge and Mamie returned to their seats and Mrs Skeene-Mitchell moved to the piano where she was to be accompanied by another of the soloists, Mr Sidney Woodward of Florida. The tune was instantly recognisable as 'God Save the King' but they had changed the words for the occasion. Mrs Skeene-Mitchell sang beautifully.

"'O Thou Illustrious one,
Whose genius as the sun
Illumines our race;
'Twas love that brought thee here
To fill our hearts with cheer,
And may our love sincere
Repay thy grace'!"

There was a rustle of paper and to Coleridge's horror, every guest except he, had been secretly given a copy of the words and all stood and sang at him.

"'As meeting brought its cheer,
So, parting brings its tear,
Its grief and pain;
And when the ocean wide
Shall bear thee on its tide

May winds propitious guide
Thee home again!

Though earthly joys must end,
And friend must part with friend
Yet Love abides.
Our hearts where mem'ries dwell
Would fain their story tell,
But, speechless, beat farewell,
A fond farewell'!"

A farewell made fond by its heartfelt sincerity.

Coleridge's excitement had made the voyage to America pass in the flash of an eye. His sadness on leaving made the voyage home seem to last an eternity. He longed to hold Watha and squeeze baby Gwen to his face so that he could smell her beautiful, pink face.

He sat on the edge of the bed in his cabin. The distant pistons pumped and hummed in his ears as they shunted the great liner across the glassy Atlantic. His trunk of trophies sat by the door. There was a mirror fixed to the dressing table opposite the bed and he was sitting on the edge when he caught his reflection's eye.

He thought of his father. Surely his father in Africa would have heard of his success by now. Surely now he would be proud – proud enough perhaps to make the journey to see him. Coleridge wondered what it was that was holding him back – shame?

It would be so much easier for the father to track down his son than for he to make the journey back to the father. So why had he not? His father had never even written.

He had had this conversation in his head many times before and had always reached the same conclusion. He knew he could drive himself mad imagining reasons and scenarios for everything that he couldn't possibly ever know for sure. He always changed the subject of his thoughts from things he might never know to things that he did know, and so he gazed at his reflection in the cabin mirror and thought of Watha and one-year-old Gwen. He had missed her first birthday. What time would it be in England now? But just to see his father's face, he thought, just once – how wonderful that would be. How dim he had been, to believe that that vile little con man could be his father. An honest mistake though, born out of an unconscious hope. He couldn't remember or even imagine his father's face – he might never know. The things he would say to him; the things he would be able to ask him. How wonderful it would be if one day – if one day his father did come back to him.

After disembarking back in England, an overnight stay in an hotel and a whole succession of train journeys later, Coleridge found himself wearily walking from West Croydon Station towards his home. He had cabled Jess to tell her approximately what time he would be arriving and he knew that she had laid on a 'Welcome Home' party for him. He would be home by about 11a.m. and everyone would be there.

Jess had put all of Coleridge's post in his Music Shed, all except one. A telegram had arrived at his home the day after he had left Boston harbour. The telegram stood on the mantelpiece over the fire. It had come all the way from a place she'd never heard of – Freetown, in the Gambia.

Jess had given it to Coleridge to read in the kitchen soon after he arrived. She knew he would have wanted to know straightaway and she was right. He told Jess he'd deal with it once everyone had left. He asked that it not be mentioned as he didn't want to spoil the occasion and the trouble that people had gone to on his account. He put it on the mantelpiece as he joined the party.

It was a wonderful party. A string quartet, a sub-group of the Croydon Symphony, was squashed into the corner and played his 'Characteristic Waltzes'. Later William played the piano as people chatted away. Guests drifted in and out during the course of the day, and a few hours after the light, buffet lunch that Elsie had helped Jess, Kathleen and Coleridge's mother prepare, only the hard core of the closest remained.

Kathleen chatted easily with Coleridge's mother, Mrs Evans, as Watha played on the floor around the ankles of the remaining and very contented guests. It was much less jammed in the drawing room since the quartet and the others had left and a lot less formal.

Everyone had been keen to hear about America and what he had got up to there. Coleridge dug out his gifts and mementos. Some, he had been given, others he had brought back himself for family and close friends – all very much admired.

"The white people couldn't reconcile the absence of a Yankee twang in a man of colour," he said. "As soon as they found out I was English they were quite different. That's 2,000 years old...." Coleridge said about a piece of Indian pottery.

William was examining a smoothly polished, cedar-wood tobacco jar.

"The inscription inside is a prayer for rain," Coleridge told him.

"Best not try and read it aloud, then!" William joked.

"This is so beautiful," Jess said taking her gold, treble clef locket back from Kathleen.

"At the same time I was sorry for the coloured people generally. I heard some pitiful stories about their treatment."

"What's this for?" Watha interrupted.

"It's a peace pipe bag that once belonged to White Cloud who was Chief of the Chippewas." Oscar's gift to Coleridge.

"Who are the Chippewas?"

"Father's talking, Watha," said Jess.

"They wear beautiful moccasins just like yours, you lucky boy," Kathleen told him.

"For example, I met a young, coloured lady of great educational attainments and of very refined tastes. She had been travelling on the other side of the line drawn south of Washington. She was in the omnibus for coloured passengers, when a hulking lounger wiped his feet on her hair!"

They were horrified.

"Think of it if the aggrieved parties were whites!" William said. "Your father would have been very proud."

Coleridge looked at him and the frost-cloud blew in. He looked at Jess. She had already told them but had neglected to tell them that he didn't want to talk about it. Unfortunately, the subject could not now be politely ignored but Coleridge wasn't sure what he should say on the matter. Perhaps it was better that it was out in the open, but just at that moment, Coleridge didn't quite know how he felt about it.

"Freetown…" he said sadly. "It can be hard to be accepted sometimes, even in the country that gives you birth – it's hard to be unacceptable. The reception in America was overwhelming – it's a wonderful country but very foreign. He must have been incredibly brave to come over here to live, don't you think? I could move to America but I lack courage to do something like that."

Coleridge looked at the telegram on the mantlepiece. He looked into the fire beneath. Only William, and Jess to a lesser degree, had ever heard Coleridge talk about his father.

"He came all the way from Africa to London. I couldn't have done that. At first everything was fine for him apparently. He studied at the Royal College of Surgeons. But the good people of Croydon soon decided that they didn't want a young, coloured doctor. So shortly after I was born – a few months or so, I believe, he went back to Sierra Leone and did very well there, I was told. And my mother…my birth mother…." His voice trailed off, distractedly. "I'm not sure how many of you know, but she was very keen on poetry. She especially liked Samuel Taylor-Coleridge's poems apparently, so…. Well, that was where my name came from. After he left we moved back to Holborn. I was still a baby."

Mrs Evans looked at the floor. She remembered it all in an instant and all too clearly. Not like it was yesterday but as if she were actually there all over again, in that dreadful, pokey, squalid flat – her last known address. Colonel Walters had always kept an eye on his friend's young wife and baby but it soon became clear to him that she wasn't managing, so he convinced her to let him arrange an adoption. She had asked for money in return.

Colonel Walters and Mrs Evans had seen a look of indifference in her dulled eyes as Walters took the amount she had asked for from his pocket and handed it to her. Only they had seen the indifference with which she gave up her child.

Mrs Evans had only ever been in that dreadful flat once and yet there it was again, as clear as day – even down to that smell. The girl had moved out soon afterwards and no one ever heard of her again. She was probably dead. Colonel Walters and Mrs Evans had vowed never to tell him about the money.

"…my mother… well, it must have been very difficult for her too."

Coleridge stood and took the telegram from the shelf above the fire.

"He was, apparently, a very charming and clever man. He was apparently a very fine doctor. He was …most fastidious in his appearance."

Kathleen smiled fondly.

"Of course, I was far too young to remember any of it – far too young to remember what either of them looked like."

Coleridge kissed Mrs Evans on the cheek.

"Do you remember stitching that large patch on my trousers for my first day at the Royal College, Mother?"

"Oh yes," said Mrs Evans with a sad nod and smile.

"And that tiny violin I had for years? Do you remember?"

She laughed a little. William smiled. He felt dreadful that he had set Coleridge off down this melancholic path and at an event that was meant to be so celebratory.

"You see…," Coleridge said rather absently and with his back to the room. "In my heart, I always thought he might come back one day."

He turned the telegram over not sure what he was looking for.

"He must have moved, at some point, to Freetown… in the Gambia. Would you all excuse me for a moment?" he said, putting the telegram back on the mantelpiece. "I'm terribly sorry. Please excuse me."

He left the room. They heard him walking quickly up the stairs. For a moment, no one knew what to do then William jumped up and went after him.

He found him in the bedroom, hunched on the edge of the bed holding a handkerchief. He had tears rolling down his cheeks. Silently grieving for a man he never knew and now could never meet. It was too late – everything, always too late. William sat next to him and didn't say a word.

Coleridge tried to sniff as quietly as he could as the tears fell from his eyes onto his trousers. William looked at the floor. Coleridge sniffed and wiped his eyes. He slowly leaned towards William and rested his head on his friend's shoulder. William put his arm around him and held him as he quietly cried.

Coleridge would have stayed there forever but knew that he couldn't. He had to get on and get back. He wondered how he could put this from his mind. He had to finally accept that his father was gone. Strange to grieve for losing someone he'd never had.

He had to lose himself. He always found that the best way to do that was through work. Everyone demanded that he work anyway. He had a family to support. He had to get back to devoting himself to everyone again; to the

Pan-African movement, to writing, to his new African American friends, to his pupils, to conducting, to composing and to his dear children, Watha and Gwennie.

He would be a wonderful father to them, he promised himself as he sat there, in his bedroom, being held by William. He would never leave them and would show them such love and be there for them and provide for them. He would give them the best that he possibly could. He would be a father to them and give them everything a father should.

He would never leave them. He promised them both he would never leave them.

CHAPTER 12

The morning's rehearsal had gone tremendously well and the chorus and orchestra applauded Dr Sargent and themselves at the end. The whole trilogy was a highly emotional journey.

Since their conversation that morning, neither Avril nor Bunty had made any mention of the old lady that they had seen staring at them from the other side of the road. They had carried on talking about their names. Bunty explained that her real name, Gwendolen, was a Welsh name.

The rehearsal had finished a little later than planned and the Royal Albert Hall had been given over to the technical crew, dancers and actors for the 'tech'. The two young women had had eaten their sandwiches together on the steps outside and later that afternoon, had gone into Kensington Gardens near the bandstand where they sunned themselves with about six other members of the chorus that they had become friendly with during the course of the day.

The summer of 1932 was a scorcher. Bunty, Avril and the others had already changed into their costumes as these were so much lighter and allowed the air to circulate more. They were also a lot more fun than their normal, everyday clothes and they drew admiring smiles from those who passed by the happy group of Red Indians lounging in the London, summer heat.

Since the late 1920s, Samuel Coleridge-Taylor's ever-more lavish and much loved epic had become the jewel in the Royal Albert Hall's summer programme and so seeing people dressed as Red Indians sunning themselves in Kensington Gardens, had become almost normal over the years.

An old family friend of one of the group had joined them and his regalia was naturally more breathtaking than the others, because Chief Oske-Non-Ton was an actual Red Indian Chief. He was very down to earth though and had a wonderful sense of humour. But he wasn't the only one with some authenticity about him. Bunty had a genuine Red Indian artefact, a heavily embroidered peace-pipe bag.

One of the group had spotted Avril's book and they had begged 'Oscar' to read parts of the Longfellow poem to them – as if they could get any more immersed in the mood of the occasion! He had such a deep, rich voice and the most beautiful American accent. The happy group sat there in a circle on the emerald lawns of Kens-ington Gardens, listening to him read.

"'On the border of the forest,
Underneath the fragrant pine trees,
Sat the old men and the warriors
Smoking in the pleasant shadow.
In uninterrupted silence
Looked they at the gamesome labour
Of the young men and the women;
Listened to their noisy talking...'."

Avril lay back on the warm and neatly trimmed grass. She closed her eyes. It had already been a long day but she didn't feel a bit tired. She saw the wigwams and children playing by the brook that fed the lake in the Land of the Dakotahs. She saw the mountains capped with the bluey-white snow that covered the peaks and the deep, green and ancient forests of pine. She could smell the needles and the earth and the dried prairie grasses as they baked in the sun.

"'...To their laughter and their singing,
Heard them chattering like magpies,
Heard them laughing like the blue-jays
Heard them singing like the robins...'."

"Hello Avril," said a voice.

Avril shielded her opening eyes from the sun and looked up at the silhouetted young man she had arranged to meet there. She had said he wouldn't be able to miss them.

"Emlyn!" she said sitting up as he joined the group. "You made it."

"Look at you," he said. "You all look very authentic."

"This is my friend Emlyn Williams, everyone. He's coming to the show tonight."

"This is Chief Oske-Non-Ton," Bunty said.

"He met the composer on one of his trips to America," said one of the others.

"Call me Oscar."

"And this is my new friend –"

"Bunty, actually – Bunty to my friends. Pleased to meet you."

The others introduced themselves and then went back to lazing about on the grass, resting their own voices, as they listened to Oscar read.

Some distance away, the other side of the band-stand, the old woman was watching the group. All around, people walked and chatted or sat on the benches but she was just standing there, watching. She reached into her bag and took out the piece of paper, but hesitated. She knew that the girl went by a different name and was almost certain that she would be singing that evening, but could that really be her? The old lady's eyesight wasn't what it had been. Could that be the Gwendolen? The old lady was almost sure. She was certainly about the right age, she thought. But what if she was wrong? Would she be pleased to see her? She didn't want her to feel awkward. Her hand shook as she held the neatly folded square of musical parchment.

Perhaps it was she who felt most awkward. Maybe the girl wouldn't want the others to know who she was. Not many people knew of the rift that had formed between the mother and daughter. The woman longed to make things right. She longed to give her the paper and to make things complete, but not yet. She put the paper back in her bag. She would wait until the young woman was on her own and away from the others.

She watched as the group of braves and squaws in the distance stood up and brushed themselves down. She watched as they happily made their way back towards the Hall. In less than two hours' time, the performance would start.

She turned and started walking back towards the bus stop. She was staying only one more night at Claridges and then it was back to Bournemouth the following morning. She had decided that she would wait for the girl at the end of the performance or perhaps during an interval, and give her the paper then. But for now, she thought, a cup of tea was in order.

As she walked towards the bus stop, she thought back to that day in 1906. Could it really have been over twenty-five years ago that she had bumped into him and had their acquaintance reunited?

He had just returned from a second trip to America and was conducting at the Bournemouth Winter Gardens. She had been determined to talk to him. The old lady smiled as she recalled what a fool she had made of herself over him. She had known that he frequently left straight away at the end of a performance, so she had left the auditorium as soon as the applause began to die down so that she could catch him. He had left by a rear entrance but she had been waiting. In her hand, she held her programme and a neatly folded square of paper.

"Excuse me, Mr Coleridge-Taylor. Mr Coleridge-Taylor," she called to him. Coleridge realised he wasn't going to be able to get away and so he turned a little wearily and smiled politely as she approached him.

"I wonder if I might presume upon you to sign this for me," she said as she handed him the paper. He was a little taken aback as people normally asked him to sign their programmes and he could see that she had one. He unfolded the paper and looked at it. Much to his surprise he recognised the writing on the paper as his own. He knew exactly what it was.

"Where on earth did you get this?"

"My brother gave it to me."

"You're William's sister? How absolutely wonderful!" he said shaking her hand. "But I can't sign this!"

"Oh – please, you must," she insisted.

He felt foolish as she bobbed about in front of him. He tilted his head and smiled at her reluctantly, considering her almost family.

"Well if you're sure," he said taking the pen she had produced.

He wondered what on earth he could write on the page of music that he had once tried to toss in a fire. He looked at her and smiled again. He started to write.

"He always speaks very fondly of you," she said to fill the silence as he wrote. "As if you were brothers."

"Well we practically are. We've certainly known each other long enough."

"I don't expect you to remember me but you and I actually met at your graduation – the day you gave that to him, I believe."

"Of course I remember you, it's –"

"Judith."

"Yes, I remember. It all seems a very long time ago."

"I might add that he didn't give it to me that day. He knew that I was such a... well he knows I greatly admire your work so he sent it to me, just a week or so ago actually. You might tell him to visit his sister once in a while! William says he'd rather die alone in Battersea than visit Bournemouth!"

"I shall be sure to tell him," laughed Coleridge thinking just how like William that sounded. He stopped writing and looked at the music on the page.

"You know, I'm very glad he rescued it. It's not half as bad as I imagined it was at the time. Your brother is very rarely wrong, you know!" He handed the page back to Judith. "We were always so eager to please old Stanford, especially me."

"Thank you so much for this," she said clutching the paper.

"It's been lovely to see you again, Judith," he said as he looked at her.

There wasn't much of a family resemblance. In fact, she didn't really look very much like William at all, but the mannerisms were the same.

"I hope you won't think me terribly rude," he said awkwardly, "but I always try to avoid the crowds."

"Oh no, of course not. Thank you so much for this."

"It was lovely to see you again," he said as he shook her hand.

"And you too."

Coleridge started to walk away, rather briskly. She suddenly felt a wave of utter foolishness. She had been a gushy, gawky schoolgirl. But what a lovely man, she thought. She could see why William liked him so much. As Coleridge grew smaller in the distance, she turned and looked at the paper. She unfolded it to read what he'd written. She glanced back up straight away and saw him trot to catch up with the tram that was arriving at its stop. He jumped on, holding onto his hat.

She read what he had scribbled for her on the page of music and immediately read it again. Although he had been in a hurry, it had clearly come straight from the heart and touched her deeply. It was too wonderful for words and she held the folded, paper treasure to her heart as she watched the tram disappear.

When he returned to London, Coleridge had made a point of sending William a telegram to arrange a meeting. He had not been back from America for more than a week but felt rotten that he hadn't seen as much of William as he perhaps should have done.

Before America, he had in fact cancelled one meeting with William and then another and both of these had been cancelled at rather short notice. It was just so difficult to find the time to do all the things he wanted to do. He had thrown himself into his work with such abandon following the death of his father two years before.

Coleridge met William outside the Royal College of Music where William had just started teaching and they went for lunch together. Despite not seeing each other for a good few months, they always managed to pick up where they left off, just as if they were back at college; as if it was only yesterday that they had been arguing about Brahms and Dvorak or slating the Russians in no uncertain terms. In no time at all they both were talking eight to the dozen.

After lunch, they walked around the sides of the Royal Albert Hall and started down the magnificent stone steps towards their old College.

"You know, they're very lucky to have you," Coleridge told him as their conversation and their time together that day began to draw to a close.

"Parry calls Dunhill and I the two babies of the staff."

They laughed. The laughter petered out and William slowed and then stopped, halfway down the steps. He took Coleridge by the elbow.

"Coley?" Coleridge was surprised by the serious tone William had suddenly adopted. "Coley. We've known each other… well, we've been friends a very long time now, haven't we?"

"Yes of course."

"Well – it's just that there's something I've been meaning to say to you, something rather important actually, but I'm not sure how you'll.... God, I've wanted to tell you for such a long time but I could never quite find the right moment – bit of a coward really. And now, here we are, and I'm dashed if I know where to begin."

"William, what on earth's the matter?"

"You see the fact is...."

"Tell me –"

"Coley, I.... It's just that I –"

"My dear boy!" called a very familiar brogue from behind them. Coleridge turned.

"Hello, Sir," he said to his mentor. Stanford shook his hand vigorously with a warm smile.

Stanford had been knighted four years earlier and was now Sir Charles Villiers Stanford. It was wonderful to see one of his favourite students again even if Coleridge did look rather wan. He sensed that he had interrupted something. William checked his pocket watch.

"I'd better run. Another time," he told Coleridge, silently communicating something else. "Let's promise not to leave it so long, Coley."

He gave Stanford a cheery nod as he trotted off down the steps.

"He's wonderful chap," Stanford said as William trotted across the road to the College. "A wonderful professor and a great composer. And as for you! It's lovely to see you again, my dear boy. You're not rushing off too, I hope?"

Coleridge had planned to get home early to get some composition in but how could he refuse? Before he could answer, Stanford had taken him by the elbow, as he tended to do when he didn't want someone to get away.

Before long, they were in Kensington Gardens chatting about College and who was still there and who was getting up to what. They talked about the children and Jess, the house and the shed with the piano in it. They talked and talked but all too soon, they were walking back towards the Albert Memorial at the Queen's Gate having circled the Round Pond.

"You should send a copy of your 24 Negro Folk Songs to Percy Grainger," Stanford said as they passed by the bandstand. "By the way, one of the tunes, 'The Angels changed my Name' is an Irish tune and so too I think is 'The Pilgrim's Song'. I suspect they reached the American Negroes through the Irish Americans. Weren't you just there?"

"Yes, I had to go straight from Southampton to Bournemouth to conduct. I haven't been home yet actually. I saw Toronto, St Louis, New York, Washington again, Chicago…. I forget where else."

"Thank God you weren't in San Francisco."

"Terrible. You know they think that more than three thousand people died – three thousand. I don't expect they will ever really know for sure how many. It's unimaginable and nearly a quarter of a million left homeless, apparently. Everyone was saying it would be impossible for the city to come back after such a dire calamity and it's hard not to agree."

He fell silent for a moment and the two men stopped in the park.

"Anyway, we did 'The Atonement' and 'The Quadroon Girl', and 'Hiawatha' of course." His own words seemed hollow to him. He was so tired. When he was tired he knew he sounded unhappy and he wasn't particularly unhappy, just tired. "I met this wonderful couple – Carl and Ellen Stoeckel. They have a music festival in Norfolk in the foothills of the Berkshire Mountains. It sounds beautiful. And, would you believe it, they have their very own concert hall in the grounds. Funny thing is they call it the 'Music Shed' too. Very different from my own! Theirs seats more than sixteen hundred – mine seats one, just about – and my spider!"

"Surely you can afford to slow down a little?" Stanford asked.

"Slow down, Sir? No, it's all far too exciting and besides, I'm only thirty-one, for goodness sake."

"I didn't mean to imply...."

They stopped for a moment. Coleridge felt his head swim – as if he'd just got up out of a hot bath too quickly. The truth was that he hadn't been feeling terribly well. He thought he might have a fever coming on. He continued but Stanford could see through Coleridge's over-compensating cheerfulness.

"I'm working on an opera." He ran a hand over his forehead.

"Really? I suppose it was only a matter of time what with all your choral work and the theatre music for Mr Tree."

"It's called 'Thelma'. I've been working on it for a while now but I'm nearly there. I'm writing this one for me, just like I did with 'Hiawatha'. It should be magnificent." He paused for a moment. They both started slowly walking again, back towards the distant gates.

"It's hard to the find time to compose," he said. "There's always so much else to do: the teaching at Crystal Palace, the Guildhall and the private students, adjudicating... the songs. I have an artist friend, Kathleen – I set her 5 Fairy Ballads. Watha and Gwennie like 'Big Lady Moon' the best. I've also set works by Rosetti, you know and Marguerite Radclyffe Hall. Do you know her?"

"No, I don't believe so."

"She's a wonderful new writer. She smokes a pipe. Quite extraordinary! And Lady Florence Dixie too, I forgot about her – I've set some of her poems too."

Stanford opened his mouth to speak but Coleridge was already talking again.

"And then there's the Pan-African group. I write for our paper. Conducting, of course – Eastbourne and Bournemouth – did I say Bournemouth? And all the rest – and the Croydon Conservatory Orchestra. That was my first job, do you remember?"

"Of course, I remember. Coleridge –?"

"I'm subsidising it myself at the moment but only until it finds its feet again –"

"Coleridge?"

"Yes, Sir?"

"Are things alright?"

"Yes of course. Good heavens, I'm always a happy man. Normally, anyway." His face clouded as the last thread holding the mask in place slipped. "I lost a rather dear friend recently. Paul Laurence Dunbar, the poet. He died in February."

"I'm very sorry to hear that."

"He'd been ill for a long time but it was still an awful shock to me for some reason. I don't think you are ever really prepared for that kind of thing, are you? Even if someone is old, which he wasn't, or ill for a long time. We collaborated together, early on."

He felt a swell of emotion; of exhaustion and upset. He didn't know where it had come up from. He had been fine with William. He hoped with all his heart that Stanford wouldn't be kind to him. Whenever he felt upset, anyone being kind to him would almost certainly make him cry and he couldn't let this great man see him cry. This wonderful mentor who had taught him so much, and not just about music, he couldn't let him see how he really felt. He couldn't let Stanford see him struggling, sinking. Other men don't burst into floods at the drop of a hat.

"Just before I went back to America," he went on, distractedly, "I had the manuscript of a new piece stolen – after a recital. Quite flattering, really... but I don't make copies."

He had meant it to sound funny, to change the mood, but it didn't.

"The jellygraph is so messy and unreliable and professional copyists are, well, to be frank they are far too expensive."

The two men reached the gate.

"I should have been a wealthy man by now."

Stanford frowned at him. Coleridge had always been so hard on himself and it had always been so painful to witness.

"Still, it keeps me busy," he continued in cheerful desperation, his quivering lip beginning to betray him.

"I don't see as much of my children as I'd like and er.... Well, I'm always rather afraid I'm neglecting my friends. It's terribly difficult to meet everyone's expectations, you know, to please everyone, but I do try. I really do try. I always find myself late for everything. There just never seems to be enough time. I'm just so tired."

Stanford put his hands on Coleridge's shoulders and turned him to him. Coleridge was close to tears but he didn't want him to be embarrassed. Coleridge couldn't look his old mentor in the eye.

"I would love to stop, Sir but I know how busy you must be," he said.

Stanford patted his student – his friend, on the shoulder.

"Look after yourself, my boy. It's always lovely to see you."

CHAPTER 13

Some weeks had passed since William's meeting with Coleridge. The journey into town from Battersea was much less trying for him than it had been when he used to live in Croydon. After the train, William normally took the electric tram from Victoria and that made it much more manageable. At least he could breathe on the tram and underground trains were far less comfortable and far more expensive.

That particular morning however, William had waited and waited but no tram had come. He hadn't been able to decide whether to carry on waiting or to go for the underground train instead but it was nearly 8.30 and unless he did something quickly, he knew he'd be late. William decided to take an underground train the two stops to South Kensington. It was only two stops.

As he walked down the steps to the underground platforms he realised he had made the right decision as it was so much cooler down there than up at street level that morning. He found it difficult to breathe above ground in the still air where any dew or breeze had been scorched away in an instant by the morning sunshine. Not much air would have circulated around on the tram anyway, even if all the windows had been opened.

The electric train echoed in the black tunnel as it hummed and clicked its way towards the platform. This particular station was always busy with foreign visitors in addition to the normal, daily commuters. The dwarf train, like a child's toy, lit up the tunnel as it approached the platform. The brakes gently squealed, and it stopped with the smell of static and grease in the air. The gatemen at the ends of each carriage opened the doors and called 'Victoria Station' to those inside, and William stepped aboard.

The air in the already crowded carriage was thick with tobacco smoke and there was nowhere left to sit. They called the carriages on the tube trains 'padded cells' as they didn't have windows. Instead there were ventilation slats, near the oppressively low ceiling, that you could open. William wasn't near the slats. The nearest one was a good few feet away with people standing in front of it and it was only open an inch. He knew he wouldn't be feeling any benefit of it.

Once aboard, he closed the door and held on. He closed his eyes and imagined the tiny hands of a cool breeze on his face. His collar felt tight but it was only two stops.

The train seemed to wait an age. He was squeezed against the padded side by the other passengers and even once it had started moving, it seemed to crawl along to Sloane Square, so much slower than normal. Once there, it was delayed while someone tried to get their luggage onto the carriage. This always annoyed the passengers as the same rules of etiquette applied to the tube trains as applied to the trams and omnibuses – feet off the seats, if you have a seat you must not describe an angle of forty-five with your knees thereby occupying the room of two persons, step on and off quickly (if your time is not valuable, that of others may be), do not spit on the floor (you are not in a hog sty but in a train and travelling in a country which boasts refinement), do not stand and ponder your location in doorways thereby rudely blocking the access of others, and so on and so forth and especially; do not introduce luggage or large parcels onto the carriage as the underground train, like the tram and the omnibus, is not a van.

Luckily, some people had got off so there was a little space for a moment but more got on and replaced them and it all seemed to take an age. He had however, taken the opportunity of moving nearer the ventilation slats.

William shut his eyes again. A warm dew formed on his upper lip. He wouldn't think of it; if he started to worry about it, he would surely bring it on. The dip in his throat, behind his collar stud, was wet and a trickle of sweat ran between his shoulder blades and down his back under his shirt and jacket. He felt slightly light-headed. He tried to breathe slowly and calmly. The air was hot and it smelt. He leaned into the train's forward movement as it pulled out of the station.

Once he arrived at South Kensington, he decided not to wait for the lift with everyone else and be enclosed in a sardine can all over again and so he took the stairs instead. His were the only footsteps on the iron stairs and they echoed around the dark green and cream tiles of the stairwell.

He stopped halfway up. He was beginning to feel breathless. He paused for a moment. He looked down through the gaps in the black iron, spiral staircase to the dark and moaning pit below and immediately wished he hadn't. He closed his eyes, strengthening his grip on the handrail. He was alone so it didn't matter if he looked silly for a moment. He knew what the warning signs were and although he had little control over them, there were certain things he had learnt do to slow the onset of an attack or minimise the effect.

He opened his eyes and took out his watch without letting go of the rail. It was seven minutes before nine. His students would already be accumulating in the lecture theatre, the same old lecture theatre where he and Coleridge used to sit. His stomach butterflied. They would all be waiting for him. He started up the stairs again.

He felt a pang of ache in the tops of his thighs as he continued upwards, and as he neared street level the air became noticeably warmer.

He arrived at the top of the stairs long after the lift had arrived. He should have just taken the lift, he thought. He would have been halfway there if he had just taken the lift.

Stepping out of the station was like walking into an open oven. What little air there was, stank. It was the sickly juice of bletted fruits baking stickily on the pavement. It was acrid, sour and sweet. It was fish head, horse dung, coal dust and unwashed labourer. He took a slow, deep drink of the foul air and walked towards College.

His senses, and his sense of purpose, seemed more acute than ever but the others on the streets that day moved as if they had no souls, as if they were sleepwalkers. It was just like the time he had had a dream in which he became conscious for an instant. Colour and light and sound and smell exploded with vividness as he awoke in that dream world. It had a clarity that the real world did not possess. The world he now found himself in had that same clarity and was similarly inhabited by automata, dead behind the eyes.

A man walked as if William wasn't there and bumped his shoulder. It was the man's fault but William found himself apologising. The man continued without turning.

William's breathing started becoming strained. He would just get to College but he wouldn't stay, he decided. He would tell them he wasn't feeling one hundred percent. He would sit and rest for a while there and then tell them that he had to go home.

As he approached the Royal Albert Hall, a soulless child with a hoop saw him stumble a little. The child's knowing smile was far too old for her face – it was malevolent. He was wheezing as he passed her and she stared as he struggled.

He undid his collar from the stud – his breathing, shallow and increasing in rapidity. Each breath was becoming more snatched as the familiar panic began to seize him. He had to get inside. He had to get into the shade and the cool. He had to sit down.

The Royal College in sight, he started down the grand stone steps. People stood here and there on the vast and wide, white, stone staircase. People walked and chatted but there was nothing on which any sound could travel and their automata movements slowed as if preserved in syrup.

He started down the steps. He walked towards the side so that if he stumbled he would have something to hang on to. It wasn't as good as a handrail, the thick, stone wall.

The panic rose and his head swam, his hand resting lightly on the bevelled wall to steady himself. His knees were struggling to hold him up and he gasped and swayed but steadied himself. He was afraid he couldn't do it and it was a long way to fall. He would have to go back up but he was afraid he was going fall. He had only just started down the stairs, so it was nearer to go back than to go on so he turned but his head swam again. He had to get off the steps, far too far to fall, but he couldn't breathe and he couldn't move and he couldn't go down and couldn't move up and his gasping and wheezing and panicking.

He slowly continued to turn, holding on as tightly as he could, to face the Hall and the climb – just a few steps to the top and the friendly old Hall was in front of him. He lifted his knee to take a step but he couldn't breathe. He couldn't breathe at all and his legs were buckling. Heads slowly turned as peripheral people watched, in horror, the man swaying on the steps. His gasps for breath, too short and too shallow – the distant shapes moved towards him slowly at first and then they ran. He reached out. His heels over the edge of the steps, he swayed. Someone shouted for him to 'stop' and he couldn't lift his leg high enough to climb – it kept catching his toe. He put his foot down again but it wasn't quite on the step, his knee folded under him. His ankle twisted sickeningly and he fell backwards. His arm snatched out at the air, dragging oxygen into his thinning lungs in a deep, animal, croak scream as he fell backwards like a rag doll.

His weak body, twisted; his spine flailed viciously against the steep, stone stairs; the back of his head hit the edge of a step and split, with a dull crack, open.

He rolled, and slid on his back down some way, until he stopped. Someone shouted something. People ran. He drifted. His tissue lungs empty, William limply hung upside down on the giant staircase and a pool of blood formed on the white stone and matted his dark curls and dripped.

Coleridge had received a telegram from Stanford and had gone straight to William's bedside. A few days after the accident William was still suffering. Not only from the awful wound to the back of his head but also from the fever that had gripped him since his fall. When Coleridge reached William's rooms, on the third day, William had deteriorated still further. Judith was looking after him and had shown Coleridge into his room.

William was in bed – small and frail, his head, still heavily bandaged. His breathing still shallow, rapid and raspy, Judith left them alone in the room that smelt of sickness.

Coleridge sat on the edge of the bed near William's feet until he awoke. In time, he opened his eyes and smiled at his best friend.

"Dvorak," Coleridge said. William looked at him but didn't say anything for a moment.

"Brahms," he replied at last.

Coleridge smiled.

"What's all this about then?"

But William couldn't talk.

They looked deeply into each other's eyes, trying to find meaning or understanding but there was none. There was nothing to talk about – nothing to say.

"Are you comfortable?"

William didn't reply. He stared too deeply into Coleridge's eyes.

Coleridge looked around the small room. The window was open. It was a beautiful day outside. Children were playing somewhere. Coleridge was about to ask William if he wanted something to drink.

"I have to tell you something, Coley."

Coleridge looked at him and waited but nothing came. He said, "You don't have to, William." A weak questioning look crossed William's face. "You don't have to… because I already know."

William's eyes, still on Coleridge, reddened and filled. He slowly lifted his hand out. It hung in the air. Coleridge took his friend's hand in his and gently squeezed it – a handshake.

As Coleridge stood up from his seat near the front, he thought that if he focussed on the work of the man rather than the friend, he might get through it, and so he walked to the lectern. The air in the Holy Trinity Church in South Norwood was cool and the fresh scent of the flowers filled the air. If he just focussed on the work, he would get through it. He dreaded it but knew no one else was better placed for the task than he. He couldn't look at the coffin as he passed. He couldn't look at that face in the portrait.

He mounted the four or so steps that spiralled to the lectern and as it all came into view; the congregation, the flowers – the ugly reality of it all hit him with the force of a train. He didn't catch anyone's eye but he was aware of everyone being there – absolutely everyone, and they waited in silence for him.

He fumbled as he put his papers on the lectern. He was aware of Judith smiling up at him and that calmed him a little. He checked that the pages of his speech were in the right order, but at the same time, knew he was taking too long as he fidgeted the paper, and they watched him in silence but he couldn't look up and he couldn't delay the inevitable. He cleared his throat and read from the paper held so tightly in both his trembling hands.

"I recall that in our student days, both William and I each had a musical god. His was Brahms. Mine was the lesser-known Dvorak. We agreed that, when either of these composers was really inspired, there was not much to choose between them. But he... he insisted that when Brahms lost inspiration he became merely 'dull', whereas Dvorak became 'commonplace'. How we used to argue over that vexed question, as to which was the greater crime – to be dull or commonplace."

He looked up. He tried to smile. He couldn't bear it.

"He was extremely critical, in the best sense, and he had a way of seeing through superficiality. This must have been rather alarming to anyone who tried to deceive him.... as to his or her attainments musically."

"On many occasions, we sat next to each other at concerts and during the progress of a work, we would both look up at each other at the same moment. I doubt if there is anything that can draw musicians, or for that matter any artists, to each other more, than the knowledge that they each appreciate the same point in other people's work."

"In these days when it is customary to applaud all that is ugly and meaningless and to decry the beautiful and the natural, it is a relief to find music that always has melody, and more important, form. Such was the music of William Yeats Hurlstone."

They watched as Coleridge began to be overtaken and as he struggled against the swell.

"William was a very kind friend. A shrewd observer. A brilliant pianist and a scorner of humbug – such was

Mr Hurlstone personally, and ...." His face began to buckle like a child's. He sniffed and his notes swam in the tears filling his eyes as what was to come, came. "...and his early death is no less a real loss to English music than it is a... a very great grief... to his many friends."

He folded his notes and put them in his breast pocket. He returned to his seat and hung his head. Jess squeezed the back of his hand. He didn't hear the rest of the service.

Coleridge retreated to a very dark corner at the very back of his mind and when he looked out at the world, it was as through a very distant window. He was unaware of what he was saying to people, or what they were saying to him but from their reaction to him, he seemed to be acting normally but he was acting and it was a lie.

His person, in the world, was operating as normal – a world, so random there was no rhyme or reason. Everything a person did with their life, all that work, all that knowledge could be lost forever in the blink of an eye. All that talent – removed from the world leaving only an unclear memory.

Questions without answers are not worth the asking but all he could ask was, 'why?' It seemed very cruel to be given such a friend only to have that friend away taken away.

His mask of gentlemanly normality in the world was as thin and as fragile as the surface of a soapsuds bubble, but underneath was an ocean of emotion that was out of control. It never took anything of much significance to puncture the surface and release the torrent beneath and whenever it came out, it was always as fresh as the day it was first suppressed. Always a small thing; finding a letter, something with his handwriting on it, thinking what he would have thought or said in a particular situation, passing through a place they'd shared, passing that tearoom where they'd meet – all of these, that never had any significance before, would trigger that very great grief.

Coleridge sat in his usual wind shelter on the promenade at Eastbourne. He looked at the sea as it deeply breathed – sighing like a great sleeping animal as it gathered up the shingle, shuffled and sorted it, then laid it out again. Dissatisfied, it would unconsciously begin over again with an obsessive's relentless compulsion.

He looked at the horizon and straightened the trouser creases on his thighs. He closed his eyes and felt the breeze on his face – seeing and hearing nothing else but the breeze with that chill in it.

He thought of the funeral pyre of Hiawatha's bride on the mountaintop and of the forest. In the silent death of such an icy winter, the summer sounds and scents were lost but the frozen air was thick with the incense of burning pine and eucalyptus and the snapping and crackling of the flames and the smell of her burning ermine robe. The smell of her hair burning; of her small and disease-ravaged body burning as it gave itself up to the flames, blazing like an inverted waterfall, unnatural and unthinkable. Only then did Coleridge truly understand what Hiawatha had felt. The warrior king, that great teacher and peacemaker who had done all these things and more, only to be handed such a cruel injustice in return, such a suffering. He understood too Hiawatha's final, mournful cry.

'All my heart is buried with you,
All my thoughts go onward with you.
Come not back again to labour,

Come not back again to suffer,
Where the Famine and the Fever
Wear the heart and waste the body.
Soon my task will be completed
Soon your footsteps I shall follow
To the Islands of the Blessed,
To the Kingdom of Ponemah!
To the Land of the Hereafter!'

That very great grief was never far from Coleridge's side, but in time, the gaps between releases of grief grew a little further apart and their ferocity seemed a little more manageable – not because the surprise attacks were any less vicious but because they had simply become familiar.

Wearing a veneer of false normality became, in time, normality. Coleridge even began to be able to talk about William a little. But it was not until a couple of years had passed that he grew more able to dwell on what he had gained from knowing William rather than what he had lost by losing him.

He returned to work straight after the funeral. He had fallen back on his old and relentless routine and this diversion brought him some comfort. He returned to his beautiful children, to Watha and Gwennie, who filled his cup back up with the life he had once breathed into them and he drank of it so deeply. He would never give them cause to doubt the depth of his love, and everything he would do he would do it for them – in memory of their Uncle William.

CHAPTER 14

'Aldwick', was at the end of a Cul-de-Sac called St Leonard's Road in Waddon, Croydon. At the top of the stairs on the left were the rooms of Watha and Gwen and on the right, Coleridge and Jess's room overlooked the garden – the garden being to the side of the house rather than the back. Their bedroom window also overlooked the shed, the Music Shed, where Coleridge composed. Directly at the top of the stairs was a box room where Coleridge had his upright. He had wanted to put it in a room out of the way but it hadn't been possible for it to turn the tight corner at the top of the stairs and so his music room sat between the bedrooms of his children and of Jess and himself.

In 1908, Watha was eight years old and Gwen was five. Coleridge was just thirty-three but his greying hair and tired eyes made him look older. The children had been pretty tired that evening too. As tired as that evening some weeks earlier when Coleridge and the children had returned home after a day amongst the London crowds, cheering the German Kaiser who was visiting London, Union and German flags in hand. What a splendid day that had been, Coleridge recalled as he played the piano that evening.

He was playing some old Gilbert and Sullivan tunes in the box room and the children had been in bed for an hour or so, so Coleridge played as lightly as he could – barely stroking the keys with the pads of his fingertips. Gwen loved to hear him play and would stay awake as long as she could so that she could listen. The lighter he played, the more she had to concentrate and the more she had to concentrate, the harder it was to stay awake.

Once her mother had gone up to bed, it would be a short while before he would stop softly playing, put his head around her bedroom door and blow her a good-night kiss before retiring himself.

Coleridge had been a little concerned about Gwen ever since returning from his few days away conducting and adjudicating. She seemed withdrawn. He was sure something had happened while he was away but mother and daughter both seemed tight lipped and denied anything was wrong. Watha also said he didn't know what had happened and Coleridge knew his innocence was genuine. It broke his heart to see little Gwennie unhappy.

As he softly played, he became aware of Jess putting the lights out downstairs and listened to her wearily climb the stairs. He listened as she went into the bedroom and changed, as she washed her face in the basin, as she climbed into bed and opened her book.

He stopped playing and very gently put the keyboard lid down. He closed the music on the upright's stand. More than a 'music maker', Sir Arthur, he thought. He remembered that evening when 'Hiawatha' had had its first outing at the Royal College. Old Sir Arthur and his 'Muse' – Coleridge had forgotten her name. That was the night he first realised the seriousness of his mistake. Rather unjust, he thought, that years on, he would still be paying for it.

Coleridge waited until Jess had settled before he stepped out holding the candle in its holder by the ring piece. He opened Gwen's door very quietly and peered around into the dark, little, rose-pink room of dolls and bears and ponies. Gwen looked up at him over the covers as the golden candlelight fell on the exposed or shiny parts of the room and made deeper shadows of the others.

"Did I keep you awake?"

"No. Go on playing," she whispered sleepily.

He smiled at the five-year-old bundle, all snuggled up and desperately trying to steer her way through the tidal waves of sleep. He entered the room and sat on the edge of her bed. She tilted her head to the side so she could see him better and blinked.

"What's wrong?" he asked. She still wouldn't tell him. "Tell me, little Shuh-Shuh-Gah?"

"Which one is that again?"

"You know – the Shuh-Shuh-Gah is the little heron. Now don't change the subject."

"I'm... not meant to tell you."

So something had happened. Coleridge was angry but didn't show it. He counted to ten. He knew parents should always show a united front but what on earth could have happened? What would drive Jess to tell his own daughter to keep something from him? He waited. He wasn't going anywhere until she said more.

She thought very carefully before asking, "Don't you want me anymore, Daddy?" He thought his heart would break that she could think such a thing. "You would never send me away would you?" she asked.

"Of course not. What would ever make –" he said as he took her hands and rubbed them.

"I don't want to go to the big house," she went on.

A bemused frown puzzled his brow. Where on earth could she have got such an idea? Coleridge was upset but did his best to allay her fears. Perhaps she had had a nightmare. Perhaps Jess really didn't know why their daughter was withdrawing from them and the world.

She pulled a sad, little 'poor me' face. Coleridge kissed her cheek and tickled her but she fought the giggles as hard as she fought the night so he stuck out his bottom lip and opened his eyes up wide to make her laugh. She couldn't help smiling at his silly face. Still pulling the face he began to sing in a hushed, whispery voice, Jack Point's part from the 'Yeoman of the Guard' – so miserable-sounding that it cracked a smile on Gwennie's face.

"Heidy! Heidy! Misery me, lacka-day-dee!"

She giggled at him. He held up his finger, beaming, so that she didn't wake her brother in the next room. They giggled together secretly. He kissed her goodnight.

He stood in the door, intentionally holding the candle high so that it didn't make him look a fright, but instead, rather rosy and jolly.

"Goodnight, Gwennie – little Shuh-Shuh-Gah."

He blew her a second kiss from the door. She waved the wave of a five-year-old and rubbed her dreamy eye with a tiny fist and made it squelch. As the candlelight narrowed with the closing door, she rolled over to dream of dolls and bears and ponies.

Jess was sitting up in bed with her book. He changed into his pyjamas, washed and climbed in. He pinched out his candle and lay down on his side to sleep.

Eventually, Jess finished the chapter she was on and closed her book. She made a 'hmm' noise as if to say she 'hadn't seen that coming'. She was looking forward to the next chapter. It was just getting good. She took off her reading glasses and sipped her water.

"A wonderful opportunity –" she said, neither asking if he was still awake nor questioning that her enthusiasm would be shared. "I have been arranging for Gwendolen to go to boarding school next year."

Coleridge opened his eyes. So that was it. He frowned in disbelief. He skewed his body so that he could look at her. It was a stupid idea on so many levels, not least of which was that they couldn't afford boarding school. He was speechless. Jess made no real secret of the fact that Watha was her favourite. She spoke to Gwen as if she were a rather unwelcome guest in their house. It was very strange, as she had so wanted a girl before Watha had been born. He relaxed back onto his side again, away from her.

"Have you spoken to her about this?" he asked.

"No of course not," she said simply.

He turned his head towards her again but too tired to move his body. He couldn't see her face but he knew when Jess was being honest. He was even more confused. There was still something else but as neither mother nor daughter was admitting anything had happened, it was impossible to question either further on the subject. But boarding school, he asked himself incredulously, he would not have her send his daughter away to boarding school.

"If you do that," he said with a sigh, "then the boy must go too."

Jess looked over at him in silence. He waited for a moment then turned his head, resting his cheek on the downy pillow. He knew she would never send Watha away. He closed his eyes. She thought for a moment. He had a point – it wouldn't have felt or looked terribly fair. She turned and put out her candle and the subject of boarding school was never raised again.

Jess had been testing the water. She had been considering boarding school for Gwendolen but boarding school had never really been her preferred option. Her preferred option had been tried that day but it had so upset the five-year-old Gwen that it had come to nothing and so they had returned home and she had forbidden Gwendolen to speak of it – ever.

This was the fatal, hairline fracture that would one day develop into a rift between mother and daughter as wide as the Grand Canyon. Coleridge never did get to the bottom of it and it would not be until Gwen was a grown woman that she would be able to confront her mother about what had actually happened that day when she was only five.

The weather-beaten shelter on the promenade at Eastbourne marked the passing years in nicks and cuts and curling paint and stains. It was painted each Spring, but Coleridge rarely went in season and so when he was there, at the season's end, it always looked tatty and tired.

During his visits, over the years, it had been painted white, turquoise and a dark green. It was white that year but he could see the turquoise from many years before where the paint peeled. It had been turquoise when the shelter was brand new 11 years before and it had also been turquoise back in 1897, when he had sat there with William. He picked at the paint on the seat as he looked out to sea.

William had been dead for four years. Time really does speed up, as you get older. Long gone were those childhood summers that seemed to go on and on for an age. Time quickens cumulatively; faster and faster with each passing moment, faster and faster towards the final destination. There had been a time, in England, when different parts of the country had had their own time zones and it was only when the trains really took a hold, that time had to be standardised across the nation for the purposes of the timetables. Coleridge felt his time quickening, years flashing by in what felt like months, and yet, paradoxically Gwen and Watha would be enjoying each year as if each were a decade. That relativity, led Coleridge to make sure he savoured each moment spent with his children, to make each one special for them, to create wonderful memories for them. He decided that he would not buzz in and out of their lives in a hurry to catch up with the world operating in his time-zone, and did his best to operate in theirs; to slow his watch to match theirs, make time for them and make it special. Unfortunately, however, time away from his children was inevitable in his work. His travelling was constant and his work schedule, relentless. In what seemed to him to be the blink of an eye, 1908 had become 1909 and 1909 had become 1910 and more layers of paint had been applied and peeled away and applied and peeled away.

Four years, almost to the day, since his return from the success of his second visit to America, Carl and Ellen Stoeckel had invited him to conduct at their music festival. As usual, 'Hiawatha' was to be the centrepiece. Although it was to be another long voyage and a significant amount of time away from England and his children, it was a wonderful opportunity and he couldn't refuse. The Stoeckels were paying well and he was to have all his expenses paid during his stay, even down to staying with the Stoeckels in their own home. He was also aware that his hosts sometimes commissioned works from composers and so the trip could lead to additional work for him, he reasoned.

Coleridge descended the stairs carrying two large cases. Jess and the children, now ten and seven, stood by the open front door. He kissed Gwen and Watha and gave them both a big hug. He hated leaving them. He loved returning to them more than anything but you cannot have the one without the other, as perverse as that seemed. You couldn't have the exquisite reuniting without the painful parting. He barely looked at Jess as he donned his hat, coat, his white gloves. He picked up his cane.

"I'll send a telegram from Belfast and another when I arrive," he said as he stepped out. He walked down the steps from the porch and waved to the three of them from the pavement as he started to make his way towards the station.

Coleridge was in Belfast to conduct a concert at the Grand Opera House. He had made arrangements to join his liner there rather than to travel all the way back to Liverpool to board it. It was a very peculiar experience for him, as it seemed that apart from one or two others whose travel circumstances had led them to the same notion, he was to have the liner almost entirely to himself for that brief prologue to his voyage.

Arriving at the Cestrian uncharacteristically early, Coleridge found himself in the unusual position of having time to kill and so, once his luggage had been stowed, decided to take the short walk to the Harland and Wolff shipbuilding yard.

The yard stood on Queen's Island in the River Lagan and had been built on land reclaimed following the straightening of the river over sixty years earlier. Coleridge had been impressed by his own stately liner, but nothing could have prepared him for what he saw at Harland and Wolff. The first sight was of the newly-built, Thompson dry dock; over one hundred feet deep and stretching nearly two hundred feet into the city like a great, yawning amphitheatre. It would be in this dock that the new ships' propellers, electrical wiring, fixtures and fittings would be installed and the hulls would be painted before taking those first uncertain steps down the longest slipway in the world.

The yard was a seething anthill of deafening industry; a maze of criss-crossing railway tracks scraped and screeched innumerable handmade frames and plates to the bloated, embryonic twins. Steam cranes lifted and swung parts of hammered out hull and white hot rivets were used to pin them into place by the multitude of workers who crawled over the giant clanging gantry as the two, fat sister ships slept in the womb of Belfast.

Coleridge looked up. The scale was terrifying. He had to tip the brim of his hat back to see properly. He stared at the ships' names already emblazoned on their sides. The names, like the eyes of beached and paralysed whales, stared back down. They were two monstrous divas at a dress-fitting. Perhaps one day, he thought, perhaps one day he himself would have the very great privilege of travelling to America on one of these already world famous ships, for even though far from finished, there was not a man, woman or child on either side of the Atlantic, who had not already heard of Olympic and of her sister – Titanic.

Coleridge set sail on 7th May 1910, heading for Boston. Once there, he travelled straight to New York where he met his host for the first time and rehearsals started that very day.

Mr Stoeckel watched from the back of the hall as the first rehearsal wound to a close. The pieces were the Bamboula Rhapsodic Dance and a new composition, which Coleridge had taken with him and had corrected during the voyage. As the piece ended, Mr Stoeckel approached the stand, his loud, lone clapping echoing around the hollow room. Coleridge announced to the orchestra that there would follow a fifteen minute break.

"This is a wonderful orchestra," he said to Stoeckel as he leant over the conductor's stand after the first run-through of the new piece. "I never directed anything like it. They can read anything beautifully at first sight!" he panted.

The admiration was mutual. Before engaging the orchestra, Stoeckel had taken the precaution of consulting the Musical Union as to whether there would be any objection to playing under an Anglo-African conductor but no objection was raised and Coleridge was allowed to conduct as he came under the rule of 'visiting conductor'. American musicians didn't suffer fools gladly and saw straight through showy 'flim-flam' – had no respect for it, but it appeared that here was such an unprecedented level of buzzing synergy between orchestra and conductor that the festival's resounding success was surely inevitable. Conductor and orchestra understood exactly what the other was doing, wanting and even thinking, the perfect union of horse and rider.

At the end of that first day, Carl Stoeckel chatted to the very accomplished, professional musicians in his orchestra and it became apparent that the respect and admiration that Coleridge had for them was more than reciprocated. In fact, they couldn't praise him highly enough.

At that time, it was generally conceded by all American orchestral musicians, that the greatest conductor who ever visited their shores was the late Gustav Mahler of Vienna – who, for some time, was also the conductor of the Philharmonic Society of New York. Stoeckel only employed the best and the most experienced in his orchestra and many of these had also played under Mr Mahler's baton at some time or other. In the eyes of this handpicked orchestra, Mr Mahler's only equal ever was Samuel Coleridge-Taylor and they showed him the same reverence that they had shown to Mr Mahler. It was they who dubbed Coleridge, the 'Black Mahler'.

An insignificant minority of the chorus, however, harboured a different view. Mr Stoeckel had informed the members of his choral society that they were to be directed in 'Hiawatha' by its composer who was a man of colour and that if they had any objection, then it should be stated immediately. Of the nearly eight hundred members of the chorus, only one withdrew; however one of the soloists also withdrew, being of Southern birth. It was no great loss. There were many volunteers who were more than willing to take his place and to have the honour of performing under so great a composer and conductor as Mr Samuel Coleridge-Taylor.

After three days of rehearsals in New York, Coleridge and Stoeckel took the train to Connecticut. Stoeckel had brought lunch with him; a large, cheery hamper basket. Coleridge declined the wine, as he had developed a penchant for the American ginger beer on previous visits and hankered after it when at home.

After their lunch, Coleridge smoked and admired the passing countryside while Mr Stoeckel dozed his way across the state.

The Stoeckel's estate lay in the rural town of Norfolk in Litchfield County. The stately house lay in 70 acres of rolling lawns and glorious gardens. Mr Stoeckel's valet drove them in a shiny Model T motorcar from town and soon they were passing down the mile-long drive, lined with statues of the great and the good from the world of the Arts, and with torches that were lit to guide the members of the audience to the Music Shed during the June festival.

Although both men were weary from their journey, Mr Stoeckel asked Coleridge if he would like to stop by the Shed. Coleridge was filled with the same sense of anticipation and excitement as when he first visited America and so was very keen to see the venue.

The Music Shed was a huge, wooden, pentagonal-shaped concert hall set right in the middle of the estate. When they entered, the orchestra and choral society had just broken rehearsal so that others could start setting out the seats. Hundreds of people hovered all around the hall and chattered away, some prematurely tucking into their packed lunches. An excitement rose in them as they saw their great benefactor enter the Music Shed to sneak a preview and then they noticed who was with him – the great, English composer and conductor.

They smiled like happy children when they saw Coleridge. They whispered behind hands and nodded to him as he passed. Coleridge felt like visiting royalty. Mr Paine sat on the conductor's podium, mopping his forehead and engrossed in the task of examining pages of music.

"We are all looking forward to Verdi's Requiem Mass, this evening, Mr Paine," called Stoeckel as they approached the conductor of the Mass and interrupting Mr Paine's reading. To Coleridge, Mr Paine looked like he was in a bit of a flap over something or other but his manner soon changed when he recognised Stoeckel's voice and then again when he saw Coleridge.

"Oh, Mr Coleridge-Taylor it is such a very, great pleasure to meet you."

"We always try and get a composer at out festival," Stoeckel said, "and circumstances effectually prevented the appearance of Mr Verdi himself. But, I am very happy to say, we could manage to get Mr Coleridge-Taylor here!"

"Rather. I suppose you heard that one of our number pulled out at the eleventh hour," Paine said. Stoeckel hadn't felt the need to tell Coleridge about that.

"Not Miss Alma Gluck?" Coleridge asked rather anxiously.

"Oh no," Stoeckel said reassuringly, "Miss Gluck will be singing." Coleridge had conducted Miss Gluck in Washington in 1904 at the Hilyers'.

"Thank goodness! That girl is the best Minnehaha I ever heard sing the part," Coleridge told them in relief.

The Stoeckels, being a warm and welcoming couple, had felt a little embarrassed by the attention that Coleridge received from the audience that first night, being himself, the only black person in the auditrium, but both Carl and Ellen were struck by his dignified and modest bearing and his disarming affability.

Coleridge and a number of other musicians were staying at their house and that evening, following the festival's opening, they held a sumptuous dinner party. Mr Paine could hardly tear himself away from Coleridge's side.

"Your rendition of the Verdi's Requiem this evening," Coleridge told him, "gave me many new spiritual ideas that I had not observed in the work before."

Before very long into his stay with the Stoeckels a rather blissful routine had established itself. Coleridge took breakfast in his room each morning and then went downstairs and played the piano for an hour or so. Then he would take a stroll. Rehearsals during the day and a chance to mingle with other musicians then the evening concerts, all rounded off by the most wonderful dinners and after dinner conversation.

They would take tea in the afternoons. He seemed particularly partial for the Stoeckels' tea and his hosts were most gracious. He commented politely on the unique and beautiful pen that Ellen had left in his room for his use and what a kind thought he had found it.

He was always seen to be very carefully groomed and put on his white gloves whenever he stepped foot outside but was always ready to take them off to shake a well-wisher's hand. He never asked many questions of those who stole a moment to speak to him – he never had to, and he always seemed genuinely interested in whatever they had to say to him. This, with his pleasing personality and modest demeanour always resulted in him managing to draw out those with whom he conversed.

On the final night of the festival, Coleridge's night, Mr Paine mounted the stand and gave a brief speech of introduction to Coleridge-Taylor in front of the vast choir, the orchestra and an audience of two thousand. When Coleridge entered from the side, the entire chorus rose to their feet and applauded vigorously with the orchestra – the string section rapping their instruments with their bows. The audience also rose to their feet, to applaud Coleridge, and handkerchiefs flapped over the heads of the multitude like dying doves. Coleridge acknowledged the applause gracefully and a truly magnificent performance followed – arguably the best ever performance of 'The Song of Hiawatha' trilogy.

Another dinner party followed, this one held in honour of the composer. Coleridge sat beside the flamboyant violinist Miss Maud Powell.

"So how about writing me a Concerto, then?" she had kept on saying, primarily he thought to make him giggle but as she went on, he began to realise that perhaps she actually meant it.

Americans – extraordinary!

Opposite him sat Mr Henry Burleigh and Mr Paine was a little further along, also opposite. There were twenty-five around the table, including the most prolific and prominent musicians of America, and towards the end of what had been a wonderful dinner – relaxed, friendly and warm – Carl Stoeckel rose to his feet, sounded his glass with a butter knife and made a speech.

He said what a successful festival it had been, how very much he had enjoyed that final evening's performance and how he so loved the work, 'Hiawatha'. He told them how much everyone in America, black or white, loved it; how it united people. Coleridge felt the same humility that he had felt that evening some years before at the Hilyers'.

"It is difficult for people in Europe to understand," Stoeckel concluded, "the unfortunate and unreasonable prejudice, which still exists not only against Africans but also against Native American Indians in the United States – but the fact is here and we must face it and do our best to overcome it. I know of no incident, in my life at least, that has done so much to dissipate this feeling as this visit by Mr Samuel Coleridge-Taylor to our great land. Tonight was truly one of those rare and, dare I say it, historic occasions that strikes a blow at the root of prejudice." The guests clapped in agreement. "Now I know he hates making speeches so I have not asked him to say anything so perhaps..." he began, but before Stoeckel could ask them all to be up-standing, Coleridge timidly rose from his seat, scraping the heavy chair behind him.

"It's true I never make speeches," he said as he stood and unfolded a scrap of paper to read the notes he had made. They turned to him and smiled in delighted surprise. Stoeckel sat and grinned encouragingly at Coleridge. Coleridge making a speech? This truly was a historic occasion!

"But I do not feel," Coleridge went on, "as if I could leave this table without expressing the gratitude I feel for all that has been done for me... by our hosts Carl and Ellen Stoeckel, by the Litchfield County Choral Union, by the orchestra, by the conductor Mr Paine and by all the others who have been so good as to be interested in my work."

"If I had retained the rights to 'Hiawatha' – I won't go on about this but I might have been a very, very rich man today but the truth is that I only ever received a small sum for it. But for me, to hear what it means to other people – well, there is no better payment I could receive than that and so, in a way, I do feel like I am a very rich man."

"Tonight's performance of the piece was, I think, the very best I have ever heard. I do not believe that it has ever been better done. Everybody – the chorus, soloists, orchestra and audience were all with me and I have never – never in my life known anything like that. This is one of the happiest days of my life. It has been simply royal and I thank you all, from the bottom of my heart."

Later, the diners adjourned to the library where they, perhaps rather inevitably, enjoyed some impromptu music. Miss Gluck sang some African songs in which Coleridge was hugely interested, never having heard those particular songs before. Later still, Coleridge stepped into a quiet room with the composers Mr George W Chadwick and Mr Horatio Parker where they talked about contemporary music.

It was clear to them that Coleridge rated Dvorak and Grieg highly but didn't care much for most of the modern Russian Music. In fact, Chadwick and Parker both greatly enjoyed Coleridge's wicked sense of humour and amusing English delivery as he dismembered the untouchable Russians and both of them had laughed like drains. Coleridge enjoyed making people laugh, even though sometimes he wasn't absolutely sure that what he was saying was so comical.

"Now I don't include Tchaikovsky in this category," he told them. "It's that Rimsky-Korsakoff! Good

Heaven's above, he's largely just clever orchestration, don't you think – all a very rum bunch. You know, I've spent several pounds on Russian scores and to be frank I rather wish I could have my money back!" They threw back their heads and roared with laughter.

Both composers were flattered to hear that Coleridge had conducted their own works. He told them that he should like to give Parker's 'King Gorm the Grim' and Chadwick's Cantata, 'Noel' at the Royal Choral Society. He won them all with his heartfelt, liberal and progressive disposition towards the works of others, excepting the Russian composers of course, and everyone found him warm, modest and highly amusing.

Next door, in the library, Carl Stoeckel and some others were discussing Coleridge's graceful attitude on the conductor's stand. Stoeckel likened him to a well restrained, panting war-horse, when waiting to begin. It was as if Coleridge loved to get into the thick of the music, Stoeckel observed, whereas when he had risen to speak publicly, he had seemed almost to shrink within himself.

"He brought with him to this country what he termed a conductor's jacket," Stoeckel told the small group quietly. "He was very particular about changing from street attire into this jacket to conduct, although I think I am right in saying that all of the orchestra and most of our conductors work at rehearsals without coats. I told him that in New York it would be entirely good form if he chose to work without his coat at rehearsals but he always went at once to his dressing room and donned his conductor's coat!"

"What a dear man he is," Ellen said, standing and moving to the piano and sitting on the stool. She started to play the most beautiful, slow and lyrical tune as they talked but the conversations soon petered out, preferring instead to listen to her play than converse. In the other room, Coleridge couldn't help overhearing and excused himself to stand in the doorway.

"What is that lovely melody?" he asked when Ellen had finished the piece.

"It's an old African song called, 'Keep me from Sinking Down, Good Lord'. I don't believe that it has ever been in the books. It was taken from the lips of a slave by a music teacher who went south and who in turn, gave it to my late father-in-law."

"Would you play it again for me and permit me to take it down?"

She did and Coleridge notated it on the back of his impromptu speech.

Most of the others had left early that next morning but his hosts had asked Coleridge if he might like to stay one day longer rather than spend his final night at the New York hotel. Coleridge could not refuse.

After a light, early lunch on that June afternoon, Carl took Coleridge for one last ride in his motorcar. They drove off the main road and through fields of the fragrant Kalmia that was in full blossom. Coleridge was delighted by the wild and freshly scented landscape of north-western Connecticut.

They stopped in one of the fields and the two men lay in the long, dry grass and loosened their collars. Coleridge had brought a book with him that he had hoped to re-read that afternoon, but instead the landscape transported him to the land of the poem itself to Japan.

Carl Stoeckel's breathing slowed and deepened as he drifted off and Coleridge looked at the pale, blue sky above, intermittently marked with dashes of chalky cloud. He closed his eyes and saw the willow-patterned land where Yoichi Tenko, the painter in the poem, dwelt by a purple ocean. He saw Kimi, the child of Tenko's brother, a pearl-fisher lost at sea in his junk. He loved the music inherent in the words and phrases written by Alfred Noyes. His creativity raced as the story unfolded before his mind's eye.

Sawara was a student of the painter, Tenko. He was 'lissom as a cherry spray' and Kimi fell in love with him and he with her.

'"I can teach you nothing more…".' said Tenko.

So Sawara sailed away over the glassy sea to seek his fortune, but before leaving, promised Kimi he would return.

She waited by the water's edge but the days soon turned to weeks and the weeks soon turned to months.

Far away, Sawara's growing fame as an artist 'illuminated the sky' – but still he sent his love no word, or at least, no word was received by her.

A wealthy, travelling merchant offered Tenko great wealth in return for his niece's hand and knowing she would never agree, the greedy artist told Kimi that Sawara had married someone else. In her desperate, lonely grief, she finally succumbed and agreed to the marriage arranged by her uncle.

The tragedy was that just a short while after the wedding, Sawara did indeed return as he always promised he would. He had felt so unworthy of her before and so had sought his fame and fortune first and found it and now returned to her to claim the bride he loved.

On telling Sawara that she had married someone else, she suddenly knew her wicked uncle had lied to her and had sacrificed her happiness for his own financial gain.

In her grief and despair, Kimi collapsed on the beach and the young hero rushed to the side of his dying love. Trembling, she lifted her head, but then, like a broken blossom, she died.

Overcome with her beauty, even in death, Sawara felt suddenly inspired and was compelled to paint her as she slept in death with perfect, swift and inky strokes from his bamboo brush. Tenko approached and on seeing the completed painting, sad and beautiful and painted by the hand of one who loved his subject in life, spoke the final words of the poem.

'…"You have burst the golden gate!
You have conquered Time and Fate!
Hokusai is not so great!
…This is Art," said Tenko.'

Coleridge had taken breakfast in his room and was all packed up ready for the long journey home. He was sitting at the small desk writing with Ellen Stoeckel's exquisite pen when there was a gentle knock on the door.

"Please come in."

Carl Stoeckel entered. He couldn't help but notice Coleridge hurriedly hiding the notes he had been making in the desk drawer.

"I'm afraid it's time you were returning to your own Music Shed," Carl told him.

"I'll be down in a minute. I'm nearly finished."

Stoeckel smiled and closed the door behind him. Coleridge retrieved the notes and slowly stood and walked to the large, open window for one last look at that perfect view. The green of the velvety lawns stretched like baize all the way to the forest edge where it was pinned by the talons of ancient trees. The hills and mountains behind them, ruffled and rolling, were capped with snow, pale blue.

He glanced at the notes he had made. They were very provisional but the musical themes were there and sound and the subject matter was certain.

It was to be a cantata – a new and great choral work that he would write for his own pleasure just as he had done with 'Hiawatha'. This, he was sure, would bring him back success as a composer. The world's perfect love of the 'Hiawatha' cantata would be eclipsed only by 'A Tale of Old Japan'.

CHAPTER 15

Coleridge purchased some music parchment in Boston and had spent every moment of the voyage home working on the new piece. The Atlantic seemed as still as a millpond for the crossing and nearly two weeks after leaving the Stoeckels', he arrived at West Croydon Station on the last train home.

Jess had stayed up to meet him and unbeknownst to her, so too had the children and they sleepily descended the stairs to greet their loving father after hearing the door. After a quick cuddle and chat, they all settled down for the night.

The next morning, Coleridge began working his way through the pile of correspondence that had collected for him in the upstairs, box music room. Many were final demands for payment of bills, many were rejections and a few were late payments made to him for various pieces of work and engagements but there was not enough to cover the bills – there never seemed to be.

The Dorothy Perkins roses, that grew up the side of his garden Music Shed, bloomed with the summer months and then all too quickly, withered with the Autumn. Then bloomed and died back again.

The children were growing faster than ever. Watha was a very handsome twelve-year-old; a quiet, intelligent and sensitive boy, truly his father's son. He had large eyes and long lashes, a warm olive complexion with pink, rosy cheeks and dark wavy hair. Gwendolen was nine in 1912. She had a mop of curls and a pale, freckly face. She was much more boisterous than Watha and had a cheeky smile and sharp sense of humour.

At thirty-seven, Coleridge looked increasingly older than his years. His schedule remained relentless and his work was still bought for full and immediate payment as it had always been. It had always been a hand to mouth existence, sailing close to the wind, only just managing to make ends meet by the skin of his teeth. Despite this, he always remained cheerful and genuinely considered himself to be 'very fortunate'.

One February morning, the day before the premiere of 'A Tale of Old Japan' at the Croydon Grand, Coleridge was working in the Music Shed. Jess knocked and entered with that morning's post and a cup of tea. He flicked through the unopened letters to find the one he had been waiting for. Jess never understood why he would always read the envelope's outside first to try and guess whom it had come from and what it contained when he could have just as easily have opened it and found out in half the time.

Coleridge stopped sifting the unopened envelopes when he found the one that might be the one he'd been waiting for. He looked at Jess and ripped it open – no cheque. He read it through before speaking but she knew what it said.

"They've rejected 'Thelma'. The music is fine, they say but the libretto is impossible, unstageable apparently."

"Coleridge, all that time – all those years you spent writing it! I told you not to invest so much in it. I told you.... Well, something else will have to turn up, I suppose."

"'A Tale of Old Japan'," he said. He looked at her. "We'll have a motorcar out of that. I promise, Jess. And there's 'The Forest of Wild Thyme' for Tree and 'Endymion' at Brighton." He paused, suddenly noticing what Jess was wearing. He tried to remember before asking, but couldn't. "Where are we going?"

"You can't have forgotten! You have to play. Remember? For Mr Jaegar? Honestly, Coleridge, what are we going to do with you?"

"I hadn't forgotten. Do I have time to drink this?"

"Not really," she answered. "We can't be late. Everyone from Novello with be there. Everyone from everywhere will be there. Unless, of course you don't want to play – I could say you are unwell."

"No. I will. I want to. I can never forget all he did for me at the beginning and all the way along. He's been very good to me – very loyal and frank. It's the very least I can do for him now.

The late king Edward VII had knighted Mr Edward Elgar in 1904 and six years later, the King had died of his bronchial asthma, just as William had. Sir Edward sat stony-faced in the chapel.

Jess sat with their old friend Fritz from Novello. She glanced across at Lady Alice. She looked at how her hands were neatly folded on her lap. Jess neatly folded hers. She looked at the veil that stopped just above the upper lip, so becoming. She noticed Lady Alice's marble expression of cold serenity – regal and dignified, and Sir Charles Villiers Stanford with Sir George

Grove, Messrs Parry, Dunhill, Vaughan Williams and a host of others.

When his moment came, Coleridge stood and walked the centre aisle to where his violin was propped in its case. He looked out over the congregation and happened to catch Ralph Vaughan Williams' eye. Funny how, Coleridge thought, he had always hoped Ralph would come into his own one day and, albeit nearly eighteen years after their graduation, there he was doing rather well for himself with his English Hymnal and his little Book of Carols.

Coleridge picked up his violin and glanced up to the organist for the nod. A special arrangement of Sir Edward's 'Nimrod' from the 'Enigma Variations' for violin and organ had been prepared. Coleridge played perfectly. He always did, but this particular occasion meant so much more to him. This was his tribute, his way of saying thank you for all that had been done on his behalf by the old ogre of Novello. Coleridge was all too aware of how 'Hiawatha' had made the fortunes of both Jaegar and Novello but never really minded that, not like Jess did, although from time to time he couldn't help but wonder what it might have been like to be a ridiculously wealthy man. Coleridge never knew that the man that he was paying his tribute to, had not said one kind word to anyone about either Coleridge or his music since 1898 and Coleridge played on, in humble gratitude, to the father of his career – to a man who hated him, was disgusted by him and who couldn't bear to sit in the same room as him. Coleridge had been deeply touched to be asked to contribute in this way – at the memorial service for the late Mr Auguste Jaegar.

The next morning, Gwen knocked on the creaky shed door and pushed it open. Coleridge gave her a squeeze as he put down his pen.

"Has Watha gone to school without you?"

"He's still upstairs, but I'm ready now," she said as she pulled out the report book from her satchel stuffed with stuff; her pencil case and various bits of assorted, little-girl paraphernalia that nine-year-olds should never be without.

"Miss Sully says you need to see this."

She gave him the booklet and he read the page that she had opened it to. He felt overwhelmed with pride when he saw the marks that his daughter had been given in all her reports. Although her eyes were almost level with his as he sat, he looked down his nose at her comically as if he were wearing pince-nez.

"What does this mean?" he said in a mock-serious voice.

"It means I'm top of my form," she smirked.

"I see," he said sounding as much like Old Jaegar as he could.

He was just about to give her another big hug when she told him that he was meant to write something to say that he'd seen it. He turned and leaning on the piano, wrote on the open page. He closed the book, swivelled on the stool and handed it back to her with a wink and then went back to his work as she trotted off.

"Has Watha gone yet?" Jess asked some minutes later as Coleridge joined her in the kitchen. He told Jess that he probably had by now and that Gwen had left a while ago. He filled the kettle, putting it on the stove. Jess stepped out, casually sashaying into the dining-room nursing her cup of tea.

"I forgot to give you this," he said as he handed her an elaborately painted copy of 'A Tale of Old Japan'. "Kathleen painted it for you. Isn't it beautiful?"

"Yes I saw. It's very clever. I shall thank her when we see her this evening." She continued drifting, through the dining room and into the hall.

"She should steal the show if she keeps her promise," Coleridge called after her absently but with a smile in his voice. He watched the kettle as the water started to heat and stir inside.

Watha was indeed on his way to school. He had walked down to the end of St Leonard's Road and turned left into Warrington Street. He wore his satchel and his shoe bag on his back as if he were on a trek to climb Ben Nevis. He hummed happily but tunelessly as he walked along, skipping a step every so often so as to avoid the cracks in the pavement.

At the end, the turned left into Epsom Road and then left again into Duppas Road. At the crossing at the bottom he waited for a moment for the milkman and coalman to pass in their carts. He knew the journey to school like the back of his hand. He could walk it in his sleep, which was just as well, as he was still half asleep.

On the other side of the road, by the gates to the Recreation Ground between home and school, was a group of four boys. Two were sitting on the wall. The boys weren't from Watha's school, in fact he had never seen them before and everyone in Croydon had seen everyone before. They weren't much older than him.

He felt nervous for a moment but didn't think too much of them then immediately remembered that he had seen one of them before, the ginger-haired one. He had seen him on the High Street when out with his father. The boy had said something but Coleridge had covered his ears in time so that he didn't hear what the boy had said. But Watha knew anyway. He had seen the boy's venomous mouth move, 'Niggers'. His father removed his hands after they passed but in time for Watha to hear the gob of spittle hit the pavement behind them as they walked on. A rush of fear rose in Watha when he recognised the boy.

The gang watched as he crossed the road. He couldn't change direction now, he thought, it would be too obvious and besides, going through the Recreation Ground was by far the quickest route. He didn't want them to see he was afraid.

He lamely walked through the gates without giving the boys a glance, even though they eyed him like vultures. His pace didn't quicken but was steady, though perhaps the steps he took were a little wider apart than normal.

Shortly after he'd passed through the gates, he heard two boys jump down from the wall. He could feel their eyes burning into his back. He could hear them all walking in the same direction as he. He was about twenty feet from them when half a brick flew through silently through the air to land about five feet in front of him. It was hard to ignore, the brick being about the size of a cricket ball. He wasn't sure if there was enough distance for him to be able to outrun them and even if he did manage it, they would then know where he went to school and would probably be waiting for him when he came out. He knew the brick had been meant to hit him but he carried on walking and they kept on following.

Then his pace slowed.

His father had always told him to ignore bullies and to just walk away but would anyone ever be proud of him if he always ran away? Wouldn't his father be prouder of him still if he were to stop and face them? As he wondered what he should do, his pace decreased still further until he found himself at a standstill. Then, he slowly turned around.

Miss Sully had taken the register. She had given her class a reading assignment to give her time to glance through the stack of report books and ensure that all the parents had seen them. Her class was generally good and so there were very few, if any, opportunities to stamp her authority on them. They all rather liked her in fact but Miss Sully believed that for children to learn, it helped if they were a little afraid of the teacher. Not that her children weren't learning, they were learning very well indeed and this had been commented upon, but even so, an opportunity had presented itself to the pretty young woman to instil a spoonful of healthy fear into the class and it was not to be missed.

They finished reading the passage. Her props had been set. She told them to stop and the children looked up, instantly knowing that something was in the air and they waited with trepidation.

Miss Sully closed the final report book and put it on the top of the pile. One report book, however, was at the very front of Miss Sully's desk. She took off her glasses and pinched the bridge of her nose in a well-rehearsed and pained show of exasperation.

Still pinching, she opened the drawer to the desk and took out the ruler. She placed it on the desk. There was a horrified silence as the children waited to hear who had done whatever it was and who was going to get hit across the knuckles for it.

In a world-weary way, Miss Sully said, "Gwendolen Coleridge-Taylor, will you come here, please."

Gwen was genuinely puzzled. The other children breathed a sigh of relief that it wasn't them. Gwen lifted her chair as she stood as they had been instructed to do, but even so, it still scraped a little. She walked to the front as Miss Sully stood and walked around to the desk to meet her. She picked up Gwen's report book.

"You know that you must never scribble in this book, don't you?"

"I didn't," said Gwen.

"Didn't you?" The teacher opened the book." Then, perhaps you can explain this," she said, holding the open book an inch from Gwen's nose. "Perhaps you would like to share your scribblings with the rest of the class?"

Gwen took hold of the book. Miss Sully held Gwen's shoulders with splayed fingertips and turned the child to be judged by her peers.

"Read it," she instructed as she picked up the ruler and folded her arms across her bosom behind the girl. Gwen read quietly.

"'Oliver Hops,
He made some tops,
Out of the morning glory.
He used the seed,
He did indeed,
And that's the end of my story'."

Her voice trailed off. An unseen smirk tried to manifest itself on every young face.

"Well?" Miss Sully said at last. "Where did that come from?"

"Father," Gwen replied.

A giggle chuckled its way around the room but was swiftly stifled by the teacher who was not so amused. This was not the answer she had been certain of receiving and to her horror she began to think she might blush. She loved Mr Coleridge-Taylor's music.

"I see," said Miss Sully. She thought quickly. "Then kindly tell your father that he is not to scribble in your report book again. Now go back to your seat. Go on."

Gwen sucked her lips between her teeth so as not to laugh as she walked back to her seat. She allowed herself one big grin to her best friend, before turning to sit down, stony-faced.

Watha looked at the boys. They were still walking towards him and he stood his ground but suddenly their paced quickened and they were after him. He spun on his heels and ran as fast as he could towards the pavilion but they quickly caught up with him. He was shoved in the back and fell face first – skidding along the cold, wet grass. His satchel was ripped off his back as he was kicked in the side, and the bag slung onto the pavilion roof. The ginger-haired boy kicked him in the side ribs again as hard as he could.

Watha rolled over and crawled a little way forward but they had a hold of his blazer and two of them yanked him up on his feet. They tightened their grip and twisted his arm up behind his back in a half nelson, then he was frog-marched out of sight, behind the pavilion.

The same two held him against the back wall as the ginger-haired one walked towards him.

"I bloody hate darkies," he said. He hoicked up some phlegm and spat it in Watha's face. The thick, foamy, creamy spit dribbled down his face but he didn't cry out – he was too angry and his sides were bruised and ached. He struggled to get free, but it made the four boys laugh menacingly.

Watha was then punched in the stomach again and again. He was punched in his face and his lip and eyebrow swelled almost immediately and split. Blood trickled down his face. He was dragged down to the ground and pinned on his back there. They pulled his legs apart and then each took a turn at swinging a kick at him, as hard as they could.

When they'd each had a go, they let go of him. He turned to his side and was sick on the grass. One gave him a final kick in the ribs as he coughed and spluttered up some blood and the breakfast his mother had given him and the boys ran away laughing and shouting, 'go home – go home nigger boy'.

He crawled to the side of the pavilion and sat with his back against it. His shirt had been pulled over his shoulder and some buttons had come off. Blood ran down his face. His shorts were ripped at the back and his shoe had come off. His knees were stained green from the grass and he was covered with mud, thick mud and blood.

Twenty minutes or so later, when he realised the pains he felt in the various parts of his body would only get worse, he struggled up into a tree and onto the roof of the pavilion.

The groundsman shouted at him angrily from across the Recreation Ground and began running in the way that old men run, yelling at him to 'get down off that damned roof'. Watha ignored him and collected his bag. He climbed back down the tree, jumping the last three feet and twisting his ankle, as the groundsman approached.

As he got closer to the boy, the groundsman noticed Watha's state. He asked him if he was alright and Watha told him that he was. He told him that he oughtn't to go climbing on roofs and that he'd better be off on his way home.

Coleridge was pondering a musical conundrum as he sipped tea in the shed. He looked out passed the rose thorns that framed the dusty window and into his garden. He heard the gate at the bottom of the porch steps swing open and rattle shut but couldn't see who it was. It was too late for the postman. He stepped out to see his son – muddy, dishevelled, limping, bruised and bloodied as he climbed the steps to the front door.

He rushed to him and knelt on the steps. He checked the boy over. He held his face. A quick assessment told him that there was no serious damage done. He squeezed his boy to him hard enough to show how loved he was but not hard enough to aggravate any unseen bruises and Watha put his head on his father's shoulder. Coleridge felt his quiet and gentle boy's body gently convulse as he broke and silently sobbed.

Elsie had worked for the Coleridge-Taylors more regularly during those last twelve months – normally Monday to Friday from twelve until four. She mainly helped Jess with the cooking and cleaning. Jess's parents had insisted that they take a maid on more permanently.

Elsie liked Mr Coleridge-Taylor a lot but generally found Mrs Coleridge-Taylor a bit stuck up and bossy. She also seemed to look for problems and was overly critical of her work; she was very hard to please.

That evening, Elsie was helping Mrs Coleridge-Taylor dress for some big 'do' or other that they were going to. Mr Coleridge-Taylor was all done up in his black tie and tails in the front room downstairs. It was a very special occasion, Elsie was told – it was the premiere of 'A Tale of Old Japan'.

Coleridge was reading his newspaper and smoking a cigarette as he waited. After his bath, Watha had spent most of the day on his bed. Behind Coleridge as he sat, Gwen was brushing his hair. She tried parting it on the right, which was not the way he normally wore it. He was so engrossed in his paper that he was oblivious as to what she was actually doing with his hair. She tried brushing it all upwards, even at the sides, so that it all stood on end. He looked like a paintbrush, she thought with a smirk.

"I need to go soon, Gwennie," he said, so she brushed it back to how it normally was. But then a wicked thought crossed her mind. Making him look like a paint-brush had sown a seed of revenge for getting her into trouble at school that day and here was an opportunity.

He turned the page of the paper and flicked the end of his cigarette into the ashtray. With one hand, she carried on gently brushing his hair so as not to arouse suspicion. With the other, she silently undid the broad, blue satin ribbon that she wore around her waist. She quickly tied it into a very large bow and oh so gently, laid it on the very top of his brushed hair. It seemed to balance perfectly and he was totally unaware. She smirked again and took her hands off it for a second. He inhaled on his cigarette and turned his head to read the other page. It stayed in place beautifully. She put her hand over her mouth because she was convinced that she would burst and splutter out a loud guffaw. She walked out of the room on tiptoe but had to steal one last glance. Sure enough, there he was, sitting with his back to her with a huge, blue, satin ribbon bow in his hair.

Just as Gwen reached the top of the stairs there was a knock on the front door. Elsie came out of Mrs Coleridge-Taylor's bedroom, passing Gwen on the narrow landing. Gwen watched from behind the stair rods at the top, like a prisoner, as Elsie descended the stairs and opened the door. Gwen rushed into her room.

A brief moment later, there was a knock at the sitting room door and it opened, Coleridge stood and folded his paper away, turning to see Elsie come in with their visitor.

"Sir Herbert Beerbohm Tree to see you, Sir."

Elsie and Sir Herbert looked at Coleridge. He couldn't comprehend the bemused look that appeared on Elsie's face. Neither could he understand the smile of admiration on Sir Herbert's.

"Sir Herbert, you're early!" Coleridge said, still blissfully unaware of the flamboyant bow in his hair. Elsie left the room to help Mrs Coleridge-Taylor finish dressing.

"My dear fellow," said Sir Herbert as he stepped forward and warmly shook Coleridge's hand. "To never be afraid of trying something new is the quality that I think I admire most in you. Ready to go are we?"

Ten minutes, and a good laugh later, Coleridge was indeed ready to go. He had folded the sash as he talked with Sir Herbert and put it on the banister in the hall where the two men stood with young Watha.

Watha's cuts and bruises had been cleaned up as best they could. He looked like a baby prizefighter with his two big shiners and cut lip but he was fine and Sir Herbert had been very encouraging to the boy. He had told him to always remember to hold his head high while he continued about his own business, no matter what any cowardly bully should ever do or say.

Sir Herbert stopped talking suddenly and looked up the stairs. Jess appeared at the top in the most beautiful, green dress that shimmered purple like a bluebottle in the spluttering gaslight. The bodice was elaborately embroidered with an 'Arts and Crafts'-style leaf motif. The tiny buttons were of black velvet, as were the cuffs and collar and the dress ruffled as she moved. A fine lace framed her throat and wrists and she lifted her dress at the knees and descended the stairs showing the black, velvet shoe toe tips as she stepped daintily down.

Her hair was brushed to the side in a French-pleat and put up. Her black, velvet hat was decorated with peacock feathers and had a most becoming veil that came down to just above her lip. Around her neck, she wore the treble clef necklace from America.

It was as if the Queen or Lady Alice Elgar herself were descending the stairs of the modest West Croydon home; her Lady-in-Waiting, Elsie, standing proud behind her.

Gwen, in her nightdress, crouched on the upstairs landing and peeked through the balustrade bars.

"Mrs Coleridge-Taylor!" Sir Herbert exclaimed in admiration as he kissed her hand. Watha smiled at how beautiful his mother looked.

Coleridge however, was looking passed his wife at his wilful daughter who stared right back with a cheeky grin. She knew he wouldn't leave without saying something of the blue ribbon incident.

"Excuse me, Sir Herbert," Coleridge said as he squeezed passed Jess. "But I can't leave without first doing this...."

Gwen leapt to her feet with a high-pitched squeal as Coleridge charged up the stairs, two at a time. She ran up and down on the spot for a moment, not knowing which way to run then darted into her room, slamming the door. He immediately opened it and saw her desperate attempt to escape under the bed but he grabbed her by the ankles and pulled out the squealing, squirming wriggler as he laughed and roared and growled like a giant, tickling tiger. And then he tickled his little girl to within an inch of her life as she giggled and shrieked and begged him to stop.

The coach that had been organised to take them to the theatre arrived outside the Croydon Grand at seven. Sir Herbert, Jess and Coleridge got down from their carriage and the horse and coach trotted off.

The theatre had taken on a distinctly Japanese feel for the premiere of 'A Tale of Old Japan'. Red and black dragons with the detail picked out in gold leaf, stood by the doors, which were themselves framed with pagoda roofs. Japanese art covered the walls and large, ceramic lions were placed here and there. Celadon vases were filled with yellow chrysanthemums and a bonsai tree was on every table in the smoky, dress circle bar area. The female staff, who waited on them, wore kimonos.

Sir Herbert had stayed with Coleridge at the box office, as there seemed to be some sort of mix up with the tickets, which promised to embarrass Coleridge if he were to face it on his own. Everyone knew Sir Herbert Beerbohm Tree and he carried some clout.

Kathleen found Jess. Coleridge had dared her to come in full African, princess regalia and she had risen to the challenge. Her lime green and orange dress was wrapped around her beautiful mahogany skin. On her head was a large hat made of the same material, elaborately folded like an oversized table napkin. Her eyes were bright and her smile, beautiful. She was attracting a great deal of attention in her fabulous costume and Jess found it difficult to focus when talking to her, she was just too annoyed.

To Jess, Kathleen had come to the premiere dressed inappropriately, in gaudy bed linen, and the attention she was attracting, she believed was proving a distraction from her husband, whose night it was.

When the three minute bell sounded, Jess was finishing a story about how she caught a conductor somewhere or other trying to pass off some of Coleridge's compositions as his own work and how she had heroically stepped into the fray to put the man right.

"Afterwards I introduced myself," she told Kathleen, "and told him that the waltzes were actually Coleridge's work. He said that I was mistaken but I assured him I was not as they were written originally for violin and piano."

"That's terrible. How can they get away with that?" Kathleen asked, genuinely appalled, but Jess's eyes were sifting the people in the room and she never answered.

"I never thanked you for the little book you painted, did I?" Jess's tone was clipped. Kathleen's irritation mounted. Why was Jess always so angry anyway, she asked herself.

The book had been a peace offering. Kathleen had always tried very hard to be liked by Jess and never understood why she was not – why she was not only cold towards her but often downright hostile and rude.

"No you didn't thank me."

Still oblivious, Jess's eyes flitted about, perhaps to see whether she was being noticed, Kathleen thought, or perhaps to see if there was someone 'better' she ought to be speaking to. Kathleen looked deeply into Jess.

"Jessie, is everything alright?"

"Hmmm?" Jess purred with a terse, disinterested smile.

Jess would go through phases. Sometimes she would be civil but when Kathleen spent any deal of time with her husband, Jess seemed to seethe about it but not actually say anything, which seemed to Kathleen terribly unfair. Kathleen had given her that book in good faith and it was clear that she was not even going to be thanked for it. She had painted it for Jess with her own hand and it had taken her hours.

Kathleen found herself fighting to keep a lid on her irritation as it started to rise up in her. Jess turned towards the door, turning her back on Kathleen, snubbing her very publicly. Kathleen stepped to the side so that she stood in front of Jess again and so that she could not be ignored; so that Jess couldn't look at anyone else in the room, anyone who might be of more use to her or Coleridge's career than Kathleen was. She looked Jess in the eye and spoke through gritted teeth.

"I don't know what I have done to upset you, Jessie," she said quietly and with all the hurt and anger of a little home truth. "But if it is anything other than me just being another woman, then I am truly sorry for it, I truly am. If it is because I am a woman and because I am a friend of your husband, an old and dear friend I might add, then I am truly sorry for you. I am not competing with you, Jessie. None of us are. Not me, not Marguerite Radclyffe Hall and not your own daughter for Christ's sake."

Sir Herbert appeared. Kathleen turned to compose herself for a moment. Thankfully, he hadn't heard.

"Sir Herbert," Jess cooed. "We thought we'd lost you."

"Not only have they not allowed him to conduct at the premiere of his own bloody work," he raged to the two women in hushed voice, "and not only is he having to pay for our seats but he is having to pay for his own damned seat as well. It's an absolute outrage – the damned, bloody nerve!" Sir Herbert noticed the look of hurt on Kathleen's face and the pinched, faux smile on Jess's tilted head. "What?"

"Here we are," Coleridge cheerfully said as he joined them with the tickets.

Sir Herbert took Kathleen's arm and Coleridge took Jessie's – all of them angry and all of them pretending not to be.

A few minutes later, an excited hush descended in the Grand Theatre, Croydon as the theatre lights were dimmed and the opening chords of the world's first performance of the sumptuous, tragic and triumphant cantata, 'A Tale of Old Japan' were heard.

The opening bars heralded the hope or perhaps the promise, that a new and wonderful phase in his life was about to start – a phase of wealth and revived recognition.

CHAPTER 16

It was a couple of minutes before seven. The three minute bell had sounded two minutes earlier and the Royal Albert Hall auditorium was full, all except for the seat to Dr Collard's right. He could put his coat on it he thought, but decided not to – someone might arrive yet. A few rows behind him, Mr Joseph Beckwith was saying how wonderful it was to see his very old friend, Colonel Walters again, and that it had been simply too long. The two old men were shaking hands and discussing things noticed in the programme, picking over any inaccuracies.

The orchestra tuned; discordant and beautiful. Warming up, the great kettles thrummed as the keys were turned to make them sound springy, like rubber bands deeply twanged. Oboes and bassoons were hooting and bleating. Violins and cellos were plucked and tuned and keys turned on bows; the harpist, the startled-looking flutes, the Clarinet – all of them running through bits of scales, all of them athletes running on the spot waiting for the starting pistol. The horn section, men without upper lips, were showing off noisily, playing tantalising phrases of a few notes of favourite parts, the parts the audience would know so well. A few notes to tease and torment for those who knew and as a sampler for those few who didn't; an amuse bouche. All of this happening at one and the same time in one glorious blaze of sound. Adrenalin pumped, blood coursed and hearts pounded in the throats of the costumed chorus as they waited in the tunnels to process in to their seats.

When the signal came, the chorus – hundreds and hundreds of them, coiled in and filled the rows; all in the most wonderful costumes, all holding their copies of the vocal score and the audience applauded. The noise of the thousands clapping was deafening and there she was!

The old lady saw her. Filing in the way that they did, made it easier to sift through the choristers and she fixed her eyes on her as the young woman found her seat. She was sure it had to be her. Judith tried to fix the girl in her mind so that she would remember where she was sitting. The old lady lifted her eyes and gazed on the magnificent backdrop of mountains, forests, lake and wigwams. It was so large that it drew you in, as if you were really there in the Land of the Dakotahs. She wondered what her brother would have made of it all.

She tried to see from where the drop had been hung but it disappeared far too high up to see, reaching high up into the dark. She looked at the ceiling covered with the representation of both the night and the day sky and she looked back down to the girl. There she was. Water flooded down the log-shaped chutes and splattered into the lake surrounding the conductor's stand. It was all too magnificent in the warm half-light of the buzzing auditorium.

The orchestra, themselves lit only by small, electric lights on their stands were reflected in the waters of the dark lake in the centre. The hall was filled with the hum of excited chatter and of the multitude rustling programmes and of latecomers finding their seats just in time. The smell of electric light in the hall gave a very different atmosphere to the old theatre lights – the air itself seemed charged.

The old lady looked up again. This time she was looking at the audience. She looked around to the right, to the edge of the lower dress circle. Peering closely, she saw a young man of mixed race with a white woman about the same age as she. The young man was very close to the woman. He must have been in his early thirties. There could be no doubt in her mind. This young man was the son, Hiawatha Coleridge-Taylor, born in 1900 and the old woman was, Jessie. A woman Judith had heard a lot about from her late brother, William and she was also all too aware of the rift rumoured between mother and daughter.

The young man however, seemed very attached to his mother and she to him. She saw him tilt his head to say something to her, the back of one hand to his mouth and a finger half pointing towards the chorus. Mrs Coleridge-Taylor nodded. She had a strange, almost regal look on her face. She had been told Jessie had airs. She traced her gaze across the Hall to where the handsome young man had been pointing and it was to her, to the young woman in the chorus. Judith smiled. She had her confirmation. The boy had been pointing out his sister in the chorus – his sister Gwen.

There was a ripple of applause that turned into a deafening wave as Dr Malcolm Sargent was spotted taking large, rapid steps to his stand and bristling with baton in hand. He trotted across the lake, with water splashing into it, using the narrow footbridge and the applause swelled.

Once across, he spun on his heels to the audience and with his palms on his thighs and a very happy grin on his face, he bowed. The applause, that couldn't have got any louder, exploded and raised the roof. He stood straight, nodded to them all once again and, fizzing with energy and excitement, turned to his orchestra and chorus.

The lights dimmed in the auditorium. The orchestra readied themselves. Without taking her eyes off the conductor, the First Violin rested her instrument under her chin. It needed to be comfortable as it was to be there for a long time. The others followed her lead. The applause quietened down to silence. Everything was silent but for water gently cascading.

Dr Sargent ushered the chorus to stand, which they did with such discipline, it was as if they were one. And then the quiet. The orchestra and the chorus focussed on Dr Sargent.

A silence, pregnant with expectation and possibility filled the Hall; the only sound was the whispering of the laughing water. Dr Sargent lifted his arms and they hung there – crucified and breathless, straining at the leash. Suddenly the orchestra laughed. Something had happened – a false start, perhaps? Dr Sargent had clearly said or done something accidentally or maybe intentionally to disrupt the tension of the moment to relax them a little more. The moment passed. He made sure they were ready and primed once again.

Energy seemed to shoot through him and out through his baton and fingertips as he lifted his hands once again. All eyes were on him. The orchestra and chorus were with him; they saw only him, they knew only him and they waited for his signal.

Then he gave it.

The horns started with their fanfare – the opening of 'Hiawatha's Wedding Feast', the great work. The strings beat out, deep and rhythmic, slow and steady, just like Native American Indian drums beating around a smoky fire. It had begun.

Coleridge knew where he was instantly, but as is often the case in dreams, the place wasn't as it looked in reality. The Royal Albert Hall's organ had gone for one thing and the colours were brighter than ever. The Hall was packed to capacity and the orchestra was playing but all he could hear was the sound of his own breathing and the ticking of the bedside clock as he slept in late.

He was looking down from behind two people in the circle during an extravagant musical performance. He was standing behind a man and an old woman. There was an empty seat next to them so he sat down and leant his left elbow on the railing to look at them. They seemed unaware of his presence as he looked.

The woman was about sixty-five or seventy. He spoke to them but all that could be heard was the sound of his own breathing and then – then he recognised them. The old woman was Jess and the man was his beautiful boy but decades had passed. He spoke again but they were unable to hear him. All was silent but for the sound of his breathing and the tick, tick. All movements were slow and numbed as if this world were gripped by some terrible, partial paralysis. He looked at Watha. His grown up son, his boy, had a single tear rolling down his cheek. Watha slowly rested his cheek on his old mother's shoulder as he silently mouthed the words that Coleridge knew so well.

"'…Farewell, O Hiawatha. Farewell forever…'!"

Watha's face buckled then grimaced and he buried it and his grief into the breast of his stony-faced, unflinching, unemotional mother. He clung to her.

Coleridge called to them again, to tell them he was there but they couldn't hear and they wouldn't look and Watha, his son, wept. Coleridge wondered what could have happened to so upset his boy.

Coleridge looked out across the vast Hall but a light from behind him shot across the floor and cast his boy and wife into silhouette. It was too bright for a dark theatre and should have caused heads to turn but no one seemed to notice.

Coleridge turned and squinted into the brightness of it and a form appeared in the doorway. He shielded his eyes to see the outline of the person; a person distorted by light but even so, the frame seemed familiar. The stance was unmistakable. The size and build and the way the person moved was all too familiar but how could it be possible, he wondered as a joy filled him and he stood.

The light around the person started to fade and his features became more distinct – his thin, pale face, those large, dark eyes and floppy hair.

Coleridge was filled with such overwhelming happiness at seeing him again and put his hand out to him but William didn't take it. He just stood there, smiling kindly, smiling fondly.

After a little while, William turned to leave. Then, as the light began to burn as brightly as before, he looked over his shoulder at Coleridge one last time as brighter and brighter the light intensified, until it burnt Coleridge's eyes, and William dissolved back into it.

He pressed his eyes shut against the glare but tried to follow William through the door, but the numbness in his body seemed to drain away with the paralysis he'd felt. The light on his eyes, he started to feel his skin again. He felt the sheets under his chin and they were warm. The downy pillow under his head felt soft and familiar. He lifted his hand to shield his eyes from the dusty shaft of light that blazed across his pillow. His eyes were wet. He stretched and yawned where he lay, being careful not to wake Jess who slept on soundly beside him.

He rolled out and sat on the edge of his bed. The shard of bright, new April sunlight splintered between the gap in the curtains. He loved the month of April best of all and the birds were in fine voice that morning.

How wonderful it had been to see William again, he thought to himself, even if it had been just in a dream. And how wonderful it was that the joy he had felt would be carried through into the rest of that day and of the next and of the one after that. The word for it was, 'Wunderschon'.

Two hours later and the children had risen, washed and dressed and had left for school. Jess was busying herself in the kitchen and Coleridge had already completed a significant amount of work in his shed and was enjoying breakfast.

He gulped his coffee and buttered his cold toast. He put a dab of marmalade on the corner and crunched into it. The coffee made the marmalade taste even tastier and vice versa.

His fingers were stained with ink and smelt of paper. He could smell the daffodils in the vase on the table. Today was a big day. It was the day his Violin Concerto was to set sail for America and to the Stoeckels who had commissioned it for Maud.

The premiere date had been set long ago and it was due to be premiered in London later that same year of

1912, in the September. He had had ample time to complete the work but unfortunately the first version of the Violin Concerto had been returned to him as unsatisfactory. He had been deeply hurt. Maud Powell hadn't been happy with the main section that he had based on the slave tune he'd heard Ellen Stoeckel play on the last night of their festival nearly two years before.

They were the ones paying for the piece and if they didn't like it then he simply had to rewrite it rather than debate the issue, he had told Jess philosophically. He had given himself plenty of time to write it. He knew he had spent too long on it just for it to be rejected. He never dreamt it would be rejected. He hadn't left himself sufficient time for a re-write.

The amendments however, would have been so substantial, that he decided very early on that it would be far simpler and quicker to start again from scratch than to adapt a work already written, even if it did mean burning the candle at both ends to get it completed in time.

Anyway, it was done. The rewrite, that he had been afraid could never be completed in the time left to him, before the American premiere, had been completed; every part for every instrument had been written out by him by hand.

Composing was the part he loved but the bulk of the work was just copying, as Coleridge never utilised the services of a professional copyist.

All the parts had been copied and placed in sequence, each wrapped in tissue, in the new trunk bought for the purpose and as soon as the trunk had been filled, he would take each out again and double-check it. There was insufficient time for any more errors.

Three months should be enough time for the new Concerto to arrive and be adequately rehearsed. He knew that all his hard work would be rewarded and although very tired, and with a sharp aching in the back of his hand from non-stop weeks of writing, he was happy – he was very happy with the piece and the fact that he had met his deadline. He was very much looking forward to personally ensuring the safe passage of the piece.

He sipped his coffee, had another bite of marmalade toast and started to read a letter.

"How wonderful!" he called through to Jess, next door in the kitchen. "This man was in the chorus of a production of 'A Tale of Old Japan' in Shanghai!"

"Have we had the Stoeckels' cheque yet?" Jess asked.

She knew that payment was not due until the piece had been both received and approved by them and also that it hadn't even left the house yet.

"No." he said simply, then adding under his breath, "They're waiting for the rewrite. I hope to God Maud approves this time and that the Stoeckels like it."

"'Many Thousands Gone' does work better than 'Keep me from Sinking Down, Good Lord' – it's true," said Jess.

"I think so. I hope so."

"Look, Coleridge if you don't go now…."

"It's all packed. It's all there. I've checked the parts a million times."

He took a last, massive bite of toast and stood, taking a final gulp of coffee. He went out into the hall where his bag and the wooden trunk housing the precious Concerto patiently waited for him. He put his hat on.

"I've been thinking about 'Hiawatha'," he called as he put his arms through his coat sleeves. "The Royal Albert

Hall – a huge pageant. The chorus all dressed as squaws and braves, a huge backdrop and a ballet. Tree could direct it."

Jess appeared in the hallway wiping her hands on a small towel.

"Coleridge, you'll miss the boat!"

"I didn't say goodbye to the children."

"I told them not to disturb you. They were late for school. You'll be home again in no time."

He looked at her and blew her a kiss. She blew one back and smiled. His white gloves on, he wrestled the small trunk and bag through the open door.

The West Croydon Station porter had very kindly left a trolley outside Coleridge's front door to make the walk to the station that much easier. He had told Mr Taylor that it was really against regulations as it was station property, but that as it was him... and with a nod and a wink, it was there as promised. Coleridge loaded up and set off, on the twenty-five minute walk towards the station.

Coleridge bought an extra seat ticket so that his trunk could sit next to him on its end, rather than be put it in the luggage compartment. He didn't want to let the precious cargo out of his sight. The contents of the trunk had a personality and a life of its own, he had put his soul into it; he couldn't just put it in the luggage compartment, it didn't seem right.

The train set off and was on its way on what was one of the first of many perfect Spring days before Summer blistered in. After the English winter months, one awakes each morning hoping that it will be Spring and then, one morning, it suddenly is. It was hard to define how he knew it was Spring. Was it the warmth, the smell, the chirping of the happy birds? It was difficult to pin down but it was on that very singular day of the year, as his train cheerily chuffed its way towards town, that he knew Spring had arrived. Coleridge watched the world go by from his compartment window, making his way into town with a Violin Concerto as travelling companion. He crossed his knee and patted the trunk with a contented smile.

At Clapham Junction, he changed for the all-stations train to Southampton. The train was full of so many people who were to be making the same journey to America. Everyone was so excited and with such good reason. There was a certain amount of horseplay from some quarters on the train and so Coleridge was careful not to let the Concerto trunk very far from sight.

Children laughed happily in the train carriage and there was a couple in the row of seats just up ahead who were clearly just married. Perhaps they were emigrating. There was an elderly lady, rather wealthy-looking. He guessed she was visiting relatives there or possibly an American herself, returning home – who knows, he pondered happily.

It was a swift and very pleasant journey but the excited smiles on the people's faces grew a little more obvious as they approached the end of that leg of their journey. Once at Southampton, it was not very much more than a hop, skip and a jump down to the dock where a mass of passengers from Europe were already disembarking from the Belfast-built Nomadic and boarding the ship for the trans-Atlantic crossing.

A young porter offered to carry Coleridge's trunk up the gangplank and into the great liner but he had told the boy very kindly that although he would probably think him very foolish, he would rather put the trunk in stowage himself.

"Right you are, Sir."

A few minutes after the boy had arranged cover for his post, they were both in the bowels of the ship. Under the watchful eye of the amused young porter, Coleridge placed the trunk, making sure that it was securely fastened and safely sandwiched between two other trunks, both brand new and both very expensive.

Back on board some minutes later, Coleridge sent two telegrams from the onboard office. One was to the Stoeckels the other was to Jess. Hers read, simply, 'Wunderschon'. The man in the office had told him that his was the first passenger telegram to be sent.

There was not much else to do once the Concerto had been safely stowed below deck, except perhaps to spoil oneself with a leisurely promenade or a sit down in a deckchair before the ship disembarked. So a leisurely sit down it was.

He couldn't believe he was where he was. He stretched out his legs and crossed them at the ankles. He put his hands behind his head and occasionally he'd glance up to watch all the expectant, happy people bustling about, passing the time of day – the parasols, the children, the lovers, the wealthy and well-to-do, the normal and the everyday, the maids and valets, workers, the crew – all blissfully happy, sharing one common joy and all very eager for the off.

From his seat on deck, as the time neared, he couldn't see much of the dock, as every single passenger seemed to be on deck for the departure. People were waving and calling to friends and relatives on shore. The noise of the hat and hanky-waving crowd was both deafening and joyous. Coleridge smiled with a satisfied sigh from his comfy deck chair.

He looked at his watch. It wouldn't be long before the 'all ashore who are going ashore' and he tipped his hat over his eyes, smiling contentedly. On board that ship, where he'd once hoped he would be and which for just a few more moments would remain in the dock's maternal embrace; a magnificent and fat fledgling on the bunting and ticker tape-strewn occasion of her maiden voyage.

She had already made headlines all over the world, not least because of her sheer scale and engineering wizardry but also because of the marvellous technical and material advancements that made her unsinkable. She was also internationally recognised as the most luxurious and opulent liner there had ever been. But words and headlines were truly insufficient to do justice to the jewel in the crown of the White Star Line, Titanic.

CHAPTER 17

14th April 1912.

The news was met with that incapacitating mixture of bewilderment and horror that appears in the place of 'fight or flight' when what had been inconceivable, happens. With the greatest innovation, always came the greatest tragedy; with unimaginable glory came an unimaginable horror, with an 'advancement' an even greater regress. Never had there been a ship so magnificent and never had there been an accident so catastrophic. She had been lauded as 'unsinkable', but how quickly the cheers turned to jeers at such an unnatural arrogance. Never had nature been so challenged; never had fate been so tempted. The pride felt in Belfast, the city built to build her, turned overnight to abject dismay. The city was never to mention that ship's name again.

Coleridge had watched from the quayside as the doomed vessel full of excited souls set sail with his precious Violin Concerto, a work in which so much love and time and hope had been invested but all that paled into insignificance against the magnitude of the human horror.

He had neither the time nor the money to accompany his Concerto all the way to America; it had never been an option. But he could dream, he had told himself as he sunned himself from his deckchair watching the people pass by as he pretended, just for a few blissful moments, to be a fellow passenger. How sickeningly lame that innocent pleasure seemed after the event.

He could recall the faces of those he saw, especially those he had spoken to – that young, porter boy who had asked if he could help Coleridge with his trunk, the ladies and gentlemen he had tipped his hat to, those children running and laughing, that newly-wed couple on the train, that elderly lady – all of them gone forever. All of them drowned. His Violin Concerto, like all those people, and everything they had, whole family lines – gone forever. His Concerto, safe and snug in its trunk under a mile of inky-black and ice-cold water.

Everybody always remembered where they had been when they first heard the news that the Titanic had sunk. The mood at Gwen and Watha's school had been very sombre and all the children had been told to go back home almost as soon as they had arrived that morning. Hiawatha had gone to a friend's house leaving Gwen to make the short walk home alone.

She walked slowly and enjoyed the beautiful Spring day. Everywhere, the streets were quiet. It was a most peculiar day, no one ventured out unless it was unavoidable and a day of national mourning was declared.

Her father had been so happy when he had returned from Southampton and they had all enjoyed hearing how he cheekily stayed on deck until the very last minute. He had been so crushed when the first Concerto had been rejected but so pleased to be able to complete it for the second time and send it safely on its way, but when she opened the front door to her house that morning, the day the news broke, Gwen heard her parent's voices straight away and her father was inconsolable.

"Listen to me…" her mother was saying.

"All those people, Jess. Children; whole families. I saw them all."

"You can't think about that now."

Gwen closed the front door as silently as she could. Her parents were in their bedroom. She had never heard her father crying before.

"I can't do it all again."

"Coleridge…"

Gwen started to climb the stairs, stepping over the squeaky one. She didn't want her father to know she was home and could hear.

"Well I can't, can I – not in two months. It's just not possible. It's too much…."

At the top of the stairs, Gwen turned and stood outside her bedroom door for a moment. She wasn't meant to be there and she wasn't meant to hear. She didn't want her breathing to give away her presence and without a sound, she turned the handle to her room and opened it.

"You could have been on that ship."

"But in two months? You tell me how that can be done?"

Gwen stepped into her room and started to slowly close the door behind her.

"We could have lost you, you stupid man, but you were spared so that you could…."

"But you never listen to me, Jess. You never listen. You tell me how – in the time? Tell me how?"

"I don't know. But we haven't any money, Coleridge. You don't have a choice."

Gwen shut the door to her bedroom and sat on her bed as the muffled voices continued for another twenty minutes or so. From her room, she couldn't make out the words but that was right; she knew that the conversation wasn't meant for her ears. She waited there until the conversation had finished. She heard her father walking quickly down the stairs. She heard the front door open and then she heard it slam shut. A door had never been slammed in the house before. And then a silence descended upon the house, upon the whole nation.

Gwen had seen her father's eyes mist over before. Sometimes, when he was hearing or reading something very sad she saw it, or when he mentioned Uncle William. She had also seen tears stream down his face when he had been laughing, when something really tickled him.

He seemed so utterly crushed – so exhausted and overwhelmed. She had never known him to collapse under it all like this. She had never heard him slam the door and it all disturbed her world.

She wondered if the perception she held of her father, as being in some way indestructible and super-human, was not wholly accurate. What if he was really as frail and uncertain and frightened as she was? If that was the case, then what had led her to her faulty perception? Had he always been hiding from her how he really felt and who he really was? She might never have witnessed it if she hadn't been sent home from school early that day. What else hadn't she witnessed?

Coleridge cancelled the few engagements that it was possible to cancel. It was only a handful really and didn't release a significant amount of time but he cancelled them nevertheless and got straight back to work. There were many engagements however, that he could not cancel, that had paid in advance – and he resented the time spent away from composing, for what was then the third time, his Violin Concerto. And now it must be completed in a fraction of the time that he originally had.

The timescale was totally inadequate. He hated to rush composition as it would, no doubt, be substandard work and totally unsatisfactory. It was sure to be rejected, so why even begin again, he ranted in inner panic. He'd be reminded by Jess that he couldn't afford not to begin again and he knew that this was true. It just had to be finished on time and so he had to rush; there was no other option or choice to make.

He referred to the original notes he had made to try and recall what he had put down before and why. He worked like a maniac all through the day and through most of the night. He tried to focus on the separate chunks so as not to be overwhelmed by the scale of the task. He made a decision not to analyse anything as he went along, he just got on and did it. He didn't stop to reread or rewrite, he just wrote. He could always go back at the end if there was time. He just had to concentrate on pressing forward and getting on until the end.

A new trunk was delivered. He set time aside each day for copying work, copying as he went. He had never worked like that before. Normally, he would complete the one part and then the others, each in its turn until all were done. But this was like an advancing army of parts, advancing blind, all pressing forward and not one breaking rank. He was not to be disturbed. He would almost certainly not have time to double-check that all the parts were all there, so he had to be sure everything was right first time round. He kept checklists; he didn't have time to make mistakes. He couldn't afford to forget something so he had to go carefully. At the same time, he had to work quickly. He had to concentrate. He had to focus, to stay awake.

As one week and then another went by, Coleridge found himself falling further behind in the schedule he had made for himself and things seemed even more hopeless than ever. He extended his working day and did anything to wring even more time out of each day. He decided to stop copying as he went along and to focus solely on getting the piece composed. By the end of week three, the piece was completed and he became his own copyist.

After supper, he would go back to the shed to work and in the blink of an eye he would find that it was dawn. He copied every page of the music for each member of the orchestra. As one part was completed he would light a cigarette and smoke it as he checked off the part on his list. He aimed to have four parts copied per day. He normally managed three. The trunk was not even half full. He was gripped by panic whenever he stopped to think about it. To make up the time lost from the early weeks was not possible and to dwell on it paralysed him. It was better not to think about it, better by far to just press on.

He gripped the pen tightly and his inky fingers developed a dent in which his pen rested. Pain shot up across the back of his hand and up his arm from the constant writing. At the end of the day it would take a little longer for the pain to pass until eventually, the periods when he was not in pain narrowed to nothing but he pressed on and on and started to pile pain on pain. He could rest later. He couldn't stop. He knew that he might deeply regret any time with his feet up if he failed to meet the deadline. He would send Gwen or Watha out for more music parchment or ink when he ran out. He would go to bed for a few hours' sleep before getting back to the shed and picking up a fresh piece of parchment.

And so it went on – for over five weeks.

In the final days of May, and against all the odds, the Violin Concerto and all the parts were completed. Coleridge had lost some weight and his hair was noticeably greyer. His eyes had lost much of their sparkle. His sense of humour had all but deserted him and he didn't really seem to find enjoyment in things as he had done before. He never seemed to feel hungry and when he got to bed, although he got off alright, he found himself awakening earlier and earlier each morning.

Sometimes when he stood up too quickly, he felt his head swim for a moment. No one commented upon how tired he looked or how unhappy he seemed but he knew. He felt empty and spent and everything was too much. He felt tearful all the time and fought it.

It would be weeks until payment came through for the Concerto and so he knew he would have to return, straight away, to his normal work routine if he was to avoid actual financial ruin. They expected it of him anyway and besides, never had ruin moved closer in on him than then. Nothing ever seemed to slow down. The relentlessness only ever seemed to get worse and worse and the harder he worked, the less he seemed to gain and the more he seemed to lose.

Coleridge buttered the triangle of cold toast and put a dab of marmalade on the corner. He used to love marmalade toast with a cup of coffee in the morning. It was a simple but profound pleasure but he wasn't hungry that day and he didn't actually want it. He was going through the motions but without any pleasure or other emotional involvement. He had the newspaper open and although his eyes were reading it, he wasn't able to take any of it in.

He took a sip of coffee. He had spent the previous evening scanning each part, one last time, for any obvious errors. He found none but suspected that this just meant he hadn't spotted them rather than there being none to spot but he could do no more. It was finished, and in time, and this was quite an achievement but there was no pride. He had put everything neatly back in the new trunk, each part wrapped in tissue paper, but decided not to check it anymore. He didn't have fresh eyes and there wasn't any more time. He told himself that he just had to accept that he had done his best and that that would just have to do – that 'good enough' would have to be good enough on this one occasion.

"I told you you could do it," Jess told him from the kitchen as she distractedly rinsed the suds from her teacup, a distant smile fixed on her face. The money would soon be on its way from America. The teacup sparkled in the morning sunshine that knifed its way across the small kitchen. She yawned.

"I didn't sleep at all well last night. I think it might be time we got a new mattress, Coleridge."

"I didn't tell you, did I? I had a dream, a little while ago, in which I met William Hurlstone." He understood.

Jess stopped.

Her smile faded and turned as cloudy and tepid as the used dishwater in the sink. She put the teacup on the drainer. She turned and looked at him through the kitchen doorway but his eyes remained focussed on the blurred page of newspaper he wasn't reading – his voice, flat and devoid of feeling.

"We couldn't shake hands," he continued.

She couldn't take her eyes away from him.

"This means I shall die soon."

He bit his toast.

Jess wanted to say something but didn't know what to say. She just stared at him as he munched. It was as if some deep and unconscious thought had been channelled aloud but without his knowledge. She watched him from the doorway.

There was nothing to say.

He decided that this time, he would not travel with the trunk any further than he had to. So he left it on the platform at West Croydon Station for the porter to load onto the train, then turned straight around and went home. He hadn't even stopped to check that it was loaded.

Maud Powell and the Stoeckels' orchestra would have less than a week in which to rehearse the Violin Concerto before its American premiere. The morning following the premiere, it would start on its return journey to arrive just in time for the London premiere. Directly after this, it would be sent to the publishers. The London premiere date had been set at the outset and there was no room for manoeuvre so just as long as all things remained equal, the timescales should be feasible.

After leaving the trunk on the platform, Coleridge knew that unless he received a telegram from the Stoeckels to confirm safe receipt, the Concerto's return would almost certainly be the next contact he would have with them. He had sent a telegram in early May, reporting on his progress but had had no reply. So until the piece came back, he would not know if its first performance was well received or whether it had even been acceptable to the Stoeckels and Miss Powell; or if they had been so disappointed again that the event had been cancelled, the orchestra dismissed and his shame reported across the world. Once back in England again, the London Orchestra would have a few days to rehearse it.

Everything he touched, he told himself, was late despite his best efforts. The world seemed to conspire against him. Too much seemed to go wrong for it to be down to chance alone but he struggled on against it whilst just maintaining his mask of cheerfulness and normality. Events conspired against him and the more he successfully struggled against them, the tougher the next challenge seemed to become and so the struggling continued, increasing exponentially time on time and there was no one he could tell about it. Each had their expectations of him but each was unaware of any expectations other than their own. William had never had expectations of him. William would have listened.

Coleridge had grown used to the hole left in his life by William – a gap that nothing and no one could ever fill, it being William-shaped. It had become familiar to him over the years but the hurt the hole caused him was as deep and as raw as the day that William was ripped out of his world and since then, his world had started to unravel.

The Croydon Symphony Orchestra no longer played at the Croydon Grand and had not travelled anywhere to perform in years, neither had it made any money. Coleridge had been subsidising it out of his own pocket in the hope that it would one day return to its former glory – 'Glory is like a circle in the water, which never ceaseth to enlarge itself, until broad spreading, disperses to naught.'

It had proved increasingly difficult for him to retain the services of good musicians at the Croydon Symphony for very long. At that time, the orchestra was made up of amateurs, student amateurs, semi-professionals and retired professionals. The orchestra had been relegated to the hall of the Holy Trinity Church in South Norwood and in early June, the posters outside publicised the orchestra's final performance – a concert that, it was hoped, would pay the outstanding hall rental bills.

Coleridge and one of his students had set out the chairs but they had over-estimated the attendance. It turned out that less than half the seats were occupied. Tickets had been on sale in the post office for a week or so but Coleridge stood at the door in order to sell tickets to those who had not bought one beforehand.

In order to wait for latecomers, the concert started a little later than advertised, but no latecomers came. Coleridge asked the audience to fill the first few rows rather than sit dotted around the hall and they rather reluctantly did so. As they shuffled about he recalled the concerts that Colonel Walters used to organise for him, playing to a hall packed to bursting.

People had parted with their hard earned pennies to attend and even if it was just the hall of the Holy Trinity Church in South Norwood, Coleridge conducted with the same fervour as when he conducted elsewhere – like at the Convention Hall in Washington or at the Stoeckels' magnificent Music Shed, when he was the Black Mahler.

As he conducted, his eyes fell on each of the musicians he had assembled. The oboist's instrument was held together at the mouthpiece with a length of string. The timpanist, also the curate and not a natural musician by any stretch, scrutinised his music through cloudy pince-nez, in need of a good wipe. The orchestra pushed its way through the piece like a tired, old steam train straining up a steep incline.

Coleridge brought in the flute but when the flautist blew, his upper false teeth popped out slightly, making members of the audience both wince and smirk. The orchestra played on around the gap left by the flautist as he corrected himself.

The piece plodded towards its conclusion but the orchestra seemed to have too little steam left to get it across the finishing line. The timpanist sounded the cymbals a fraction too late and much too loud. This made the double-bass player jump and the old man's instrument slid across the floor a little way. He fumbled to save it but hit it in the neck, sending it skidding off the edge of the stage. Coleridge continued on as the old man mouthed, 'sorry' to him.

What they lacked in skill, Coleridge made up for in energy to get them over the line. He was determined that they would reach the end of the piece and he pushed them onwards but all together, they were far too heavy for him to carry. He mouthed to them to 'keep going – keep going' and eventually, they limped over the final bar.

Coleridge ushered them to stand and he turned and bowed to the flutter of polite applause, made more generous by relief. He didn't look any member of the audience in the eye and tried not to entertain the feeling of utter humiliation, which had never been so very far away that it couldn't sidle up at any time.

Before the applause had died down, he had put down his baton and walked up the aisle and out into the street. He normally tried to leave before the audience but never quite like this. He didn't look back. He was always the one to pick up the pieces but not this time. This time he had to walk away. He took off his conductor's jacket as he walked the short journey home, hoping as he went, that he would be able to jump onto a tram or hail an omnibus for part of the way.

That was the end of the Croydon Symphony Orchestra, a poor animal that should have died a natural death many years before but that had been kept alive artificially solely by Coleridge's monumental efforts. It is hard to weep for a death like that but his was an investment of time, energy, life and money. It never showed him the slightest return, not even out of courtesy. He had been entrusted with its care. He had been asked to. He had taken it in his arms and had fed it and nursed it, but the hopeless creature had withered before his eyes. It had been an unnatural act to try and keep it alive, driven by pride and selfishness. And now, it was enough. Enough.

Watha ran to the front door when he heard the letterbox flap and the ruffle of letters hit the mat. He walked slowly back towards his family in the dining room as he sifted the morning's post, trying to guess where they were from and what they contained. Watha liked breakfast time on Saturdays. They rarely ate breakfast together during the week so it made Saturday mornings all the more special. He gave the letters to his father. Gwen munched on her toast and jiggled her legs under the table. Jess refilled the coffee pot in the kitchen then returned to the table and to her half of the newspaper.

Watha told his father that one of the letters was from America so Coleridge opened that one first. He was waiting for some word and had been disappointed when no telegram came. He opened the letter. A cheque was clipped to the folded letter, a good and very welcome cheque. He held it between his thumb and index finger as he read.

"Thank God. It arrived. It's from Maud Powell," he said skipping to the end. Jess dabbed the corners of her mouth and took the cheque as he read on.

"Rehearsals started in haste. The Stoeckels are, 'very pleased and will be writing shortly'. Thank God." His eyes darted across the page and then they stopped and he smiled. "Maud says receiving the Concerto was 'like receiving a bouquet of flowers'."

"I'm sure," Jess sounded irritated. "Just as long as they send it all back in time for the first London performance. Don't do that Gwen!" she snapped. Gwen stopped jiggling.

Coleridge unfolded the newspaper cutting that the Stoeckels had also enclosed. His face broadened into a huge smile – the first in quite some time.

"Well I'm blowed! Do you remember Dr Miller?"

"Yes, and the thirteen pounds he wrote you I.O.U.'s for. You know, that's very nearly as much as you sold 'Hiawatha' for."

"Well, apparently he borrowed a pound from someone else and didn't return that either," Coleridge said as he skim-read. "But they tracked him down and Miller told him he didn't have the money to repay the pound and that everything he 'owned' was on hire. He didn't even have the money for the cost of a stamp."

Coleridge was silent for a moment, and then laughed.

"You will not believe this; he told the man that if he sent him ten shillings he'd able to post the pound on!" Jess chuckled as she tried to read her paper.

"Who's Dr Miller?" Watha asked.

"Well amazingly, or perhaps stupidly, the man sent Miller the ten shillings but – surprise, surprise, Miller vanished again!" Jess laughed as Coleridge read on in disbelief.

"Who's Dr Miller?"

"A vile, little confidence trickster who your father made friends with once," Jess told her boy. She sipped her coffee. Coleridge suddenly gasped.

"That's not the best bit. Listen – he's now on trial... for bigamy!" Jess snorted on her coffee and a bit of it came out of her nose.

"No!" she gasped as she dabbed her mouth again and nostrils. Watha and Gwen started giggling.

"Bigmy?" asked Gwen.

"Big – am – y," Coleridge pronounced for her. "A bigamist."

"What's that?"

"A very, very bad man" Jess told the girl. Coleridge folded the cutting and put it on the table, holding it there with his palm. He tried to look as serious as he could.

"Guess how many," he said. Jess thought for a moment. The children looked at her.

"Not more than two?"

Coleridge smiled and raised an eyebrow – there were to be no clues.

"Not three?"

"Four?" Gwen chimed in.

"He was marrying his fifth wife," Coleridge said. Jess clapped her hand and napkin over her mouth and snorted as she laughed.

"In church, I might add, in the sight of Almighty Whoever...." The children laughed at their parents' growing giggling fit as Coleridge continued. "...when wife number three suddenly appeared at the back and, walking down the aisle, declared – denouncing him in front of the entire congregation as 'a very... much married man'!" Coleridge threw back his head and laughed. He hadn't laughed so much in years and it felt good. "...Five wives! No wonder he was always so short of money!"

Jess threw her napkin at him as they all laughed. The strain of the past few months made the relief and the laughter all the more hysterical. Uncontrolled, tears streamed down his face as he counted up five fingers to Jess who giggled and snorted like a stuck pig and Watha and Gwennie laughed at their parents laughing.

It was a wonderful morning. It was one of those perfect times that would be remembered for years afterwards, especially by Watha and Gwen. They wouldn't be able to help themselves smile when they thought about their mother and father laughing so hard that day; that wonderful Saturday morning when they were all so happy and all so together.

CHAPTER 18

As the audience stood and made their way to the stalls, circle and dress circle bars and toilets, they chattered noisily about the second part of the 'Hiawatha' trilogy that they had just seen.

Snow had fallen from the ceiling of the Royal Albert Hall onto the audience and lake during 'The Death of Minnehaha'. All had been in semi-darkness. Only the end of Dr Sargent's baton had been illuminated for the orchestra and in the round, the dancers had acted out the scene. Minnehaha, in her finest ermine robes, had been brought in on the stretcher illuminated by fiery torches and had been laid, reverentially, on the pyre in the centre. The Indian braves then pulled from under the stretcher, white fabric, which was stretched to the edges of the round as the snow continued to fall, transforming the fertile prairie into a still and barren winter wasteland. The spectacle itself was breathtaking but it was the music, that wonderful music lamenting the loss of Hiawatha's love, that brought tears to the eyes of all who witnessed it.

Bunty found Avril sitting on some steps deep in the Hall's backstage labyrinth of tunnels and corridors that ran beneath the floors and up behind the organ. It was easy to be late, not so much because of the complexity of it all but because of the circular nature of the corridors and the scale. If you made a mistake, you might not have enough time to retrace your steps to rectify it.

Avril had found a quiet step which was far enough away but not so far that she could no longer hear the vast chorus whispering in the rooms assigned to them. A little further along was the room where the orchestra took their break. All of them only had about ten more minutes until they were due back in position for the overture and the final part – 'Hiawatha's Departure'.

"Avril?"

Avril looked up and smiled but Bunty looked serious.

"You're to see Dr Sargent."

"Now?" Avril asked nervously looking for a clue from Bunty as to what it was about.

"He said you're to come right away."

Avril stood. Bunty couldn't imagine what it was about. All that was clear to her was that Avril must be in a whole lot of trouble about something. It suddenly felt terribly inappropriate to be dressed as squaws.

They walked the long tunnels, like naughty school-girls about to get the ruler, up some steps and finally, towards Dr Sargent's room. This was right at the back of the hall, behind the auditorium and almost directly above the Artists' Entrance.

Outside his door, Bunty stood back a little as there was really only room for one to stand in front of the door and it was Avril he had asked for. Bunty encouraged her to knock with a 'let's get it over with' nod. Avril knocked.

"Come in," called a voice from behind the door.

Avril turned the knob. She stood there.

"Hello there," he said in a kindly voice.

Bunty was rather surprised at his tone. It wasn't what she had been expecting.

"We don't have long," he said to Avril. "You're to come with me."

Dr Sargent walked towards her and ushered her out as he checked his watch. Bunty flattened herself against the wall as they passed.

She watched them walk briskly in the direction of the Artists' Entrance. They turned the corner at the end. Around the corner and out of Bunty's sight, Dr Sargent took Avril's hand.

She didn't know where she was being taken but those words 'we don't have long. You're to come with me' rang in Avril's ears. Someone else had said those words to her many years before. In fact it had been exactly twenty-four years earlier, in 1908, when Avril was five. She had replayed the memory many times wondering if it was real or just a five-year-old's imagination that had created it, but deep down she knew it was a real memory – horribly real.

"We don't have long. You're to come with me," Avril had been told that morning. A small, packed overnight bag had appeared by her side. There had been no discussion or warning about the trip. She had taken the train with her mother. Later, they made a connection to somewhere near a place called, Northampton.

It was a fast train and they arrived at a quiet village in the mid-morning. A pony and trap was waiting for them. The driver jumped down and lifted the little girl up. She had asked to sit up front, next to him and this had been allowed.

It was lovely being in the countryside but when she asked where they were going, she was given no answer. It wasn't a very long journey and quite soon the trap was making its way up a long avenue lined on both sides with enormous poplars. There were fields on either side and in the distance a large and stately, sandstone pile loomed. The toothy turrets and gothic style made the house look more like a castle than a house.

"You like rabbits?" The driver had said to her as he manoeuvred the pony and trap around the potholes in the road. She nodded.

"Well there's a warren over there," he said, pointing, "and a foxes' lair down here."

She smiled up him but he was silhouetted against the sun. She couldn't see him clearly. He touched her on the head and ruffled her reddy-brown curls.

As they neared the house, she saw a scarecrow. Rooks cawed in the trees and a long way off, possibly behind the stately house, peacocks cried out. Standing in front of the great house was a very pretty lady with her arms folded. She walked towards the carriage as it pulled up in the parking area built to accommodate a great many visitors at any one time. She was smiling and greeted them warmly. The driver lifted the child down from her seat. The lady was in her late twenties. She knelt down in front of little Avril and parted her fringe so that she could see her freckly face properly.

"Hello dear," the lady said.

"Hello."

They passed the porch pillars and through the arched, dark-wood, double-doors into a circular entrance hall. A large staircase dominated as it gracefully spiralled upwards. The floor was of black and cream marble tiles. A splendid mirror in a gold, rococo setting stood over the fireplace. To the right was a doorway to an enormous room full of books and a great many musical instruments. At the other end of the vast room was a doorway to another spacious room which looked, from that distance, to be a bit cosier.

A fire crackled and echoed in the hall fireplace there. At the bottom of the stairs where they stood, was a red, two-seater sofa with gold-leaf arms and legs. The lady sat Avril, still in her coat, on this.

"You'll be alright here for a moment won't you? Of course you will, darling."

The lady smiled at her, then the two women walked to the distant but cosy room. Avril's little legs stuck out parallel to the floor. She put her hands in her lap as she waited patiently, her overnight bag on the floor next to her.

She could hear them talking in hushed voices in the distant room but couldn't hear all the words, just the odd one here or there. The women's hushed voices echoed in the otherwise silent house. She heard one of them say 'finalise' and a little later the other, her mother, had said 'very well-behaved'. The fire crackled and echoed. And then she heard another word, one she hadn't heard before. She didn't understand it – 'adoption'.

She looked at her toes. Her shoes were very shiny indeed. A man joined the two women. Avril looked through the large hall doors to the cosy room at the end to see him shaking Mummy's hand. Avril looked at her shiny toes again and then heard footsteps. All three grown-ups were coming back.

The man was very handsome. He had a splendid moustache that was pinched at the ends and twisted with a slight curl. His hair was dark and greased flat but his eyes were crystal blue and twinkled. He had a dimple in his chin and dimples in his cheeks when he smiled. He took great, big steps towards her and lifted her up high.

He gave her a squeeze. He was very nice. His shirt and collar smelt clean and his cheek had a little cologne on it. He held her sideways against his chest.

"How would you like to live in a beautiful house like this, then eh?" he asked.

The three grown-ups stood in front of the majestic mirror. The pretty lady smiled sweetly at the child in her husband's arms, but Avril didn't understand.

She looked into the mirror at the backs of the grown-ups' heads. She wanted to go home but it was too far away – it had taken hours to get there. They seemed to be very nice but she just wanted to go home. Her mother noticed her looking over their shoulders and into the mirror rather than at them, so she turned around and spoke to her daughter's reflection.

"This is to be your new father, Gwendolen."

The little girl's eyes squeezed out great, big tears and her face flushed hot and red. Her mouth quivered and twisted, opening as she cried.

"How would you like to have me for your father?" asked the kind man.

The little girl sucked in massive gasps of air and cried and wailed her heart out.

"I want Daddy! I never said goodbye. I want to see Daddy!" she wailed in inconsolable disbelief – in not understanding and for being so far from home and her father. She screamed and she sobbed. She didn't hear the rest of the conversation nor would she be able to remember much else of that day.

Her mother had told her not to speak of it but Daddy had known that something was wrong with his little 'Shuh-Shuh-Gah'. She had been listening to him play the piano very late that night when she should have been fast asleep. She cherished every single moment with her father but she couldn't tell him what had happened – she couldn't tell him that Mummy had wanted to leave her with those strangers.

"Why am I telling you this? Avril suddenly asked Dr Sargent. They were standing at the top of the stairs that led down to the Artist's Entrance. Dr Sargent stared at her in disbelief. "What did you ask me?"

She looked down the stairs sadly. Someone was standing in the street the other side of the frosted glass-panelled door. They waited for a moment.

"Anyway, I was so upset," she told him, the anger and sadness still so raw all those years later. "So hurt and I sobbed so bitterly that I suppose they decided not to go ahead with it. I never asked her why she wanted to get rid of me and she never told me. My father never knew."

"I had no idea," said Dr Sargent.

"Perhaps she wanted to make me into a great artist like him. Perhaps she thought that you make an artist by abandoning them as a child just as he'd been left. I honestly don't know what she was thinking. I've given up driving myself mad trying to work out why. All I do know is that he knew nothing about it and would never have agreed to it if he had."

She looked down at the person in the street and wondered for the first time who it could be that Dr Sargent had brought her there to meet. It was then that Avril remembered what he had asked her and that had released that torrent of sad memory. He had asked her about her name.

"The choice of name, Gwendolen, was hers," Avril said.

She hung her head as she felt her lip begin to quiver out of control.

"And so that had to go. I've been having some help in dealing with things, you understand. She did some other things to me too – later on as I grew up. I won't go into it all. Anyway, as part of the recovery, we came to the conclusion, the doctor and I, that it might be an idea to change my name. My father used to call me 'Shuh-Shuh-Gah', the little heron from the poem, but I couldn't call myself that. His favourite month was April, he often said so, so I chose Avril. You know, she wasn't even going to let me say goodbye to him. She didn't then and she didn't … she didn't let me say goodbye to him that other time."

She looked up into Dr Sargent's eyes.

Dr Sargent said, "You do know that he… is here, don't you? He's here tonight so that you can say good-bye to him properly – so that we all can. So that we can all say 'thank you'."

She smiled, nodding, and a tear rolled out. Dr Sargent kissed her head and she dabbed her sticky, pink and puffy eyes dry.

"Now, you have less than five minutes," he said to his young friend. He squeezed her shoulder and left her alone for the person who was waiting outside.

She took a deep breath and started to walk down the stairs. She didn't have long – the third and final act was about to start. She saw the figure standing outside the Artists' Entrance door through the frosted glass and then the figure suddenly receded. The figure started to leave.

Avril quickened her pace down the steps. At the bottom, on the left, was a thin counter and window into the caretaker's office. Avril glanced at him as she passed.

He nodded his head towards the person outside, who was walking away from the door.

Avril stepped out into the balmy, August night. The person who had been waiting had walked out of the lamplight; then out in the dark, Avril heard the footsteps stop. She waited.

She heard the person turn and slowly walk back towards the door. The light illuminated the woman's feet first, then her ankles and then she stepped fully into the lamplight and stopped for a moment, holding her bag close to her – standing a little way from Avril.

It was the old lady who had been staring at her and Bunty from across the way that morning. She stepped closer.

"It is you isn't it?" she asked. Avril nodded.

"I knew it!" the old woman said in triumph.

Avril suddenly felt unsure of herself – not knowing who the old lady was or what she wanted with her or even if she was the 'you' the old lady had meant. She couldn't help her puzzlement from expressing itself on her brow so the old lady explained.

"I knew you would be busy at the end – people to see and all that, so I hope you don't mind me asking to see you now. It's going wonderfully well, by the way – absolutely thrilling, but always little sad."

Avril smiled, still not understanding.

"Anyway, I know you don't have long so I'll be very quick, I promise."

The old lady noticed then that Avril's eyes were pink and swollen from crying. She suddenly felt a pang as if she were intruding. The girl had her father's eyes, sure enough. The old lady started rapidly rummaging inside her bag.

"Right, well to get to the point I was turning out some old things and... isn't it funny how you find things, and..." She took out the yellowing piece of paper, neatly folded. She looked at it fondly for a moment. "It's funny the things that you keep. ...It's funny the things that mean so much. ...Little things."

She looked deep into Avril's eyes and smiled. She held the paper out for Avril to take.

"I've come to give you this. I've had it an awful long time but... I think that now it must really belong to you. It's from your father."

Avril took the piece of paper and slowly turned it in her hands, as the old lady continued.

"Such a perfectionist – a wonderful man. He threw that away because it wouldn't meet with their professor's approval, you know. He wanted so much to please everyone all the time. He tried so very hard. He threw it away into the fireplace but my brother... my brother William... well, I think he liked it so much that he rescued it and Coleridge, your father I mean, he let him keep it."

"Uncle William," Avril said sadly. "I remember when he died. My father missed him terribly."

She slowly started to unfold the paper.

"And William gave it to me – all such an awful long time ago now, I'm afraid. I was such a fan of your father's, you see. Years after they graduated I bumped into him in Bournemouth, he was conducting there. I believe he had just returned from one of his American visits, and I asked him to sign it for me.... Silly really but he was so very, very famous and as I say, I was such a fan. We all were. Anyway, he was very kind to me, very gracious and...."

Avril looked at the paper as she opened it. She recognised her father's writing instantly.

"It's for you – it's from him. You'll understand."

Avril read.

'To the very special sister of a very special brother, I leave this little scrap of music, with all my love, always.'

Avril's hand shook slightly. The old lady smiled at her kindly. Avril put her hand to her mouth.

"There, you see," Judith said as a gentle peace swept over her; the last loose end now neatly tied.

Avril folded the paper and thanked her. She told Judith that she had to get back as the final act was about to start, but asked her to wait at the end so that they could talk properly. Avril kissed her powdery, pink tissue cheek.

Just before going back in, Avril turned and called to her once again just as she was disappearing into the night.

"You will wait at the end, wont you? Promise me...."

William's sister gave a cheery, little wave and was gone.

Back inside, the caretaker told Avril the three minute bell had already sounded for the final act. She thanked him and started to climb the stairs.

She could almost feel the warmth from her father's smile on her face. She could almost feel him holding her hand protectively just as he did when they walked together when she was a child. She felt like a child again. She held the precious page of musical parchment as she climbed the steps. She had never had such a strong feeling of his presence before, since his passing.

The yellowed paper was curled at the edges like flower petals – like the petals of that single, yellow chrysanthemum plucked from the bunch for her to carry as she and her father happily walked home together that hot day in late August 1912 – that last day.

CHAPTER 19

Gwen skipped along to keep up with him. His warm hand held hers protectively. In her other hand, Gwen held a large, sherbety-yellow chrysanthemum that must have had a thousand petals on it, all gathered up into one fresh and perfect sun-burst that nodded as she walked.

Coleridge held his rolled-up paper, the Croydon Guardian, under his arm and the pompous bunch of blooms, soggily wrapped up in paper in his hand.

The crystalline sap had risen in the trees months before and he had a strange mixture of feelings; the joy at spending time with his little girl on such a beautiful day, but at the same time, some anxiety. Anxious because the Violin Concerto still hadn't been returned from America and rehearsals for the London premiere were due to start the following week.

The breezeless air was full of the scent of freshly cut but rather parched lawns and aromatic, hedge conifers against a chewy tarmac smell that came off the hot road and pavement. They walked back from the newsagents on the corner of Waddon Road. In the distance a steam train was heard pulling into West Croydon Station and a tram hummed and rang its way down the London Road as horses clopped and cartwheels turned. They were nearly home.

Coleridge had returned from Birmingham a few days earlier. The date was 28th August 1912, not two weeks since Coleridge's birthday.

The happy pair turned into St Leonard's Road, and were soon climbing the steps to the front door of the white house on the end, the one with the piano in its side-garden shed.

Coleridge's keys rattled against the door as he unlocked it. Gwen ran straight up the stairs to her room with her chrysanthemum. He put his hat and white gloves on the side and turned to go into the dining room. He stood in the doorway for a moment and looked at Jessie in the kitchen. She must have heard him come in but didn't say anything. He opened up his newspaper on the table and remained standing as he flicked over the pages. At last, Jess wiped her hands dry to acknowledge him. He looked up at her and handed her the flowers.

"Aren't they lovely?" he said.

Jess looked puzzled. She had an awful lot to do that day and didn't feel that he had been particularly helpful so far.

"Thank you," she sighed as she took the flowers. She put a vase in the sink and started to unwrap the paper on the draining board. She filled the vase and started trimming off the stem bottoms and unwanted leaves. Coleridge stopped turning the pages.

"It's in!" he said triumphantly.

"These are beautiful," said Jess, beginning to fall for the flowers just as Coleridge and Gwen had done when they first saw them, the last bunch in the bucket, outside the newsagents.

"Did you hear? The Croydon Guardian has printed my letter. I don't believe it," he said with a chuckle.

"Which letter?"

"I wrote a reply to that article the vicar from the Purley Debating Society wrote, the one about The Negro Problem in North America." He folded the paper over. "Listen," and still standing, he read aloud from the Guardian.

"It is amazing that grown-up, and presumably educated people, can listen to such primitive and ignorant nonsense-mongers; to men who are without vision, utterly incapable of penetrating beneath the surface of things. No one realises more than I that coloured people have not yet taken their place in the scheme of things, but to say that they never will is arrogant rubbish, and an insult to God in whom they profess to believe. I personally know hundreds of men and women of Negro blood who have already made their mark in the world, and this is only the beginning. I might suggest that the Purley Circle engage someone to lecture on Alexander Dumas, a rather well known author, I fancy, who had more than a drop of Negro blood in him. Who is there who has not read and loved his Dumas? And what about Poushkin, the poet? And the Creole Elizabeth Barrett Browning and Du Bois whose Souls of Black Folk was hailed by James Payne as the greatest book that had come out of the United States for 50 years?

"I mention these because not only are they distinguished people, but people of colossal genius. The fact is that there is an appalling amount of ignorance amongst people regarding the Negro and his doings. If the Purley lecturer (I forget his name, and am away from home, the Birmingham people having engaged me to direct something that has come straight out of my ill-formed skull) – if the vicar is right, then let us at once and for ever stop the humbug of missions to darkest Africa, and let the clergy stop calling their congregations 'dear brethren', at any rate whenever a black man happens to be in the church. Let us change our prayer books, our bibles and everything pertaining to Christianity and be honest.

"Personally, I consider myself the equal of any white man who ever lived, and no one could change me in that respect – on the other hand, no man reverences worth more than I, irrespective of colour and creed. May I further remind the lecturer that really great people always see the best in others? It is the little man who looks for the worst – and finds it. It is a peculiar thing that almost without exception all the most distinguished, white men have been favourably disposed towards their black brethren. No English person was ever more courteous to me than a certain member of our own English Royal Family and no American more so than President Roosevelt. It was an arrogant 'little' white man, who dared to say to the great Dumas, 'and I hear you actually have Negro blood in you!' 'Yes', said the witty writer; 'my father was a Mulatto, his father a Negro, and his father a monkey. My ancestry begins where yours ends!' Somehow I always manage to remember that wonderful answer when I meet a certain type of white man (a type, thank goodness! as far removed from the best as the Poles are from each other) and the remembrance of it makes me feel quite happy – wickedly happy, in fact!"

Coleridge had a cheeky smirk on his face as he looked up. He couldn't quite believe that they had actually published it. He would have to send a copy to Kathleen – she'd love it.

Jess stood in the doorway to the kitchen in silence. He couldn't read her expression. He looked down at the page of text and for a moment it didn't quite come into focus. Looking up had made him feel slightly dizzy. He had felt a little under the weather all morning in fact. His collar felt hot, tight and constricting and he ran his finger around the inside to stretch it a bit. He splayed his fingers on the mahogany table and closed his eyes for a moment. He closed his eyes and steadied himself. He closed his eyes and he saw the mountain range and its cool breeze refreshed him.

High on the mountaintop in the Land of the Dakotahs, the handsome brave looked out across the land, his valley and the great lake. The waters lapped at the pebbly margin and the coral and turquoise clouds shone in the bluey-green sky, illuminated by the fiery, setting sun. Then he saw the others – all the others. Far away, in the distance and from every corner of the land, came together all the tribes. All the tribes that had once been at war with each other but whom Hiawatha had united together in peace as one great people – all were coming to that place by the water's edge to honour him.

The tribes assembled in their thousands, by the edge of the great lake – the Maklak, the Absaroke or 'Crow', the Yavapai 'people of the sun', the Dakotah and Lakotah Sioux, the war-like Pekwatawog, the Blackfoot, the Umoh'hon (which means 'against the current'), the gentle and peace-loving Hopi people, the Cheyenne, the Delawares, the Pawnees and Ojibways, the Inuit from the Land of the White Rabbit, the Dene and the Cree, the Iroquois from the swamplands, the Chippewa and the Klickitat from beyond the mountains, the Shawnee, the Mohawk, the Seminole and Muskogee, the fearsome Apache, the Comanche and the Cherokee – all. All the tribes; with their squabbles and shaky alliances, conflicts, gripes, vengeances and grievances all left far behind them. These tribes, who had laid down their arms, held against each other from time immemorial, now met in peace, forgiveness and trust to honour the man who had united them – meeting there in the sure knowledge that a respect that is demanded is not a respect at all but fear mistaken for respect. Meeting there in the knowledge that true respect does not come from what a person says but from what a person does and how he acts – acting from his unshakable and noble values. Meeting there in the knowledge that true respect is earned and that the great man they came to honour had more than earned their respect in this way.

All the united tribes and all the people of those tribes, all dressed in the dress of their people – adorned with the porcupine breastplates, beading and feathered head-dresses of their tribes – all gathered by the edge of the lake and all looking to this simple, strong and gentle man standing on the mountain who had so changed their lives and the lives of the generations to come.

His hands lifted towards the sun, both palms spread out to catch it. He raised his strong arms and between his parted fingers, fell the sunshine on his features and flecked with light his naked, brown shoulders, as light flecks an oak-tree through rifted leaves and branches. The thousand, thousand strong let out a deafening cry and drums were beaten, as ancient thunder in the mountains, in thanksgiving to this man, the son of the Mudjekee'wis, the West Wind, sent by the Great Spirit and Master of Life, the Gitche Man'ito – this humble hero who had given so much and who had asked for so little, who had toiled and suffered with them and now, on the pebbly shallows of that inland sea, waited by a single bark canoe for his final journey.

Coleridge opened his eyes.

"Did you hear?" he asked her.

"Yes. Isn't it wonderful," she said, sounding rather disinterested, as she passed through the dining room with the vase of chrysanths. Coleridge started to pull out a chair.

"No, you can't sit down," she said. "You'll miss your train."

Coleridge put the chair back under the table. He felt slightly queasy and really just wanted to sit down but he knew she was right and that he ought to go. He had a number of students in Crystal Palace to teach that afternoon.

In the hall, he put his hat and gloves back on, despite the August heat. He picked up his cane and his case. He opened the front door. Gwennie ran down the stairs holding her doll by the arm and ran straight into the front room where Jess was. He saw Jess place the vase on the mantelpiece and then step back to see if that was the place for them or not. He didn't say anything to Jess but to him, the flowers looked a little top-heavy up on the mantle. She really had no taste or discernment at all, he thought with a loving smile as he stepped outside.

He walked down the steps to the road and towards the end. He turned left into Warrington Street, then right onto the Epsom Road. He crossed at the off-kilter crossroads and walked up Waddon New Road. He slowed, partly because of the oppressive heat and lack of cool air but partly also because he was nearing the spot where he had lived as a student all those years before. He passed it every day but that particular day was different. It suddenly dawned on him that he had never lived anywhere that was more than a stone's throw from this small corner of Croydon, south of London. He had walked past his old rooms many times before but seldom thought much of it but as he approached, from the other side of the road, he slowed.

He saw the curtains twitch in what had once been his room – the room where he had composed 'Hiawatha's Wedding Feast'. He stopped but looked straight ahead. He didn't have to look back at his old rooms to know that she was standing on the step outside the door. He heard the landlady – what was her name again? – opening the door, leaving it open for the young composer and the girl on the doorstep. He heard the rap on his door as whatever her name was started back up the stairs. Then the boy came out – young and not so very bad looking and composing for the fun of it. What wisdom pearls he could give the boy if he could and if he thought for one moment they would be believed. And there she was on the doorstep, with his Musical Times, Miss Jessie Fleetwood-Walmisely – asking if he'd accompany her with some rather spurious Schubert duets.

She'd told him that she'd miss seeing him once he graduated. Then she had walked away. He had pretended he was going somewhere, but had just walked around the block and then returned home, he remembered – all those years ago.

Coleridge carried on up Waddon New Road, across and up Ruskin Road. A motorcar sped past and croaked its horn at him as he crossed London Road. It had made him jump. He walked to the ticket office at West Croydon Station. It was shady there.

"Crystal Palace, please," Coleridge said as he put the exact money on the brass plate under the tickets window.

"Coming back today, Sir?"

"Yes, please."

Coleridge climbed the white wooden steps over the tracks, over the footbridge to the other platform. He walked along a little way and turned to face the few people lined on the platform opposite. They stared. He looked at his watch. It was 1.28pm.

What little air there was, smelt of coal and soot and tarmac. He took a deep drink of the hot, still air and straightened his back as his head started to swim again. He looked at the people opposite.

There was a silence, a profound silence. He couldn't hear the sound of the roads or anything. He was alone on his platform. The people opposite were waiting for the Victoria train. They were white and they were staring at him and nothing moved for an age; broken or unwound automata peopled this world. They stared at him in the stillness. He felt uncomfortable. He felt faint but didn't want to show it – hot, airless, silent and still.

He looked up the track, with the heat coming off the hot steel and way off into the wobbly distance. There was no sign of the train. He looked the other way – nothing, nothing either way.

Beads of cold sweat started to form on his brow.

He looked at his watch. It was still 1.28. It hadn't changed. It didn't tick. The people stared and still, nothing moved.

He could hear the sound of the Victoria train far away, approaching the other platform. Coleridge took off a glove and took out his handkerchief to dab his brow. He tapped the glass front to his watch with a fingernail.

The sound of the train grew louder. He ran his finger around the inside of his collar again. It was moist or was it his finger that was wet? He heard the chuffing of steam as the train approached and slowed. He stuffed his hanky back into his pocket. He heard the growing sound of the brakes gently being applied, gently screeching and his head swam.

He dropped his cane and it clattered on the platform like a baton. The brakes screeched. He turned to pick it up – the train pulling in and cutting him off from the people opposite, the steam and grating brakes screaming. He stooped to pick up his cane but his legs folded underneath him and he fell as the train finally stopped.

He had awoken from unconsciousness almost immediately, his cheek on the hot tarmac of the platform. He felt some pain in his body from where he had landed. He began to get up. His body ached.

He checked his watch. It was 1.30pm. He looked up. The Crystal Palace train was already there. He must have been unconscious when it pulled in. He struggled to get up but the whistle sounded. People stared at him from the windows of his train as he struggled to stand but the train was already pulling out. No one helped him. They stared.

Unsteadily, he stood. He had taken a layer of skin off each knee and gone through the trousers. He had taken a lot of skin off the palm and wrist of his right hand. He had a graze above his eye and on the end of his nose. His wounds, especially those to his face, bled. They were sore and covered with hot, black grit. His students would wonder where he was but he knew he had no option but to struggle home. He wouldn't be able to teach in that state. He had a fever.

Gwen was putting a different outfit on her doll when she heard the front door open. She heard the hat being placed on the table and the cane in the stand and then there was the familiar pause while the gloves came off but instead of coming into the front room, she heard the sound of her father stumbling up the stairs. She waited for a moment and then put her head through the doorway. She saw her father reach the landing and turn towards her parents' bedroom.

"Gwennie," he moaned quietly as he disappeared out of sight. Gwen, holding her dolly by the arm, ran up the stairs and straight into the bedroom. Her father was lying face down on the bed at an angle. His shoes were on and he was quietly crying, unaware that she was even there.

Gwen turned in panic and ran down the stairs two at a time. She ran through the dining room doorway and into the kitchen.

"Father wants you," she said to her mother frantically.

Jess was polishing the best tea service for the visitor she was expecting later that afternoon.

"Father is ill. He wants you quickly."

Jess looked at Gwen. There was a look of horror on the little girl's face that she had never seen before. Something in the pit of Jess's stomach dropped and turned. She pushed passed the little girl and hurried up the stairs.

Gwen sat on the bottom step of the stairs, with her doll on her lap and didn't move. She didn't move for the rest of the day, despite all the comings and goings. First, Coleridge's mother, Mrs Evans – or 'Grannie' to Watha and Gwen, had arrived and had promptly left to telegraph to cancel Jessie's visitors. Another neighbour had gone to fetch the doctor and collect Watha who was at a friend's house. Lots of other people had come and gone too but Gwen didn't stray from her step.

Late that afternoon, around teatime, Grannie was standing in the hall with her hat and coat on and with her arm around Watha's waist. There was a knock on the front door. Jess appeared at the top of the stairs like a ghost. The depth of her concern was marked by her efforts to conceal it. She descended the stairs like Lady Alice at a weekend house party. She was marble. She had a look of stony, serenity on her face and it looked hideously out of place – a look that should be reserved only for the monumental angels of Highgate Cemetery or Bandon Hill. She opened the front door expecting their normal family doctor.

"I'm afraid Dr Collard is on his rounds," said the young man on the doorstep. No disappointment showed on her face. Nothing would ever show itself on her face again. She would never remove the mask of granite purity that she assumed that day.

"Dr Duncan, do come in, won't you?"

She led him up the stairs, Coleridge's own mother and her children no longer visible to her.

"But I thought I heard you were getting married tomorrow," she went on as they disappeared from sight at the top of the stairs.

"Come on children. Hats and coats," said Grannie with weighty reluctance. Inside she was raging but again, she couldn't show it for the sake of the children. No matter how much she disliked Jess, she would never undermine her decisions or motherhood – not in front of her own children.

"Hat and coat, Gwennie, please."

"But I haven't said goodbye," said Gwen.

"Your mother says that children are not wanted when people are unwell, now pop your coat and hat on, there's a good girl."

The children would spend that night, and as it turned out, the next few nights, staying with their grandmother a short walk away.

Coleridge was covered with one sheet and a very thin blanket. There was a bowl on the floor. His condition had grown steadily worse since he had arrived home. He was sweating profusely. The fire was burning in the grate and yet he still complained of feeling cold. He had heard the voices of the people on the stairs as Jess and the doctor arrived so had straightened his hair up a bit with the flat of his hand. The door had opened slowly so as not to wake him in case he was asleep and Dr Duncan and Jess came in.

"She shouldn't have bothered you, Dr Duncan. It's just a bilious attack. I generally have one once a year."

That night, Coleridge drifted in and out of sleep, and an unconsciousness that was not sleep, and was awoken the next morning, feeling more tired than he had ever felt in his life. He was awoken by the sound of a trunk being dragged up the stairs.

The trunk clunked against each step as it was dragged. At the top of the stairs, he heard it being dragged into another room and the door close. It must be the Violin Concerto back from the Stoeckels, he thought, with the relief of that particular weight lifting.

Jess left the trunk in the upstairs music room next to Gwen's. She had spent that night in Watha's room but hadn't slept much. Instead of trying to force sleep, she had occupied herself for most of the night by trying to tidy up a bit and organise the upstairs music room. In the process, she had found some pieces; old waltzes, sketches, songs and quartets mainly. Things he had penned in a morning, never to return to. She had put all the finished but unsigned ones on the side.

She looked around the room. It was very tidy – too tidy. Coleridge was tidy when he worked, but never that tidy. It was then that she realised that she had ruined his room. It wasn't him anymore; no longer a place of work, it was pristine. She had managed to remove all trace of Coleridge from it. It looked packed up for a house move, especially with the trunk on the floor. She knew he would be upset with her if he saw it now.

She picked up the stack of finished pieces from the edge of the piano stool and closed the door behind her. A terrible thought shot across her mind but she forced it out and papered over the crack as quickly as it had entered.

Dr Duncan had called it pneumonia, most probably brought on by exhaustion and overwork but he was such a young and inexperienced doctor, she told herself, she was sure it wasn't serious. Dr Duncan had said that Coleridge was at a critical stage and that a close eye should be kept on him for a few days as things could go either way. Of course she would do so, she had told him, but she told herself that Dr Collard would tell her it was just a fever – just a fever and nothing more, she was sure – that's what Dr Collard would say.

She slowly opened the door to their bedroom not wanting to wake him, not really thinking that she proba-bly already had with all that trunk-clunking up the stairs. He looked at her as she came in. He was drained of all energy. He smiled at her with his eyes only. She smiled back. She moved his glass of water and put the pieces of music on his bedside table as she sat on the edge of his bed.

"How do you feel today?"

"Actually, I feel much better."

"That's good."

She stood again and opened the curtains wide and the window an inch. The stale air in the room was thick with the smell of sickness.

"The Concerto has come back," she said, still almost whispering.

"Thank God. What's the date today?"

"Don't worry. There's plenty of time. Can you believe it – they sent it to the wrong address! That's why it took so long. On top of everything else!"

She looked at him. He was too tired to talk. She didn't know what to say and a one-way conversation promised to be uncomfortable and would inevitably sound trivial.

"That's why it took so long... can you believe it?" she repeated, weakly. "It's in the next room. I'll check the parts this afternoon."

"I wish I could drill a hole through the wall so that we could do it together."

"I could bring it in here, if you like," she said.

She moved with new purpose to the door.

"What are those?" He asked about the papers she had placed on the bedside table.

"Oh," she said, picking up the music. "I was going to check. They're unsigned most of them. I was just tidying up."

She put them down and moved to the door again.

"Jess...?"

She turned to him.

"Would you like me to sign them for you?"

She stopped in the doorway for a moment and looked at him. His eyes were closed. She could pretend she had already left the room, she thought. She could pretend she hadn't heard him. Silently she left.

Coleridge opened his eyes and reached for the papers. He opened the drawer of the bedside table, took out a pen and began to sign each of the pieces.

Jess dragged the trunk out of the upstairs music room across the landing and into their bedroom. She undid the buckles and opened it up when the front doorbell rang. She left the trunk and hurried out again and down the stairs to the door, straightening the dress she had worn a day or two too long as she went. She opened the door to Dr Duncan. He had promised to drop by that morning. She hadn't told him that he shouldn't trouble himself and so, there he was in his top hat, black tie and tails.

"Dr Duncan!"

"Don't worry. The wedding isn't until twelve. Anyway, she'll keep!"

Coleridge had finished signing. That, and quickly combing his hair for the visitor, had taken some effort. He felt so sick, so tired. As the door to his room was opening, he managed to hide the comb under the covers.

"Good morning, Dr Duncan," Coleridge said trying to sound as breezy as possible. The room looked a mess with the trunk and pile of manuscripts at the side of his bed.

"It's the Violin Concerto back from America," she explained, feeling the need to. "We were going to check the parts together. Make sure it's all present and correct before sending it off for the London rehearsals. I hope I'm not doing wrong but he was so anxious about it arriving in time, to find out whether it contained the right number of parts...."

"No. I think that's a splendid idea," said Dr Duncan as he opened his bag. "Do let him go on."

Dr Duncan sat on the edge of the bed and held Coleridge's wrist. He popped a thermometer under his tongue.

"How are you today, Mr Taylor?"

"Do you know – I feel absolutely fine," he answered deliberately and almost believing it himself but it sounded ridiculous with the obstacle under his tongue. He was far from fine. He closed his eyes and tried not to chew on the glass thermometer as it rattled against his teeth. He hated being ill. It felt like such a monumental waste of time and he detested being fussed over and the centre of attention.

Dr Duncan hid his concern, as doctors do, as he made a note of his observations. Coleridge was getting worse – a lot worse, and there was less and less that could be done about it.

Waiting for the thermometer and feeling slightly redundant, and more than a little ridiculous in his wedding garb, Dr Duncan looked in the trunk and gave a, 'may I?' look to Jess. She gave him an, 'of course you can' glance back. Dr Duncan reached into the trunk and pulled out one of the bundles of papers.

"Good heavens," he said. "This all looks rather involved. All Greek to me, I'm afraid. I can barely even hum."

Under the ribbon holding the part together, was tucked a letter, 'To Mr Samuel Coleridge-Taylor'.

Coleridge opened his eyes with a sigh and Dr Duncan read the thermometer and gave the letter to Coleridge. He made another note.

Jess put an extra pillow behind Coleridge's shoulder to sit him up a bit but he was a dead weight. He leant and was struggling with the envelope. The flap was gummed right up to the corners. Coleridge accepted the doctor's offer of help and the envelope was opened for him. Dr Duncan handed it back to him. Coleridge took out the letter. Some small photographs slipped out onto the bed covers. Coleridge started to read.

"It's from Carl and Ellen Stoeckel. Unfortunately I wasn't able to conduct it myself," he explained. "Other commitments…. I often have other commitments."

He read a little further.

"It seems to have been acceptable this time. They say they were sorry I wasn't there in person but they had some photographs taken."

He put the letter down and gathered up the pictures to look at them. Coleridge communicated that he wanted to show the young doctor so they both leant in.

"This is Carl Stoeckel," he said pointing to Carl in the picture. "That's Ellen, his wife. That's Mr Paine and…. This is Maud Powell, the soloist."

He closed his eyes.

"…The violinist."

Coleridge's hand relaxed. Dr Duncan took the pictures from him.

"And there you are," said the doctor pointing to the huge portrait that the Stoeckels and orchestra were proudly seated around. A portrait of the composer, a portrait as tall as the man himself. Coleridge opened his eyes.

The photograph had been taken on the lawns outside their grand home the afternoon before the premiere – those beautiful lawns that rolled on and on and the laurel was in flower and the palisades of pine-trees and the thunder in the mountains....

"Oh yes," Coleridge said. "I didn't see that. There I am."

"So you were there after all," said the doctor as he put the pictures on bedside table.

"Have you ever been to America?"

Dr Duncan shook his head.

"Then you must. I've been three times. It is a beautiful country, you know – the most extraordinarily cheerful people."

"You always seem pretty cheerful to me too."

Coleridge's eyes slowly closed again.

"Well yes, I am I suppose. I'm always a happy man.... You see, I want to be nothing else, nothing else than what I am – a musician."

Coleridge drifted off to sleep. Dr Duncan stood. Coleridge's hand relaxed. Jess took the letter from his bed and put it on top of the pieces of music with the pictures. He had signed the pieces. She picked all of it up and put it in the trunk, closing the lid.

"I'll drop by a little later," Dr Duncan said quietly as he and Jess stepped out of the bedroom and closed the door slowly and silently. "Dr Collard asked me to tell you that he was very sorry he wasn't able to be here himself just yet. His mother died, you know."

"I didn't know," she said. "I'm very sorry to hear that."

They walked the rest of the way down the stairs and to the front door in silence. Jess wished him good luck for his wedding and thanked him for calling.

Jess let Coleridge sleep for most of the day but when he awoke, he had seemed so keen to check the parts, that this is what they did that afternoon. Everything was, of course, all present and correct. He slept for the rest of the day.

That evening, he ate a little soup.

Jess slept in Watha's room for the second night running but only when she wasn't drifting from room to room in the dark and empty house. The house was eerily quiet without the children. Not that they were generally noisy, it was rather that there was nothing and no one in the house to stir the air around. The Music Shed stood still. The kitchen stood still. The front and dining rooms stood still and the children's rooms all stood still. Even the air outside seemed to stand still – even time. Time barely moved. Nothing moved except Jess, drifting from room to room like a ghost, lost and alone and with nothing to do, drifting absently about the empty house.

During that night, he deteriorated further and his fever grew worse. He was much weaker. He ate a little more than the day before but seemed to sleep most of the time – a very deep sleep. Dr Duncan had left instructions that she was to contact the surgery the minute Coleridge turned any worse but to Jess, the deterioration seemed so slight and so gradual and besides, she thought, he could just as easily get better. She didn't want to waste anyone's time. She knew Coleridge wouldn't want her to waste anyone's time.

The day after that was 1st September and he seemed to be much better that morning and that was a joy to her. His fever was the same but it didn't seem to bother him in quite the same way. He and Jess had had quite a chat.

He had seemed to her slightly different in himself however. He had said some peculiar things but had spoken them clearly and strongly and matter-of-factly. What he had said should have made sense but instead seemed rather nonsensical. He had also reached out in front of him because he thought he saw some threads hanging down in front of his eyes, but there weren't any there. His eyes wandered round the room. He had talked of visitors coming into his room, he had been sure of it, but there had been none.

He had had a nap that afternoon and when he awoke was the most lucid he had been since the onset of his illness. Just before 4pm, she took him some tea, which she helped him to drink. He sipped. She moved the cup and waited a little while and then let him sip some more.

As she sat on the side of their bed, feeding her husband sips of tea, she looked out of the window. Life, for everyone else, was going on as normal.

He felt helpless – like a baby. He felt humiliated. He felt abandoned. He was annoyed that there was so much he should be doing. He was frustrated.

He wondered where everyone was. Why was it just he and Jess? He assumed that Kathleen and his mother would know he was ill but could not understand why they had not visited. Dr Duncan was very nice but where was Dr Collard? The people that he would have expected to be there were notably absent. He wondered if he was dying but if that were the case, surely there would be more people around. He worried that he might be dying because if he were to die, it would mean leaving so much undone and he couldn't bear leaving a mess, letting people down or leaving so much unfinished.

As he neared the end of the cup, she saw his bottom lip trembling and his eyes misting. She pretended not to notice. She put the cup down.

"Is that enough?" she asked. He nodded. She dabbed at the corners of his mouth. She dabbed at the tears appearing in his eyes.

"If I die, everything will go wrong."

"No one's going to die," she said.

"They'll call me a Creole," he said with a sad, cheeky smile. She smiled back at him. She looked at her beautiful Coleridge – so gentle, so full of love, generous to a fault, funny. He was the cleverest person she had ever met, a wonderful father and here he was wasting away before her eyes and it broke her heart. "I shall meet such a crowd of musicians."

She couldn't bear it. She looked away, ahead at the window.

"When my father left...." he couldn't finish the sentence. Jess closed her eyes to stop her own tears. He must not see her upset, she thought. She stared at the window.

"When my father left –"

"Coleridge, he would have been very... very proud of you."

Coleridge really wanted to know for sure. "Would he?" he asked. He believed that his father might be proud and he certainly hoped, but he couldn't say, with his hand on his heart that he knew. "Do you really think so?"

"Yes. You know that."

She looked at her knees. She looked at the floor but looking down made the tears roll across her eye and put everything out of focus. She looked up at the wall again but the tears rolled out.

"And I need to know," he went on, "if everything has been alright for you?"

"What do you mean?"

"Have I been acceptable as a husband?" he asked simply.

She stayed with her back to him. She tried to stifle the sob that was rising up in her and spoke as naturally and casually as she could.

"Yes Coleridge – as a husband, as a father, as a son I'm sure and as everything else too…. As everything you are and have been…. to all of us, you've been more than acceptable."

He nodded.

"Do I really have to tell you all these things?" she asked.

"I wish I could have conducted it, though – the Violin Concerto."

He was tired again. He touched the side of her back. He wanted to see her face but she wasn't turning around.

"I don't like to see children in mourning clothes," he said quietly.

"Coleridge, will you please not talk like that."

"Where are they, anyway?"

Jess sniffed and stood up to leave.

"At your mother's."

"Is there time…?"

She turned to him but he had his eyes closed.

"Time?" she asked.

"Is there time for one more of Mrs Caudle's Curtain Lectures?"

"He's asleep," Jess had whispered as she quietly let Kathleen into the house. Mrs Evans had asked a neighbour to watch the children and had arrived some minutes later. Jess had sent for the doctor. It was early evening and he had been getting steadily worse and worse again. He had been drifting in and out of consciousness but the periods of consciousness were becoming fewer and further between. Although he was sleeping, his breathing had become more laboured and rasping as the afternoon had gone on and on one occasion, she hadn't been able to wake him. He was sleeping too deeply.

The three women had sat around the dining room table and sipped their tea in silence, as they waited for the doctor to arrive. None of them could speak what they were thinking.

Coleridge sat in a train station waiting room. The oversized clock ticked noisily somewhere and thick, sepia smog and steam obscured all sight of anything through the windows, misted with nicotine. He sat neatly and waited patiently. He had on his hat and white gloves and his cane lay across his knees, his bag on the floor to the side. He looked at his watch and rubbed his wrist where his watch normally was. He would be slightly lost without it, he thought and he scolded himself for forgetting it before remembering that it wasn't working properly anyway. In front of him, a nurse sat at a desk. On the corner of her desk was a heap of buns under a bell-jar, then a bell sounded and she looked up at him.

"The doctor will see you now, Mr Taylor," she said.

Kathleen answered the doorbell. It was Dr Collard but Coleridge slept on.

He knew where he was. He would know the Royal Albert Hall anywhere. But more than this, he had been at this performance before. He had observed it from a different seat. This time though, he was down in the stalls. There was no sound except the sound of his own deep breathing and of the ticking clock at his bedside.

There was a conductor he didn't know, which was strange because he thought he knew them all. The conductor was standing on a lake and was surrounded by a choir of hundreds of squaws and braves.

He looked up at the circle and saw Jess, an old woman, and his boy – all grown up into a handsome young man. Watha leant his head against his mother and sank his face into her in inconsolable grief. But where was Gwennie?

He looked at the Choir. He scanned the rows. There she was. She had grown up too. She must have been about twenty-eight or so but it was undoubtedly her, he thought. She was singing her heart out, a very fine young woman. He felt such pride and such comfort to know that they were all alright.

He looked to see whom he was sitting next to. To his right was a person he didn't know but on his left and staring straight ahead at the spectacle was Dr Collard although he too was an old man.

"Doctor Collard?" Coleridge asked him but he didn't turn or even acknowledge his presence there and although he wasn't talking, Coleridge could somehow hear his voice – soft and gentle as if whispering into his ear. That wonderful speaking voice that Dr Collard had.

"Hello Coleridge."

Coleridge looked at the old man. How could he hear him when he wasn't even talking?

"Look at us," the doctor's voice said. "Everyone has come together. Look at everything you've done. You've done so much for all of us. Coleridge…?

"Have I?"

"It's alright if you decide to go now. No one will think any the less of you if you were to decide that enough was enough. You don't have to do anything for anyone anymore because... you already mean everything to all of us."

The voice stopped.

Coleridge turned his head and looked at the chorus and the orchestra playing. He admired the skill of the first violinist. He admired the skill of the conductor. He saw his daughter sing but couldn't hear. He smiled.

He smiled and a peace filled him.

Jess, Kathleen and Mrs Evans entered the room. Dr Collard had asked for a moment alone with Coleridge and was sitting on the edge of the bed. Jess closed the door. Dr Collard stood and looked down at Coleridge breathing so deeply. He didn't know if Coleridge had heard his words. The three women stood by the door.

None of them moved. None of them spoke. They looked to the doctor. Coleridge had been unconscious for over two hours. They knew that nothing else could be done.

Coleridge's mouth began to move. They strained to listen to what he was trying to say. His voice was so quiet, so tired and so weak. His eyes were closed, his words almost inaudible. He was saying his children's names.

Kathleen folded her arms. She put her hand to her mouth and tilted her head to the side. Her face crumpled and she cried, silently and unnoticed. Coleridge's mother began to gently shake and her eyes grew wide as panic and disbelief rose up in her. She wanted to cry out, to scream. Her son was dying right there in front of her and she could do nothing – nothing at all about it. Jess stood as if of marble. They couldn't speak.

"I'm sorry.... My promise.... Thank you."

He had his arms over the covers. They watched him. Would he say anything else? His arms by his side, he was unconscious and breathing much too deeply – too deeply asleep and sinking deeper.

Just then, his fingers moved a little and then his hand. Very slowly, his arms began to rise as if lighter than air – as if lifted by invisible strings and then they began to move. His hands gently swayed in the air over him. They all knew what he was doing. They all knew what he was seeing.

Jess suddenly felt embarrassed for him and the unseemliness of it all. She hurried over to him to put his hands back down under the covers. It was important that everything was perfect and perfectly dignified for the moment.

"Don't Jessie," Kathleen said softly.

Jess stopped.

"Let him." Kathleen said.

Jess turned and looked at Kathleen. She looked at Mrs Evans. It was clear she agreed with Kathleen. But their faces, seeing them for the first time – Kathleen and his mother – their distraught, grief-filled, horrified faces. Jess had wanted everything to be nice because it wasn't really happening, it couldn't be, but just then it all suddenly came into focus for her and it was vivid and ghastly. It was hideous and ugly and no amount of pretending would ever make it 'nice'. He was actually dying in front of them, right there and then, and she had been the last to permit herself to know it; their faces had shot her denial down. But he couldn't. He couldn't leave her to do it all – to go on. There was too much, too much left. He couldn't. He couldn't.

Kathleen said, "Let him, Jess. It's what he loves best in the world."

His thumb and forefinger were held lightly together, his hands gently swaying in the air over his bed, conducting an unseen orchestra as the dark of evening outside began to fall.

CHAPTER 20

Watha sat in the sun on the step outside Mrs Evans' open front door while she buttoned Gwen's coat just inside. The children were so excited that they were to see their father again. It was 2nd September and Jessie had given her mother-in-law strict instructions not to say anything to the children. She was just to tell them that they were to see their father and to bring them home at once.

"Come on," Watha said impatiently as he stood with his hands in his pockets, scuffing grit with the toe of his shoe. Mrs Evans' bag slid down her forearm and interfered with her coat buttoning. Gwen had managed to button them out of sequence and kept saying that she could do it herself. The boy started to walk towards the gate.

"Watha, wait please!" Mrs Evans said but the twelve-year-old had opened the squeaky gate and started to walk towards home.

"Wait!"

"Is father better now then?" Gwennie asked.

"Gwennie," Mrs Evans said finishing with the buttons. "Your Mother feels that it's important – "

"But we are going to see him, aren't we?" Gwen interrupted. Mrs Evans stepped out of the house holding onto her granddaughter's hand. She locked the front door.

"Yes," she said. "We are going to see him."

Gwen beamed excitedly as they started down the road, her grandmother holding her hand tightly. Mrs Evans scanned the distance, trying to keep Watha in sight.

"But you have to understand, Gwennie...."

Watha was a long way off in the distance. He was walking quite quickly and hopscotched on the paving, avoiding the cracks. He dragged a stick along the railings. He didn't look back. The morning sun burned his eyes and he squinted. He turned the corner.

"Watha!" shouted Mrs Evans after him as she quickened her already brisk pace to a trot.

"Watha!" she shouted at him from some distance away. He had heard her but pretended not to. He carried on. Besides, he was nearly home and didn't want to have to wait. He was nearly at the newsagents at the corner. He could hear his grandmother in the distance shouting for him.

Reluctantly, he thought he'd better wait at the shop and so he slowed as he approached it. He could hear his grandmother in the distance. She was running down the street holding his sister's hand. Why was she running? It sounded like she was screaming his name. It sounded like she was shouting that he wasn't to look, but at what? There was nothing there but the sandwich board outside the corner shop with the day's headlines on it. He slowed as he approached.

His grandmother had passed the board on her way to collect the children from her house and knew exactly what it said but that was not the way for the boy to find out. They were not to know until they got home, Jess had told her. But he was already there, standing in front of the newsagents and the sandwich board and was reading what it said.

He heard his grandmother screaming for him in the distance. He could hear her running but the horror strangled him as he read the notice on the board 'Local composer' – as he read his father's name 'Samuel Coleridge-Taylor' as he read 'dies aged thirty-seven on 1st September 1912'.

The boy's mouth hung open – his eyes widening. He could hear his grandmother calling for him. He could hear her running. Hot air filled his chest and he screamed.

He ran as fast as he could as the tears flooded from his eyes. He cried as he belted down the streets to his home. He cried as he ran and didn't care who saw him – his distress, his horror, his grief.

Outside his house, there were three motorcars parked. The front door was open. He could see that the hallway was full of people, all in black. He ran up the steps to the front door and pushed past the strangers with their teacups and saucers.

Two people were standing to the left in the doorway to the front room. Watha pushed them out of the way but couldn't move any further. The room was full of people. They turned to look at him and then turned back again and he tried to make sense of the ghastly tableau set before him.

They were standing, posing, opposite the window. Just one of them Watha knew, it was his father's friend, Kathleen. She was looking at him with a smile of such sadness. They were posing around a chair.

Watha was out of breath and wanted to say something but no one seemed to see him except Kathleen and there were no words.

On the chair in the centre, surrounded by bunches and bouquets, posed Watha's mother. She sat at a slight angle, her face serene. On her lap and around her feet, pages of musical manuscript were artistically strewn. She held some pages in her limp left hand and propped up under her right hand and resting on her knee was a death mask of Watha's beloved father, eyes closed but mouth slightly open, cast in plaster - white and jagged around the edges.

A flash of camera bulb and the picture froze all the faces in time – looking out at anyone who looked at the picture in years to come; all looking into the camera lens but Kathleen. She was looking to the side, at her dear friend's distraught boy.

The sitters relaxed. Kathleen went straight to Watha and kneeling, gave him a big hug. Watha was just like a little Coleridge. The photographer reverently removed the papers from around Jessie's feet. She stood and placed the death mask on the mantle. She moved the vase slightly so there was a space.

"Let me do that, Jessie," Kathleen said taking the vase of wilted yellow chrysanthemums. Jess placed the dead face in the centre of the mantle and took the vase back from Kathleen without looking at her.

That day and the next were a blur for Jess, Watha and Gwen. They were never left alone. There was always someone in the house. There was always coming and going and all too soon, the day of the funeral arrived.

On the 4th September, Jess had arranged for the photographer to return to take some portraits of the children on the day of their father's burial. Their mother's favourite picture from that session was taken on the front porch. Watha was seated and looking to the side and into the middle distance with his arms loosely folded and in his best jacket and shorts. Gwen sat on her brother's left with her head on his shoulder looking into the middle distance the other way.

St Leonard's Road was full of carriages and a number of motorcars but most would be making the short journey to Bandon Hill Cemetery on foot. The hearse horses' hooves breaking the silence, waiting – all their neighbours, standing in silence outside their homes.

When the pictures had been taken, Gwen and Watha were taken back indoors where the grown-ups were waiting. Watha looked up and saw the mahogany coffin carried passed the door. It was covered with lilies and carried in silence from the dining room and through to the front door.

A little while later, the main undertaker nodded to Jessie from the door. She stood and took the hands of the children. The others started to drift out slowly and with that genteel, hands-clasped, politeness peculiar only to funerals.

The procession started slowly down the road. The coffin was in the hearse in front. Jess and the children were in a carriage behind it.

As they turned the corner out of their road, they saw the people for the first time – the hundreds and hundreds of people – all along the way they stood, all the way to Bandon Hill. All the way, they lined the footpaths on both sides of the road, four or five deep. The men held their hats. Some people crossed themselves. Some tossed flowers under the hoofs of the hearse horses. All were strangers, many were crying. And so it was for the whole short journey.

The numbers of people swelled the nearer they got to the chapel in the cemetery. The roads had been closed. Thousands had turned out to pay their respects to

Coleridge, the most popular composer of the day, on his final journey. There were a great many black people present and that surprised the children. There were hundreds of them – hundreds and hundreds, all lining the streets. They didn't know these people or where they had all come from but they all knew and loved their father.

The carriages stopped on Plough Lane and the final part of the journey to the chapel was made on foot. There were people everywhere, standing in silence as the summer faded.

"'O Loveliest Light, from whom all planets borrow...',"" Sir Charles Stanford read from the chapel pulpit.

"'All rays that kindle life or sweeten death,
Burn into consecration all our sorrow,
And touch with fire divine our faltering breath;
The shadowing veil of anguish rend asunder,
Lay thy pure gleam upon his quiet brow,
Who, in thy glowing mystery of wonder,
Rejoins the chorus of immortals now.

O source of Song, from whose pure fountain springing
All harmonies are poured, all lovely lays,
Blend here thy rapture with his own strong singing,
Who shed thy beauty on our changeful days.
Thy bourne of birth the soul of song regaineth,
Though sunset deepens here where morning shone;
The harp is still, the melody remaineth,
The Singer passes, but the song lives on.

Peace to him now! Death is not dust and ashes,
Nor life a sound that dies upon the wind;

Beyond the grave a fairer splendour flashes
Than human eye hath seen or heart divined.
Peace to him now! While in our hearts insistent
Burns evermore his God-reflecting fire,
In spheres of light and song and beauty distant
He dwells beyond our dreaming and desire'."

William's sister Judith had made the journey up from Bournemouth to attend the funeral and sat next to Dr Collard near the back of the chapel as they heard Sir Charles reading Mr Berwick Sayers' 'In Memoriam'. Mr Alfred Noyes also wrote an 'In Memoriam' in addition to the words that were later to appear on the stone marking the burial site,

'Too young to die –
His great simplicity,
His happy courage in an alien world –
His gentleness, made all that knew him,
Love him.'

The coffin was lowered into the ground and the final prayers said.

The mourners viewed the floral tributes laid along the outside wall of the chapel, led by Jessie with the children, Mrs Evans and Kathleen. The cards had been set so that they could be read from a standing position as long as one's eyesight was keen enough.

"Look at this one," Jess said to Kathleen, stopping.

Jess had seen a large tribute in the shape of Africa with Sierra Leone highlighted in red flowers. Kathleen knelt to read the card.

"'From all the sons and daughters of West Africa resident in London'."

Towards the end of the procession, Sir Charles Villiers Stanford walked with Sir Edward Elgar. Their hushed conversation had started off cordially enough. Sir Edward had said something he intended to be innocuous about what a marvellous contribution the music publishers made in the careers of young composers. But he instantly saw that his comments were particularly poorly chosen and actually quite provocative and so began digging a grave of his own by going on and on about how mindful of artists, the publishers really were. How they encourage and promote and where would we be without them, and such like, until Sir Charles could bear it no more.

"I'm glad that your experience," he said tersely, "leads you to think that the big publishers are often everything that is considerate." Sir Edward prickled with embarrassment at the tactlessness of his comments. "But I can tell you of many cases where they are not." Sir Charles went on – his words, almost spat. "I seem to remember a conversation where Mr Auguste Jaegar said that 'Hiawatha' was the biggest success Novello had had since Mendelssohn's 'Elijah'. If by accident, Sir Edward, you happened to see the accounts of Messrs Novello concerning 'Hiawatha', it might open your eyes a little as regards the 'considerate treatment of composers'".

Far up ahead by the chapel, Jess knelt to read another of the tribute cards.

"Kathleen," she said. "Listen to this one. 'We always wished him well in life and now we wish him peace in death. Sent with much love from all his brothers and sisters and other relatives in distant Sierra Leone – his family who always longed to meet him one day'."

Jessie Coleridge-Taylor was left next to penniless but a charity concert held for her raised £1,440. Some funds were also raised from the sale of some previously unpublished signed works that she had managed to unearth and King George V later awarded her a Civil List pension of £100 per annum.

The Society of Authors urged the publishers, Novello to grant her a share of the massive revenue generated by 'Hiawatha' when it publicly emerged that the publishers had paid just fifteen guineas for the original cantata. But despite her stoic lobbying and letter writing and that undertaken on her behalf, she maintained that Novello consistently refused to grant her a royalty on 'The Song of Hiawatha' trilogy.

In 1914, less than two years later, the Performing Rights Society was formed in Great Britain with the aim of ensuring that composers received fair payment for their work.

The popular appeal of 'The Song of Hiawatha' continued to grow and grow with the decades, right up to the beginning of the Second Great War. But there was one very special performance, at the Royal Albert Hall in 1932, held twenty years after Coleridge's death, when all those who needed to remember him, came together one more time.

Kathleen was there and Coleridge's old friend Fritz, from Novello. The Coleridge-Taylor's one-time maid, Elsie was also there. She had often told the tale of how she and Sir Herbert Beerbohm Tree had found Mr Taylor with a blue, satin bow tied teetering on his head.

Chief Oske-Non-Ton attended, and a man who as a child had set Coley's hair alight during a carol service and who had lived with that regret all his life.

The First Violin had been adjudicated by Coleridge as a child.

Havergal Brian was there as was a woman from Liverpool who had become friends with Coleridge and his wife whilst holidaying in Eastbourne as a child; his mentor Colonel Walters and teacher Mr Beckwith, Jessie Coleridge-Taylor with her handsome son, Hiawatha. It seemed that everyone there; the audience, orchestra and chorus all knew the man in some way and all loved him for himself and for the music he left that so united them.

Judith, the sister of William Hurlstone was there but sadly passed away herself later that same year.

Dr Collard was there – sitting next to what seemed to be the only empty seat in the entire house, and Avril – Avril was there.

The final resolution of the piece began with a tumultuous crash of drums and cymbals. With the scrap of music in her hand, dedicated 'to the very special sister of a very special brother', Avril sang with the chorus as the orchestra blasted out the closing, rending bars.

"'And they said, 'Farewell, forever!
Farewell O Hiawatha!'
And the forests, dark and lonely,
Moved through all their depths of darkness,
Sighed, 'Farewell, O Hiawatha!'
And the waves upon the margin,
Sobbed, 'Farewell, O Hiawatha'!"

Avril looked away from her score for a moment. She knew the words anyway and she wept as she sang them.

"'...And the heron, the Shuh-Shuh-Gah
From her haunts among the fenlands,

Screamed, 'Farewell, O Hiawatha'!"

She closed her score and sobbed as the others sang, crying for the father she missed so much and then she looked up. She looked up at the huge backdrop and it seemed to her to crackle into life. She saw the stream waters rippling in the mountain valley and the wigwam village with its curling smoke. She saw the multitude on the margin and the warrior King standing alone in his bark canoe as it drifted out on the still waters of the lake. She saw the deepening of the sunset and the dazzling beams spike behind the luminescent, coral and turquoise shards of cloud reflected in the still water. He started to turn to look at her. He stopped and smiled. She saw him lift his palms to heaven as the clouds rolled apart and with the colours, phosphorescing, burning brightly through them, in that blaze of light, the image of the man dissolved.

"'Thus departed Hiawatha
Hiawatha the Beloved.
In the glory of the sunset,
In the purple mists of evening
To the regions of the home-wind,
Of the Northwest wind Keewaydin
To the Islands of the Blessed,
To the Kingdom of Ponemah,
To the Land....
....the Land....
...of the Hereafter'!"

As the lights inside the Royal Albert Hall dimmed in the musical afterglow, a single beam shone out and illuminated a point at the very back. Every head turned to see where the light fell and they instantly rose in rapturous ovation at what they saw.

High up on the back wall was illuminated a portrait; a portrait commissioned by the Stoeckels; a portrait that had been photographed many years earlier with his Violin Concerto's first orchestra and in place of the man himself – as tall as the man himself. It was the portrait of an English composer, young and handsome and happy – the portrait of Samuel Coleridge-Taylor.

Bibliography

Coleridge-Taylor, Avril. *The Heritage of Samuel Coleridge-Taylor.* London: Dennis Dobson, 1979.

Coleridge-Taylor, Jessie. *Coleridge-Taylor: Genius and Musician, A Memory Sketch.* Bognor Regis and London: John Crowther, 1943.

Sayers, W. C. Berwick. *Samuel Coleridge-Taylor, Musician* London: Cassell, 1915; revised ed. 1927; republished by Afro-Am Press, 1969.

Self, Geoffrey. *The Hiawatha Man, the Life and World of Samuel Coleridge-Taylor.* Burlington, VT: Scolar Press, 1995.

Tortolano, William. *Samuel Coleridge-Taylor: Anglo-Black Composer, 1875-1912.* Metuchen, NJ.: Scarecrow Press, 1977.

Lightning Source UK Ltd.
Milton Keynes UK
18 June 2010

155796UK00001B/7/P